Kirov Saga:
Roll of Thunder

An alternate history of the Pacific War
Volume I

By

John Schettler

A publication of: *The Writing Shop Press*
Roll of Thunder, Copyright©2016, John A. Schettler

KIROV SERIES:

The Kirov Saga: Season One
Kirov - Kirov Series - Volume 1
Cauldron of Fire - Kirov Series - Volume 2
Pacific Storm - Kirov Series - Volume 3
Men of War - Kirov Series - Volume 4
Nine Days Falling - Kirov Series - Volume 5
Fallen Angels - Kirov Series - Volume 6
Devil's Garden - Kirov Series - Volume 7
Armageddon – Kirov Series – Volume 8

The Kirov Saga: Season Two ~ 1940-1941
Altered States– Kirov Series – Volume 9
Darkest Hour– Kirov Series – Volume 10
Hinge of Fate– Kirov Series – Volume 11
Three Kings – Kirov Series – Volume 12
Grand Alliance – Kirov Series – Volume 13
Hammer of God – Kirov Series – Volume 14
Crescendo of Doom – Kirov Series – Volume 15
Paradox Hour – Kirov Series – Volume 16

The Kirov Saga: Season Three ~1942
Doppelganger – Kirov Series – Volume 17
Nemesis – Kirov Series – Volume 18
Winter Storm – Kirov Series – Volume 19
Tide of Fortune – Kirov Series – Volume 20
Knight's Move – Kirov Series – Volume 21
Turning Point – Kirov Series – Volume 22
Steel Reign – Kirov Series – Volume 23
Second Front – Kirov Series – Volume 24

Season 4 Premier: Tigers East

Kirov Saga:
Roll of Thunder

An alternate history of the Pacific War
Volume I

By

John Schettler

Kirov Saga:
Roll of Thunder

By
John Schettler

Part I – *Climb Mount Niitaka*
Part II – *Day of Infamy*
Part III – *Ultimatum*
Part IV – *The Lost Convoy*
Part V – *Rook's Gambit*
Part VI – *Wolf in the Fold*
Part VII – *Aftermath*
Part VIII – *Banzai!*
Part IX – *Rock of the East*
Part X – *Bitter Dregs*
Part XI – *Plan 7*
Part XII – *Too Many Cooks*
Part XIII – *Feather Light*
Part XIV – *A Roll of Thunder*
Part XV – *The Gates of Hell*

Author's Note:

Dear Readers,

This is the alternate history of the war in the Pacific, extracted from many volumes of the long *Kirov Series* and re-edited into one continuous narrative. There are already 90 chapters featuring action from the Pacific, far too many to assemble in just one volume, particularly if a print trade paperback version is also being produced, as is the case with this Pacific War Series. That history will therefore be presented in a series of Battle Books, this being the first 45 chapters. This volume will present:

The war begins with the Japanese Pearl Harbor Operation, where the first carrier to carrier battle of the war begins to set the history off on a very different course. Then comes the story of the US "Pensacola Convoy," and the alternate history US battle with the French Pacific Fleet in the New Hebrides. As the Japanese land on the Philippines and MacArthur is forced to flee to Australia, the war progresses with a detailed presentation of Yamashita's Malay Campaign and the exciting Battle for Singapore.

Karpov's initial duels with the Japanese Navy are covered, including his attack on the *Kido Butai*, and the opening rounds of his Plan 7 operation against Japanese occupied Kamchatka. The Japanese invasion of Timor follows to recount the fate of the Australian Sparrow Force, along with the Battle of Badung Strait, the Battle of the Java Sea, and the British effort to reinforce and hold the strategic island of Java. Even as the Japanese invasion there proceeds, this volume will conclude with the dramatic events off Java that led to the arrival of a most unexpected visitor. The material above will present 45 chapters, 400 pages; about 132,750 words.

In editing this, I have revised certain segments to eliminate information not needed for this narrative, and also included small segments of new material in places to improve the flow. I worked a bit so that a reader who is new to the series can jump right in without having to read all of season 1 and 2. So if you are a Pacific War fan, I hope you will enjoy my spin on this history, though be advised that it will be heavily influenced by the underlying premise of the series as a whole—*what if a modern day ship of war suddenly found itself transported into the midst of WWII?* How would it, or how could it, influence the course of events and shape the outcome of the war, and by extension, of all the history that follows.

The battlecruiser *Kirov* was that ship, launching a series that has become much more than I ever expected from the story, and this is but one of the many subplots presented in that series, which has covered wartime action on every key front.

Volume II for the Pacific War will then continue with the story concerning JS *Takami*, the Battle of the Coral Sea, Halsey's raid on the Marshalls, Japanese Operation FS and the landings on Fiji, the Battle of the Koro Sea, US Marine Landing at Suva Bay, Karpov's Landings on Sakhalin Island, and finally the battle between *Kirov* and an unexpected challenger in the Sea of Okhotsk, (another 45 chapters in all). It will then probably take at least one more volume of this same length to cover the remainder of the Pacific War, or possibly two, all chapters I expect to write as the *Kirov Series* soon moves into 1943.

For those many readers who have written and asked me to cover the Pacific in the next release for the Battle Book Series, here it is. For new readers just interested in military fiction and the Pacific Theater, this book will also give you a good flavor of what the Kirov Series is all about.

Enjoy!

- *John Schettler*

Part I

Climb Mount Niitaka

"The fate of our nation depends on this battle—All hands will exert themselves to their utmost."

—Admiral Togo
Flag signal message from BB *Mikasa* at the outset of the Battle of Tsushima Strait. This message was repeated by CV *Akagi*, fleet flagship, as the attack on Pearl Harbor was launched.

Chapter 1

Admiral Yamamoto was a very careful man, and too much was now at stake to allow for anything to slip his notice. All the planning was complete, the long days of rehearsals off small bays on the coast of the Home Islands now concluded. All the selection and posting of ships and officers were carefully considered and assigned. Now it remained only for him to relay the final order, and as he read it through one last time, a strange feeling came over him, as if all these events had already been lived through, fought through, concluded. Was it merely his confidence in the certainty of the outcome that led him to feel this way? If so, then why was this strange thought surrounded by such an intense feeling of presentiment?

It is simply adrenaline, he thought. Here I sit, ready to transmit the order that will soon set my nation on an inevitable course of war, and one that I had hoped to prevent. That was not to be, and so if war must come, and if I must lead it, then let every detail be well considered. Let nothing be overlooked, and then let the hawks fly into this gray sky, and cry their warning to the Gods above.

Now he read the words he had written one last time:

'The Task Force, keeping its movements strictly secret and maintaining close guard against submarines and aircraft, shall advance into Hawaiian waters and, upon the very opening of hostilities, shall attack the main force of the United States fleet in Hawaii and deal it a mortal blow. Upon completion of the air raid, the task force, keeping close coordination and guarding against enemy counterattack, shall speedily leave the enemy waters and then return to Japan….'

The navy is ready, he thought, and it is perhaps the best trained and most capable fleet in the world. Only the Royal Navy of Great Britain could match it, and even though the Americans may claim to have more ships, they will soon see that they have built far too many battleships, and not enough aircraft carriers. We will teach them a very hard lesson, and then, for the next six months, I will rage across these seas and hand Japan the Southern Empire Tojo and the others covet so dearly. This, at least, is the certainty I feel in my gut. But then comes the shadow of darkness and doubt, as though some dark nemesis is waiting for me out there, hidden in the mists of the sea, like a denizen of the unseen realm of the Gods themselves. What is it, this shadow, this warning, this unsettling feeling of imminent doom?

Every man must face and make peace with his own fear, he thought. I give this order today, and then each and every man aboard the ships I send east must face their own inner demons. Some will embrace them like long lost brothers, others tremble at their approach. No man faces the prospect of death lightly, and yes, I know this order condemns thousands to that fate, tens of thousands, perhaps hundreds of thousands.

The United States will be the most dangerous foe we could ever contemplate facing. This, too, I know to a certainty. What were the words of that American Bible Preacher I met once at Harvard when I studied there? Ah, yes, I could never forget them: "He who chooses the beginning of the road chooses the place it leads to."

That one simple phase holds all the emotion I feel now, the clarity of the beginning, the feeling of destiny that lies heavy on my heart, the sense of impending doom, for I cannot see the place this road might lead to, I cannot see the end of this war, and that is my greatest fear. Yet a man can only take one step at a time. The navy is finally ready, and so now we take the first....

* * *

Yamamoto had every reason to be confident, in spite of his many doubts and fears that day. The Imperial Japanese Navy that would undertake this journey was one of the largest and most professional forces in the world. Yet the world this navy would sail in was much different now. A young Russian navigator named Anton Fedorov, and his Captain, one Vladimir Karpov, had seen to that. How they came to be in this world was a very long story, and one for another book to tell. Yet the fact that their presence here had changed things would soon be most apparent, for the Japanese navy was not quite the same as the one that had started the war in his old history books.

There were 10 carriers Fedorov could name by heart, with two that had originally been designed as battlecruisers, the fleet Flagship *Akagi*, and the *Kaga*. But there were also ships on the register that had never been built in the history he knew so well. One was another *Kaga* Class ship, for a third battlecruiser, the *Tosa*, had also been converted to an aircraft carrier in this world, forsaking her appointment with the scrap yards. The other familiar names were still all there. *Hiryu* and *Soryu*, both ships built between 1934 and 1936 as full fleet size carriers, were soon followed by *Zuikaku* and *Shokaku*, perhaps the finest fleet carriers in the world in 1941. They were fast at 34 knots, well protected, with excellent range and a compliment of 81 aircraft.

To these seven ships, another project that was nearing completion as war broke out was the all new *Taiho*, a ship designed with much thicker skin in its armored belt and flight deck. It was not the same ship the Japanese would commission in 1944 in Fedorov's history, though it stole that name and many design features from the old *Taiho*. The idea here was to build "battle endurance" into a carrier, making it an armored knight and allowing it to take hits and still survive as a battle worthy asset.

As such, *Taiho* would get 152mm belt armor, 50% thicker than that on a *Mogami* class heavy cruiser, and a tough armored flight deck 80mm thick. It would also bristle with a dozen 100mm AA guns, and over fifty 25mm cannons, with a compliment of 65 aircraft. Said to be the toughest carrier in the fleet, it was also fast, delivering an amazing 33 knots with all that armor. The Empire's accelerated building program saw it delivered to the fleet almost two years early, Japan's 8th, and newest, fleet carrier.

This same idea of creating a tougher fighting carrier had perhaps been born in the long standing duel between the big gun advocates and the carrier faction. It resulted in a pair of ships unlike any that had been seen before on the high seas, when two more fast battlecruisers that had been in the shipyards were also slated for conversion to carriers.

With war on the minds of the Imperial General Staff, and the need for carriers now taking the highest priority in the shipyards, these two projects were put on the fast track by creating a hybrid ship. The forward segments of the design, which had already been completed as a battlecruiser, would be left as they were. Their two twin armored turrets bearing 40cm guns were left in place. Everything aft of the main armored conning tower was cancelled, and instead an armored deck occupied that entire space, with the underdeck areas cleared for hanger storage sufficient for 24 aircraft.

The Japanese had been the first to launch such ships, commissioning both *Gozu* and *Mezu* in 1938. Like *Taiho*, they had thick skin, with 200mm belt armor, 100mm armored deck, a sturdy conning tower protected by 200mm, and those two heavy turrets. Weight was saved with that slightly thinner belt armor, lighter conning tower and the removal of all the aft superstructure along with that third aft turret. It produced an excellent, sturdy 'battlecarrier,' a new class in the navy that could run at 32 knots, sting hard with those four 40cm guns, and also throw 12 fighters and 12 dive bombers into the battle. The fleet was so pleased with the ships, that they took the third *Yamato* class battleship and ordered its immediate conversion along this same model, designating the new design *Shinano*. This order was cut shortly after the ship was laid down in 1940, and not after Japan's disastrous defeat at Midway in the history before Fedorov came to this world. Thus *Shinano*, like *Taiho*, was also on the list of ships that would make an early appearance in the war, now on schedule for completion some time in 1942.

The eight fleet carriers and those two hybrids would also be joined by a number of smaller carriers, and the first of these were three converted ocean liners. *Hiyo* and *Junyo* were both liners purchased by the Empire for this purpose, and completed before the war, a full year early, with 48 planes each. They were hefty at over 24,000 tons, and could make only 25 knots, but added some middleweight punch to the Navy's carrier divisions that was very useful. A third liner owned by the Nippon Yusen shipping line was first slated to become a troop ship, and then reconverted to a carrier to become the 20,000 ton *Taiyo*.

In the lightweight division, several sub tenders had been built with the deliberate intention of converting them to aircraft carriers in time of war. One was the *Ryuho*, at 16,700 tons, the "Great Phoenix" rising from the original design of the sub tender *Taigei*, or "Great Whale." Two smaller tenders were also converted to light carriers, the *Zuiho* and *Shoho*, which were 11,000 ton ships carrying only 30 planes, but relatively fast at 28 knots.

At the bottom of the scale came *Ryujo*, a design that managed to squeeze 48 planes onto her small 10,000 ton frame, and could still run at 29 knots. This ship proved to be top-heavy, and this flaw had not been corrected by the time war broke out, and so she was dry docked in Yokohama, along with the venerable old 7,400 ton *Hosho*, the ship laying the claim as the first aircraft carrier ever built.

All told, Japan would deploy eight fleet carriers, her two new hybrids, three medium carriers converted from liners, and the three light sub tender conversions, making the IJN unchallenged with all of 16 aircraft carriers in late 1941. No nation on earth could match the IJN in this category. By comparison the US Navy had seven carriers, and the vaunted Royal Navy had eight, so Japan's Navy had more naval air power at its disposal than both those allied nations combined. This was not something Fedorov knew at first, though he soon discovered the changes.

There were also a few differences in the battleships, one prominent exception being the second *Yamato* class ship, *Musashi*, which was also completed in time for the show, joining the fleet nine months early. With those two 72,000 ton monsters on the sea, Japan could also claim the largest and most powerful battleships ever built. And seeing the need for fast heavy gunned ships capable of running with her newest carriers, the Empire was adding a pair of excellent battleships to her list of commissioned ships, inspired by the British design for HMS *Hood*.

The two new ships were *Satsuma* and *Hiraga*, and at 42,000 tons they were heavier than any of the Empire's older battlewagons dating to the 1920s. Each carried nine 16-inch guns on three triple turrets, and their long, sleek hull and powerful engines saw them running at 30 knots. Nothing in the fleet battleship division was faster, and only the super heavyweights could hit harder, which made these ships the equal of most any other battleship then afloat.

Japan's "Battleship Row" was then finished off by their older designs, ten more ships in the 27,000 to 32,000 ton weight division. *Nagato* and *Mutsu* had eight 16-inch guns, but could only work up to 26 knots. Next came the four ships in the *Kongo* class, *Hiei*, *Kirishima*, *Haruna*, and *Kongo* itself. They were a little faster at a hair under 28 knots, which was enough to see them often working with the carriers. The last four, *Ise*, *Hyuga*, *Fuso* and *Yamashiro* were much slower at 23 knots, but had good punch with their twelve 14-inch guns distributed over six turrets. Later in the war, those that survived would be eyed as possible battlecarrier conversions.

Next came the heavy cruisers, and the startling new innovation here was the B-65 Super Cruiser project, one conceived in Fedorov's old history, but never built. But here in these altered states, the seed of that project fell on good ground, and the result was a superb new class of ships that embraced the idea of the 'pocket battleship' first pioneered by the Germans.

There were two completed in the class, *Amagi*, and *Kagami*, and they featured the same long forecastle, clipper bow, and swept decks of the *Yamato* class, only with nine 12.2-inch guns. They were also well protected with 210mm belt armor and 180mm on the conning tower, and they were very fast at nearly 34 knots, with an 8,000 nautical mile endurance. Some called them fast battlecruisers, but the Japanese classified them as super Type A cruisers.

The cruiser classes beneath these two fearsome leaders were among the best in the world, with speeds pushing 36 knots, good 8-inch guns, and the world's premier torpedo on reloadable turrets, the dreadful Type 93, soon to be called the 'Long Lance' by historian Samuel Morrison.

Both on paper, and on the wild Pacific Ocean, this was a navy that was second to none. The British and Americans might have more destroyers, and better submarines, but these surface ships, particularly the lavish carrier divisions, made the Imperial Japanese Navy a dangerous and capable force, and one that now threatened to raise havoc all throughout Southeast Asia. All Yamamoto's plans were therefore very well founded, and he had every reason to be confident, in spite of his many doubts. But then there was that shadow… that feeling of impending doom, the sense that there was something out there, and its stealthy approach was like the coming of death itself, a dark hunter, and unseen threat that he could scarcely comprehend.

Anton Fedorov was standing on the bridge of that unseen threat, and beneath his feet was a ship more powerful than any named on his list of Japanese warships—the battlecruiser *Kirov*, 32,000 tons of doubt, death and unseen terror. A freak accident had sent it to this place and time, but those events have been told elsewhere. The history of this war, and that of the entire world, had already been blackened by the fire of that ship's missiles. Yet the man perhaps most responsible for the shape of the world, particularly in the Pacific, was Vladimir Karpov, the Captain of this ship. He had once set out to assure the rise of Japanese power would never happen in these waters. He had once thought to smash this powerful navy even before it could ever grow to the massive force it was in late 1941.

But that plan had failed, so now Karpov had another plan. If he couldn't stop the rise of Japanese power on the world stage, then now he would defeat it in battle. Yet Japan was much more powerful than it ever was in the old history, soundly defeating Russia in the years between 1905 and 1908. The Japanese then occupied huge swaths of Russian territory in the Pacific. They had landed in Vladivostok, occupied all of Primorskiy Province, pushed out army divisions as far north as the Amur River, and seized all of Sakhalin and half of Kamchatka. The damage had been so severe, that Russia was now divided, with one state ruled by Sergie Kirov, the man who had assassinated Josef Stalin before he ever had a chance to come to power. Another interloper from the future ruled a second state, the Orenburg Federation occupying all the lands once held by Kazakhstan and adjacent outlying states. Ivan Volkov ruled there, but his story is again too long to include in this narrative. Finally, there was the Free Siberian State, where Karpov had slowly seized and consolidated power. Karpov knew his ship has caused all this damage to the history, and so now he and his ship would see that it was redressed.

Fedorov folded the note paper he had been referring to as he concluded this extensive briefing with Karpov on the bridge of *Kirov*. He had run down his list of Japanese ships, their numbers and capabilities, making particular note of the newcomers he discovered as he sleuthed this altered history. "And let us not forget that they also have another good port in the north," he concluded.

"Yes," said Karpov, "*our* port, Vladivostok. We shall have to do some long range reconnaissance of the Golden Horn Bay to see what may be berthed there. We already know they have strong air units based there, and at Port Arthur as well, on the Yellow Sea."

"Those ports are both real strategic assets," said Fedorov. "Even if they do decide to negotiate with you, I doubt if either one will ever seriously be on the bargaining table. I think they would sooner give you back all of Kamchatka than yield Vladivostok."

"Then it will have to be taken from them."

"Most likely," said Fedorov, "but how? Your divisions in the east are a long way from being in any position where they could pose a threat to that port. It's over 2600 kilometers from your main eastern command at Irkutsk to Vladivostok, and that is as the crow flies, cutting straight through Manchuria and the entire Kwantung Army. The Trans-Siberian Rail line going around the Amur River route is over 3200 kilometers. The only other way to take it by force would be by amphibious assault, and for that you'll need a good deal more than this ship."

"Your assessment is fairly grim, Fedorov."

"But those are the facts, sir. The Japanese certainly know all this as much as I do. You can threaten and make demands, but I do not think you can take Vladivostok from them by force, and they will know it."

"Then what do we put on the scales of war that would be heavy enough to break them?" Karpov was pacing now, finally realizing the true scale of the foe he was sizing up. What do they need more than anything else if they are to pursue their war aims?"

"Those aircraft carriers," said Fedorov. "Without them they have some marvelous battleships and cruisers, but they will not be able to project naval air power. To lose them would mean they would be forced to restrict their advances to areas where they could quickly seize land based airfields and build up air power. If the Americans have carriers, they can establish sea dominance very quickly, neutralize those heavy surface units, and then easily interdict Japan's effort to supply its overseas bases. Japanese sea power lies in the *Kido Butai*. Take that away from them and they are a third rate navy again, still dangerous, but manageable, and doomed to eventual defeat. They would not even match the *Kriegsmarine*, considering that Germany's U-boat arm is far more potent than the Japanese submarine force, and their surface units are every bit as good as the Japanese, except perhaps for the cruisers."

"This was what I came to realize," said Karpov. "And there is the Ace I have in hand with this ship. *Kirov* alone can emasculate this *Kido Butai*."

"But yet," Fedorov held up a finger, "even in defeat the Japanese remained tenacious. They will not yield one island, let alone that port. It is too strategic, and by this time, too much a part of their economic and military infrastructure. They use it to supply their forces in Manchuria."

"And on the rail line they took from us," said Karpov sourly. "What you say is very sobering. Yes, I cannot push my eastern divisions that far from Irkutsk, even if we could defeat their Kwantung

Army. Nor can I conduct an amphibious invasion until I collect more transport ships… But the Americans can."

"Sir? You think you can convince them to take back Vladivostok for you?"

"Consider this," said Karpov. "The US fought long bitter campaigns through Central and Southeast Asia, throwing their troops at one island outpost after another."

"The navy's leapfrog strategy," said Fedorov.

"Exactly, and it took them at least three years before they could get close enough to the Japanese home islands to deliver that knockout blow—strategic bombing. Wasn't that what really broke Japan?"

"After their navy was broken first," said Fedorov.

"Well then," Karpov rubbed his hands together. "I can offer the Americans another route, the northern route. What about an advance through the Aleutians? They are pointed like a sword, right at the Japanese mainland."

"They are still too far away to support strategic bombing, sir. Adak is 3500 kilometers from Japan, and Attu is just under 3000. It's the same distance to Guam and the Marianas, and the Marianas are much more strategically positioned. The B-17s can't handle that range anyway. Their B-29s could do it, but they won't have them for another year."

"Yes, but the Aleutians could become a base to attack Kamchatka."

"Still 2000 kilometers away."

"And then Sakhalin Island."

"But you don't control any of those territories, sir, except northern enclaves in Kamchatka the Japanese have not yet occupied."

"True," said Karpov, "but with the American's help I could control them, and contribute troops and material to the war effort to take and hold them. Imagine those B-29s basing from Sakhalin Island a year from now? We could defeat Japan much sooner—cut years off the war in the Pacific."

"Assuming the American's agree. Don't forget, if Japan takes the Philippines, which is likely, then you'll have a man dead set on structuring the American war effort to take them back—General Douglas MacArthur. I suppose your plan is worth presenting to the Americans, but it will involve a good deal of diplomatic wrangling."

"So I need some leverage with the Americans too," said Karpov, thinking. "A good deal of leverage…" He smiled. "Thank you, Mister Fedorov, you helped me clarify my thinking on all of this. Now to see about getting us into the Pacific as soon as possible. That's where the action will be."

Fedorov knew the man well enough to realize Karpov had not yet revealed all that might be clarifying in that mind of his. The Captain has plans within plans, he thought. What did he mean about getting leverage with the Americans? He was a little ill at ease, but decided to say nothing at this point until he knew more. Instead he calculated their ETA in the Bering Strait.

"We should be at Big Diomede in four sea days at ten to twelve knots average speed in this ice."

Chapter 2

In spite of every effort, nature had a way of imposing her will on these events. Fedorov had plotted a skillful course through the ice, and they passed through the East Siberian Sea, entering the Chukchi Sea two days later, which brought Marine Sergeant Troyak up on deck to breathe that cold Siberian air that was so familiar to him. He had been born on the peninsula that reached towards the Bering Strait, and so this was a taste of home for him, and many other crewmen as well.

Fedorov had done his best to brief the crew, talking to them in small groups, seeing their astonished faces, hearing their many questions and answering as best he could. It took all of two weeks since they first left Severomorsk to finish that job, and soon the crew settled into a sullen silence, sitting with the impossible notion that they had left the world they once knew. It was the accident, Fedorov had told them, right in the middle of those live fire exercises in 2021. The explosion aboard the submarine *Orel* had blown a hole in time, and *Kirov* slipped right through. That was the only way to explain it.

"You mean like that American aircraft carrier in the movies?" one seaman had asked.

"Yes," said Fedorov, "something like that I suppose."

"They went to stop the Japanese at Pearl Harbor!"

Yes, they did, thought Fedorov, though they failed in that movie, hardly firing a shot. Now here we are, and with Karpov dead set on doing the very same thing. Only Karpov won't be so cautious. When it comes to war, that man has a special appetite, and this ship will fight. The crew must know that. I must do everything possible to prepare them. They have lost everything they ever knew, parents, wives, family, friends, and here they are at the edge of the world, being asked to fight a war that ended long before any of them were ever born. For some the shock will be too heavy, and Doctor Zolkin will be a very busy man these next two weeks.

Fedorov had already spent his own time with Zolkin, discussing his concern over what might lie ahead. They were going to war, aboard the most powerful ship in the world, and he knew Karpov had every intention of using that power.

"He would say that might makes right," he told Zolkin. "Yes, I first thought I had to entrench here and stand against him to try and prevent even more damage to the history, but honestly, what good would that do? Even if I found allies aboard ship, men like Troyak and his Marines, I'd be setting one crew member against another. I'd be doing the very same thing we found so distasteful in the way he took command here. But here he is, with that lout Grilikov and 60 security men aboard."

Zolkin took a long breath. "Our own little private war aboard this ship would come to no good," he said.

"Yes," said Fedorov, "but Doctor, something is different about Karpov now. He's quieter, more inward, less boastful, yet still surrounded by this aura of darkness that is difficult to penetrate at times. He offered me a position as his *Starpom*, second in command, and in that moment I realized that I would have much more control over what happens here in that role than I would likely have in the brig."

"Probably true," said Zolkin.

Fedorov was quiet for a time, thinking. "Karpov is going to confront Japan," he said flatly.

"What? Alone? With this single ship?"

"That remains to be seen. Like I said, he's very careful now, and very calculating. He's got some plan in mind, and it's all aimed at recovering our lost territories from Japan."

"I hope he doesn't get any ideas about dropping an early nuke on Tokyo!"

"Thankfully, that hasn't come up. No. I think he'll show some restraint in that, and as *Starpom*, I'll have some say in it all as well."

There came a whistle through the overhead intercom, and an announcement for all senior officers to come to the bridge. Fedorov shrugged. "I'd best be off. Thank you Doctor, it was good to get some of that off my chest."

He rushed to the bridge to report to Karpov, wondering what was happening, and heavy with thoughts of all he had discussed with Zolkin. When he got there the Captain was already quite concerned.

"Well Fedorov," said Karpov. "We've picked up some Japanese military signals traffic."

As if on cue, communications officer Nikolin looked over his shoulder, giving the Captain a thumbs up. He flipped a switch to put the broadcast he had stumbled upon on audio, but it was simply Morse code.

Fedorov listened, thinking, remembering.

"Nikolin, is that standard Morse?"

"No sir… I think it's—"

"Kana Code," Fedorov finished for him. "Probably the Wabun variant. Switch your decoder to that system. It should be in the database."

In another five minutes they had deciphered the message. Nikolin could make no sense of it, but to Fedorov it was crystal clear: *"Kono junjo wa, 12 tsuki 2-nichi 17-ji 30-bu ni yūkōdearu: Rengō kantai shiriaru #10… Niitaka yama nobore! 1208, Ripīto, 1208!"*

"What does it mean sir? Should I call for Mishman Tanaka?"

"No need," said Fedorov. "Just run it through the translator here." They had their answer soon enough: *"This order is effective at 17:30 on 2 December: Combined Fleet Serial #10. Climb NIITAKAYAMA! Climb Mount Niitaka! 1208, repeat, 1208."*

"A code within a code," said Karpov, looking at Fedorov.

"Except it is one of the most famous code signals ever transmitted sir. That is the Japanese signal authorizing the attack on Pearl Harbor. That message was historically first transmitted at 15:00, Tokyo Time, on December 2, 1941. No doubt we may hear others. 'East Wind Rain' was the Japanese Foreign Ministry alert code for the start of the war, and 'The Black Kite Eagle and Hawk Will Fly' was used for the Army. This one was for the navy, 'Climb Mount Niitaka,' and it took them all night to broadcast it effectively so all fleet assets would get the message."

"My God," said Karpov. "Where would the Japanese Strike force be on December 2nd when they got this message?"

Fedorov ran to his navigation station, quickly retrieving a pad device where he had stored his research on this campaign. A few taps later he had a map. "About here, sir. The *Kido Butai* refueled at 42 degrees north and 170 degrees east; at 20:00 hours—today. The fleet rendezvous point on December 6th was at 34 North, 158 West. That's our best chance to get close. If I punch in our present position, that would put them nearly 4000 kilometers south of us on the 6th. About 2160 nautical miles. That's 72 hours sea time at 30 knots, but we'll be lucky to make even half that speed given the ice conditions now. Ice minimum was in September, but it's been building up ever since."

"Damn!" Karpov was not happy. "I had hoped we would get there sooner."

"We have no chance to catch them before the attack sir," said Fedorov, actually somewhat relieved. The thought of further meddling in the history always made him uncomfortable, and meddling was but half a word for what Karpov had in mind.

"Given these sea ice conditions, it could take us a week to get down through the Bering Strait. Even trying to catch them as they withdraw would be a very close shave.

"Before that, I want to send them a message," said Karpov. "Mister Nikolin, come with me to the briefing room and we'll go over what I want." He looked at Fedorov now.

"Mister Fedorov, the bridge is yours. We're in a horse race. Ice be damned. I want to get as close to this *Kido Butai* as possible. Give this old grey stallion the whip!"

* * *

Kirov would not be able to navigate the thickening ice floes and get up enough speed to cross the enormous distance that separated the two forces. The sailor who contemplated taking part in their own version of "The Final Countdown" would be disappointed, at least on that score. When this was clear, Karpov determined to fall back on his Plan B, or so he indicated to Fedorov. But he secretly had a hidden agenda in these proceedings, one that saw his presence here a two edged sword. He could not get close enough to prevent the Japanese attack, nor did he ever wish to. The outbreak of the war was not his concern, only how it would end.

Nikolin was ferreting out more in the signals traffic. They began to pick up information about unusual troop movements by the Japanese. They were pushing patrols up the northern neck of Kamchatka, and merchant ships docked at Petropavlovsk, unloading fresh troops and supplies. There was also movement in the Kuriles and Aleutians. The Japanese had occupied the old outpost at Nikolskoye, and they were building a small airfield. Tyrenkov, Karpov's intelligence Chief ashore at Irkutsk, believed these troops were staging for the seizure of Attu Island, then an American protectorate. It was yet another omen that war was imminent.

The message Karpov had Nikolin send was to the Japanese authorities, a diplomatic nicety, as he really could care less what response they gave. He had it delivered through the Siberian embassy in Vladivostok, and Nikolin's radio signal was just a reminder to indicate he meant business. It was, in fact, the harbinger of his "Plan 7." He told them that Siberia was fully aware of their plan to strike Pearl Harbor, and even stated the present estimated position of the *Kido Butai* in his signal to make that stick. He said that unless Japan agreed to cede territories, withdraw south of the Amur River, and relinquish control of the Trans-Siberian Rail Line, that Siberia would have no other recourse but to declare war. As Fedorov had advised him, he did not expect the Japanese to bow to such demands, for that rail line was now vital to Japan's northern Imperial holdings.

Then, just to stick in a quiet knife, he had Nikolin transmit the position of the *Kido Butai* in the clear as they expected it for December 3 and December 6. He knew from his discussions with Fedorov that the American carriers would be too far away to do anything about the matter on December 3, but if they picked up that signal, and turned after this warning to sail east....

The Japanese are likely to achieve at least historical damage on the American fleet, he thought. If my warning prompts the U.S. Navy to risk those two carriers, all the better. And if the Americans get lucky, perhaps with a little assistance from my long range helos, they just might put some hurt on this *Kido Butai*. Either outcome suited him fine.

He smiled, for indeed, he had plans within plans within plans.

* * *

Mount Niitaka was the 'New High Mountain' as it was called, on the Japanese possession of Taiwan, was climbed for the first time by Japanese explorers in the year 1900, a most grueling ascent, studded with perilous cliffs, steep stony walls, and slide zones where the risk of avalanche was very great. It was so named because it was even higher than the sacred heights of Mount Fuji on the home islands, and it was symbolic of a great task to be performed.

On the morning of December 2nd, 1941, that was the code phrase that was flashed to Admiral Nagumo's *Kido Butai*, Climb Mount Niitaka! Japan was about to embark on their arduous expedition onto the steep, stony cliffs of WWII.

"*Climb Niitakayama,*" said the Lieutenant. "The operation has finally been approved!"

Vice Admiral Chuichi Nagumo gave the man a quiet look, his white gloved hands still gripping his field glasses as he studied the wild sea. Those last numbers in the signal, 1208, were simply the date, December 8, 1941, which would be Sunday the 7th in Hawaii on the other side of the international date line. Yamamoto's long planned operation was finally about to reach its terminal phase.

It had been a long, silent journey from the Kuriles, with the sudden rising winds and sea of a winter storm to brave as they went. Yet the Admiral was not bothered by the weather. His real concern was in being spotted and in wondering whether this whole affair would ever come to fruition at all.

He was a navy veteran, having graduated from the academy in that fateful year of 1908, too young then to see action when Admiral Togo faced down that strange Russian ship off Oki Island. Ever thereafter, it was said that that enemy ship had been emboldened by the soul of the legendary sea Dragon, *Mizuchi,* and the shock of that encounter had done much to spur the development of the Japanese naval building program. They were determined to get sea dragons of their own.

Now Nagumo had them, right there in the *Kido Butai,* six of the eight fleet carriers with over 440 planes at his command. The words of the Commander in Chief, Admiral Yamamoto, were still fresh in his mind that night. The two men had met just before the fleet departed home waters.

"We have received certain intelligence from the breakaway Russian Republic of Orenburg. Sakyamuno labored all night to get this information to Urajio by rail." That was the name the Japanese had given to Vladivostok when they took it in 1908—Urajio.

"What is it?" Nagumo eyed the diplomatic pouch carefully.

"A very strange document," said Yamamoto. "It contains a map of the American anchorages at Pearl Harbor, the exact positions of their ships, or so we are to believe. There is one thing notably absent on the map—there are no American carriers."

"How could this information be accurate? It will be two weeks before we are in range to attack. Anything could happen in that time."

"That is what is so strange about this map," said Yamamoto. "It appears as if… well as if this has already happened! It even indicates our planned flight approach for the first attack wave! How could the Russians have this? I am in doubt about the entire mission now."

"You suspect a security breach?"

"This man—Volkov—he clearly seemed to know all the details of our attack," Yamamoto shook his head. "Sakyamuno told me that it was imperative we focus our effort not only on the battleships and cruisers we may still find there, but also on the submarine pens… here." Yamamoto pointed to the map. "Also note these fuel tanks that were discussed as potential targets."

"It was determined we could damage them, but not destroy the oil," said Nagumo. "Remember, they are surrounded by dikes."

Yamamoto nodded. "Yet this man, Volkov, insisted that they must be attacked, along with the dry docks and ship repair facilities."

"The Prophet," said Nagumo with a dismissive look. "I have heard of his many predictions. He flits about in that antiquated airship, whispering in Hitler's ear one day, and in Tojo's the next."

"Yes," said Yamamoto. "He predicted there would be a fire in Moscow, and the Soviet Government would flee to Leningrad. He predicted what happened to Sergei Kirov as well!"

"Guesswork," said Nagumo. "I could have predicted that myself."

"Nonetheless, I am inclined to consider the possibility of a third wave strike to target these things. Can it be done?"

"Genda argued strongly for this," said Nagumo. "In fact, he still thinks we should invade Hawaii!"

"That will not happen this time out." Yamamoto smiled. "Give thought to this. If such a third wave could be mounted, then perhaps Genda's voice should be heard. I will leave this up to you. But there is more here."

"More?" Nagumo eyed the leather pouch again, and Yamamoto handed him a second page.

"This is where the carriers will be."

"Another prediction? This renegade dictator cannot possibly know this. Predicting where the American carriers will be before they even leave port is ridiculous."

"Our men on the Hawaiian Islands confirm that the carriers have been moving in and out of the harbor. One departed today. This paper says there are only two operating out of Pearl Harbor, not four as we first thought. A third is on the American West Coast, the fourth was called to the Atlantic. It indicates that the Americans will try to reinforce their mid-Pacific islands, one carrier to Midway, another to

Wake Island, most likely ferrying aircraft or delivering troops and supplies."

"Most regrettable," said Nagumo. "If they accommodate this man and do as he predicts, then I will not get a chance to destroy them at Pearl Harbor."

"Let us not put too much faith in this report," said Yamamoto, "but if it is true, those carriers will not be able to interfere. Just the same, do keep a wary eye over your right shoulder as you turn south for the final approach. If all goes well, you should receive the final go order sometime after your refueling operation on December 2nd."

"Climb Mount Niitaka," said Nagumo. "Someday I will go there to see the real mountain. I have heard it is a difficult height to master."

"The one you already have in front of you will be trouble enough," said Yamamoto. "Do not forget the words of Admiral Togo at Tsushima!"

"How could I forget them?" said Nagumo. "That is where your hand was injured."

"Aboard the armored cruiser *Nisshin*," said Yamamoto. "We fired almost every round we had during that fight, and the ship took much more damage than this old left hand of mind. Yes, I lost two fingers, but the Russians lost the war—twice…"

"It was the second victory that mattered most for us," said Nagumo. "That's when we finally put them in their place." He smiled.

"Just the same," said Yamamoto. "Now we are about to strike the most dangerous foe we have ever fought. Remember Togo's words, and remember the *Nisshin*. I know you had your reservations about this plan, but if you are asked to climb this mountain, when you get there, fire every round you have."

Nagumo put that remark beside their discussion about a third strike wave, and though Yamamoto had politely left the decision to him, he nonetheless felt that the Commander In Chief was urging him to strongly consider Genda's exhortation for that third strike.

Chapter 3

The flags rose on the main mast of *Akagi* precisely on schedule, at 5:45 AM in the pre-dawn hour of December 7th, 1941. Time and Fate were stubborn, and determined to restore their dignity, no matter how badly ruffled their skirts were by the violations of *Kirov* and crew. They had conspired that day to bring the *Kido Butai* to precisely the right place, at precisely the right moment, to launch the most infamously famous attack of the war.

Strangely, it would not be the Japanese that would actually initiate hostilities. It would be the US destroyer *Ward*, which fired on a Japanese midget submarine that was creeping up behind a tug towing targets for live fire exercises near the entrance to the harbor. That was the first hit scored in what would soon become a long desperate struggle over 63.8 million square miles on the largest body of water known in the universe. And in Fedorov's history, the last hit would come many years later, again delivered by the Americans. It would be scored by Bafford E. "Loopy Lew" Lewellen, commanding the US Submarine *Torsk* as it stalked a Japanese cargo ship escorted by a frigate on August 14, 1945. *Torsk* would sink the escort with a newfangled sonar guided torpedo aimed by a gizmo the crew called a torpedo data computer, the legacy of the terror brought back to this tumultuous past by a ship called *Kirov*.

1945 was very far away when Admiral Nagumo stared down the staircase of *Akagi's* three flight decks, descending one after another to the bow of the ship as it turned into the wind. *Akagi* had not yet finished its conversion as it had in Fedorov's history. One day it would have only one flight deck, extending all the way to the nose of the bow, but not this day. He knew what the flags on that mast were now saying to every member of the *Kido Butai* that could see them. They were the same flags Admiral Togo had raised at the Battle of Tsushima, the same words Admiral Yamamoto had pressed him to never forget. *"The fate of our nation depends on this battle—All hands will exert themselves to their utmost."*

Nagumo had a lot on his mind, the weight of that statement hanging right over his head on that mainmast. He had been entrusted with command of this operation, and the cream of Japan's fleet carrier divisions, in what he always thought was a risky, and highly dangerous operation. There were too many things that could go wrong. The long sea journey east, the risk of early detection, the prospect that they would arrive and find an enemy fully alerted and ready for battle. And there was one other question he wished he could answer now, in spite of the strange file Yamamoto had shared with him—where were the American carriers?

In spite of Japan's clear superiority in that category, any carrier on the sea was deemed to be a threat by Japanese navy planners, and always a target of the highest priority. There were only three in the Pacific, with two more scheduled to transfer there soon, hoping to arrive before war came, but they would not get there in time. In spite of warnings that had come from many quarters, the British, US intelligence, blunt threats broadcast by Tojo himself, and that final secret message delivered by Vladimir Karpov, the US was woefully unprepared for the outbreak of the war.

The war fighting elements of the US Fleet were organized into three large Task Forces. TF 1, commanded by Vice Admiral Pye, was the heavyweight, with 6 battleships, 6 cruisers, 18 destroyers, 12 submarines, and 5 minelayers. It was also supposed to have a carrier, CV *Saratoga*, but this ship was fresh from overhaul in Seattle and off to San Diego to pick up her planes.

An old battleship man who had served on five such ships in his early career, Pye had boasted that there was little danger to the fleet at its new forward base in Pearl Harbor. "The Japanese will not go to war with the United States," he said as late as the 6th of December in staff meetings with Fleet CinC Admiral Kimmel. "We are too big, too powerful, and too strong." Thus, in spite of the war warnings, he had his powerful task force sleeping quietly in the harbor, with his overconfidence about to be roundly skewered in a matter of hours.

The other two task forces were at sea. TF 2, under Vice Admiral William Halsey, had three battleships, *Arizona, Nevada* and *Oklahoma*, with 18 destroyers and 3 cruisers. The battleships were to conduct night fire exercises west of Hawaii, while Halsey organized a new TF 8, and slipped away with *Enterprise* along with the heavy cruisers *Northampton, Chester, Salt Lake City* and nine of those destroyers.

Halsey took this force out on November 28th, heading for Wake Island to secretly deliver 12 Marine fighters. The planes were flying off the deck for Wake on December 2, just as *Kirov* reappeared in these troubled waters, and the signal to attack Pearl Harbor was delivered. He had planned to return to Pearl by December 6, but was delayed by a storm in Fedorov's history—weather that was not going to occur in these altered states. The swirling, ever random moods of sea and sky would simply not obey the dictates of Fate and Time, and this would soon have a dramatic impact on the Japanese plans.

Vice Admiral Brown's TF 3 was designated the scouting force of the navy, led by CV *Lexington* under Admiral Newton, along with eight cruisers, 9 destroyers, 17 submarines and 12 minelayers. Like Halsey's special mission, Newton organized a smaller TF 12 and took "Lady Lex" and heavy cruisers *Chicago, Portland* and *Astoria*, with five destroyers, out to deliver planes to Midway.

It is often said that a single day can make all the difference in the world, and Fate was also to change the tabular record of movement for this group, when Newton went on his way 24 hours early, thus finding himself one day ahead of schedule on his return leg to Pearl. Instead of being 500 miles southeast of Midway, and effectively out of the game on December 7th, TF 12 was a little over 500 miles further on, steaming just 150 miles west of Kauai Island, northwest of Pearl.

The night firing exercises went off without a hitch, and Halsey had a mind to dismiss his three slow battleships and send them back to Pearl on December 5th. In Fedorov's history, this is what he actually did, which doomed all three to become proverbial sitting ducks in the harbor. But with *Lexington* ahead of schedule, and his own task force unhampered by foul weather as it was in the old history, the *Enterprise* group was very near *Lexington* on the way home.

Rear Admiral John H. Newton was Commander, Scouting Force, getting a rare chance in the seat of a carrier commander for this one special mission. Otherwise his senior, vice Admiral Wilson Brown, would normally be in charge. Seeing the close proximity of the *Enterprise* as a unique training opportunity, Newton sent a message to Halsey asking if he would care to organize an impromptu fleet exercise involving all the assets they presently had at sea. The signal was simple, but Halsey could read between the lines. He smiled, realizing Newton knew he was about to be bumped back down to the cruisers as soon as they made port. With nothing else other than a dull cruise home, Halsey agreed.

It was to be a cover and converge exercise, where the three battleships and the two carrier groups would stage as if they were a covering force for some other operation, and then converge on a rendezvous point. Thus those three battleships were not detached, and as Halsey looked at his map on December 6, he got a screwball idea.

"Hell, we always come into Pearl from the west. Why not make this rendezvous point up near Kauai? This time we'll swing north of that island and come home from the northwest. We can have the battleships inshore, and the carriers and cruisers covering."

What Admirals decide they often do, and this became the plan for the morning of December 7th, 1941. It would mean the two carriers would not be where Volkov's report predicted, nor would Battleship Division 1 be waiting in the harbor with the rest of Pye's ships. Instead, the American carriers would mount morning search patrols as part of the exercise, and aboard CV *Enterprise*, Scouting Squadron 6 was tapped for the job. Halsey had planned to send out such a mission anyway, having his planes search out in a 150 mile arc, and then just sending them on to land at Ford Island. There, they would have arrived just as the Japanese attack began, with six destroyed in that chaos as they tried to land. This time, Halsey decided they would fly an out and back mission, and return to the *Enterprise*.

Scouting Six had 9 planes, led by Lieutenant Commander Hopping. They would each take a slice of the search arc, with names that would begin rewriting the history of that eventful day, Teaff, Kroeger, Gallaher, West, Dobson, Dickensen, Hilton and Weber. It was Ensign Teaff in plane 6S-2 that would score the jackpot, for his slice of the morning sky would take him directly at the point on the sea where Nagumo's *Kido Butai* was now launching the first strike wave. Commander Mitsuo Fuchida was up to lead them, and they soon darkened the skies above those carriers like fitful bats, their dark wings barely silhouetted against the gloaming dawn.

The planes howled away on their mission, cruising through the grey early morning, lulled by the quiet songs from a radio station on Honolulu. When they had gone, preparations were made for the second wave, and Lieutenant Saburo Shindo would be among the first to fly, leading nine A6-Zero fighters in three *Shotai*. He would take the first *Shotai* up immediately, with extra fuel tanks to loiter over the task force on a defensive watch until the second wave was up.

The Japanese had every hope that they would catch the Americans by surprise, as a seaplane off the heavy cruiser *Chikuma* had reported the fleet was there with at least six battleships, but with no carriers present. One of those six was the *Utah*, now designated a target ship. The other five belonged to Admiral Pye's TF 1. The three notably absent were now rounding the northern shores of Kauai Island, about 10 miles north of Princeville. They were simulating a shore bombardment on that island, screened by the carriers and cruisers. Amazingly, they were just far enough west so that the first strike wave could not spot them.

Events were now about to careen in a wild new direction, all because of the fickle weather, Lexington's hasty efficiency, and a crazy yearning by a cruiser screen commander to try his hand at carrier operations. Then came the message Karpov had quietly arranged, and the altered states were about to alter yet again….

* * *

"What do you make of this?" said Halsey, looking over the strange signal that they had just received on fleet channels. Captain George Murray leaned in closer, his eyes tight.

"Who could have sent it?"

"Came in properly formatted," said Halsey. "Looks like it's from Chief of Naval Ops, but the signal faded out and we lost it. This is all we got, but by god it's a mouthful! This thing is telling me the Japanese fleet is a couple hundred miles northwest of our planned rendezvous point!"

"Could it have been a sighting by one of our PBYs, or perhaps a sub?" Murray was very interested now.

"Well we need to get someone out there and take a good long look. This little exercise we've planned may become something else sooner than we expect. Let's get Scouting Six up right away."

* * *

"Squadron Leader to Little Lost Lambs... report status by assigned order." Lieutenant Commander Hopping was in Plane 6S-1 polling his sheep.

"*Little Lamb 2, all clear,*" same the voice of radioman Jinks on Ensign Teaff's 6S-2. And one by one the others in the flock all called home, until Ensign Weber's radioman Keaney was about to sign off with the last all clear. But Teaff's keen eye thought he saw something, probably another oiler like the one they had overflown ten minutes earlier, the Richfield tanker, *Pat Doheny*. But the longer he looked, the more he saw, until his eyes finally widened with the shock that was soon to ripple through the entire US Pacific Fleet.

"Holy cow! Jinks! Do you see what I see off the port bow?"

"Who the hell are they?" asked Jinks.

"Christ almighty! Those are aircraft carriers. Damn things are launching planes! Get on the blower and report!"

"Squadron leader, this is Little Lamb 1. Big Bad Wolf at 20 miles! My position: two-sixer point three north, one-five-seven west. Repeat Big Bad Wolf! Big Bad Wolf! Carriers!"

Jinks was so rattled that he sent that message right out in the clear, and it hopped into Lieutenant Commander Hopping's head like a thunderbolt.

"Little Lamb One. Confirm. Did you say carriers?"

"Roger Sheep Leader. Five or six big flattops, and they're launching planes! Mother of God… It's the Japanese!"

Hopping needed no further persuasion, and he wasted no time, passing it on to the *Enterprise*, where Halsey got the news at 07:00 hours, just as a ward officer was reporting the three battleships had successfully made their simulated bombardment run off Kauai. He was about to give the order to send the battlewagons home when the news hit him like an electric current.

"Get hold of that crazy cruiser Commander on Lady Lex! Looks like this is no goddamned drill! Then get word down below. I want Bombing Six up on deck in fifteen minutes!"

Those orders were stiffened further in a Fleet Signal, where Halsey ordered all torpedoes to be rigged with warheads, all dive bombers armed with bombs, all fighters to be ready for action, and the destroyer screen was to immediately attack any submarine spotted. The battleships were ordered to load all main guns, for real this time, and ready ammunition was to be moved up from the main magazines. The American ships at sea were to lock and load for action. Halsey had orders that he was to "intercept and destroy" any enemy force encountered, so there was no question that his carriers had been ushered off to ferry planes simply to remove them from harm's way. *Enterprise* and *Lexington* were out there to fight, even if the odds were stacked very high against them.

At 07:10 it was Saburo Shindo's three Zeroes who thought they saw something out of place in the second wave of planes forming up. There was one stray goose, and it seemed to be edging around the flank of the main carrier fleet, dipping in and out of the few clouds puffing up in the rapidly brightening sky. He banked right, taking his whole *Shotai* with him to investigate, and was soon surprised to see what looked to be an American fighter!

The word was flashed to *Akagi*, and then he immediately dove on the enemy, sending Ensign Teaff into a banking dive as he tried to evade. The first air to air duel of the Pacific war saw hapless Teaff pounced upon by three well trained Japanese pilots, and he and his radioman Jinks would become the first American casualties.

* * *

Captain George Murray was at the Admiral's side, worry in his eyes as the ship was jolted into full battle readiness. "Don't forget those three fat pigs up north of Kauai," he said. "What'll we do about them? The Japs will find them sooner or later. Should we have the battleships turn east and rejoin us?"

"All they'll do is slow us down," said Halsey. "Yes, the Japs may find them, sooner or later, so I'd rather make it sooner, and ram them right down their throats. Signal Van Falkenburgh on the *Arizona*. Make sure he got that enemy sighting report, and tell him to get up there and give 'em hell."

Murray gave Halsey a look, seeing the fire in his eyes now, the grizzled war face he would become famous for. He knew the Admiral's order was going to send those ships into harm's way, and possibly to their doom, and he said as much.

"Well hell, Captain," said Halsey. "We call them battleships for a reason! If this isn't the fight they were built for, then what is? That order stands."

Aboard *Arizona*, Officer of the Deck, Ensign Henry Davidson handed Van Falkenburgh the signal, who read it silently before handing it off to Lieutenant Commander Samuel Fuqua, the ship's First Lieutenant and Damage Control Officer, and third in line of command. "Shall we sound battle stations again?" asked Fuqua.

"Better make sure they know it's not a drill this time," said the Captain.

Fuqua nodded to Davidson, who went off to sound the wooping alarm signal, and Fuqua was already heading to his station at Central Control in the conning tower. The fate of BB *Arizona* was going to be much different this time out.

* * *

Admiral Nagumo was equally stunned by the news signaled by Lieutenant Shindo's fighters. The breach of radio silence was only permitted in this extreme case, and the moment the breathless Lieutenant rushed in from the radio room, Nagumo knew the worst—they had been discovered. His precious *Kido Butai* had been certainly spotted now, and radio operators on the *Akagi* also heard the frantic enemy sighting report go out in the clear. The lines on his forehead deepened with concern, for his orders were to abort the mission should he be discovered here—yet now that was simply too late. The first wave was on its way. To call it back now and attempt evasion would be extremely dangerous. So instead his mind turned to the nature of this sighting. Was this a land based plane searching north off the islands, or could it have come from an enemy carrier?

He remembered the briefing file Yamamoto had shown him, indicating the enemy should be far to the southwest on this day. He did not give it much credibility then, nor would he do so now. If that plane was off an enemy carrier, then that ship had to be within 150 miles. He immediately turned to his Fleet Air Officer, Masuda Shogo.

"The second strike wave is spotted on deck and about to launch, but that plane could have been from an enemy carrier. In this event, should we hold back the planes from *Zuikaku* and *Shokaku*?"

"That would weaken the second wave considerably!"

"Yet I am inclined to order this. We have been spotted, and the enemy may be closer than we realize. To set loose all our arrows on

Pearl Harbor would mean we have nothing left to defend the *Kido Butai.*"

"But sir, Genda insists we can organize a third wave."

"Only after recovering planes that are already in the air," said Nagumo. "Kusaka?" Nagumo wanted the opinion of his 1st Air Fleet Chief of Staff, who had been in the thick of the planning for this attack.

"The seaplanes off *Tone* and *Chikuma* can launch an immediate search to the south and west. And the twelve fighters that were to accompany the planes off *Zuikaku* and *Shokaku* can be placed on fleet overwatch at once."

"And if we do find the enemy close enough to attack us?" Nagumo continued to press.

"We can order the second wave planes from the other carriers to depart on schedule. Those from Hara's 5th Carrier Division can delay their launch if necessary. Then, if nothing is found, they can either be sent on behind the second wave, or held for the third wave Genda has planned."

Nagumo had never warmed to the idea of a third wave, but this suggestion achieved his purpose in leaving something in the fleet to strike a seaborne enemy if one was found close at hand. "Very well," he said. "That will be the order. See that Air officers Wada and Shimoda are informed at once—but by flag signals. Even if we have been sighted, fleet units will continue to maintain radio silence."

Quick orders were sent to the fast scout cruisers *Tone* and *Chikuma*. They were to mount an intensive air search in a 180-degree arc north, west and south of the fleet's position. Nagumo would take Yamamoto's advice to keep one eye over his right shoulder as he continued south, and this caution would begin the first carrier to carrier battle in history. As an additional measure, he ordered his escorting battleships, *Hiei* and *Kirishima* to move out ahead of the carriers with an escorting screen of destroyers.

That last ship, the *Kirishima*, had a most interesting fate line, for somewhere in the skewed nexus points of Time, it had encountered a strange beast of a ship from another world, chasing it fitfully through the Timor Sea, only to be mined and beached on a razor sharp shoal near the Torres Strait on the 26th of August, 1942. Yet that whole line of causality was now coming unraveled, save one steely thread that would remain strangely entangled with the monster *Kirishima* had faced. It was embodied in the raging soul of a man named Sanji Iwabuchi.

He had graduated from the Naval Academy several years after Yamamoto, and ended up also serving on the armored cruiser *Nisshin* for a time before moving on to an assignment aboard *Hiei*. There his irascible disposition soon saw him sent off to command shore batteries and seaplane tenders, a rather ignominious demotion that he resented for some time. When he learned that there was a secret operation known as Plan Z going on, he wanted in very badly, longing for another at-sea assignment on a real fighting ship.

It was just his luck that the screening force needed men who were familiar with the two *Kongo* class battleships assigned to the *Kido Butai*, and with seaplane operations being planned from the cruisers *Tone* and *Chikuma*. Iwabuchi's experience in both finally paid off, and he was given a post on *Kirishima* as an aviation liaison officer. The Lieutenant was overjoyed, particularly since his post would put him on the bridge as liaison officer for sighting reports received from cruiser *Tone*. That was where he had transferred his flag after *Kirishima* sunk on his ill-fated pursuit in that earlier thread of lost history, and so the strange bridge that connected the two ships was already being built, and under the surly supervision of Sanji Iwabuchi.

Events were developing rapidly. A signal had been received from Strike Commander Fuchida—*Tora! Tora! Tora!* In spite of every warning, the Japanese had achieved surprise. The reports were soon coming in from the first wave striking Pearl Harbor where the planes were swooping down on battleship row. The clear skies over the harbor were soon stained with the ugly black smoke of fires from the first hits, and daring Japanese pilots raced in, twenty or thirty feet above the water, to deliver their specially modified torpedoes. Fighters danced above, some sweeping down to ship level where they flashed past the stunned American crews, guns blazing.

The absence of Battleship Division 1 saw the berthings in the harbor changed. *West Virginia* was berthed where *Arizona* might have been, about 75 feet astern of *Tennessee*. The open water off Ford Island where *Nevada* should have been, was now empty, and the *Oklahoma*, which had berthed outboard of the *Maryland*, was also gone, exposing the latter ship to the devastating torpedo attack Japan was now delivering. In those first five minutes, 40 torpedoes were launched, and 23 of them scored hits.

All of Pye's battleships, save *Pennsylvania*, which was berthed across the harbor on a protected dock, were gutted by multiple hits. The target ship *Utah* was not overlooked either, and was soon to be logged by the Japanese as a killed battleship. The eager Lieutenants crowded onto the *Akagi's* bridge were making notes on every hit being reported, with newly arriving signals stacked up on the clip boards.

And so, as the Kates, Vals and Zeroes continued to tip their wings and dive, Battleship Division 1 turned north with *Arizona*, *Nevada* and *Oklahoma*, into the winds of uncertainty. The crews were ready and standing to arms, while pilots on both *Enterprise* and *Lexington* were already climbing up onto their wildcats and SBD Douglas Dive Bombers.

Vladimir Karpov was also standing to arms, hands clasped behind his back on the bridge of *Kirov*, which had finally freed itself from the wintery grip of the ice in the Bering Strait. Now the monster the Japanese would come to call *Mizuchi* was racing south at 30 knots into the storm of steel and fire that would soon become the greatest naval conflict of all time.

Karpov smiled, his mind on missiles and mayhem, and just retribution for the Japanese Empire that had dared to set foot on Siberian territory, a smile that was a warning to all enemies far and wide.

Part II

Day of Infamy

"There is heroism in crime as well as in virtue. Vice and infamy have their altars and their religion."

— William Hazlit

Chapter 4

They fell from the sky like dark birds of prey. Flight after flight, one *Shotai* after another, their dark green wings painted with the red fireball of wrath. The Kates were swooping low, their bellies laden with the heavy water lances that would soon open the steel hulls of the enemy battleships. Above, the Vals plummeted down in their dive bombing runs, and beyond it all, the white winged Zeroes circled like hawks as they searched in vain for opposing enemy aircraft. Yet in spite of every warning, the surprise had been complete, and soon the Zeroes were off to other targets, some to the sleeping airfields at Hickam, Wheeler and Ford. There they came in low, guns blazing as they strafed the tightly packed planes on the concrete tarmacs.

Fuchida's jubilant signal, *Tora, Tora, Tora*, still echoed on the airwaves, as it would resound through the history of these tumultuous hours for decades to come. Some events were simply so weighty in their impact, with a gravitational pull on the stream of causality that doomed them to reoccur.

And this was one of them.

Japan's decision to attack Pearl Harbor had been all but pre-ordained when the Strike South Camp found itself largely unopposed in this retelling of events. For the Empire had already taken every province to the north of any value. Its troops garrisoned the long Trans-Siberian Rail as it wound its way up from Old Vladivostok, now called *Urajio* by the Japanese. Once it reached Khabarovsk, it then skirted the long bend of the Amur River, up and over until it reached Chita, a little over 200 miles from Lake Baikal. Those steel rails formed the Empire's northern border, and beyond the line, the endless stretches of tree sewn taiga held no interest for the Japanese. Even though there were vast reserves of oil and other resources there, Japan knew little about them, nor did it have the means of finding and developing those resources in that vast wilderness.

So instead, the eyes of the Generals and Admirals looked south, to the rubber plantations and proven oil fields of the Dutch Pacific

Colonies, largely defenseless, like ripened fruit on a low hanging bough. The only caveat in taking them was the growing presence of the American military in the Philippines. All the sea lanes that would carry that oil and rubber back to Japan would have to transit waters within easy reach of US forces in the Philippines, and so war with the United States was deemed inevitable. The American bases in the Philippines would have to be attacked, and the islands occupied, and if this were so, then the navy, largely through the voice of Admiral Yamamoto, strongly argued that the American navy must also be attacked, and if possible, destroyed.

The plan was worked out in exacting detail and rehearsed by the attack squadrons over many weeks of intensive training. As bold as it was risky, it would involve the cream of the Japanese carrier fleet, the *Kido Butai,* with the lion's share of the navy's best pilots. They would strike perhaps the strongest military bastion in the Pacific at that time, the massive combination of Army muscle and land based air power, and the hardened steel of America's Pacific Battleship Squadrons all packed into the corner of one small island, Pearl Harbor. Almost all of America's offensive war making power in the Pacific lay in that one place, quietly asleep on a balmy Sunday morning.

Off to the north, Admiral Nagumo sat in his Red Steel Castle, the carrier *Akagi,* flagship of the *Kido Butai,* and his thumping heart echoed the reports of exploding bombs and torpedoes as his first strike wave delivered its attack. His ship was the perfect example of the pivot in naval strategy that he would now so ably demonstrate. For *Akagi* was conceived as a fast battlecruiser of the *Amagi* class, in an era where battleships still reigned supreme. Now it had morphed into an aircraft carrier, the new queen of the seas insofar as many in the Navy were concerned.

Japanese ship naming conventions selected the towering strength of mountains to name their battleships, which was how *Akagi* began its career before its conversion. The ship now beneath Nagumo's feet had therefore been named for Mount Akagi, one of the three fabled "mountains of Jomo." That was the ancestral name of the province right there in the heart of the main island of Honshu, no more than 100 kilometers from Tokyo. Roughly translated, the ship's name was the "Red Castle."

Akagi had also seen many upgrades over the years, but strangely, her three tiered flight decks that had been revamped and overshadowed by one main upper deck in Fedorov's history, still remained. A small island superstructure had been added by 1938, on the port side to keep it clear from the vented steam and smoke of the downward facing stacks, which were on the starboard side of the ship. That tall island had been packed with long vertical bundles of sand bags to protect it from the shrapnel of war, two thick bands below the conning tower windows, and one row above. There stood Admiral Nagumo atop his Red Castle, surrounded by Lieutenants and Commanders of every stripe.

An hour earlier, the ship had turned into the wind, and at that moment, with that single turn of the wheel, Japan as a nation had set her course for war that would lead her empire either to renewed glory, or to complete destruction.

"Now we climb our Mountain," said Nagumo as he watched the planes taking off.

"May we find the lost treasure!" said his Fleet Air Officer, Masuda Shogo. He was referring to the legend associated with the rust iron red of the volcanic caldera on Mount Akagi, where it was said that the lost treasure of the Tokugawa Shogunate was secretly buried hundreds of years ago, and never found again. Those who have sought to discover it would have to first brave the icy cold winds that blew down the flanks of that mountain, the *Karakkaze*. That was what the pilots now called the bite of the wind when the carrier increased her speed and turned just before the planes would launch, the *Karakkaze*. Into that wind, Japan would now send the best trained naval aviation pilots in the world, and in some of the best combat planes designed to date.

The Aichi D3A1 *KanBaku* dive bomber the Allies called the "Val" was a relative newcomer, entering production just two years ago in December of 1939. With excellent range at almost 900 miles, it was a superb dive bomber, very stable in the near vertical dive it was capable of, which gave it lethal accuracy in the hands of a skilled pilot.

The Nakajima B5N2 *KanKo* Torpedo Bomber, known as the "Kate," had a distinctive long windowed canopy for excellent visibility, good speed, and exceptional range exceeding 1200 miles. It was superior to its American counterpart in every respect, for the lumbering Douglas TBD "Devastator" was a plane that too often failed to live up to its threatening name.

The Japanese plane was 100MPH faster, had a third more range, and carried the world's premier aerial borne torpedo, the Type 91, with 800 kilograms of striking power and fabled reliability. By comparison the American Mark XIII was plagued with problems in 1941 and 1942, with many surface runners and duds weakening the striking power of the TBD squadrons. The US flyers would be lucky to get the torpedo to run true a third of the time, and then even luckier if they got a hit and it actually exploded.

The Japanese Type 91 had several unique features that made it so advanced for its day. First there were wooden tail fins added to the torpedo to stabilize the airborne segment of its attack. They would be shed upon entry into the water, where a special PID controller system would take over to minimize roll in the sea. While the American plane had to come in low and slow, the Kate could race in at cruising speeds exceeding 200 MPH, much faster than the maximum speed of the American TBDs. For the Pearl Harbor attack, the Japanese had further modified the wooden fins to allow the torpedo to run in the shallow waters of the harbor instead of descending to 100 feet, as most torpedoes would do after hitting the water. The *Gyorai*, as they called it, the Thunderfish, were already tearing the bellies of the American battleships open when Nagumo got the urgent sighting report from Lieutenant Saburo Shindo's fighters off *Akagi*.

The men in those Japanese planes were as good as they came, many recruited at the age of 15 through the Japanese Yokaren program. Eager to find fresh young minds and bodies to mold and train, the Japanese staged formation flights over schools to arouse interest and stir the imagination of the young boys. Many times the pilots would even 'bomb" the school yards with small rubber balls attached to tiny parachutes, a gift to the young boys who stood in awe below. Recruitment followed soon after, and the one percent who made the grade entered a rigorous Spartan training regimen, grueling and very tough, where physical beatings would follow any lapse or failure, to harden the young boys into fighting men.

There at Tsuchiura on Lake Kasumigaura, the 'Misty Lagoon,' the discipline bordered on sadistic, and yet to the boys that made it that far, failure was unthinkable. If they were to be expelled from the training school, their family would be so dishonored that they might be forever ostracized. A discharge for poor performance was feared as the ultimate shame, but being human flesh and blood, for some that failure came in the form of suicide. Those who survived were as tough as hardened steel, and with skills to match the determination and willpower this rigorous training program had instilled in them.

Yet there was an artistry to their flying that was almost Zen like, for many had actually sat in long hours with Zen Monks and priests, who instilled in them the virtue of fighting with no mind. Their actions would then become instinctive, reflexive, without contamination by the discriminating consciousness. That was the Cherry blossom on the insignia inscribed on his left sleeve, and with it were the iron anchor of the navy and the wings he had labored so long and hard to earn.

The third plane to rise from those carriers was the Mitsubishi A6M *Reisen* "Zero," a plane the Allies called the "Zeke." It was a real shadow dancer in the skies, light, quick, and with whisper soft responsiveness at the flight controls that led many pilots who flew it to say it seemed as though the plane was a part of their own bodies. With the wings and fuselage built as one piece, the plane had strength and durability for the rigorous stresses of a dog fight in which it excelled. It could out range and out fight any Allied plane that opposed it in late 1941, hitting hard with two 20mm Type-99 cannons on the wings, and a pair of 7.7mm machineguns on the engine cowling.

Allied flyers who inspected one they had recovered from the

Aleutians in 1942 would say that it was "built like a fine watch," with a dash board that was a "marvel of simplicity," and it was the scourge of the skies over the Pacific for many long months, until the Americans finally built planes like the Hellcat, P-38, and Mustang to match it.

One famous Zero pilot was the man who had planned the entire operation, Minoru Genda, and he had reveled in the skies with his white winged plane for months before the war, honing his skills to a fine and perfect art. One maneuver he devised to shake off an enemy fighter coming from behind became the famous *Hineri-Komi*, or "turning in." It was a kind of pitch back maneuver, and it was refined to perfection by another Japanese Ace, Mochizuki Isamu. The plane would start a loop, and pitch over to one side at the top with a right rudder side slip followed by a hard left rudder that ended up putting the plane behind the attacking enemy. It was widely adopted and taught at the Yokosuka Naval Air School, becoming the bane of many an Allied pilot in those early months of the war.

So by the time these Japanese boy recruits had left the school yards behind to become men, and reached the decks of those carriers, they had hundreds of hours of flying experience behind them, uncompromising discipline, chiseled skill, and the planes to use every ounce of that ability. They had also formed a close knit comradery that was even tighter than traditional family circles. Only their fellow aviators knew just how hard it had been to get where they were, enduring deprivation, humiliation, endless physical hardships and beatings, the constant pressure to succeed, and fear of failure.

Admiral Nagumo's flyers were truly an elite class, even as the war was just beginning, and many would stop and bow to the wall in the wardroom where another onetime Captain of the Red Castle, one Isokoru Yamamoto, had ordered that the name of any flyer who ever died in action should be inscribed. It would take a wall full of those names, he had once told them, before they would ever reach the lofty heights their ship was named for, or before they would ever truly climb the mountain that was before them now.

"Order the planes from 5th Carrier Division to launch

immediately, but they will assemble over the task force and await my order to move out." Nagumo was listening to an urgent inner voice, something was itching at him, a thrumming sense of warning and alarm. He had earlier ordered those planes to be held back, but the thought that they would be sitting on the flight decks, armed and fueled, seemed too great a risk at that moment. If there were American carriers close by, he wanted to face them with a sword in hand.

His sixth sense was serving him well, for at that moment the planes of Bombing Six off the USS *Enterprise* were already in the air, and heading northwest to the point signaled by Ensign Teaff in plane 6S-2. They would soon be spotted by Lieutenant Saburo Shindo's fighters, and the level of alarm now became a burning certainty in Nagumo's mind. The enemy was there, and he already knew exactly where the Japanese carriers were. He knew that miles and miles ago, thought Nagumo, though he would never know how the careful stealth of his approach to this attack had been undone. Somehow the enemy had wind of his carriers, and he was coming in for the kill.

The orders flashed to *Zuikaku* and *Shokaku* could not come soon enough, the fitful flag signals snapping in the stiff breeze with an almost frantic movement—*launch all ready aircraft!*

Chapter 5

Vice Admiral Bull Halsey was well named. He stood on thick short legs, which supported his barrel chested torso and well muscled arms. His big head sat at the top, with wild brows and the glint of mischief in his blue eyes that was often mistaken for anger. A no nonsense man, his disposition could flare that way on a moment's notice, but a wry grin would just as easily tug the corners of his heavy bulldog jaw. Under fire he would soon become cool and unperturbed, preferring to wear a broad white helmet on the weather bridge during any enemy attack, and personally watching the fall of every bomb that was directed at his ship as if he were evaluating the enemy pilot in a training drill.

But this was no drill… Even as the ship beat to quarters for its first official action of the Pacific War, Halsey was deep in thought, wondering whether he would be able to hurt the enemy he had just stumbled upon. Scouting Six had flashed the report, but only from a single plane. He could either get on the radio and ask Lieutenant Commander Hoppings to confirm the sighting, or he could take it as the war warning it was, and do something about it. Minutes later, when the news came that Pearl Harbor itself was already under attack, any shred of hesitation he may have had left him completely. He had already put the ship on its toes, and ordered Battleship Division 1 to get up north after that sighting.

Now he was sending Lieutenant Commander William Hollingsworth out with Bombing Six, 17 SBD-2 Dauntless dive bombers. Lieutenant Commander Eugene Lindsey's TBDs were still arming, but they would be up on deck soon. And he already had Wade McClusky up overhead with 16 Wildcats. It was going to be one hell of a morning, and the only question in his mind was how to coordinate his attack with Newman's task force, the man who had proposed this impromptu exercise that now saw his ship sitting right on the edge of the enemy attack on Pearl.

Captain Fredrick Sherman on the Lady Lex was about 75 miles northeast of his position, and would need time to get close enough to launch an attack if this sighting report was accurate. But Halsey knew that every minute counted now. If his ship was sighted by the enemy, McClusky's 16 Wildcats would be a fairly thin shield, and if he kept them all here on CAP, who was going to escort the strike wave in? He thought of Putman's 12 Marine Wildcats, delivered to Wake just 48 hours ago, and realized they would do a lot more good here on the *Enterprise* than they ever would on that island.

"Damn it," he swore. "Where the hell is *Lexington?*"

Captain Murray had no answer for him, which did little for Halsey's mood, but every instinct in the Admiral's body was urging him to attack.

"Alright," he said. "Notify Young that he can take in everything we have, including half McClusky's fighters. That means we arm what's left of Scouting Six."

"That'll be the ten SBDs, sir. Hopping took out the other eight."

"Fine, get 'em armed and off this ship heading northeast. We can't wait for *Lexington*, but be damn sure they know where the bar is out there, and they'd better show up for the fight."

He couldn't be too hard on Newman and Sherman, for the *Lexington* was coming all the way from a position off Midway. In fact, had it not been for Newman's suggestion concerning this exercise, the *Enterprise* would already be back at Pearl Harbor, and right under the gun. So it was just good Joss that *Enterprise* was here, he thought. Halsey believed in luck, lived by it, and would always knock on wood whenever he made an overoptimistic prediction. Now he hoped his Joss was good that day, for from his perspective, the whole navy was counting on him now, and he was going to do everything possible to find and fight his enemy.

The strike group would become 27 SBDs now that Bombing Six had been augmented with the rest of those planes from Scouting Six. Along with the 18 TBD Devastators, and eight Wildcats in escort, Halsey would throw 53 planes at the Japanese that morning. They formed up at a little after 09:40 and were heading off into the brightening skies to look for that fight.

And they would soon find it.

* * *

Saburo Shindo was still up when they came, flights of dark blue planes against the pale sky. He had been the first to find and shoot down an American carrier based aircraft, for the planes Halsey had sent to Pearl in the old historical timeline never had that mission. Instead they were up in that strike wave, raw, untried pilots for the most part, yet feeling strength in numbers…. Until they saw what they were up against. Shindo and the two other fighters from his *Shotai* off the *Akagi* were not alone.

The skies above the Japanese fleet were thick with swarms of aircraft. Many were the strike planes still taking off from the 5th Carrier Division, and they were already breaking away in small groups and heading south. Yet all the fighters, 15 Zeros off *Shokaku* led by Lt. Tadashi Kaneko, and another 15 off *Zuikaku* led by Lt. Masao Sato, joined the standing CAP assigned to the fleet, which amounted to 36 additional fighters, nine from each of the four remaining carriers. So the 45 American strike planes escorted by 8 Wildcats were now going to be facing 66 Zeros, and the result was a cold, unflinching mathematical carnage.

The brave Wildcats surged ahead to almost certain doom, while the 18 torpedo bombers broke off and dove for the deck. The dive bombers had to maintain altitude if they were ever to mount an attack, and of the 27 that flew out that day, 10 were killed outright, and another seven forced to break off and evade. *Shotai* after *Shotai* ripped through the formation, savaging the American planes like hawks streaking through a flight of lumbering geese. Planes were burning, trailing long smoky tails, and several exploded, careening down out of the sky in a mad cartwheel of death.

Others broke formation and maneuvered, pulling hard on the stick and yoke of their dive bombers, but no match for the nimble Japanese fighter planes. Yet the rear gunners were blazing away at any enemy plane that lined up for a kill, and some were scoring hits. Of the ten SBDs that managed to get over a target, six more were tailed by lethal Japanese fighter pilots, and gunned down as they braved that last final hour. Two pilots had been so rattled by the swirling air battle that they found themselves too low to get into the fight. They broke off and sped away, finding a bank of sea mist to hide them as they desperately headed home.

Saburo Shindo saw them briefly, noting their heading, and quickly radioed the strike planes to the south. An order had been given that if any clear sighting report emerged in the hours ahead, all 5th Carrier Division strike planes still carrying bombs and torpedoes were to break off from their approach run to Pearl Harbor and look to find the American carriers at sea. Shindo's frantic call urged his comrades to follow the American dive bombers, and that was the only reason he decided to spare them, for they would have been easy kills, just as all the others were.

The American Wildcats fought their desperate defense, getting three kills, but losing five of eight planes, with the other three damaged, out of ammo, and looking to escape.

Down on the deck, the torpedo planes were struggling to line up on targets as the skies around them puffed up with dark deadly blossoms of fire and jet black smoke. The Zeroes came down after them, getting eight, and three more were so badly damaged by the enemy flak that they broke off, jettisoning their torpedoes and trying to find a way out of the death trap. Seven actually got torpedoes into the water, but four of those had launched much too soon, the planes being harried by the hot tracer rounds of enemy fire, and the jittery pilots wanting to just drop their fish and run for their lives. Those four had no chance to score a hit, but three brave men held on, one with the right wing of his plane on fire, painting the sky with a dark line of smoke that was aimed right at the carrier *Kaga*.

They all got off a clean shot, then banked away in a wild retreat, one with a bright winged Zero right on its tail. Two of the three torpedoes ran true, but one soon bobbed up to the surface where it was easily spotted in time for Captain Jisaku Okada to make a ten point turn to avoid the attack. *Kaga* turned, but her 42,000 ton displacement responded sluggishly. Okada could see that he would avoid the first torpedo, but there were two, and the second could not be evaded. He clenched his jaw, about to endure the shame of being the first sea Captain in the Japanese Navy to be struck by the enemy, but that fate was reserved for another that day. The last torpedo would have struck home had its engine not failed, sending it diving into the depths to be forever forgotten.

Thus far, the American attack had been a terrible disaster, but there were still those last two SBDs who had kept on in their dive when the other two broke off, the last of the Mohegans from Bombing Six—and they were right over the Red Castle. Down came the bombs, a pair of 500 pounders delivered by two intrepid American pilots—Ensign G. H. Goldsmith and Lieutenant John Van Buren. Their Joss was very good that day, and Van Buren put his bomb right on the nose of the unwieldy carrier, where it would strike the low bow flight deck and explode. Goldsmith's bomb just skirted the starboard side funnel where it blew away part of the cowlings on the steam vent and shotgunned shrapnel into the guts of the ship, killing fifteen sailors.

To the angry Japanese fighter pilots above, they looked in horror to see *Akagi*, the fleet flagship, had been hit twice, bleeding dark black smoke like a harpooned whale.

The Red Castle was on fire.

* * *

In the ninety minutes it took the planes of *Enterprise* to launch, assemble, reach their presumed target and die, the *Lexington* had trimmed 45 miles off the range and was already spotting planes on her long deck for takeoff. The crazy cruiser skipper who had wanted his chance as a carrier commander was about to get his wish come true in a way he never expected. But in many ways, the *Lexington* was even more ill equipped than *Enterprise* was for this fight.

The ship had just delivered 18 old Marine Vindicator dive bombers to Midway, clearing her decks for the action that was now underway. Lady Lex could send up 18 SBD-2 dive bombers in Bombing Two, and an equal number from Search Two. Behind them there would be only 12 TBD-1 torpedo planes, all watched over by 17 obsolete F2A-3 Brewster Buffalos. Ten would fly escort, leaving only seven left for CAP, and one of those failed to make it off the deck that morning due to engine problems.

Lieutenant Commander Jim Thatch and his wingman Ensign Eddy Sellstrom were in two of those Buffalos, the last planes off the deck that day. Historically, they would have to wait until February 20, 1942 before they trained their guns on an enemy plane, a Japanese Type 97 flying boat near Rabaul. This time their baptism by fire would come much sooner. They were up with Lt. Stanley and Ensign Haynes, and Lieutenants Butch O'Hare and Marion Dufilho were the last two in the CAP formation.

Those six men were *Lexington*'s shield, in six lumbering planes that had been very well named when they were dubbed Buffalos. They were so heavy that when the British received them, they ended up cutting the loads of ammo and fuel, and replacing the guns in a vain attempt to get more performance out of the plane. In the end they made trainers of the few they received, for the Buffalo was simply outclassed in every respect by their own fighters. A few surplus planes delivered to Finland were derisively called "flying beer bottles," though the planes still bested the older Russian fighters they faced. In the Pacific, they could not even match the early Japanese A5M Claude, let alone the acrobatic Zeroes they might soon encounter in this desperate hour. The plane was almost as fast as a Zero at 320MPH, but the Japanese plane was far more maneuverable. The stubby fuselage of the buffalo would soon come to be called the "flying coffin" by Marine pilots, and it was a very fitting rebuke.

The strike wing started on its way after receiving a better report on the enemy location. It was going to be a very long run for the TBDs, for the action was almost beyond their 'point of no return' for the Devastator, which had a fairly short strike radius. Down on the flight deck before takeoff, Ensign Chuck Hamilton was fresh from the strike briefing room, his cheeks red in the morning wind.

"Did I hear that right?" he said to a mate, Lieutenant Ed Hurst. "They said the Japs were spotted 175 miles out."

"You heard it right," said Hurst as he started to climb up the wing of his plane.

"But sir, those torpedo planes have a combat radius of only 200 miles, if even that. How are they supposed to get home?"

Hurst gave him a look, rubbed his nose. "Now you're starting to sound like Walkie Talkie," he said, referring to a squadron mate who always seemed to be talking aloud to himself on the hanger deck, Gunner Talkington. "Don't you think the Brass know that? They'll move the damn ship after we take off, that's all. Besides, if the Torpies can't do the job, we will. Now get in your goddamned plane."

All told, *Lexington* was going to send out 58 more planes to look for the Japanese, and they had a fairly good idea how to find them. On the way in, they could hear the action then underway as the *Enterprise* group ran into the buzz saw of those enemy Zeroes on CAP defense. More than one man swallowed hard as they heard the frantic calls of their comrades, some yelling for their mates to turn, others to bail out when their planes were scorched with fire. They had been told they were going up against five or six enemy carriers, yet the futility of what they were now doing never entered the minds of the pilots. They kept on, steady on the stick, though a good number prayed, while others silently said their inner goodbyes to loved ones they left behind in the states.

Yet now fate would play a cruel game. When the planes of Carrier Division 5 responded to the urging of Saburo Shindo, they eventually spotted those two wayward US planes and started following them. But the American pilots had their return heading wrong, and instead of leading the enemy back to the *Enterprise*, they had turned 15 degrees to starboard and they were now leading them directly back to *Lexington*.

The Japanese had 27 B5N Kates off *Shokaku*, all expecting to launch their torpedoes at the battleships in Pearl Harbor, and all equipped with torpedoes designed to run shallow. The Kates off *Zuikaku* were too far along and had been sent on to Pearl, but the dive bombers off that carrier turned back and joined those of *Shokaku* to put a total of 54 Vals in the Japanese strike wave. These, combined with 12 Zeroes on escort, would send a total of 93 planes out in the hunt for the American carriers, and while it was *Enterprise* that had picked this fight and thrown the first punch, they were all going to find Lady Lex instead.

Those six Brewster Buffalos over Newton's Task Group would each be double teamed by a pair of escorting Zeroes, and the remaining 81 strike planes looked down to see the *Lexington*, escorted by the heavy cruisers *Chicago, Portland* and *Astoria*, with five destroyers.

Again, the results were coldly mathematical, though the Japanese torpedo bombers would find the wooden fins rigged to their lances had them running much too shallow in the rising swells, and many well aimed torpedoes would run astray on the open sea. That said, they were going to put three of those 27 torpedoes into *Lexington*, and one would get through the torpedo protection system and strike a reservoir of stored Avgas. The resulting explosion rocked the ship violently to starboard, and for a moment it looked as though the weight of that prominent superstructure would pull it all the way over. But *Lexington* righted herself, though she was soon listing heavily to port where that hit had been taken.

Another two torpedoes found her closest defender, the cruiser *Astoria*, and that ship would not survive. The Vals would do a little better, scoring five bomb hits that savaged the flight deck of *Lexington*, and a sixth that struck flush on the wide stack, blasting it open and sending a pall of heavy smoke over the entire scene. *Astoria* would also take two hits, with two on *Chicago* and one on *Portland*, and the destroyer *Flusser* was blown completely out of the water when a 500 pound bomb struck and ignited a torpedo rack, but the other four destroyers raced about to avoid harm.

Not long after their home carrier was mortally wounded, the planes off *Lexington* found what they were looking for…

Chapter 6

Aboard *Lexington*, the situation was going from bad to worse. A 500 pound bomb had exploded just forward of the center elevator, opening a hole twelve feet wide and penetrating to the hangar deck where it caused a great deal of fragment damage. Another bomb had fallen just inboard of the main island, apparently without detonating, but it was a delayed action bomb, and when it reached the 2nd deck a hapless seaman stared in horror as the spinning fuse activator suddenly stopped.

It was the last thing he saw. Another bomb had just missed the stern of the ship, but had enough explosive power to start fires on the fantail and temporarily interfere with the ship's steering when the rudder was batted to one side by the force of the detonation. Yet the most telling blow fell right on the forward elevator, punching through to deck three where it ignited to send smoke and fire into all the hanger deck spaces in that area.

Even taken together, the ship might have recovered from this damage, but not with the serious torpedo hits thrown in on the port side, and the heavy fires below decks there when that Avgas blew. *Lexington* was soon in a heavy list, and Admiral Newton's experience as a carrier commander was coming to a most unfortunate end. He could see that the situation was now beyond saving, and gave the order to abandon ship. Signals flashed to the four remaining destroyers in his screen to make ready to recover survivors in the water. As to where his planes would land when they returned, he ordered his senior flight operations officer to notify the strike leader they had to either look for the *Enterprise* or somehow make it to any land base they might find.

When that news reached the planes in flight, Ensign Chuck Hamilton swore under his breath. They had not even seen the enemy yet and the damn Japs had already put the hurts on Lady Lex. This mission had been a long shot from the beginning, with the presumed targets right at, or beyond the edge of the point of no return, at least for the torpedo bombers. He had a little more range in his Dauntless, but Hurst had told him they were going to move the damn ship, and that was not going to happen. Now they had to look for the *Enterprise*, and he had absolutely no idea where that ship might be. With a sinking feeling he tightened his grip on the stick, saying nothing to his machine gunner in the back. He knew in his bones he was probably never going to lay eyes on the *Enterprise*, and getting over to Oahu would be just as difficult.

Angry that the war was starting off so badly for the ship and his mates, he swore he'd make this run a way to get even. Seconds later, he heard the strike leader shout out a warning: *Enemy Carriers! Three O'clock!* He and the rest of Bombing Two were about to get their day in the fire.

* * *

Down on the long flight deck of the carrier *Kaga*, standing just aft of the command island, Air Commander Sata Naohito looked in horror at the dark cloud mushrooming up from the fleet flagship. *Kaga* had been steaming abreast of *Akagi*, and had only now turned away when Captain Okada had maneuvered to avoid those torpedoes, which gave Naohito an excellent view of the other ship after the turn. He had clearly seen the first hit on the short forward deck, and his initial thought had been that it was fortunate *Akagi* had not completed her planned refit to extend the main top flight deck all the way to the bow. Now *Akagi* was only using that lower bow deck to launch and recover her small detachment of sea planes, which were then stored on a much smaller middle deck just below the main deck. That hit was clearly going to prevent any further launch or recovery of a seaplane, but it should not interfere with the carrier's main flight deck operations.

We were lucky to avoid those torpedoes, he thought, and if *Akagi* had to suffer this insult, the ship was also lucky to be hit where it was, right on the nose. The American pilots were brave, but unskilled. Their minds were on the flack being thrown at them by our 5-inch batteries, and not on the weapons they hoped to strike us with. That is always a fatal distraction at the moment of attack. A good pilot must lose all sense of self in that moment. He must become nothing more than a part of his aircraft, a simple machine of death, with not the slightest inkling of his own fate coming to mind. They should not have even come this close.

He watched as a Zero chased down the last of the torpedo bombers that had made that threatening run on the *Kaga*, gunning it down with bright fire from the white wings. He could not see what the other bomb had done to *Akagi*, but from the looks of things, the heavy smoke told him the ventilation stacks on the side of the carrier had been hit. That would be a nuisance, the smoke obscuring flight deck operations, but it was also not a serious blow. For a moment he thought he saw the hot orange tongues of a fire starting on the bow of the other ship, and the smoke there became heavier. That was most likely the fuel from one of the ready seaplanes on that deck, he thought. Most unfortunate, particularly for the pilot who was waiting in that cockpit.

Yet now his attention was suddenly pulled skyward again, and he could hear shouts from other watchmen on the island above, see their stiff arms pointing. He looked to see the sky darkening with tiny black specks, and he could just hear the drone of their engines. An air duel began there as he watched, where two *Shotai* that had been on high overwatch now dived to engage the enemy planes, but the bulk of the CAP had been scattered in its pursuit of the first American strike, and many planes had dived to low elevation to attack those enemy torpedo planes.

With a sudden pulse of anxiety, he realized that all these planes could not be coming from a single American carrier. There had to be at least two, and possibly even three. For the first time the sense of imminent danger settled on him, though he took a deep breath, looking now to the elevators where he could see the last three Zeroes remaining in reserve were now being brought up to be spotted for launch. Soon the planes from the first strike wave should be returning, and Captain Okada would have to run with the wind for recovery. Behind him, he could see a few planes on the decks of *Hiryu* and *Soryu*, but with the second wave already launched to attack Pearl Harbor, the fleet was in an interval of calm where flight deck operations were concerned.

That moment of breathless calm was now about to end.

* * *

Ensign Hamilton saw the carriers ahead, heard the chatter of the Buffalo pilots as they struggled to engage the first enemy fighters coming down from above. But there were not many, and he and his mates were able to close on the targets relatively quickly. He saw the torpedo planes descending to make their runs, and there he could see many more enemy fighters swarming low over the sea, and starting to climb. He looked ahead, saw the smoke from the lead carrier, and realized the *Enterprise* strike group must have already attacked. They had come on the scene like a column of cavalry reinforcements at a beleaguered post, and now he was going to give it to the enemy for what they had done to Lady Lex.

Hurst was in his ear… *"Steady boys, let's get that stray sheep first!"* The ensign could see what his flight leader meant, for one of the enemy carriers had swung out of the formation and was now turning to resume station. A minute later they were right on top, and he tipped his wings over, following two other planes down after Hurst to begin his dive. For the first time in the war, he heard one of his mates shout out a battle cry on the radio as they dove, a word that was once imbued with a sinister hidden meaning… *Geronimo!*

Hamilton dove, still in love with his big heavy plane, and feeling the weight and solidity of the Dauntless SB2. It had a rugged feel that reassured, and yet it still handled as well in a dive as it might in level flight. The innovative diving brake at the trailing edge of the wing allowed the plane to make very good high angle dives, with great stability that led to very accurate bombing. It wasn't as maneuverable as the quick turning Japanese Vals, but it could carry a better bomb load, take much more punishment, and was just as accurate in the hands of a decent pilot. Ensign Hamilton was pretty good, and today he was well motivated.

The stray sheep he was diving on was the *Kaga*, now well away from the main formation of enemy carriers. Lieutenant Hurst knew that they would likely face a good deal less flak to go after that ship, for the rest of the formation presented a phalanx of defense, with the skies already beginning to puff up as one of the other squadrons decided to try their luck against the main body.

The enemy had seen them approaching, and though the fighters had not come up yet to challenge, the flak was pocking up the sky all around them. *Kaga*'s main weapon for a high elevation attack was her sixteen 5-inch dual purpose guns, eight on each side of the ship. They could outrange the 25mm auto cannons, but getting a hit wasn't going to be easy as the fast moving dive bombers came in.

He watched as the airspeed slowly increased, moving through 260 to 280 knots. The enemy ship appeared under the cowl of the plane, and he could see he was lined up well. He nudged the nose just a little to the right, reduced his throttle a bit, and set his props. Coming down from the higher altitude required him to adjust the gas mixture slightly as the plane descended. His eyes ran quickly over his instrument panel, checking the carburetor heat, and noting the indicators telling him the safety was off and his bomb was ready to release. He took a quick look over his shoulder to check his rear seat gunner, seeing he was in position for the dive, then leaned forward to put his eye to the bombing telescope. The plane passed through 11,000 feet, and at 10,000 he pushed it over for the final vertical segment of the dive.

Hamilton set his goggles firmly in place, opened the dive brakes to trim his speed, and looked for his target. The chill of the air at cruising altitude was now gone, and he could feel the muggy warmth of the Pacific beneath him.

He had a 500 pounder underneath, and a pair of 100 pound bombs on the wings. As he dove, through 8000 feet to 6000 feet, he could hear Gunner Talkington yammering to himself on the radio as always, which brought a smile. Then he squinted to be sure he had his target in the crosshairs, and hit his bomb release. 700 pounds fell away, lightening the plane, and the Ensign pushed himself back in the seat, his stomach muscles tight, yelling at the top of his voice like all the others when they let that payload go. It was one more way to keep the blood in your head when you pulled out of that dive—yell for all you were worth. He didn't want to black out, even for a moment on his first real combat dive, so he stayed focused, breathing hard as he closed those dive flaps to pick up speed and make good his escape from the bright flashing fire of the Japanese 25mm guns that had now joined the battle at lower elevation. He wanted to see his enemy beneath him when he pulled up, inwardly crossing his fingers that his aim had been true.

It was a strange feeling coming in like that, the noise of the plane, the sharp crack of the flak guns, the fitful calls on the radio, and the sensation of terrible speed, as if you were strapped on a meteor plummeting down through the sky. He had been lined up well, the plane very stable when he pulled to release those bombs, and now he had every expectation for a hit. He heard Talkington's shrill voice yelling and knew the other man had just released his eggs too. But Walkie Talkie's voice was suddenly cut off, and Hamilton turned his head to look for his mate.

The plane had been hit. A 5-inch shell exploded right in front of the Dauntless, the shrapnel shattering Talkington's wind screen and taking him in the left shoulder with a severe wound. Other fragments had scored his wings, and these early versions of the plane did not have self-sealing fuel tanks. The resulting fire was going to end his mate's dive the hard way, and that was his war, over before it started. He wasn't going to have to worry about trying to find the *Enterprise*, thought Hamilton grimly. The only place he was ever going to land that plane was in the deep blue sea.

* * *

As the attack came in, Air Commander Sata Naohito ran for his station on the aft quarter of the island, a very small platform, just above the flight deck, and beneath the Type 91 AA fire director that was trying to feed the 5-inch guns the best firing angle to engage the planes. It had done well enough against Walkie Talkie's plane, but not before he had released his bombs, which were now falling with very good accuracy. Naohito saw them coming, specks in the sky at first, yet growing ever larger, as though the heavens had hurled them directly at his station, and with deadly precision.

Down they came, the 500 pounder just barely missing the flight deck, while one of the smaller 100 pound bombs struck and exploded directly beneath his station. He had just stepped up onto the circular stairway around that fire director when the shrapnel took his legs from under him. Some struck the windows of the bridge itself, fifteen feet above, and the glass shattered from that impact. As he fell with the pain, Naohito felt the cold spray from that 500 pounder that had narrowly missed the ship, and could see white spumes of other bomb splashes bracketing the carrier. Then he felt a larger impact, and knew they had taken a direct hit with a heavy bomb. Hamilton's aim had been dead on, and he was getting his payback for Lady Lex, for Pearl, and for old Walkie Talkie all in one. In that ten-minute slice of the war, both ships in Carrier Division 1 had been hit and were now on fire.

Commander Naohito might have bled to death then and there, were it not for the fact that some of that shrapnel had also struck the Type 91 director, and gunnery officer Lieutenant Commander Miyano Toyosaburo had come out from the bridge to inspect for damage. He saw Naohito slumped on the winding stair, and immediately ordered men to his aid. Talkington's hit, even with that much smaller bomb, had done just enough damage to put that director out of action, and though he did not know it, he had helped the next squadron get through that flak defense to press home the attack.

Though this was their first real combat experience, and they were up against very steep odds, the American pilots in their sturdy Dauntless planes were going to wreak havoc. Hamilton's 500 pound bomb went right through the main flight deck, shaking the ship violently when it exploded to immolate the hanger deck spaces below. Though they were mostly empty of planes now, there were fuel canisters, hoses, tools, winches, and a rack of ordnance for the dive bombers was still at the ready. A fire started, and Japanese fire control on the carriers was going to prove for the first time here that it was not up to the task.

On the bridge above, Captain Jisaku Okada felt the concussion of the hit, and the intense vibration under his feet. First hit, second hit, it did not matter. His face burned with shame as he rushed to the shattered window to see what had happened. The dark black smoke was pouring from the center of his flight deck, where a slight elevation created a small bulge. He could see the hot wavering flames there, and the only consolation he could take was the fact that almost every plane on the ship was already in the sky. Even those last three zeroes that had been spotted managed to get off the deck just before the American dive bombers came in, and now they were savagely attacking the ship's tormenters.

But how will I recover my planes if that fire is not soon controlled, he thought? Thankfully, there are many other decks free of harm, and no danger to the pilots should they return soon.

But the shame of being struck here was bad enough, let alone the thought that his planes might now have to land elsewhere, and he might have to return home without an air wing. He turned to a young Lieutenant, ordering him below to get a firsthand report on the damage. Trying to sort out what was being shouted over the voice tubes was useless.

Another bomb landed very near the forward port side of the ship, and then *Kaga* rocked yet again as it was struck heavily near the bow. This time it blew away one of the big support girders there, causing the entire edge and corner of the flight deck supports to crumple and collapse right before Captain Okada's unbelieving eyes. It looked as though the ship had struck something in the water, with the bow segment of the long flight deck rutted and bent. He did not think the damage was severe enough to inhibit landing operations, but the hit amidships had already decided that fate, and the sudden secondary explosion that now shook the Captain from his feet would decide the fate of the ship itself.

Hamilton's hit was now greatly compounded. The fire amidships had reached the ordinance rack, and three more 500 pound bombs that had not been properly stored went off one after another. The resulting explosion blew a massive 40 foot hole in the main deck, while also blasting deeper into the ship where it cut numerous steam pipes from the engines in the boiler spaces.

When Okada pulled himself to his feet, he saw the jet black smoke laced with hot white steam, and knew at once what had happened. There, through all that smoke and steam, he could dimly see the blood red circle of the *hinomaru* painted on the bow segment of the flight deck, Japan's famous rising sun that would soon become an aiming point for industrious American pilots in the years ahead.

The symbolism of that insignia was rooted deep in Japanese culture, for the Emperor himself was said to be a direct descendant of the Sun Goddess Amaterasu, his authority thereby springing from divine origins. Seeing that emblem shrouded over by the choking black smoke and vented steam that was the life blood of his ship, was a great blow to Captain Okada, and he never forgot the ominous feeling he experienced at that moment.

Part III

Ultimatum

"We are not diplomats but prophets, and our message is not a compromise but an ultimatum."

— **Aiden Wilson Tozer**

Chapter 7

Admiral Nagumo saw the explosion plume up from the center of his sister ship, and his eyes tightened. There was a collective groan from many of the younger officers, but Nagumo said nothing, standing stone still on the bridge. It was then that a damage control officer rushed in to report the hit to the lower forward deck of his own ship had been managed, and the fires were under control.

"We are still fully operational," the young officer said hopefully, then he stopped and gaped out the window at *Kaga*, the intake of his breath a sharp punctuation to his optimistic report.

At that moment, all the fears and reservations Admiral Nagumo had harbored concerning this mission were made a real and tangible thing in the sight of *Kaga* burning off his starboard side. The enemy planes were still attacking, torpedo bombers swooping down and leveling off to make runs on Carrier Division 2 in the center of his formation. He could already see that *Hiryu* and *Soryu* were beginning to turn away to port, knowing there must be torpedoes in the water.

He also realized that, in spite of the awesome spectacle of his powerful *Kido Butai*, it now seemed as fragile as a lotus blossom. Throw a handful of planes at it, for that was the sum of all that got in close enough to attack his sister ship, and look what could happen.

They had been nearly two years planning, working out every conceivable detail of the operation. His squadron pilots had been all assigned to specific berths and targets. Genda had worked out the details to the letter, and the men had rehearsed it all for many months. The long cross Pacific approach had been conducted with perfect secrecy, save one lonesome Russian steamer that they had seen on their far horizon, which they allowed to pass unharmed. Everything had been working flawlessly, and the reports coming back from the first wave strike on Pearl Harbor had been ticking off the hits like a grandfather clock tolling midnight.

The names of the enemy battleships had been memorized by his pilots, and now the wardroom aide had been carefully painting the dark silhouettes for every hit obtained, his brush tipped in blood red paint. His enemy was feeling the power of the *Kido Butai, California, Tennessee, West Virginia,* all striped red with numerous bomb and torpedo hits, and doomed to sink. *Maryland* had been screened off from torpedo attack by the *Vestal*, but it had already taken three bomb hits from his skilled Val dive bombers, along with two more on *Pennsylvania*. On the other side of Ford Island, the battleship *Utah*, now only a target ship, had taken three torpedo hits and two more bomb hits. The Americans were going to have to fire at some other ship, for *Utah* would also sink, along with the heavy cruiser *Detroit*, with the *Raleigh* also damaged but still afloat.

Yet in spite of the heavy toll he had inflicted on his enemy, all Nagumo could see was the *Kaga*, the one thing that had gone wrong, and the only thing that seemed to matter to him now. *Kaga* was burning, clearly out of action, and now her speed was falling off considerably with the loss of steam to her engines. The time for gawking at the display was over, and he turned to give orders, his eyes hard on his Fleet Air Officer, Masuda Shogo.

"Signal the destroyers to render assistance to *Kaga*," he said slowly. "The *Kido Butai* will now make a ten point turn to come around on the course taken by Carrier Division Two."

They were not turning their backs on *Kaga* just yet, but they were certainly looking away. Nagumo knew the smoke from that fire would be seen for a hundred miles, and he wanted to get his fleet as far from this place in the sea as possible. Considering the stricken carrier's loss of speed, he knew it could no longer run with the others. The destroyers would help provide good flak coverage, and if it became necessary to abandon the ship, they would be ready to take on survivors, and help her commit *seppuku* with their torpedoes.

One look at this second enemy attack had also confirmed the assumption made by many others when they saw it coming. There were now at least two enemy carriers nearby, and possibly more. They believed three were here, in the Pacific, and now he found himself wondering how the enemy could have discovered them so quickly.

I have struck a very hard blow, he thought, but the tip of my sword has already shattered. It is my duty to return this fleet intact, for this war is only just beginning. At the same time, here is the opportunity before us to find and destroy those enemy carriers as well. But at what further cost to me? This very ship has already sustained a hit. Yes, the damage was controlled, and we have lost little more than our pride in being the first ship struck by the enemy, yet fate would decree this, would she not? This is the Red Castle, the flagship of the *Kido Butai*. I have little doubt that *Kaga* has taken a blow that was meant for me, but we will all feel it now, each and every one of us.

News came on a runner that the dark enemy on his horizon had been found. Fleet Air Officer, Masuda Shogo, reported that an enemy carrier had been spotted and attacked, and that it was seen to be badly burning as the strike planes retired. They had traded *Kaga* for at least one American carrier, and still enjoyed the tremendous advantage of odds here. Yet at that moment he was powerless. All his planes were already in the sky, and soon to be looking for friendly decks to land, their fuel tanks low, guns running empty after the long morning battle. A minute later Commander Shogo reported Fuchida was returning with the bulk of all the first wave strike planes. Now he had to recover them, each and every one, and it would take a good deal of time before he could spot new planes for offensive operations.

What would come out of the skies in that interval? He had seen at least a hundred enemy planes in this attack. Was there a third carrier out there launching on his position even now?

"Sir," came the senior officer of the watch. "Commander Fuchida reports enemy ships are approaching from the south! Three battleships!"

Nagumo whirled around, his face taut, eyes narrow. "Battleships?" There, it had finally come, the answer to yet another question that had been gnawing at the back of his mind. There were three dark silhouettes on the placards unblemished by the ward aid's red paint. He looked at the tally, noting their names, *Arizona, Oklahoma, Nevada*. There could be no doubt as to why those ships had weathered the first strike unscathed—they were not in the harbor. They must have been far to the south and east when Fuchida led the first wave in, yet they have been laboring all morning to find us here, and now they come when I haven't a single armed plane to throw at them.

"Sir, Admiral Mikawa with Battleship Division 3 asks permission to close and engage the enemy."

Vice Admiral Gunichi Mikawa had planted his flag aboard the battleship *Kirishima* for this sortie, a most capable man, former Chief of Staff of the 2nd Fleet, and an Admiral on Navy General Staff and with Imperial Headquarters. Nagumo could not deny him this hour, though every instinct in his body was warning him to turn now, use speed instead of steel, and to disengage.

"The *Kido Butai* will assume a course heading of 310 for aircraft recovery," he ordered. "The screening force will engage the enemy task force and cover recovery operations involving the *Kaga* while we do so. All first wave planes will rearm and prepare for launch as soon as possible."

"Then we will launch the third wave as planned?" asked Masuda Shogo, the light of battle in his dark eyes.

"There will be no third wave at Pearl Harbor," said Nagumo. "All planes will rearm for naval strike operations."

His Air Commander hesitated, the loss of the long advocated third strike a blow, but he immediately knew the reason for Nagumo's decision was sound. There was blood in the water here. The enemy carriers had found them and struck hard, and now they had battleships on their far horizon to the south. Nowhere, not in any of their planning scenarios, had the prospect of encountering enemy battleships at sea been seriously considered. The American ships were old and slow, just like *Mutsu* and *Nagato* back home. That was why Battleship Division 3 had been selected for this mission, as the *Kongo* Class ships that filled its ranks had originally been conceived as fast battlecruisers, though only two such ships were present in the screening force, *Kirishima* and *Hiei*.

Now a strange calculus entered his mind, and with it came a shaking realization of what was actually happening at that moment. The two Japanese battleships carried eight 14-inch guns each, but they would be opposed by twelve 14-inch guns on the *Arizona*, ten on the *Nevada*, and then another ten on the *Oklahoma*. The Americans would have a decided advantage, with 32 big guns against only 16 for Mikawa's force. Nagumo knew it was unlikely those ships were steaming alone. There would be cruisers and destroyers in that enemy task force as well. How could it have been missed? The frenzy of the unexpected carrier attack had overshadowed all else.

Now the fleet was facing a strong enemy surface action group, with *Kaga* out there like a wounded bison, and unable to stay in the herd. And here they were with no planes ready to strike these unexpected American battleships. Now he realized Nagumo's turn to the north, so quietly veiled as instructions to recover and re-arm for further operations, was actually a forced disengagement. The Admiral was preparing to retire, or at the very least he was laboring now to get his carriers as far from those battleships as possible.

He gave Nagumo one look that indicated he understood everything in his superior officer's mind, and then went off, sharply issuing the orders that had been given. Nagumo turned again to look at *Kaga*, his lips tight, cheeks taut. He had no choice, he thought. He had to leave his sister ship behind....

A single 500 pound bomb, flown and delivered on a single SBD-2 Dauntless, by a singularly motivated pilot who had lost all worries about finding his way home, had now changed everything.

* * *

It was a lonesome feeling when the first planes eventually made it back to *Enterprise*. Halsey was out on the weather bridge watching them come, thinking the main body had to be right behind these early arrivals. Two planes looked like they still had their bombs in place, and he made a mental note to go see the pilots and ask them why... until he saw the planes first after they landed. The damage from enemy machine gun and flak was plain to see. One SBD even had the canopy shattered, the pilot flying in the open air the whole way home, and damage to wings, tail fins and engine cowlings was visible even from his perch above the flight deck. Eleven SBDs made it back, along with three Wildcats and six TBDs. That was all that was left of his wing, just 20 of 53 planes that he had launched only two hours ago.

To make matters worse, he had already received word of the fate of the *Lexington*. Newton had abandoned ship, moving his flag to the heavy cruiser *Portland*, which was also hit, but had managed to control the fires. *Chicago* had it a little worse, and was still fighting fires amidships. *Astoria* was gone, along with destroyer *Flusser*, and the remaining four destroyers in TF 12, *Porter*, *Drayton*, *Lamson* and *Mayhan*, were circling the stricken carrier trying to get as many men off the lifeboats and out of the water as possible.

On top of all this, the news came back from Pearl with reports on the heavy damage there. Captain Murray was at his side now, seeing that grim bulldog look on Halsey's face, only now he seemed a dog without a bone.

"We got hit real hard today," said Murray.

"Don't I know it," said Halsey. He was thinking of the men lost now, not the ships. They could, and would, build more ships, but the men could never be replaced. Fresh faced recruits would soon flood every branch of the service as the startling news of the Pearl Harbor attack rippled across the country. Yet it was all standing force that was lost today, the ships, planes, and men who had been in navy blue and khaki in the years before the war, and Halsey was silently counting the men.

There were over 2500 out there on the *Lexington* alone, and now he had word from Van Valkenburgh that his heavy division had sighted the enemy and was preparing to engage. There were another thousand men on each of those battleships, hundreds more on the escort ships. Now he was considering the wisdom of so boldly ordering them north to attack, as was Murray, though he said nothing to Halsey about it at a moment like this.

"What about the boys off *Lexington*?" said Murray. "They'll be running on fumes in another twenty minutes."

"Word is they're inbound now, and god help them," said Halsey. "I didn't know where we'd put the damn planes, until I saw what was left of our own air wing."

A straggler from the *Enterprise* group had run into trouble, dived to evade a pursuing enemy fighter, eventually losing it in low clouds. The delay had been very fortunate. By the time he climbed to a cruising altitude, he spotted a flight of planes and heard some loose chatter on the radio that told them they were friendly. It was a group of planes off the *Lexington*, and they were more than eager to follow him home.

"They hit us at Guam," said Murray. "No doubt Wake and Midway will be next. At least those planes we delivered were there in the nick of time, but we haven't heard anything else for a while. MacArthur ought to be on his toes in the Philippines."

"Mountbatten warned me about this," said Halsey, with a strange edge in his tone. "Remember when we entertained his highness here aboard the *Enterprise*? He took part in that little destroyer attack exercise when we transferred him to the *Balch*. Well after that, he told me he was appalled by the poor state of readiness at Pearl. Said the Japanese had a history of starting things by launching surprise attacks, and Pearl Harbor looked like ripe fruit. Well, he was right, wasn't he."

"Admiral… Do you think the Brits knew about this in advance?"

"If they did, they might have made their warning just a little more official, but that hardly matters now."

The real scope of what was happening descended on Halsey like a dark cloud. They had been receiving war warnings for months, whispered intelligence, signals that had been decoded, oddities in the behaviors and schedules of Japanese diplomats in embassies all over the Pacific. Now the storm had finally broken, a roll of thunder that would soon become a raging torrent that would make a misnomer of the name they had given to the ocean this war would be fought on. Yes, they had been hit hard, treacherously hard, but they were already fighting back. This action was not yet concluded. The Admiral wanted to see what was left after the last of the planes came in, and he was keeping his fingers crossed behind his back as he waited on word from Van Valkenburgh on the *Arizona*.

Halsey looked at Captain Murray, his brow furrowed, eyes set, and that big jaw jutting forward with sudden confidence behind the anger that was so apparent in what he said next. It is said that history never quite repeats itself, but it rhymes. In this instance it was a haunting echo of a statement the Admiral made when he saw the damage inflicted on the men, ships, and facilities at Pearl Harbor.

"George," he said. "Before we're done with them, the Japanese language will only be spoken in Hell!"

Murray nodded silently.

Chapter 8

Karpov stood on the bridge of the battlecruiser *Kirov*, the smile barely faded from his expression as his mind now turned to the action that lay ahead. Behind him stood Anton Fedorov, unmasked and newly recruited to the Admiral's camp, seeing no other way to be relevant in the situation, and realizing that the power he was handed in Karpov's offer of *Starpom* would otherwise have to be won by conflict, and possibly even blood on the ship. That was something he was not yet prepared to foment, and the fact that they were now on the edge of momentous events made it even more imperative that his voice be heard at the command level, and without Karpov's suspicion poisoning their relationship.

"Well," said Karpov. "It's begun, and that damn ice has delayed us just enough to miss the main event. But better late than never, eh Fedorov?" He looked down the long forward bow of the ship, remembering every occasion when those missile doors would open and the weapons would snap up, hearing the soft hiss of the inclination jets fire to aim them before their engines would erupt with bright fire and the billow of hot white smoke. He remembered every target, every kill, and every heated moment when the ship had faced the danger of enemy attack. One by one, those missiles had been expended, *Kirov's* power slowly diminishing each and every time it was used, until at one point, there in the Coral Sea, they had finally fired the last of their AA missile suite. The ship had been reduced to the level of a fast cruiser, with only a fraction of the power it now held beneath that deck....

But that was in another world, he thought. Now the ship is here, just as it was in that first coming, and those decks are full of missiles as before. A man rarely has a second chance like this, and I must make the best of this one, particularly now that Admiral Volsky is out of the picture, and the ship is mine.

Karpov's eyes played over the hatches where the S-300s were stored, straying to the long broad compartments that harbored the dreadful *Moskit-II*. Now he remembered that first tactical briefing after the ship's arrival. Perhaps only Fedorov remembered it now, as every other man aboard seemed oblivious to all they had experienced and endured before that strange moment of Paradox came upon them. But it was still all clear to Karpov. He could hear Fedorov's voice in his mind, cautioning him about the need to respect the offensive power of the ships from this era, and telling him that even the 8-inch guns on these enemy cruisers could land fatal blows on *Kirov* if they ever got close enough to do so.

Kirov was like the world's best heavyweight, he thought, fast, lean, with lightning quick reflexes and ring savvy unlike any man to ever put on the gloves. With that ship, they could dance and move out of harm's way in half a heartbeat, and when they attacked, they had the most murderous punch ever seen. Yet, for all of that, there was but one flaw they had to live with. *Kirov* was a heavyweight with a glass jaw. One good punch from their opponent might be all it would take to deliver a knockout blow that would end the ship's reign as the world champion. Fedorov's first warning was in his mind now…

"Do you have any idea what a 15 or 16-inch shell would do to this ship if we should be hit? Even an 8-inch shell could easily penetrate the forward deck and ignite the missile fuel and warheads there, and my guess is that this ship would literally be blown to pieces in that event. We are not invulnerable."

And he could remember exactly what he had said in response… *"But our advantage lies elsewhere. True, we have only armored certain segments of the ship, the citadels, the reactor cores. But we do not have to come anywhere near an enemy ship to deliver a barrage of precision guided firepower on the enemy. Our missiles can fire from a range of 250 kilometers or more! Our cannon can use rocket assisted munitions and range out to 50 kilometers if need be. We can stand off and destroy any fleet we encounter, and they will never even see us. The only equivalent weapon the enemy might deploy is a fleet of aircraft carriers, and we can find them with our helicopters first, and sink them before they become a threat. Should any dare launch an air strike at us, our SAM defenses will be more than enough to protect us."*

Volsky had chimed in with another warning, and one Karpov knew only too well now. *"What you say is true for a time,"* The Admiral had said. *"It was fortunate that we replenished our primary missile inventory for the live fire exercise before we were able to complete our scheduled maneuvers. We find ourselves with reloads aboard for our Moskit-IIs. But yet there is a limit to what we can accomplish, yes? We now have forty Moskit-IIs in inventory instead of only twenty, and ten each for our other missiles. That means we have a gun with 60 rounds, and after they have been fired, all we have left are the 152mm cannon and a few torpedoes, twenty, to be exact. Certainly no ship in the world can match us now, yet we must be very judicious as to how we choose to actually use the weaponry we have."*

Very judicious indeed, thought Karpov. Experience can be a very hard teacher. The awful sound of Japanese dive bombers swooping down in a near vertical attack was still fresh in his mind. His own lightning quick reflex for war had saved the ship that time, but it took half the *Kashtan* close in defense missiles in one massed salvo to do it. Even then, one plane got through, smashing savagely into the battle bridge on the aft segment of the ship, and it was only the 200mm armor on both the roof and deck of that compartment that had saved them. Again, that had happened in another time, another world, or so he now reasoned it. But the recollection of those events was still a stern schoolmaster in his mind.

That had been a moment of grave peril, and he knew he must heed the warnings long ago expressed by Fedorov and Volsky, and listen also to the voice of his own experience in fighting these many battles. One thing he could also never forget was the sheer determination of the men who fought on the ships of this day and age, and particularly the singular mindset of the Japanese, willing to give all in the moment of attack, embracing death if it could not be avoided, and willing to stop at nothing to deliver harm to their enemy. Look what it took to force Japan to finally surrender, he thought, the horror of Hiroshima and Nagasaki. That thought was echoed by the recollection of his own voice as he had answered Volsky that day.

"You are forgetting one other thing," he had told him. *"We have nuclear warheads aboard."*

Yes, at that moment they held power that was inconceivable to any generation of men who had ever lived or walked upon this earth or sailed its seas. At that moment they had Hiroshima, Nagasaki, or any other city they might choose, right in the palm of their hand, and all they had to do was clench their fist. Volsky had been quick to rule out use of those weapons from the very first, he thought, but I had them in mind right from the outset. I must admit that my deployment of that awesome power was less than judicious. I was young and brash back then, and believed nothing could harm us. I wanted to show our enemies just what we could do to them unless they fell into line, and yet, expending one of those precious warheads to kill an old American battleship and a few escorts was really a waste. It certainly had a very dramatic effect, but did it stop them? Not for one moment. In their ignorance they fought on, heedless of the danger we posed, but what else could they do?

Yes, he thought. That is a lesson I found very hard to learn, and I must not forget it this time around. This entire world is at war, and by God, they'll fight to the finish. The world has never seen anything to rival the sheer unbridled terror of WWII. It makes all other wars pale by comparison. Even the so called 'Great War' that preceded it was merely a foreshock to the cataclysm that WWII would bring. Entire cities would be burned and broken, with a hundred thousand or more killed in a single hour—twice the number of dead the Americans experienced over ten years in Vietnam. And it is not just the Japanese who would fight with ruthless determination. The Americans rooted them out of one cave after another, for four long years. They would lose more lives in combat in a single weekend to take one island than they would sacrifice in all those ten years they fought in Iraq and Afghanistan. Fedorov can give me the numbers.

So now we shifted here to a time before any of those other battles ever happened. The ship itself has been made new, and I hold that pistol again, fully loaded, a gun with 60 rounds, and those three trump card warheads that could be utterly decisive if I use them at just the right moment. Fedorov won't want to hear that, but hopefully he will not be any further problem.

"You took Nikolin's report?" He turned to his new *Starpom*, and could not help noticing that there was something in the way Fedorov stood there on the bridge that was also decidedly different. Yes, he had been Captain here once. He had settled into the big chair, unwillingly at first, but in the long months at sea, through trial and fire, he had earned his place there. That experience was now quite evident in the man. Even the other junior officers can see it, sense it in him. I could see it from the very first. I knew something was different about him, and would have unmasked him in time in spite of every subterfuge, because no man can truly ever disguise who he really is. He's going to show his colors, one way or another. Can Fedorov see who I really am now? I wonder…

"Yes sir," said Fedorov. "Apparently there has already been a point of departure, and this time we had nothing whatsoever to do with it. That shouldn't surprise me, I suppose. This world, the history of these events, is already greatly changed."

"Your shattered mirror?" said Karpov.

"Yes, but what does surprise me is how true that image still is in so many ways. From what we've been able to determine, the Japanese strike force here, the *Kido Butai*, was almost identical to the one they sent to attack Pearl Harbor—six fleet carriers at its heart."

"But there's been a big change now," said Karpov.

Nikolin had been closely monitoring radio traffic, along with another *mishman* who was fluent in Japanese. They had pieced the situation together from that traffic, surmising in time that there had been a carrier action northwest of Pearl Harbor.

"What do you make of this, Mister Fedorov?"

"It's quite serious, sir. If the reports are correct, and the Americans lost the *Lexington*, that now leaves them with only one carrier here in the Pacific."

"Yet several of their battleships escaped harm," said Karpov.

"Nikolin says he is fairly certain there was also a surface engagement involving those ships, but yes, it seems they have survived."

"That would be Battleship Division 1," said Fedorov the *Arizona*, *Oklahoma* and *Nevada*."

"*Arizona?* That was the ship they made a monument of, am I correct?"

"Yes sir, perhaps one of the most famous ships in history, if only because of the way it died. It came to symbolize the entire Pearl Harbor attack."

"That honor will now have to be given to another old battleship," said Karpov. "And the Japanese? What do you think of that report?"

"It's clear they also took hits in that carrier duel. My understanding is that two of their carriers were hit, with *Kaga* taking the worst of it. *Mishman* Tanaka says he's picked up numerous radio intercepts where the Japanese are routing aircraft to other carriers, and away from *Kaga*. That ship has been detached from the main body, and from the code signals I was able to decrypt, it is being sent to Kwajalein, the closest Japanese anchorage, which tells me the damage must be serious. Otherwise they would have just ordered it back to Japan."

"Interesting," said Karpov. "Then this attack, while different in some respects, leaves the Americans in much the same position they were in the real history."

"Except for the loss of *Lexington*, sir. That by far outweighs the survival of Battleship Division 1. In fact, I'm surprised the Japanese did not go after those ships and finish them off. My guess is that the damage to *Kaga*, and the weather front building today, compelled Nagumo to retire."

"He was very cautious here, was he not?"

"Quite so, sir."

"So there was no third strike against Pearl Harbor?"

"No sir, that carrier action preempted any possibility of that happening. We have identified at least two strike waves against the harbor, but we don't really know the extent of the damage there, except to capital ships. Historically, 21 of 96 vessels in the harbor were hit, but only a dozen took enough damage to put them out of action, and then for no more than a few months. Yes, it was a hard blow, but most of the battleships were re-floated and repaired fairly soon. Also, it now appears that two of the permanent losses, *Arizona* and *Oklahoma*, survived. So this wasn't the knockout blow many think it was. That said, there's been some radio traffic that concerns me, involving one particular ship, the *Neosho*. It was a tanker that arrived at Pearl Harbor on December 6th, carrying a million gallons of aviation fuel. Nikolin thinks it was destroyed."

"With all the battleships and the loss of that carrier," said Karpov, "why should one more merchant ship matter?"

"Because it was the largest tanker in the world when commissioned in 1939, and the only one this far west in the Hawaiian Islands. That ship literally kept the American fleet fueled in the early months of the war when it started to probe west towards the Solomons and Coral Sea. Its loss would be significant, but it is how and when it was destroyed that really matters here."

"Explain," said Karpov, folding his arms.

"Historically, the *Neosho* arrived in December 6th, docked at Hickam Airfield to deliver 500,000 gallons of Aviation Fuel, and then moved to a mooring right on Battleship Row at Ford Island. It tied off right between the battleships *California* and *Oklahoma*, though the latter was apparently at sea this time around. That said, it still had another half a million gallons of fuel in its tanks, and was offloading that to the fuel tanks on Ford Island the night of December 6. It was mostly finished when the Japanese attack started the following morning, and managed to slip off Battleship Row unharmed in the middle of the attack. It made it across the harbor to Merry Point, near the US submarine pens and the big oil tank farm that was adjacent to that area. Nikolin's report indicates something changed here, and that could be very significant."

Something had changed… That was an understatement if Fedorov could have known the details of what really happened. It seemed a small thing, the simple movement of a weather front, but it had huge effects on the outcome of the attack. The same weather that had masked the approach of the *Kido Butai*, and also served to delay the return of the American carriers, had instead moved faster than it once did. It allowed *Enterprise* and *Lexington* to get much farther east, giving them the opportunity to intervene, but also exposing them to the grave risk of counterattack.

The front swept through the islands on the morning of the 6th, where it found *Neosho* still at sea, enroute from San Pedro in California to deliver its aviation fuel. There, the rough seas for the heavily loaded tanker slowed it down considerably, and it was very late, arriving at Pearl Harbor in the pre-dawn hours of the 7th instead of the 6th. Running late, the ship's skipper, Captain John S. Phillips, obtained permission to move directly to the berth at Battleship Row to begin offloading fuel for Ford Island Naval Air Station.

To do so, ships always took the west channel, swung up and around Ford Island to reach Battleship Row, so their bows would be pointed west towards the harbor entrance when they berthed. This saved a lot of tug time turning the ships around if they had to sortie, and also helped manage harbor traffic. So *Neosho* was on the move that morning when the Japanese attack came in, and she was still fully loaded. The ship took the west channel, swung up past the old *Utah*, came around a few destroyer anchorages, and was right in the channel near Battleship Row when the attack started. It never reached its berthing near the *California*, because something happened to break a tiny link in the chain of causality, and it was going to make a great deal of difference in the months ahead.

Chapter 9

Yes, something had changed, a turning of the wind, a sea change as any old sailor might put it, and that wind had conspired with Fate to do a great many things. *Enterprise* and *Lexington* were early, *Neosho* was late. Battleships that should have been berthed in the harbor were out to sea about to open a long range gun duel with the heavy ships in the screening force, where *Kirishima* and *Hiei* were squaring off against Battleship Division 1. There was plenty of room on the Row, and an enterprising Captain Phillips thought he'd make up for lost time by berthing directly at Ford Island instead of first going to Hickam. And one more thing was about to happen, a few stray rounds from a Japanese Zero that would also have an impact far beyond their weight, and one no person in this time period would ever know about.

It was a Push Point on the history that no man could see that day, a small thing that would cause dramatic and catastrophic changes in the Meridians of time.

When the attack on Pearl Harbor started, one thing did ring true, the reflexive instinct of Captain Phillips to get his ship away from those battleships. He saw the planes coming in, the torpedo wakes streaking in to hit *California* right off his bow, and he quickly ordered a hard turn to starboard to head for the same refuge he had selected historically, the berthing at Merry Point near the submarine pens. He had the same good luck in getting there as he did in the old history, his AA guns even shooting down a Japanese plane on the way.

Neosho made it to Merry Point, right behind the *Castor*, a general stores issue ship that had been carrying ammunition. There the two ships were to have passed through the attack unharmed. At one point in the real history, both *Neosho* and *Castor* were strafed by an enemy plane, with no loss of personnel and little more than a damaged nut on the recoil cylinder of *Castor's* number three AA gun… But that did not happen this time.

Instead of a wayward strafing, it was a dive bomber from the second wave that made that attack. The absence of Battleship Division 1 had left three less targets in the Harbor, and by the time that wave arrived, even without the planes from *Zuikaku* and *Shokaku*, Battleship Row was finished. So instead, one enterprising pilot decided to attack the largest ship he could find, and the 533 foot long *Neosho* seemed an appropriate choice, even if it wasn't a warship.

His name was Lt. Saburo Makino, with his radioman and rear gunner CPO Sueo Sukida. Both men were swooping down through the tattered Meridians of time that day, as they had been sheared and cut when the first wave attacks delayed the takeoff of a P-40 that was to have been flown by American pilot 2nd Lieutenant George Welch.

He and another pilot had just come back from a Christmas dinner and dance party at a hotel in Waikiki, and a long all-night poker game afterwards. When they saw the attack begin, the Lieutenant telephoned Haleiwa fighter strip and told them to get a pair of P-40s ready. Then he and his mate, 2nd Lieutenant Ken Taylor, jumped back in their Buick and barreled towards the airfield.

But they were just a little late.

A Japanese plane came in low and made a strafing run on that car as it sped towards the field, with the rounds close enough to force Welch to swerve off the road and barely avoid crashing. The delay of just a minute was all it took, something so insignificant that it passed the notice of any historian scrutinizing the battle in the long decades ahead. It didn't happen in Fedorov's history, but it happened here. So when Welch and Taylor got their Tomahawks up, they were somewhere else in the sky, a hot minute away, and Welch was busy trying to shoot down some other plane instead of number AII-250, flown by Lt. Saburo Makino.

That made all the difference in the world, and served to heavily underscore the tremendous effect that one man, a single pilot, a single sortie and attack, could have on the course of history. If Welch gets that plane, *Neosho* comes through the attack unscathed, in spite of the weather front that delayed her and kept her holds burgeoning with a million gallons of aviation fuel. If Welch is somewhere else, then Lieutenant Makino tips his plane over and comes down on top of *Neosho* to put his 500 pound bomb right on target. He did not even know the real significance of what he was about to do, and would not survive to learn anything more about it. The resulting explosion was catastrophic.

Neosho blew sky high, smashing Lieutenant Makino's plane to pieces as it pulled out of that dive. The ship was blown apart, the fireball so enormous that it completely engulfed the ammunition carrier *Castor* as well. Then that ship blew, with all that remained in its holds, and the fires rampaged landward, immolating Merry Point, the submarine pens and tenders, CINCPAC Headquarters building, and then sweeping right on into the big oil storage tanks beyond.

Standing there in his office near the sub pens, watching the attack across the harbor at Battleship Row, was the Commander-in-Chief of the United States Pacific Fleet, Admiral Husband E. Kimmel. In Fedorov's history he would later report that it was only a stray machinegun round that had struck the window as he watched, punching a hole through and grazing his naval jacket, just one little scratch from the fingernail of fate that raised a small weal on his torso. He famously remarked to his communications officer, Commander Maurice Curts, "It would have been merciful had it killed me."

This time Fate's mercy would come in raging fire. Minutes after that explosion, both Kimmel and Curts were killed, along with tens of other ranking officers in CINCPAC Headquarters, decapitating the US command structure in one mighty blow.

The destruction went far beyond the removal of an Admiral whose days in command were already well numbered. It took out those sub pens, destroying *Narwhal, Dolphin,* and *Tautog,* along with a pair of sub tenders. *Narwhal* would not get her 19 ships, sinking over 40,000 tons over 15 patrols. *Tautog* would never get her 26 kills totaling 72,606 tons. They once called the boat '*Tautog* the Terrible,' but that would never be. *Dolphin* had ended up a school boat after serving well in a reconnaissance role early in the war, but none of that would happen now. Those subs sunk 41 ships, more kills than the entire *Kido Butai* had inflicted just now with its attack, and their absence would certainly have some as yet unseen effect on the course of the war.

The raging inferno eventually engulfed 40% of the oil tank farm behind the sub base, burning for days after with a thick black smoke that hung over the islands like a pall of doom. The loss of that oil tanker, all its aviation fuel, and 40% of the fuel stocks in that tank farm, were going to have a far greater impact on US operations than all the damaged battleships and cruisers combined. Thrown on the scales with the loss of Lady Lex, the aborted attack on Pearl Harbor was a much more devastating blow to the US Pacific Fleet than it had been in Fedorov's history books.

He did not know that as he stood on the bridge of *Kirov* at that moment with Karpov, but he could feel it. Something seemed to hang in the tension of that moment that spoke of destiny and disaster, something far more profound than Karpov's desultory appraisal of Nikolin's radio traffic intercept reports.

"So what if this oil tanker were lost?" asked Karpov.

"It would severely inhibit American fleet operations in the next few months. Ships at sea in this era were thirsty beasts. A destroyer would need replenishing every three days, and carriers steaming at higher speeds burned through fuel at an alarming rate. *Neosho* was an essential link in the thin logistical chain out to Hawaii."

"Then why didn't the Japanese just target the fuel bunkers? You've already pointed out that the loss of those old battleships counted for little."

"Quite right," said Fedorov. "In fact, historians remain amazed to this day that the Japanese did not place more emphasis on logistical targets in this attack. Considering the fact that they went to war for largely economic reasons, this is quite surprising. Their fuel stocks had diminished to about 50 million barrels, no more than 18 months supply due to the US oil embargo. They moved south to secure every vital source of oil and other resources between Hawaii and the Middle East, yet in striking here, they largely ignored the same fuel that would be so important to their enemy. Some say it was the samurai mindset of the attacking pilots, who wanted to strike ships of war, but the same behavior was also seen in the use of the submarines."

"Submarines?" That word had always been a hot button for Karpov.

"Yes sir, the Japanese had many subs involved in this operation, and after the attack quite a few were assigned to interdict the sea lanes between the US west coast and Hawaii, but they largely ignored merchant shipping. Only 19 US merchant ships would be sunk over the next ten months, and most of those in the weeks just after the attack. The Germans tried to persuade them to alter their submarine warfare strategy, but they refused to change their preference for targeting warships. For them, a warship was their real enemy, with trained men and a potential to do harm to the empire, and something that took time and much effort to replace. By contrast, they thought lowly merchant ships were harmless, and even if sunk, might be easily replaced, and built quickly in very great numbers. The German U-boats did far better in the Atlantic than the Japanese ever did here in the Pacific."

"Yes, I remember you telling me this. Well there isn't much we can do about Japanese sub Captains wanting to kill big fish— that is, as long as they stay out of my way. As for the rest of this discussion, I find it quite enlightening. Logistics. We certainly don't have a fuel problem, if our reactors settle down and leave us in one place and time for a while."

"I've spoken to Chief Dobrynin," said Fedorov. "He's detected nothing unusual, and the reactors seem to have stabilized."

"Then the question now," said Karpov, "is how to best proceed. Where would this *Kido Butai* be at the moment? Have you plotted that position estimate I asked for?"

"I have, sir." Fedorov walked to the Plexiglas navigation screen and indicated a position northwest of the Hawaiian Islands. "Considering the weather, my best guess is that they are somewhere here, and this is the predictive plot I've laid in based on their historical route of withdrawal. Yet they've fought a naval action here, and that tends to break up a task force into smaller components. It's likely that the screening force is no longer with the carriers, and we have no battle damage assessment on the action fought with the American battleships."

They wouldn't find that out for some time either, until Nikolin determined that another ship seemed to be routing to Kwajalein as well, the battleship *Hiei*. In the duel with Van Valkenburgh's battleships, *Hiei* had taken the worst of it, sustaining eight hits of various calibers, including three by 14 inch guns. Destroyer *Kagero*, who's name literally meant 'heat haze,' also took the heat when a 14-inch shell got lucky. At the same time, the Japanese battleships put two solid hits on both *Nevada* and *Oklahoma*, and one more on *Arizona*, but the resulting fires would be controlled.

The first face off between the battleships, that both sides once thought would determine the outcome of the war, therefore proved most indecisive when Admiral Mikawa broke off the engagement after seeing the damage to *Hiei*. *Kirishima* could still fight, but the ships separated, with *Hiei* heading due west away from the action at the best speed it could make, just 17 knots. Even that was enough to get her out of harm's way, for the lumbering American battleships, maintaining formation throughout the entire battle, could not pursue effectively, nor was Van Valkenburgh inclined to do so. A pair of fast heavy cruisers might have finished the battleship off, but none were present, and bad weather set in again soon after, severely hindering air search operations, and even making it difficult for his escort of four destroyers to keep station. Even the seaplane launches from *Tone* and *Chikuma* had to be cancelled, and that, along with Nagumo's caution, ended the battle.

"If the Japanese do withdraw as they did historically," said Fedorov, "then we may hear about them next at Midway."

"They are going to bomb it?"

"Possibly. Historically they simply detached a pair of destroyers to shell it, but this course shows the *Kido Butai* moving north of that island, well within air bombing range."

"Plot a course to get me within range of those ships," said Karpov. How soon can we move to helo operations?"

"I recommend 28 knots on this course," Fedorov pointed to the screen as a blue line lit up showing his plot. "That would put our KA-40s in range to cover this segment of the anticipated enemy course in about… three hours."

Enough time to check in with the diplomats, thought Karpov. He had ordered Tyrenkov to relay his demands to Tokyo, along with specific instructions on a coded signal he would send to initiate any further discussion. He then briefed Nikolin on how he wanted him to send out that message. Now he told Fedorov about it for the first time.

"I have made demands of the Japanese concerning their ongoing occupation of Siberian territory."

"You expect them to concede, sir? You think they'll return Vladivostok simply because you demand it?"

"Of course not, but I have spelled out the consequences should they fail to do so."

"What consequences?" Fedorov still wanted to see into the darkest corner of Karpov's mind.

"First, that a state of war would exist between the Japanese Empire and the Free Siberian State, effective at 14:00 today, December 9th on this side of the international dateline. That is two hours and forty minutes from now as I read the ship's chronometer, assuming it was correctly reset. It's still December 8th in Hawaii and the United States, and Roosevelt will likely make his famous little infamy speech shortly, then Congress follows with a declaration of war on Japan at 13:10pm today. Roosevelt won't sign it for another three hours, but that was a mere formality. As for Siberia, I sign off on hostilities at 14:00, and I have also formally dispatched a message to the American Embassy at Irkutsk informing them of my demands, my intention to declare war, and my open support of the United States in the Pacific as far as I am able. I have requested their ambassador arrange negotiations concerning the use of Siberian territory for wartime purposes."

"You still think you can interest them in an Aleutians strategy?"

"That remains to be seen, but before those discussions, I intend to make myself useful, and also to put a little fire in the demands I have made of Japan. I have already warned them of severe consequences, telling them exactly what they can expect if they fail to comply. And like our old nemesis Ivan Volkov, I can make predictions as well. I've told them I will lay waste to their sea lanes and surface warships unless they begin the immediate withdrawal of their military forces from Siberian territory. The language was not so brazen, but my message was clear, at least on paper."

"Then what happens next, sir? You know very well that the Japanese will not accede to your demands. The most you can expect will be delay and obfuscation, requests for negotiations and a better equity in terms of the agreement will certainly be the order of the day."

"Negotiations? Yes, that will be quite tedious, as you suggest. You see, Fedorov, like Volkov, I am no diplomat at heart, and I have little patience for such negotiations. But I am a prophet when it comes to deciding what happens to the Japanese Navy now, and when I negotiate, I do not make concessions, but an ultimatum. At 14:00 today I expect to be at war with Japan, and I will not fail to see that they know it."

Part IV

The Lost Convoy

"There was no moon. The sea was as black as the lowest depths of despair. Far below in the troughs and now on the crest of the waves, little marine creatures flashed their phosphorescence in defiance, like little stars fallen from grace on high. The wind whistled through the rigging like the cry of lost souls. The gates of hell were opened and the devil himself roamed the night…"

— **Byron Wilhite,** War Diary, Pensacola Convoy

Chapter 10

After the fuse was lit, the fires of war spread very rapidly throughout the Pacific. In the Philippines, the principle Far East base of the US Military was presided over by a man who inwardly deemed himself another emperor of sorts, General Douglas MacArthur. He had come out of retirement to take the post, and yet, the force he had in hand was really not one to pose a grave threat to Japan, in spite of Japanese planners thinking to the contrary. The Navy had argued the Philippines sat astride the sea lanes that would carry Japan's soon to be conquered resources back to the empire. That required the Japanese Army to occupy the Philippines, a land area equivalent to the home islands, or even the British Isles in total size.

Before they could do that, it would be necessary to destroy any offensive capability the US possessed in those islands, and the one force uppermost in the minds of Japanese planners was the United States Army Air Force. It had four squadrons of fighters, and 31 B-17 bombers, the largest contingent of those planes outside the US. Those bombers really represented almost all of MacArthur's immediate offensive capability against the Japanese, the only way he could participate in U.S. War Plan Rainbow 5. Their target would be the Japanese bases on Formosa, principally at Takao, seeking to preempt and forestall its use as a springboard for further hostilities.

It was a foolish plan in retrospect, for the Japanese had 117 A6M2 Zeroes at Takao, which was more than enough to neutralize that bomber threat. Yet it became even worse when the American raid, quite literally, never got off the ground. War warnings were telephoned in, messages received of the attack on Pearl Harbor, and the only US radar on the islands at Iba Field in the north was spotting possible flights of enemy planes. Rumors were flying through the air crews at the fields, but US aircraft remained mostly on the ground. At one point two squadrons scrambled, with one bomber group, but after flying about over Manila for some time, they eventually were forced to land and refuel. Their timing had been wrong, but the Japanese would get theirs right. Their main air strikes would come in right in the middle of that refueling operation.

MacArthur had finally given his subordinates the order to strike Formosa at 10:15, and the Japanese struck an hour later, while almost every plane available was still on the ground being serviced.

Whether those bombers over Formosa would have made any difference has been debated by many historians and dismissed as irrelevant. Notoriously ill equipped to strike naval targets, they were not going to prevent a Japanese invasion of the islands, or seriously interfere with enemy staging operations for such an offensive, because it was already at sea.

As for the navy, there were two cruisers, the *Houston* and *Marblehead*, along with 13 old WWI era destroyers, and 23 submarines that might have made a difference. But US sub tactics could have learned much from the Germans, and the subs that rushed to clear the harbor ended up scattering out to sea on recon patrol duties. No provision in their orders was ever made for defensive mine laying, close in coastal defense of likely invasion sites, or even patrols off enemy harbors likely to initiate offensive operations. Thus those 23 subs were largely squandered as an offensive weapon, or even an adequate defensive naval shield. By the time they would be needing a safe harbor to replenish fuel and ammunition, Manila would be in enemy hands.

The Japanese invasion of the Philippines was going to come off right on schedule, and there was nothing that Emperor MacArthur, with all his haughty arrogance and inflated self-confidence, could do about it. One brave man had put himself, and his ships, into the fire to attack the enemy in those early days, and his name was Admiral William 'Bull' Halsey. With Admiral Kimmel and much if the senior staff at CINCPAC gone in that terrible conflagration, Halsey would return to Pearl Harbor to find himself the senior officer in the Pacific. He had one lonesome carrier and a pack of fast cruisers to run with it, and that was exactly what he decided to do.

"Come on, boys," he said to the harbor crews. "Let's get this baby turned around and out to sea in 24 hours."

When Van Valkenburgh arrived with Battleship Division 1 six hours later, Halsey went over to take his report.

"How were those live fire exercises?" he quipped.

"Gave it to the Japs real good," said the Captain. "These old ladies were as tough as we hoped they would be."

When Halsey learned there were a few bloodied Japanese ships out there, he had it in mind to get out to sea as fast as he could and see if he could finish them off. But before he did anything, he got on the phone to Fleet Admiral King in the States and asked for the one thing he needed more than anything else now, aircraft carriers.

"I'll give you all the support I can," said King, "but can you hold there at Hawaii? Should you fall back to the West coast?"

"Are you serious? We do that and it will add another 2000 miles to every fleet sortie, and it's as good as planting a 'For Rent' sign up on Opana Point for the Japs."

"Alright, do you want a battleship division? We've got the 3rd and 5th on the Atlantic coast."

"Battleships? They'll only slow me down. It's carriers I need now, and fast cruisers. Get *Saratoga* out here from San Diego as fast as she can move, and by God, unless you plan on invading France tomorrow, send me anything you've got afloat on the East coast as well."

"You can have *Yorktown, Hornet* and *Wasp*. That's the lot of them, but we won't have the new *Essex* class up for months."

"I warned you about the big Jap buildup in carriers," said Halsey, the frustration evident in his voice. "Now they've just written the goddamned book on how to use them."

"We'll get it fixed, Bill, but for now it's a come as you are party, and you'll just have to make do. I'll send along the 7th Cruiser Division as icing on the cake, and if you need destroyers, we've got them in droves."

"One more thing, Rey," said Halsey, using the Admiral's nickname, "they hit the fuel stocks here pretty hard. We can operate, but we lost *Neosho*, and we'll need tanker support as much as anything else. *Pecos* and *Trinity* were in the Phils, but word is they made a run for it last night, heading for the Dutch East Indies. We've got two more inbound, but most everything else is on the West coast."

"We'll get them moving," said King. "Now what about the Philippines?"

"You know we wrote that off in almost every pre-war plan worth its salt," said Halsey. "I never thought War Plan Orange was ever going to float with a battleship sortie to relieve MacArthur, and that's entirely out of the question now. Admiral Hart knows he's on a short least now in the Philippines, which is why he's getting those oilers out of harm's way. I give MacArthur three months—four at best—but the longer he can hold out, the better. We'll need time to get off the canvas here and back in the ring. And we'll need new bases out here, and good anchorages. You'd better tell Marshall that they ought to get on the phone with the French and twist a few arms. Where's MacArthur going to go to reorganize if the Japs kick him out of the Philippines? The only place I can think of is Australia, and for that to happen, we've got to get there before the enemy does. I can't do that in one long jump from Pearl. I'll need bases in the South Pacific."

Before he sortied again with the *Enterprise*, Halsey took stock of the damage at Pearl, appalled by the blazing fires that had consumed so much of the precious fuel his ships were going to need. Preliminary reports indicated they would lose 40% of the stocks, but that still left enough for fleet operations. Halsey knew that he'd have more oil when those tankers arrived from the West coast, and if there was no place to put it, they'd just leave it in the ships until it could be off loaded.

The situation was going from bad to worse as the scope of the full Japanese attack became apparent. In addition to the Philippines, they were hitting Hong Kong, Malaya, and Burma, and Halsey knew the resource rich Dutch Colonies would fall soon after. As he looked at the map, trying to decide how he could possibly operate now, it was evident that he would first have to build some new support structure in the Pacific so he had half a chance at using those oilers to get fuel out west. It was a task made much more difficult than it was in Fedorov's history, for two big reasons.

The first was the open hostilities between two former Allies, France and Britain, a sad chapter that both Fedorov and Volsky had seen re-written when *Kirov* shifted to June of 1940. That month, the fall of France cast doubt on the future status of all French Colonies in Africa and the Pacific. But the outbreak of hostilities between British and French Naval forces at Mers-el-Kebir, and the subsequent British Campaign against French holdings in Syria and Lebanon, had gone a long way towards hardening the attitude of French citizens in all her colonies. That meant that all of North and West Africa was soon hostile ground, and the British were already at war with the French at sea in the Med, and in Syria.

The French also had colonies in the Pacific, controlling all the New Hebrides island group southeast of the Solomons, which was a very strategic place, and also in French Polynesia. Both holdings sat astride vital sea lanes and lines of communications between the United States and Australia, and this was a development that another man named Ivan Volkov did not fail to appreciate. He was reason two, because Volkov had an embassy in Tokyo as well as Berlin, and he had used it to fill the Japanese war planners with the benefit of his much touted 'Prophecies.' His whispered words were going to complicate matters in the South Pacific for Halsey and all others concerned.

* * *

The Japanese, with well-developed plans for a movement south into the resource rich South Pacific, quickly surmised the value of existing French colonies there, and perceived their vulnerability. As such, Japan negotiated to secure permission to post troops in French Indochina, and set up military bases there.

This had all happened in the real history before *Kirov* started its long saga, but in these altered states, a most alarming change resulting from the Anglo-Franco war would now weigh heavily in the scales of the War in the Pacific. Ivan Volkov had been a very busy man with his visits to Adolf Hitler, and then to Japan, where he attempted to strongly warn the Japanese of the strategic necessity of occupying French held territories as soon as possible.

There was already a sympathetic ear for this strategy among Japanese planners. They saw the French colonies as essential to cutting sea lanes between the United States and Australia, isolating the latter, and attempting to force Australia out of the war. That, plus the fact that Japan already had a considerable commercial presence in the New Hebrides Islands, where 1300 Japanese workers labored at the important nickel and magnesium mines on New Caledonia, led the planners of the Rising Sun Empire to see the successful intervention in French Indochina as a template for what they might quickly achieve in the other French Pacific colonies.

That was the strategy they pursued, opening secret negotiations with the French and assuring the solidarity of those territories if their security could be guaranteed. To this end, Japan obtained permission to post a small security contingent on New Caledonia to protect the mines, while secretly planning a much more significant intervention timed with the attack on Pearl Harbor. In Late November of 1941, a task force was assembled in the Japanese Caroline Islands bastion of Truk, with a full SNLF battalion to move quickly by destroyer transport to New Caledonia, and specifically, the vital port of Noumea. It was to be followed by a slower reinforcement convoy with an additional full regiment, and basing supplies.

While the French in that colony had eventually sided with the Free French movement, that was not going to happen in this history, and Japan would gain a most important base in New Caledonia before the Allies could organize forces to prevent that. Further east, in French Polynesia, the Japanese influence was not yet a factor, and, in spite of considerable resentment towards the British, French Colonial citizens on Tahiti eventually opted to attempt to remain neutral.

Halsey knew he needed new bases in the Pacific, and fast, which is why he bent Admiral King's ear on the matter. Thankfully, King understood the gravity of the situation, and urged Marshall to join him in a bid to convince Roosevelt of the urgent need for quick negotiations with the French.

"Negotiations?" said Roosevelt, rising to the occasion. "I'll read them the Riot Act! If they think they've got trouble with the British now, just wait until we show up."

Halsey would get his wish, for when pressed heavily by the United States to permit US forces on the French held island of Bora Bora, they agreed, asking as a concession if the United States would refrain from declaring war on France. Roosevelt had already appointed a Navy man, his good friend Admiral William D. Lehay, as Ambassador to France, and he quickly telephoned him to plan a strategy. It would be said that Germany's response to the US Declaration of War on Japan would largely dictate the American attitude toward France, but if the French could sweeten the deal now with Bora Bora, the government of the United States would take that into full consideration.

So it was that Operation Bobcat was quickly conceived and launched, with Bull Halsey leading the charge. It was a plan to send 5000 US troops and service personnel to Bora Bora, which had an excellent lagoon that could only be entered in one place, easy to defend from enemy submarines. There they would set up a naval fueling station and supply center. Known as the "Pearl of the Pacific," Halsey wanted to crack open the oyster and get that pearl in hand before the Japanese could do anything about it. Thankfully, it was too remote to attract Japanese interest before the war. Halsey hoped that this operation could be concluded successfully without incident, and the American toe hold in French Polynesia might then help to eventually bring all those territories in to the Allied camp.

Even so, the loss of the New Hebrides was a severe blow to American war strategy, and one that would also strongly impact events as far away as North Africa. Seeing the cordon of Japanese strength slowly encroaching on its homeland, Australia and New Zealand decided that it was absolutely necessary to recall Commonwealth Divisions presently serving in Syria and Libya. This was going to mean that the British would soon lose the able services of the veteran 6th, 7th and 9th Australian Divisions, as well as the 2nd New Zealand Division that had just tangled with Rommel again in Operation Crusader before the outbreak of the Pacific war. The vacuum these troop withdrawals would create in the Middle East would soon change the balance of power there again, and give Rommel some very unexpected opportunities.

Everything was connected, with the tenuous lines of fate and destiny strung across the globe in a web of causality. In the Pacific, particularly at this tempestuous early stage, a single ship sailing along one of those Meridians could cause a change in the course of the war that would have grave ramifications. One major point of divergence had already taken place west of Pearl Harbor, and now Lady Lex was at the bottom of the sea instead of in Halsey's fast carrier group. Two more such events were now about to occur, one involving a relief operation headed for the Philippines dubbed "Operation Plum," and another involving a pair of strange ships that were never supposed to be at sea.

Chapter 11

Admiral King's pledge of three more fleet carriers for the Pacific was heartening, but as lonesome as it seemed for the *Enterprise* now, there was strange company out west that Halsey hoped to make good use of. While the Asiatic Fleet was fairly pathetic, there were a pair of unusual ships there that were part of the fleet that never was in Fedorov's history books. They had been originally conceived in the 1920s, possibly as a way to circumvent the restrictions on fleet carriers in the Washington Naval Treaty. The Japanese had begun the arms race here with their hybrid *Gozo* Class Cruiser Carrier, and the Germans answered with the *Goeben*. But the Americans also had a plan for a similar ship, one that had seen real ink on the drawing boards, but was cancelled before the war Fedorov studied. Here, however, it was another case of altered states putting ships at sea that had never been built.

USS *Antietam*, BCV-1, was the lead ship in the class, and it was soon followed by the *Shiloh*, with both ships commissioned before the war. They were 650 feet long, with a 350 foot flight deck aft that was later extended to nearly 400 feet, and hanger space for 24 aircraft. That left just enough room up front for the conning tower and a pair of triple 6-inch gun turrets, the typical armament of a light cruiser, including eight more 5-inch dual purpose guns, with four on each side edging out that flight deck. The two ships were at Davao in the Philippines when the war started, and Admiral Hart ordered them out to sea, heading south for the Dutch East Indies with those two oilers and the seaplane carrier *Langley*.

The general concept was argued for further development in the US Navy, a seeming compromise between the big gun school and the flat top camp. The Marines liked the ships because they had space below decks for a strong reinforced company or two, and provided an excellent platform for shore fire support from those forward guns, as well as air cover over a landing zone. They saw them as a perfect complement to a small amphibious landing task force, and trained with both ships in that capacity off San Diego before the war.

The Japanese were in love with this hybrid cruiser/carrier concept, and they had several more in the ship yards, and were eyeing older battleships like *Ise* and *Hyuga* for conversion to hybrid "battlecarriers." Their special SNLF battalions had not failed to see the same utility in the ships, and both *Gozo* and *Mezu* were designated for special small landing operations to the distant Pacific isles.

As to extending the idea to a larger hull, the Navy decided its successful conversion of *Lexington* and *Saratoga* would be the end of that road. From now on, all new carriers would be built from the ground up on all new hulls, and several were already under construction. So *Antietam* and *Shiloh* would be the only two ever built for the US Navy, which decided that full sized fleet carriers would do the job much better than these hybrids.

Halsey was nonetheless grateful those two ships were afloat on December 8th, and he was counting on them getting to safe water so they could operate with *Enterprise*. With Operation Bobcat in mind, Halsey sent word to Captain James Hansen on the *Antietam*, telling him he should take his small task group to Suva Bay in the Fiji Island Group, wait there, and stay out of trouble. It was a fateful order, because the French were soon going to complicate matters for the US. Those two hybrid cruiser carriers would soon be right in the middle of more trouble than they needed.

With war imminent, the US had dispatched a number of forces to reinforce the Philippines. Some were air groups, like the B-17s that arrived just as the Japanese attack began at Pearl Harbor. Others were land units intended to reinforce MacArthur's garrison, basing personnel, engineers, and even crated aircraft were all heading west on the Pacific as the Japanese offensive began. One such convoy sailed under the code name "Operation Plum," which was an acronym standing for Philippines, LUzon, Manila. It was escorted by the cruiser *Pensacola* and the submarine chaser *Niagara*, with four transports, *Republic*, *Chaumont*, *Meigs*, and *Holbrook*, and three freighters,

Admiral Halstead, *Coast Farmer*, and the *Bloemfontein* under Dutch colors. The convoy was being routed southwest instead of trying to take the more direct route which might take it too close to Japanese controlled territories. They planned to make a stop at Port Moresby and then come up through the Dutch East Indies to Davao, but the outbreak of war changed all that.

Soon the leisurely cruise on the open Pacific was given new urgency. Crews were quickly put to work, painting over white hulls and superstructures in haze grey, removing the white canvas on the life boats, and then the men were sent below to don life jackets and look through the cargo and find anything that might serve as a deck gun for the otherwise unprotected cargo ships. *Republic* found four British 75mm guns in her hold, and the crews dragged them up onto the weather deck, feeling just a little more secure when they had tied them down fore and aft, until it was discovered there was no ammunition for the guns on board.

Commander Guy Clark, the Captain of the *Republic*, shook his head. "Well at least we might look a little threatening," he said, and he gave orders that if a Japanese sub were spotted on the surface the crews were to rush to the guns and look as though they were prepping them for action. In fact, he ordered drills to that effect, though the whole exercise seemed to mirror the sense of futility hanging over the entire Navy at that moment. "Here we are rushing to serve an empty gun," he said to the Army commander aboard, Brig. Gen. Julian F. Barnes, but there was nothing else to be done.

"At least we've got *Pensacola* out there," said Barnes.

Things got edgy when a report came in that a Japanese sub had been spotted near the Ellice Islands, even though they were 300 miles away. Then late on December 8th, word came from Pearl that they were to divert their course to Fiji and wait at Suva Bay for further instructions. The Navy Brass, particularly Halsey, had decided that the waters ahead were too uncertain. If they continued, the *Pensacola* Convoy would soon be entering French controlled waters, and no one knew whether or not a state of war might exist between the US and

France. Suva Bay seemed a safe alternative, and Halsey then ordered *Antietam* and *Shiloh* to get over there to put some more teeth in the defense of that convoy.

Two days later, just as the convoy was arriving at Suva Bay, it was learned that Germany had declared war on the United States in support of Japan, and they were insisting that all Axis partners do the same. The French equivocated, afraid that they might be on the wrong side of the equation, but eventually bowed to pressure and issued a formal declaration that day, though the French Ambassador in Washington stated it was carried out with great regret.

"You can regret it all you want now," said the US Secretary of state, Cordell Hull. "But I can assure you that you will certainly regret it a good deal more before this is over."

That said, the French then made a formal request that the US send no forces to Bora Bora as they had agreed earlier. Hull smiled, looked the man squarely in the eye, and gave it to him in his best Tennessee accent. "Mister Ambassador," he said. "Don't suppose the Japanese have done away with the entire United States Navy in that dastardly attack they just pulled. Now I've got one ornery Fleet Admiral over at Pearl Harbor, and he's dead set on occupying those islands. We're coming as planned, and if you want to do anything about it, you'll have to get past Bull Halsey first."

And that ended the matter. The US was coming, but French pride, which was considerable and well wounded in this war, would not allow them to simply hand over French territory without some action in reprisal. So word was quickly sent to the French Far East Fleet, such as it was, and they were told to prepare to initiate hostilities against any American shipping entering French territorial waters. For good measure, they passed on information concerning the American plans to the Japanese, hoping they might get some support from them in the matter, and it was a bid that paid them good dividends.

In Fedorov's history, the French might have posed no threat to the *Pensacola* Convoy, or any other American shipping in the Pacific, but again, things were different now in this world. As France was falling, the carrier *Bearn* was sent packing on a mission very much like the one HMS *Rodney* was undertaking when she met her fate. The ship was carrying gold to safety in the West Indies. That was yet another ship that was to have been designed as a battleship, but when the French saw the British carrier *Argus*, they got other ideas and converted *Bearn* to a carrier. The work was done in 1927, making the ship old and slow at 21 knots in 1941, but it was a carrier, with 30 aircraft aboard, and that made it a significant ship.

In better days, the carrier had proudly served in the French *Force de Raid*, and even participated in the hunt for the German raider *Graf Spee*. Then, as France's fortunes declined, she sent her fortune abroad in the holds of that carrier, escorted by the cruisers *Jean de Arc* and *Emile Bertin*. They were supposed to transport the gold to Halifax, but never got there due to a U-boat scare. Instead they diverted to Martinique, where they would have been interned, save for a timely warning that came from Ivan Volkov.

So it was that the French ordered the little flotilla to slip away before the Armistice with Germany was signed, and it made the long, hazardous journey to the Pacific thru the South Atlantic, around the Cape to Madagascar to refuel, and then on to French Indochina at Saigon. It was there before the Japanese offensive began, when the French decided to move it out of an impending war zone to safer climes—in their colonial island holdings of the New Hebrides. There it cooperated with the Japanese as they landed troops on New Caledonia, again another insult, but at least from a nation that was a supposed ally in this war.

But *Bearn* was not alone with those two cruisers. The French also had a small flotilla at Saigon, ships they had moved to the Pacific before the war. The cruisers *Lamotte-Picquett, Suffren,* and four destroyers sailed with the carrier to Noumea, *Fougueux, Frondeur, Lansquenet,* and *Le-Hardi*. All the power the French Pacific Fleet could muster was now massed at Noumea, closing like a steel fist as the ships gathered. This war would see fleets massed with ships in the hundreds, but now, right at the outset of the conflict, the French had managed to put together a task force comprised of a carrier, four cruisers, and four destroyers. It was the most powerful naval force for a thousand miles in any direction, and the raging Bull Halsey was nowhere at hand. Vice Admiral Decoux from Saigon took command, planting his flag on the *Bearn*. The only question now was whether he knew how to use the force he had, and what he might decide to do with it.

At that same moment, the *Pensacola* convoy was heaving to at Suva Bay, a little over 700 nautical miles to the northeast, or about two days at 15 knots. The convoy ships were carrying 9,000 drums of high octane Aviation Gas on the *Admiral Halstead*. 18 crated P-40 Tomahawks of the 24th Fighter Group, and the 2nd Battalion of the 131st Field Artillery with twelve 75mm guns, and 48 more British 75s bound for Luzon were on the Dutch freighter *Blomfontein*. Most of the 7th Bomb group personnel were on the *Republic*, and 52 more Douglas A-24 Banshee dive bombers, also crated, were on the *Meigs*.

Along with all that equipment there were 4,600 National Guard personnel scattered among all the ships, considerable stores of half a million rounds of .50 caliber ammunition and another 9,600 for 37mm guns, 5000 bombs for the aircraft, 340 vehicles and trucks. The convoy code name was well chosen, for here was a ripe plum, low hanging fruit within easy reach of any enemy, and it was a most valuable, and highly volatile prize.

There was one other valuable prize at sea, enroute from California to Australia with 125 more P-40s, with their pilots, and ammunition comprising the entire 4th Mobile Depot Group. Information on the likely existence of these convoys, fetched from the archives Volkov had compiled over the years from his old service jacket, was being fed to the Japanese and French. He did not know whether they would actually form and sail on schedule, but this one did, the *Pensacola* Convoy, ringing true like a bell that resounded through the history, inviolate.

That convoy would now become the target of all that wounded French pride, and the single American cruiser in escort would find itself badly outnumbered if the French fleet ever found it at sea. But *Pensacola* was soon to get some much needed help from a pair of ships that never were, the USS *Antietam* and USS *Shiloh*, steaming at that moment in the Coral Sea.

MacArthur was eager to receive the guns and ammo on that convoy, and those 52 A-24 dive bombers, the Army version of the Dauntless SBD, would be most welcome. He pressed Admiral Hart to send out anything he had left. Gloomy, and thinking the Japanese would soon have all the Philippines blockaded with their powerful navy, Hart wanted to keep what little he had in Manila Bay, but MacArthur persisted, another point of departure that would nudge things off in a new direction. He got his way instead of Hart, and the US cruiser *Houston* under Captain Rooks, with four destroyers, was sent south looking for the *Antietam* group, and with orders to sail for Fiji.

Meanwhile, a debate was on as to what should be done with the valuable convoy. Some argued that it should be recalled to Pearl Harbor or the West coast, but George Marshall took it to Roosevelt one morning, and the president was fairly decisive.

"Where is it now?" he asked.

"Approaching Suva Bay," said Marshall. "It was the only safe place we could send it until this gets decided."

"Well, it's half way there," Roosevelt exclaimed. "Why recall it now? If it can't reach MacArthur, then at the very least it should go to Australia."

That decision made, the rest was about to become all new history. When Cliff Causton, B Battery, 148th Artillery, heard the news aboard the transport *Holbrook*, he was quite surprised.

"Australia?" he said to a fellow National Guardsman, Bill Heath. "I thought we were supposed to go to the Philippines."

Willard A. Heath had smiled when he first heard he was being assigned to a ship that bore his own first name and middle initial, the 27,000 ton ex-steamship liner, now called the *Willard A. Holbrook*. He had never liked the name, preferring William instead, and most now called him Bill, and sometimes Willie. "Too hot over there," said

Heath. "And I don't mean the weather. The Japs are probably swarming all over the place by now."

"Well hell," said Causton, "That's what these damn 75s are for! What are we supposed to do in Australia?"

"I'll tell you one thing they should do," said Heath. "They ought to scrub this damn rust bucket down real good. It smells like hell!"

He pinched his nose, for the ship they were on had been carrying shipments of jute and copra from the Philippines for many months, and the residual stench was so bad that they call the ship "Stinking Old *Holbrook*." But that would be the least of worries for Heath. Causton would also get his wish one day, but he would get to the Philippines in a very roundabout way, after years of hard fighting that would see him return there with the very man he was hoping to relieve, General Douglas MacArthur.

But first his ship would have to make the risky trip to Brisbane, not knowing that the French Pacific Squadron was going to be looking for them soon, and the altered history they were now sailing into would one day become known as the First Battle of the New Hebrides….

Chapter 12

When the convoy had first sailed from Hawaii, a pilot on board the Republic with a poet's last name for his first name, Byron Wilhite, wrote in his diary: "There's something about leaving that gets you… a feeling that creeps over you and, try as you may to down it, it remains to remind you that you may never see this place again. It's sort of like the feeling you get at New Year when, for a short moment amid all the gaiety and laughter of the party, you pause to reflect and realize that here is something slipping from you that can never be returned as it is."

That was life in a nutshell, a poetic muse that was akin to that made by J. D. Salinger when he wrote, "…all we do our whole lives through is go from one little piece of Holy Ground to the next."

Men aboard those ships had hailed from small towns all over the US: Texas, New York, and the Midwest. They had said their goodbyes to girlfriends, buddies and family, piled onto trains for the long trip to San Francisco, steamed out to Hawaii, and then slipped away into the wide empty sea. They crossed the equator where the old salts, the 'Shellbacks' who had been there once before, planned an elaborate initiation for the 'Pollywogs' making the journey for the first time. They smeared them with oil and grease, dunked them in vats of sea water, and otherwise subjected them to every indignity they could devise. But this would be nothing compared to the baptism by fire all these men would soon endure.

They had all sailed on to Fiji, an island paradise if ever there was one. Many had hoped that might be the end of their sea voyage, but their Holy Ground would lie elsewhere in this turn of events, and now they were slipping away from the pier yet again, leaving behind a place that could never be returned to them as it was, and their last moments of innocence and civility as they now went off to war. Every moment in life was like that, but some moments make you stand up and pay attention as they slip away, a last kiss, a goodbye, a heave to and out to sea moment that was heavily upon the men aboard old stinking

Holbrook that day. They could hear the dolorous song of the Tahitian Maori farewell as they slipped away, and many never forgot it. They could feel in their hearts that they were crossing yet another frontier, the thin line of demarcation between the peaceful lives they had left behind, and the peculiar form of human insanity that was war.

Things started in a very ominous way, when one of the sea planes launched off the *Pensacola* went out later that morning, and never returned. That started the men talking, tightening the straps of their life jackets, and getting down into the hold for cases of ammo for those .50 caliber machine guns, which were soon bristling from all the ships in the convoy. They were the only guns that had ammo, and Bill Heath passed a moment thinking about all the rest of the stuff in those crates below as he came on deck, his broad shoulders draped with straps of MG rounds.

One hit from an enemy bomb, shell, or torpedo, and this old rust bucket will go up like fireworks, he thought. *Holbrook* had her guts stuffed with bombs and ammo, and her decks crawling with National Guardsmen.

The convoy was stretched out in a long line, with *Pensacola* in the van, leading the others in a zig-zag course to the south. The gunboat *Niagara* was bringing up the rear, last out of the harbor and lagging behind. A small steel hulled yacht of only 1000 tons, the boat could make no more than 16 knots, enough to keep up with the convoy easily enough, but not much good in her intended role as a sub chaser.

An enemy submarine would get the better of the little ship that day, the Japanese boat I-19, which was to have a particularly fruitful war record. The boat was supposed to be credited with the sinking of the US carrier *Wasp,* destroyer *O'Brien,* and would also put her lance into the side of the battleship *North Carolina.* On this day it would cut its teeth on the little *Niagara,* and when her distress call was received by Captain Frank L. Lowe on the *Pensacola,* it was far too late for the cruiser to do anything about it. The rumors spread that they were now being stalked by Japanese subs, and the men watched the mid-day sea with fearful eyes, many pointing at possible periscopes that were never there, and even firing off their .50 caliber machineguns at them, which did little more than stir up the sea and relieve just a little tension on the boat. Somehow firing the guns was a great release, better than just sitting there on the open decks, watching and waiting.

The following morning December 12th, at a little after sunrise, an aircraft was spotted to the southwest. Captain Lowe hoped it might be his long lost seaplane, but as it lingered just out of reach of the cruiser's AA guns, he had the sinking feeling that the convoy had been spotted by the enemy.

"That had to come off another ship," he said to his XO. "Because it sure as hell didn't come from Fiji."

"What do you figure?"

"Could be off a Japanese cruiser out here somewhere, or even a French ship. Something tells me we should have waited for the Aussies to get here with their welcoming committee." He was referring to the one bit of good news they had that day, when word came the Australians had dispatched a flotilla comprised of the cruisers *Canberra*, *Perth* and *Achilles*, sending them out to rendezvous with the convoy.

"Could it be off one of their ships?" asked the XO.

"Not likely. They'd notify us by signal if they were close enough to send that plane."

Captain Lowe's instincts were correct, for at that moment, the French Pacific Squadron under Vice Admiral Decoux was already twelve hours out of Noumea, and about 450 miles southeast of the *Pensacola*, and the French were now about to launch their first ever carrier borne air strike in history.

Aboard the carrier *Bearn*, the Admiral was watching the planes lining up on the flight deck, small bi-winged PL.7s that could carry a torpedo or a pair of 450 kg bombs. There were only nine aboard, but he also had 15 single seat LN.401 naval dive bombers, the only planes in that line to ever be built. They had decent range at 1200 kilometers, or about 648 nautical miles, and could be armed with 225kg bombs. Those planes would be escorted by four of his ten old Dewotine D.373

mono-wing fighters, each armed with a pair of Hotchkiss 13.2 MGs. All these planes were obsolete by 1941, with the dive bombers being the best of the lot.

Decoux had his sighting report in hand, and steamed another three hours, slowly closing the range. At a little after 12:00, he turned *Bearn* into the wind and put his fledgling strike wave aloft, with the range to the target at about 300 miles. The planes trundled off the deck, formed up overhead, and then fluttered off like a formation of moths from the last war, about to attempt something that had never been done by the French Navy.

Forty minutes later they had the *Pensacola* convoy in sight, and alarms were ringing on all the ships, sending the tense crews to man every machinegun they had managed to get out of those cargo holds. The war's fifth carrier strike was now underway. The Japanese made three in their attack against Pearl Harbor and the *Lexington*, and the Americans had returned the favor once with planes off *Enterprise* and *Lexington*. As soon as Bill heath saw those planes, he knew the jig was up and his war was finally getting started.

He and Cliff Causton were on a machinegun mounted in the bow of the *Holbrook*, squinting up at the French planes and not knowing what to make of them. Captain Lowe on the *Pensacola* had other ideas, knowing trouble when he saw it, and he ordered his cruiser to open up with everything it had, which wasn't much, at 12:10. His ten 8 inch guns were not much good against an air attack, and he had only four 5-inch dual purpose AA guns. Those guns started puffing up rounds, but were not hitting much of anything. He might have been better served sending his float planes up to dog fight with the enemy, or by a few cases of those .50 caliber MGs that were now starting to fire from all the transport ships that had managed to get them rigged out.

The men on the 75s that had been lashed to the decks on the *Republic* ran their drill, looking as threatening as possible, but with no ammo to fire at the planes as they came in for their attack runs. The dive bombers came first, relatively slow and ponderous as they fell from above, even though the plane looked much faster than it was, with a pointed nose and sleek fuselage and canopy.

The inexperience of the French pilots showed, many with no more than one or two practice bombing drills under their belts. A few bombs fell near the *Republic*, spraying her decks with more seawater than shrapnel. One more fell right off the bow of *Holbrook*, and Cliff Causton whooped as he fired off his machinegun in reprisal, missing the swooping plane by an equal margin. He, too, had no training on that weapon. It was all new to the men on both sides, this game of war, and more theater in that first wild hour than anything else.

When the French torpedo planes came in, things changed. The pilots knew enough to come in groups of three so they could put down a spread of torpedoes. They got in low, braving the inaccurate machine gun fire and the 5-inchers on the *Pensacola*, but they made the mistake of trying to go after that ship instead of the much slower transports. Perhaps it was a point of honor, in that *Pensacola* was clearly a warship, built for this fight, while the transports seemed innocent victims and bystanders, in spite of the stream of .50 caliber bullets off the *Holbrook*, and the stream of invectives as the men shouted at the French planes, giving them the middle finger as they came in.

Pensacola was well out in front now, under attack, and putting on speed. One French PL.7 took enough of a near miss from one of those 5-inch guns to force the pilot to abandon his run, smoke trailing from his engine. The other two in the first wave came in off the port bow, with three more off the starboard side, and they were going to get all five fish in the water. Captain Lowe was watching the attack, and decided to give his horse the wind.

"Ahead full!" he shouted, wanting to run right out of the steel V those torpedoes were making as they came at him. A speedy ship, the *Pensacola* responded quickly, able to run at 31 knots when necessary, as it was at that very moment. She was able to race on through, her aft deck crews cheering when they saw all five enemy torpedoes scudding through the cruiser's foaming wake. The last three PL.7s tried their luck, with even worse results. They came in on the port side and fired a spread that Lowe easily avoided with a timely turn.

Their teeth pulled, the PL.7s turned for home, while the last of the dive bombers tried to return some of the machinegun bullets being fired at them off the *Holbrook*. There was a final exchange of fire, with a few enemy rounds tearing up the aft deck and wounding three men there, while the gunners tried to riddle the planes in return, hitting nothing much at all. Then it was over, the French batting zero in their first attack, and all planes heading home save one unlucky dive bomber and that single PL.7 torpedo plane that was downed by *Pensacola*.

As the men on *Holbrook* watched them go, they began to hoot and jeer, whistling them off like a tea kettle letting off steam in that tense moment. Bill heath was braving the stench down in the hold to bring up more ammunition in case anything came back. He opened a fresh crate, and to his great surprise and delight, found it was filled with bottles of whiskey instead of ammunition. Smiling broadly, he grabbed an armful and went topside, and he and his mates had themselves a good little celebration after what they considered to be their first victory in the war that lay ahead.

Yet the battle was far from over. When the French planes made it back to the *Bearn*, Vice Admiral Decoux was most unhappy with the results. When he finally got a full report on the composition of the convoy, he was incensed. Most of his pilots had gone after *Pensacola*, which sped away, dodging bombs and torpedoes all the while.

"You idiots!" he exclaimed. "We lost two planes, and another three on landing, and we have nothing to show for it. So we attack again, only this time use your heads and go after those transport ships!"

He reasoned he would have plenty of daylight left to rearm his planes and strike again, and the entire task force began to put on speed. This time he would send only the strike planes, leaving his ten fighters aboard, with three flying CAP.

But Captain Lowe had sent out an SOS the moment that first attack came in, and it was heard by Captain James Hansen on the

Antietam. His task force had left Davao days ago and swept down the coast of New Guinea, through the Bismarck Barrier and into the Solomon Sea. He pushed down between the Island of Naunoga and Vanua Lava in the French New Hebrides group, intending to approach Fiji from the northwest.

The Americans were about 300 miles from the action when he got news of the attack, immediately ordering all ahead full. His sleek hybrid battlecarriers churned up the sea, capable of making 33 knots, though he held his speed to 30. The cruiser *Houston* could easily keep pace, a ship that was to be called "The Galloping Ghost of the Java Coast." That ship had stayed with his task force, along with the destroyer *Alden*, while the remaining destroyers escorting the seaplane tender *Langley* were left behind and bound for Port Moresby to refuel. *Alden* was supposed to have been in Tarakan on Borneo, lingering there for a little added security, but now it would go rushing into battle with the hybrids.

"Get hold of Gates on the *Shiloh*," said Hansen as they passed through the 250 range mark. "Tell him to get 'em up and turn 'em over. The Japs must have a carrier out here somewhere."

Those initial reports had not clarified the situation. Hansen knew *Pensacola* was under attack, but no mention had been made of the French. It wasn't until he had his planes on deck, that follow up signals from *Pensacola* enlightened him.

"So now we're at war with the French? They'll have to be coming out of Noumea, and if they hit *Pensacola* an hour ago, then they'd have to be right about here." He fingered the map, his index finger falling right on the spot where Admiral Decoux was cursing and organizing his second strike. "Alright, let's get all 24 strike planes in the air, and half the fighters, that will leave us 12 fighters here on CAP."

He was going to send 36 planes at the French, twelve SBDs, 12 TBDs and 12 Wildcats. While they were still inter-war models, they were head and shoulders above what *Bearn* was carrying, and his pilots were much better trained. They were raised and spotted quickly on the small but efficient flight deck, which was angled out slightly so the planes would take off on an angle of about 15 degrees from the bow. The men had heard what had happened at Pearl, and knew the fate of the *Lexington*. Now it was time for a little payback, though their only regret was that they were not going up against the Japanese.

The strike was up and on its way, arriving near the suspected position of the enemy task force at mid-day, just as *Bearn* was spotting her refueled and rearmed planes for their second attack. When the warning came in of enemy planes, Admiral Decoux was shocked. Where could they be coming from? He was well away from any island, and from all intelligence, the only American carriers were far to the east at Pearl Harbor, or already at the bottom of the sea.

His disillusionment aside, the French began to put up AA fire just as the SBDs tipped over into their final dive. Down they came, the Wildcats right behind them to look for enemy fighters. One of those planes was being piloted by a man who should have been on the *Lexington* that day, if it were still afloat. His name was Butch O'Hare, who would get 7 kills early in the war after training with flight group leader Jimmy Thach. He was transferred into Davao when the *Antietam* needed a replacement pilot, and now he found himself in a perfect place to start notching his belt.

O'Hare saw that there were only a handful of enemy planes up, the old Dewoitine D.371s. The rest were just starting to take off, and he called out to his mates that they had caught the French napping, as usual. The six D.371s up on CAP never even tried to go after those SBDs, fluttering off to the north where O'Hare could get a good crack at them. He was on the tail of one with a good burst that riddled its feathers right from the start.

Before it was over he would shoot two of those planes down, needing only five more to equal his wartime tally in Fedorov's history. It would not be any great accomplishment if you just looked at the numbers. The top American Ace of the war, Richard L. Bong, would get 40 kills, and even this would put him far down on the list, which was largely dominated by German pilots. Eric Hartmann would get 352 confirmed kills, and the Germans would stack nearly a hundred

Aces at the top of the heap. But here, in these early days of the war, those two kills O'Hare notched counted for a great deal. They were tiny little victories where they were much needed, grains of sand in the war, but enough to start an avalanche.

Meanwhile, the Dauntless pilots were pushing their SBDs into the final leg of the dive, and one was going to put a 500 pound bomb right on the flight deck of the *Bearn*, just aft of the tall narrow island. Admiral Decoux stared at the hit, seeing it blow away the central crane for hoisting planes up on deck. The tall white sea spray of several more near misses shook his nerves, and then another 500 pound bomb crashed into the carrier about 50 feet from the stern. That one was the fatal blow, for it would penetrate the thin 25mm flight deck, plunge through the spaces below and start a raging fire that soon threatened to involve the main propulsion shafts.

In the chaos that ensued, the French simply forgot all about their launch operations. They managed to get 9 planes in the air, and the Wildcats were all over them, shooting four more down, and forcing another two torpedo planes to fly so low that they ended up ditching. Three got away. But unable to go back to the *Bearn*, they simply headed out to sea.

Admiral Decoux would see his days as a carrier commander come to a swift end, and he boiled with anger to think of what had just happened to France's only carrier. But he still had a significant force in hand, with those cruisers and destroyers. The flak they were putting up was considerable, and enough to drive off most of the 12 TBDs that came in, but not before one got a torpedo in the water that stuck it to the French carrier right amidships. That sealed the fate of the *Bearn*, and Admiral Decoux knew it when he felt the jarring impact and saw the tall white sea spray wash up and over his flight deck. Try as he might to save her, he would now lose the ship, and be forced to transfer his flag to the nearest cruiser, *Jean de Arc*.

Then something happened that no one expected at that time and place, not even the French. A squadron of three white winged Japanese Zeroes came diving into the scene, swooping down like falcons to attack the American TBDs as they formed up to make the return leg to their battlecarriers. The First Battle of the New Hebrides was about to enter Round 3.

Part V

Rooks' Gambit

"No Price is too great for the scalp of the enemy King."

— **Koblentz**

Chapter 13

They had come off the light carrier *Hiyo*, which had been stationed at Truk with her sister ship the *Junyo* to support planned amphibious landings in the Gilberts and French New Hebrides. They had once been the luxury passenger liners *Izumo Maru* and *Kashiwara Maru*, laid down at Nagasaki in 1938, but from their very inception the designers were paid a handsome subsidy to build in features that would allow for an easy conversion to an aircraft carrier. It was all part of Japan's sleight of hand before the war, a plan to quickly produce even more carriers should they be needed.

With this in mind, they were designed with double hulls, and large internal areas used as dining halls and ballrooms were positioned exactly where the navy might want its hangers and flight deck elevators. As it happened, both were purchased by the Japanese Navy before the war, now commissioned five months earlier than they might have appeared. They were very useful ships for the purpose in mind, a good escort for amphibious task forces where their 25 knot speed would serve well enough, and they could carry 48 combat planes and a number of float planes as well.

Junyo was now far to the north, escorting a Japanese SNLF battalion out to the Gilberts, and *Hiyo* had been assigned the mission of escorting in the crack Ichiki Regiment under Colonel Kiyonao Ichiki, to Noumea to reinforce the battalion that had landed there on December 4th. The Colonel had his name first entered into the history books as a Major in China, when he had been conducting a night training session with his men firing blanks. The Chinese across the nearby border thought an attack was imminent, fired artillery, and that night one of Ichiki's men failed to return to the barracks. Thinking the man had been captured, the intrepid Major formed up his battalion and went storming into Wanping, the first hostile act of the war against China that began in 1934.

Now Ichiki was a Colonel, and the men on the transports were not going to be shooting blanks, though this was not to be an assault mission. He had the 28th regiment of Kuma Heidan, the 7th Infantry, otherwise known as the Army's 'Bear Division.' It was called that because the unit had gained most of its experience in the so called "Siberian Intervention," occupying Vladivostok and Primorskiy Province and also fighting in Manchuria. Ichiki's regiment had been moved to Truk for a possible attack on Midway Island, but that was not yet scheduled, and so it was now being sent south to Noumea.

The small task force was comprised of *Hiyo*, five transports, the destroyers *Isuzu* and *Yura*, and the heavy cruiser *Chokai*. The latter had been pulled from the Malaya operation and sent out to Truk to put just a little muscle into the operations group there, which was otherwise quite lean. They would be operating in waters that would be deemed safe for some time, and so battle was not on the mind of Captain Beppu Akitomo as he took his 'Flying Hawk' south to what he thought would be nothing more than a quick ferry mission. He was to offload Ichiki's troops, and leave most of his aircraft at Noumea as well before returning to Truk to be re-provisioned.

Hiyo had 18 D3A Val dive bombers, 18 B5N Kate torpedo bombers, and 12 A6M Zeroes, with three of them up that day on a wide area search sweep. They heard the radio traffic rising like the unexpected swell of a storm, and homed in to see what was going on. *Shotai* leader Teneko Tadashi was eager to get into the war, and the sound of a rollicking battle on his radio, with heated calls in both French and English, pulled his planes in like sharks to blood in the water. They saw the American SBDs and fell on them, gunning one out of the sky in that first pass and scattering the rest.

The Wildcats that had accompanied the strike had been chasing off the last of the planes that struggled into the air off the *Bearn*. The hapless French pilots did not know where they were going, and simply fled away from the scene on any heading. By the time the US fighters realized they had uninvited guests, those three Zeroes had each feasted on one of the SBDs. The Americans reformed and raced to get to the scene of the battle, the twelve planes being enough to discourage Teneko when he saw them coming. As much as he had every desire to dance with the American fighters, he knew that this many planes were confirmation that an enemy carrier was somewhere close at hand, and that became his highest priority. So he quickly ordered his *Shotai* to break off and follow him due south to mask the real location of the *Hiyo*, which was now steaming exactly 294 miles west of the battle zone.

Teneko flashed the warning back to *Hiyo—enemy planes—possible carrier close by!* He could not provide a location, but he had carefully noted the course of the SBDs when they had found them, and surmised from this that the Americans might be to the north. So with plenty of fuel left in his long legged Zeroes, he led his planes back north again to see if he could stealthily trail the American formation home.

For their part, the US strike leader had radioed back to *Antietam* that they had just mixed it up with three Jap fighters, and were now inbound, and with three confirmed hits on the French flat top.

This was a real surprise for Captain James Hansen. "Enemy fighters? Out here?" he folded his arms, looking at Cliff Howard, the balding XO of the ship with a bulldog neck and heavy shoulders.

"Must have come out of Noumea," said Howard. "For my money, we ought to get down there and give them a good pasting, right along with the Frogs. Let's bust up their little tea party with Tojo's boys before it gets started."

"Easy does it, Cliff," said Hansen. He was a tall, straight backed navy Captain, near the top of his class, and with just enough of a cavalry officer in him to have landed this posting to *Antietam*. Yet for him, orders were orders. He had been sent to find and protect the *Pensacola* Convoy, and that was what he was fixed on doing.

"This signal says those Zeroes broke off to the south. There's nothing down there but open sea, so maybe they did come out of Noumea. That said, we've got to link up with *Pensacola* ASAP. We gave it to that French carrier pretty good. As soon as we recover the boys, I'm moving east."

That was going to take *Antietam* and *Shiloh* directly away from his unseen enemy. The *Hiyo* group had come down through the

Solomons, and was right between the long island of New Caledonia and the lower New Hebrides, a string of four islands, Efate, Erromango, Tanna and Aneityum. You could draw a line between the Japanese and American carriers now, and it would run right over the second island in that chain, Erromango, largely uninhabited and with no history to speak of in the original war.

Teneko's fighters followed the Americans just long enough to get a good heading, carefully watching his fuel diminish as they went. Yet he persisted until he finally saw them starting to descend. There, ahead through a stand of puffy white clouds, he clearly saw what he was looking for, two enemy carriers. Elated, he noted his position as best he could, and turned off to head home, now flying slightly southwest. He would find Erromango dead ahead, and knew that he could use it again to lead him right toward the enemy carriers.

Aboard *Hiyo*, Captain Beppu could hardly believe the news. He knew the Americans were thought to have four carriers here in the Pacific. Two had been spotted and engaged near Pearl Harbor, and these could certainly not be those ships, because the *Kido Butai* had put one of them on the bottom of the sea. So these must be the other two carriers, hiding out here and probably trying to get to Australia. It was just his luck that he had discovered them, and though he was outnumbered two to one, or so he believed, he would now get his chance for a big kill.

In fact, the odds were fairly even, for the Americans would now have 44 planes between their two hybrids, losing those three SBDs and one Wildcat that had developed engine trouble and had to ditch. Beppu immediately ordered his strike planes to make ready, and now the race was on to get those planes into the air as soon as possible.

By the time Teneko's three thirsty Zeroes returned, the strike wave was being spotted on deck. He took his plane in, leaping from the cockpit to run to the *Hiyo* strike leader, Lt. Zenji Abe. "Two carriers!" He pointed stiffly to the east, right off the bow of the ship, which was now turning into the wind. "All you have to do is find the big island out there, and fly right over top of it! But be sure you save something for me. I'll be right on your tail as soon as they refuel my plane."

Lieutenant Zenji Abe was eager to go. He had come over from the Fleet Carrier *Soryu*, thinking to make a move to the Fleet Flagship *Akagi*, and was disappointed when he first learned he would be sent to the *Hiyo* instead. He would not be with his old ship in the Pearl Harbor attack, and this posting to *Hiyo* seemed a lackluster affair. Yet now he would get his chance to shine. He would not get his day over the Devil's Island, as the Japanese called Oahu, but today he would give the Devil his due.

His 18 Vals had good range, nearly 800 nautical miles, and it was only a reported 300 to the enemy task force. That meant he could expend fuel he might use to travel 200 nautical miles over the target, which was more than enough to deliver his bombs to the enemy. The Kates behind him had even better range, so he knew they would make a good attack. But there were only six Zeroes along, and Teneko would not be able to make good on his promise to follow when he was told his *Shotai* would refuel and then stand on defensive CAP over the *Hiyo*.

On the long flight out, Abe put his mind into a calming meditation, but when they finally spotted the dark silhouette of Erromango, he could not help the rising adrenaline in his chest. Cruising at a little over 140 knots, it took Abe a little over two hours before he found what he was looking for.

The American carriers had moved east as Captain Hansen ordered. Even as Teneko was landing on *Hiyo* with his news, the US strike wave was being recovered. In those two hours, the service crews below decks worked like maniacs to turn those planes over and get them spotted again. Yet Hansen had no idea what to do with them. Even if he presumed there was a Japanese carrier around, he did not yet know where it was, and his only suspicion put it south of the French Fleet in his mind. The thought that the Japanese would come from the west, right over the line of the southern Hebrides, never entered his mind.

At 15:00 hours, Hansen had considered mounting yet another strike on the French, but hesitated, hoping the seaplanes off the *Houston* would tell him whether the enemy was persisting in an easterly course towards *Pensacola*. That was not happening, for Admiral Decoux had had quite enough after *Bearn* took those hits, and he was nursing a fruitless hope that he could get the carrier back to Noumea. So the French were just hovering, and *Houston's* spotters confirmed that.

"What's your call," said XO Cliff Howard. "You going to give it to the Frogs on the other cheek now? We can make sure we get that carrier, and after that, get after those French cruisers."

Hansen liked the fire in his eyes, and so he nodded, ordering the planes to be spotted again for a final strike. "This time we better load up on fighters," he said. "Just in case those Japs have more Zeroes out there. Tell Murray to get all his Wildcats up first."

That was a fortuitous order, for when Abe's strike came in they were surprised to find the skies already crowded with American planes over the two carriers. 18 of the 24 Wildcats had already taken off, forming up like a swarm of hornets over the two fast carriers. Behind them the strike planes were following them up, climbing slowly into the sky.

The seeming calm of all that open sea and sky was soon a wild swirl of planes. Abe was determined to put in his attack, and he led his Vals gallantly forward against very steep odds. The Wildcats had been forewarned by the planes returning from the strike, and they figured they had a score to settle should they find any more Zeroes holding hands with the French. This time they found much more than they expected.

The six Zeroes flying escort raged in, boldly challenging the American formation, though they would be outnumbered three to one. Yet at this stage of the war, they were among the best pilots in the Japanese Navy, even on a secondary light carrier like the *Hiyo*, and the planes they were flying were second to none. They downed two Wildcats before the numbers began to matter and they were more often forced to defensive maneuvers after that initial fitful attack. Yet they had two thirds of the Wildcats in a wild fight, leaving no more than six to go after Abe's strike planes.

Flight leader Calvin Murray was one of them, and he cut a path to get at those Vals just as they were tipping over, following one down and forcing it to break off its attack run and go defensive. The others persisted, 17 dive bombers coming down to churn up the seas with their 500 pound bombs. Six went after *Houston*, putting one bomb right amidships on the Galloping Ghost. The other eleven focused on the carriers, but the Wildcats got two more on the way down. That left nine Vals to put in that attack, and one put a bomb right beside *Antietam*, the spray of shrapnel and seawater raking the hull and one of the 5-inch guns there. The second was lucky enough to score a direct hit, but it was well forward of the flight deck, landing right on the number two 6-inch gun turret.

The resulting explosion looked worse than it was, for there was just enough armor there to protect the ship from taking serious harm, even though that gun was certainly put out of action. But now the Kates were swooping low, bearing down on *Antietam*, which seemed to be pulling in most of the enemy attacks. Captain Rooks was cruising just off the starboard side of the carrier in *Houston*, his cruiser throwing everything it had at the enemy, and he was about to make history, and pose a question to every new academy recruit for the next sixty years.

Chapter 14

The Galloping Ghost was a beautiful ship when it first sailed in dress whites. It had a lovely clipper bow, with two big triple 8-inch gun turrets right behind it, and a third turret aft. A tall tripod mainmast, that looked much like those on the old American battleships, rose high above the bridge, doubling the height of the ship well above the two stacks, and there was another small tripod mast right behind the aft turret. Now she sailed in Haze Grey war paint, her sleek bow cutting through the whitecaps as she put on speed.

In better days, the ship had hosted President Roosevelt on a long Pacific cruise before the war, attended the opening of the Golden Gate Bridge in San Francisco, but now she was rigged for battle, with four new quad 1.1 caliber AA cannons installed just before the war. Those guns opened up on the Kates, along with all the 5-inch 130mm AA guns on the starboard side of the ship, and eight .50 caliber machineguns. Their fire had been ineffective against the dive bombers, but with barrels depressed, *Houston* was throwing out a hail of steel at the oncoming enemy planes.

Torpedo planes died at an average kill rate of 30% to 50% in the early war, but the Japanese were coming in very fast, much faster than the American gunners expected. This high speed run was possible due to the unique technology of the Type-91, and that would save all but three that were downed by defensive fire, one in a tumultuous cartwheel when its wing hit the choppy seas. Three more had been harried off by a group of four Wildcats, and that left a dozen in the attack, all getting fish in the water. Of these, four were ill timed, and two others skipped on the ocean when their pilots came in just a little too low. But the last six were running true in a wide spread.

Captain Rooks saw the *Antietam* pull a hard right turn to port, slightly ahead, and knew that if he did the same he might avoid the leading torpedoes. But in his judgment, if he did that they would plow right into the *Antietam*, for he did not think the carrier was nimble enough to turn where it needed to be. In that hard moment a cruel calculus ran through his mind. Should he save his cruiser, leaving a good chance that the carrier would be hit?

Aboard *Antietam*, Captain Hansen was on the weather deck with his bulldog, Lieutenant Commander Cliff Howard, who pointed at the *Houston* with a growl. "God damn! This is going to be close. Why doesn't he turn?"

Hansen knew why.

Seconds later they saw the tall splashes that told the story. Rooks and the *Houston* had taken the fall. In that split second the Captain had simply ordered steady as she goes, his jaw set. His cruiser had already taken a 500 pound bomb, with damage in that attack that was far more serious than the one that took out the number two turret on *Antietam*. And though he had violated his primary duty as a Captain to see to the safety of his ship and crew, he saved the *Antietam* that day, for those torpedoes were going to hit her for sure if *Houston* turned.

Each of those Type 91s would put a 204kg warhead into *Houston*, and that would end her career long before she ever would earn her nickname. Her sides were ripped open, and the water flooded in. While it helped douse the fire amidships from that bomb hit, the flooding could not be controlled. *Houston* would die in what the Navy training schools would later call "Rooks' Gambit," but that Rook had protected the Queen in this deadly chess game at sea, and the planes off that queen had skewered the enemy King.

The Russian chess player Koblentz once said that no price was too great for the scalp of the enemy King. The men who went into the water that day took little solace from that, but their sacrifice was going to make a great difference in the months ahead.

Three separate carrier based task forces had now each put in attacks, one after another. The French attack had suffered from the liability of their obsolete planes and inexperienced pilots, the Americans had hit them back hard and knocked France right out of the war, at least insofar as carrier operations would be concerned, and now the Japanese had come to their aid and hurt the Americans in turn.

Antietam had been hit, but her flight deck was not involved, and she could still launch whatever she had left. *Shiloh* had been completely unscratched, along with destroyer *Alden*, shunned by the Japanese pilots. There were still three French planes out there somewhere, each one running alone on a different heading. Two eventually made it back to Noumea, but one ornery man, Captain Louis Delfino, had a crazy idea. He had flown for the Vichy Squadron at Dakar, then mustered out to French Indochina where he found himself available when *Bearn* arrived at Saigon. Fascinated by the prospect of becoming a carrier pilot, he persuaded the ship's Captain to let him train, and he was the one man who would put that training to good use that day.

Not knowing the fate of the *Bearn* when he sped away, Captain Delfino took the same heading he had flown earlier, and it led him right back to the *Pensacola* convoy. When he got there, he kept looking over his shoulder for company, but found himself completely alone. Had his mates been with him, the flack would have been fairly thick, but as it was, he was able to line up on one of the transports in an almost leisurely fashion, low and slow.

At one point, Captain Lowe on the *Pensacola* thought he might be looking at his lost seaplane, as the resemblance was very close at range. Then he spied the torpedo slung below the belly of Delfino's plane, and sounded general quarters.

He was a little too late. The men on *Holbrook* were quicker, their .50 caliber machineguns opening up with a restless chatter. The men hadn't seen a thing for well over three hours since that first attack, and they thought they had licked their enemy. For the most part that was true—all but one. The plane was coming right in on the water, not aimed at *Holbrook*, but at the ship right behind her, the *Admiral Halstead*, with those 9,000 drums of high octane Avgas. Delfino got his fish in the water, it ran true, and the resulting explosion was the loudest sound to be heard on those waters for decades.

Cliff Causton, was on the bow manning his gun when it happened, along with Willie Heath. The two men were almost blown right off the ship by the blast wave, and the fireball was big enough that portions of deck mounted cargo on the aft of the *Holbrook* ignited, forcing the stunned crew to scramble for water hoses. As for the *Admiral Halstead*, when the shocked crewmen peered through the smoke and roiling flame, they could see nothing of the ship at all, and then a rain of hot metal began to fall all around the convoy line. The ship had literally been blown to ten thousand pieces, and not a single man aboard survived.

There, too, went all the aviation fuel for the P-40s and A-24s crated aboard the *Blomfintien* and on the *Meigs*. The French had salvaged a measure of honor, with just enough of a spike of revenge to put some steel into Admiral Decoux when Captain Delfino radioed back with the news of his lucky hit. The Admiral was delighted, wagging his finger at every man on the bridge of his sinking carrier, and telling them that when they got safely off the ship, and onto those cruisers, that this battle was far from over. He also had the radio operator tell Delfino that there was no point in trying to get back to the *Bearn*, she would be gone before he got there.

The Captain had already flown 200 miles to make his stunning kill, and now he reasoned that he might have just enough fuel to make landfall somewhere—in Fiji. Those islands were about another 200 miles ahead of him, and any friendly ground behind him was well beyond his range. So that is what he did, barely making it to Fiji where he ditched his plane in the surf just off the southern coast. He was soon found by members of the local Fiji Battalion, to whom he promptly surrendered with a stiff salute, his private little war over for the moment. Later he would cross the line and join the French Normandie-Niemen Squadron to fight the Germans in Russia.

* * *

Antietam and *Shiloh* were in a quandary now as Captain Hansen tried to decide whether he should launch that second wave as planned against the French, or try to look for the Japanese.

"Those planes came in from the southwest," he said to Cliff Howard, "but we don't really know where the Japs are. If they're more than 300 miles out, we won't be able to get at them. Hell, we can barely hit the French from here, as I've been running east for the last hour."

"Bird in the hand," said his XO. "We know where the Frogs are, just like you say."

"Suppose the Japanese come at us again?"

"Then leave all the Wildcats here. Hell, the French don't have anything that will bother our boys. We busted them up pretty bad the first time out."

"I don't know," said Hansen. "I don't like piling it on the second stringers when the A team is out there gunning for us."

"Well, hell then," said Howard. "We can't very well run off east now with *Houston* going down. There's 1100 men out there and the *Alden* can't pull but a hundred out of the water. We've got to hold station here until we get those men safely aboard. So let's get after the Japs." He slapped his fist in his palm to emphasize the point, and Hansen gave him a nod.

It was going to be a long shot, but he would now launch everything he had left, eight SBDs and eleven TBDs, along with half the fighters, leaving him with ten he could hold on combat air patrol during the recovery operation. So he was sending 29 planes out this time, on a heading that followed the Japanese point of withdrawal. Along the way, some of the escorting Zeroes realized the Americans were behind them, and radioed ahead to warn the *Hiyo* they were coming. Then they broke off and went back to try and bust up the American formation, like hawks falling on a flock of geese. There were only four left, but they kept things hot and busy for twenty minutes, fighting a rearguard action. One of the TBDs took a wing hit and lost enough fuel to force it to return to *Shiloh*. The Wildcats eventually drove the four intrepid Japanese pilots off, or so they believed. In truth, the Japanese were low on fuel and had to break off the action, racing ahead to rejoin the strike planes approaching *Hiyo*.

Six more Zeroes would be waiting over the Japanese task force when the Americans finally got there. Lieutenant Commander Murray put on speed, racing ahead of the strike planes now as he led the fighters in, but this time it was even odds, with ten Zeroes against an equal number of Wildcats. It's been said that there are two kinds of fighter pilots—one that goes out to get kills every time he flies, and the rest, who secretly fear they will be the ones in the crosshairs when they fly. Jake Murray was the first kind, and he would personally put streams of hot lead into two enemy Zeroes, though he was amazed at how many others twisted away when he thought he had a good shot.

Unfortunately, the rest of his Wildcats were filled with the other kind of fighter pilots that day, young, inexperienced men, seeing their first real combat in a place they never thought they would have to fight. The Japanese were going to get six kills in that dogfight, the Wildcats claiming three, the pair Murray got, and one other that had to splash when it finally ran out of fuel.

When the strike planes got there, the combined flak from the *Hiyo*, her four destroyers, and the heavy cruiser *Chokai* was fairly thick. But the US got just a little payback as the sun began to fall. Matoba Shigehiro, Chief Engineer of *Hiyo*, was going to be a busy man that day. One of the American dive bombers put its bomb right on target, in the aft section of the ship, just behind the rear elevator. It took out a deck mounted AA gun there, blasted right on through to the deck below to destroy a boat, and kept right on going into the innards of the ship, where it blew into the engine compartments. Casualties were heavy, and *Hiyo* saw her speed quickly fall off to just 16 knots. She was now walking wounded, able to still launch and recover planes, but not nimble enough to dodge the torpedoes off those TBDs.

No one ever gave a passing thought to going after the slow moving Japanese transports. The Americans had made the same mistake the French pilots had made when they first found the *Pensacola* Convoy. They saw that Japanese carrier and went after it with single minded or perhaps myopic determination. So the Ichiki Regiment would get to

Noumea, and that was going to mean trouble and tears for US war planners from that day forward.

Out of the ten Avengers that had started the run on *Hiyo*, flak got two, and the Zeroes two more. That left six pilots pulling the stick to get their fish into the water, and one was going to get his hit, Ensign Earl Kincaid, a young buck from Texas who thought flying his TBD was just like breaking in a good horse. The other US pilots heard him *yee haw* when he saw that fish run smack into the target, right on the port side of the carrier, about 50 feet forward of the island.

Earl the Pearl had scored a hit, and Captain Beppu Akitomo cursed when he felt the torpedo striking his ship… but, to his great relief, it did not explode.

Their fight over, the American planes pulled away, got themselves back into a group, and headed northeast. Six Avengers, eight SBDs and four Wildcats came home, and Hansen told them all to land on the *Shiloh*. He waited nervously on the Bridge of *Antietam* for the next two hours, watching the recovery operation as *Houston* finally rolled over and went down. They got most everyone off, but 186 would not survive that ordeal in the sea, most casualties from the moment the bomb and those two torpedoes struck the ship.

Captain Rooks would face a board of enquiry when he eventually was flown back to Pearl Harbor, but Hansen came to his defense, telling him it was just flat out bravery under fire that had saved his battlecarrier that day. At that moment, America needed heroes. So instead of a rebuke for not turning away and saving his ship, the captain got a medal, and 'Rooks' Gambit' would be a question put to every young officer in the training schools for the next three years when they were all asked to weigh in as to what they would have done.

He had figured heavily in the outcome of that battle, for *Antietam* and *Shiloh* both made it safely east to find the stricken *Pensacola* Convoy. They had been too late to save the *Admiral Halstead* and those 9,000 drums of high octane Avgas, but what was left of that small air group would come in very handy when the French Admiral Decoux got a hair up his ass and decided he was going to continue on east and avenge the loss of his prized carrier.

Far to the south, the last element of this complex battle was coming up from Brisbane, a three ship task force led by the heavy cruiser *Canberra*, under Captain Harold Bruce Farncomb, RAN. With him were Captain Philip Boyer-Smith on the Australian light cruiser *Perth*, and Captain Hugh Barnes on New Zealand light cruiser *Achilles*. It seemed anyone could get in on this bar fight, and the arrival of that task force on the scene would now add ships from two more countries to the mix.

Hiyo, however, was out of the action. Captain Beppu decided the best thing he could do was get his wounded carrier to Noumea, where he was to have delivered his planes in any case. Getting the Ichiki Regiment there safely was his first responsibility, and so he turned away, recovering his planes and heading south with a standing patrol of Zeroes overhead the whole long way.

All that night the ships that still had any fight in them would close on the position of the *Pensacola* Convoy. The following morning the final chapter of the battle would be written, with the French fleet facing off against those three Kiwi cruisers, the US heavy cruiser *Pensacola* and destroyer *Alden*. *Antietam* and *Shiloh* would make all the difference in the world, even though their combined air wing could now only put up 28 of the original 48 planes, and most of those were Wildcats.

Admiral Decoux thought he had the upper hand with his four cruisers and four destroyers against just five enemy ships, but those two hybrid battlecarriers were just over the horizon, unseen and determined to stay in the fight.

Chapter 15

The French had learned much from Captain Louis Delfino, and they learned it very quickly. The battle they had just fought taught them that the pomp and protocol of the military, its seeming civility with fresh pressed uniforms, stiff armed salutes, and all due respect, was nothing more than a mask. Behind that mask lay the violence inherent in the machinery and weapons they commanded, and the end of their use was inevitably death—death of a plane, a ship, a man.

War was not dashing, nor gallant, nor the display of honor. It was simply a carefully controlled, yet murderous craft of destruction. Seeing the *Bearn* ravaged by bombs and fire, and finally gutted by that torpedo, had shaken Admiral Decoux's resolve, as it might any man. But seeing what Louis Delfino did, a single man alone in his plane, had forged the steel of the Admiral's resolve, at least that night, as darkness descended on his task force.

He learned where the American convoy was, and steamed hard for it all night long. At dawn, he thought he might see the tall charcoal smoke from that action, but the last fading remnant of the violence that had ended the wartime career of the *Admiral Halstead* had become nothing more than a muddy smear that slowly turned ocher in the lightening sky.

The *Pensacola* Convoy, had turned due south, thinking to evade any further enemy harassment, but Decoux had seaplanes off his cruisers up that morning, searching the rosy dawn. It was not long until they found the convoy, but soon after that report, another came in with news of the Australian led squadron to the southwest. The Admiral now had to decide whether or not to go in after that convoy, or first deal with the constable on the beat, and in doing so he took his own advice as he gave it to his pilots after that ill fated first strike.

He decided to ignore the three ships rushing to the scene, and instead put on speed, hell bent to get at the Americans. He was on their horizon at 08:00… but so was *Antietam* with its sidekick *Shiloh*. They were just about to make their rendezvous with the convoy when the uninvited guests arrived, and a Wildcat up in early morning search had seen the French coming. Captain Hansen and his growling XO Cliff Howard had every plane left spotted and in the air twenty minutes later, and Decoux looked up to see them coming, his ardor for battle suddenly dampened again.

Only six Dauntless dive bombers and an equal number of Avengers were flyable, but Hansen had ordered six more Wildcats to go up with bombs strapped to their wings. If the Japanese showed up again, they could always jettison the ordnance for a dogfight, but by now, the *Hiyo* group was far to the west, heading for Noumea with that precious troop convoy.

Down they came, six intrepid dive bombers with a hunger for revenge. They had never thought that France would be their enemy out here. In fact, *Antietam* had once called on French ports in these waters, and received a warm welcome. But seeing what they had done to the *Admiral Halstead* had fired up the pilots, and coming off a good round with the Japanese, they were ready for a fight here.

Down they came, the first flight lining up on the French cruiser *Emile Bertin*, and one of the three scored a direct hit that put a forward turret out of action. The second flight went after the Cruiser *Lamotte-Picquett*, bettering their brothers by putting a 500 pounder right amidships, and another near miss that rolled the ship heavily to starboard. Decoux ordered a hard turn, but looked to see six more planes coming in like a line of heavy cavalry, low on the water.

They were lined up well, and all six would get torpedoes off. Unfortunately, half would fail due to mechanical problems that would plague American torpedoes for months at the onset of the war. Of the three that ran true, two would find enemy hulls. Destroyer *Fougueux* would not survive the hit it took, nearly blowing off the small ship's bow. Then the light cruiser *Emil Bertin*, her bridge shrouded in heavy smoke from the bomb hit forward, could not see to maneuver out of harm's way. The cruiser took a damaging hit in the aft quarter of the ship that cut her speed in half and caused her to quickly fall out of the French battle line.

Decoux now looked to see his brave charge thinned out by the loss of those two cruisers and a destroyer. He still had *Suffren* and *Jean De Arc*, and the destroyers *Frondeur, Lansquenet,* and *Le-Hardi*, a handful of ships that now represented most of what he could command by way of a navy for the foreseeable future. He did not yet know how bad the damage was, but he did know one thing, those planes could land, rearm, and continue to stalk him for hours.

The Wildcats wheeled about, now delivering their bombs to the sea for the most part, as not a man among all those fighter pilots had any training against fast moving naval targets. Flight leader Murray straddled *Jean de Arc* with his two small bombs, rattling Decoux further, and impressing upon him just how severe the loss of the carrier *Bearn* had been. He could see, in this brief encounter, the same lesson that was being learned by navies all across the world. This was a different time, a new era at sea, a different war. The days where the battleship reigned supreme were coming to an end. It was aircraft that ruled the skies over the seas now, and nothing passed there save by their leave.

The Admiral's resolve wavered, and then, dark on the horizon, he saw the threatening silhouette of the American heavy cruiser *Pensacola*, like a mother bear out to savage the wolves that had dared to attack her cubs. Bright fire rippled through the dawn, and the long arc of those 8-inch shells hissed and whooshed in, the opening salvo surprisingly accurate. The Admiral's knuckles were white on the binnacle as the tall geysers dolloped up from the sea off his port forward quarter.

Before being pronounced Commander in Chief of the French Far East Navy, the Admiral had commanded little more than a sloop and frigate, in the early 1920s, with a brief posting to a ship of the line in 1929. The fact was, he had little idea as to how to properly fight a naval battle, and when the action opened at 18,000 yards, the tall white spray of *Pensacola's* very accurate gunfire knocked the Louis Delfino out of him in five minutes. It was one thing to give scolding orders to his pilots, but quite another to follow them himself. The simple fact of the matter was this—he had no idea what he was doing, and the American ships out there did.

He turned when he should have kept steady on, and he ordered his ships to fire when the range was beyond their means. He insisted his last three destroyers remain at the back of his battle line, thinking them no more than a nuisance. Then, when *Canberra* showed up with *Perth* and *Achilles*, he lost his nerve completely, finally employing the one thing his ships could use to prevent an even greater disaster than the one he already had on his hands—their speed. The Admiral turned about, looked for the nearest empty horizon, and sped away with his feathers thoroughly ruffled, and his wounded pride unhealed.

The Aussies came in, the big cruiser *Canberra* sighting on the wounded *Emil Bertin*. Three salvos out they saw the bright flash of yet another explosion, and then, strangely, a watchman called out that he could see a white flag being hoisted. The radio man also reported the French had put out a message in the clear that they wished to seek terms. They had no intention of dying bravely that day.

Louis Delfino was of a different stripe. There were men like him in every army, and in every navy and air force. There were men that were just a cut above the others, and then there were those you would have to stack three high to make half a man in combat. This was war, with heroes and slackers, artful warriors and clumsy fools, all thrown into the same arena.

It was no failure of the French Navy, for their ships of the line would acquit themselves very well in the Atlantic and Mediterranean. It was just the men on the scene that mattered now, not the ships. Some men had the will to fight, and knew how to go about it. Others did not. Lacking both will and skill at sea, the result of this engagement for Admiral Decoux was inevitable. He would return to Noumea, thankful to be under the protective umbrella of Japanese land based air power, all the planes from the carrier *Hiyo*. There he would stew, realizing that he would not even be master of that island, or even the port where his ships were docked. His war was a long, sullen slog from that day on, until the Americans would come calling one day... And they had long memories.

So ended the First Battle of the New Hebrides, and it was a mixed result for all concerned. The French had lost the *Bearn*, the destroyer *Fougueux*, and found both *Emil Bertin* and *Lamotte-Picquett* surrendered to the enemy and interned at Fiji. The Japanese had seen *Hiyo* limp off to Noumea, where it would remain for some time while crews tried to repair her damaged engine compartments. The Americans had lost the heavy cruiser *Houston*, but even worse, they had lost 9000 drums of Avgas on the *Admiral Halstead*. The Damage to *Antietam* would send that ship home to Pearl Harbor, and then to the west coast for a new "Triple Six" gun turret, and Hansen's air group would have to be rebuilt from planes arriving in Hawaii.

The *Pensacola* Convoy received the warm embrace of those three Aussie led cruisers, and the convoy sailed for Brisbane. For the time being, *Shiloh* sailed to Pearl with *Antietam*, where she would soon team up with the *Enterprise* and the newest kid on the carrier block, the USS *Saratoga*, arriving from San Francisco. Soon those three ships would sortie again, out looking for trouble, and just a little retribution under the command of yet another bulldog who was going to make an enormous difference in the long struggle ahead. Unlike Admiral Decoux, he had both will and skill in abundance, Admiral William 'Bull' Halsey.

* * *

So the lost convoy and Operation PLUM never got to the Philippines. Instead it made its way south and then west to Brisbane, and the main effort of the Japanese Army was raging on. They had landed at Lingayen Gulf north of Manila, and then drove relentlessly towards the city. In the south, troops arrived from their island outpost at Palau to land at Legaspi, where they raced up the lower reaches of the main island, meeting little resistance. It was virtually impossible for the defenders to try and meet them on the beaches. In the south alone, there were four broad bays and over 250 miles of beaches they could choose from to land, and defending them all with the forces available was out of the question.

Manila was a mill of rumors and fear. Some said the US Navy was coming with everything they had to the rescue. Others said it had all been destroyed at Pearl Harbor. Shop keepers boarded up their windows, sandbagged their doors, and families fled to the countryside to find lost uncles and aunts out of immediate harm's way. Like any large urban area, panic could spread very easily, making the streets a morass of animal drawn wood carts, bicycles and a few cars. People were packing up household belongings, living or dead, and it was common to see a father behind a hand cart, laden with everything he owned, including three squealing pigs and five chickens, and with his poor wife and a gaggle of children in tow.

A virtual flood of cable and signals traffic swamped every telegraph and postal office as people made frantic appeals to relatives overseas. It was war coming, sudden and uninvited, bringing confusion, an erosion of civil order, bank runs, panic buying, and all the unscrupulous corruption these activities were prone to. Yet this was merely the first swells of the storm. The tide of war would bring far more hardship and depravity in the days and months ahead.

The hardened Japanese troops faced ill-equipped Philippine divisions, where some regiments had as little as five weeks training. One even took the field having had no training at all. They knew how to hold and carry their rifles, but not how to use them. Later, in the grueling stand MacArthur would make at Corregidor, many of these same men would fight and die with great valor, but now, they were like so much debris on the beach, swept inland by the rising tide of Japanese fortunes.

There was an almost comical moment when a call came in to UAAFFE in Manila, informing them of the Japanese landings in the south. It had come from a railroad stationmaster, and is quoted here verbatim:

"There are four Jap boats in the harbor, sir, and the Japs are landing. What shall I do?"

The USAFFE Officer replied, "Just hang onto the phone and keep reporting."

"There are about twenty Japs ashore already, sir, and more are coming…. Now there are about three hundred Japs outside the station, sir. What am I to do?"

"Just sit tight."

"Sir, a few of those Japs, with an officer in front, are coming over here."

"See what they want." A moment passed…

"Those Japs want me to give them a train to take them to Manila, sir. What do I do now?"

"Tell them the next train leaves a week from Sunday. Don't give it to them."

"Okay sir."

Unfortunately, the Japanese were not about to wait until a week from next Sunday. They were establishing themselves ashore, seizing initial objectives, and pushing on. Soon they would land at Mindanao in the south and at Jolo, two outposts they would use to springboard their attack into Borneo. That was where the real plum was, the resource rich holdings of the Dutch and British oil companies.

There was oil at Sarawak near Kuching and at Miri near Brunei. There were also fields near Balikpapan, and the large island also afforded them numerous ports and airfields. These were the resources Japan had gone to war for, and they would become the heart of the new Pacific Empire they were striving to extend and build. Yet before that could be attained, the last two hard rocks of Allied resistance would have to be crushed. One would be MacArthur's stubborn defense, falling back through Manila to the rugged Bataan Peninsula, and the fortified Rock of Corregidor. The other would be the British defense of Singapore. If they could make a skillful withdrawal, Churchill believed they could hold that island outpost, for he had been forewarned by

Fedorov of how the Japanese would bluff their way into a victory there that might have been forestalled.

These battles remained to be fought, and before they would conclude, the brutality of the war would show its ugly face. The troops Japan had assembled for these operations had been combed from the best units in the Army, veteran soldiers with years of hard combat experience. Yet they were also some of the most heartless and brutal troops in the Empire, the men who raped Nanking, and the men who were responsible for the Death March on the Philippines, and many other atrocities.

No one was spared their spiteful ire. Prisoners received hideous treatment, captured civilian nurses were summarily raped and murdered, some thrown down onto the bodies of the dead patients they had once served for that act of depravity. Prisoners were beheaded, and some suffered an even more bizarre and lingering death, tied down and slowly carved up by their captors, who then literally barbecued their flesh and ate it while the helpless victim watched in utter agony.

A time would come when the US forces would advance with their own brand of cruelty, burning and blasting their way from one island outpost to another. At the end of Fedorov's history, the horrors of strategic firebombing and nuclear holocaust would await the proud conquerors that now strode so boldly into the South Pacific. But at this moment, no one could say how it would all play out. For the month of December would soon wear away, and the calendar would slowly turn to a new year, the pivotal months of 1942.

The war in the Pacific had only just begun.

Part VI

Wolf in the Fold

"The Assyrian came down like the wolf on the fold,
And his cohorts were gleaming in purple and gold;
And the sheen of their spears was like stars on the sea..."

— **Lord Byron**

Chapter 16

Another man was going to figure prominently in these events as well, though he should have not have been alive in 1941, for he had not even been born yet. At that moment, he was standing aboard yet another ship that was never supposed to be in this world, his mind running along the fine points of an agenda as long and deep as that of Imperial Japan, and with a sense of his own self-importance to rival that of MacArthur himself—Vladimir Karpov.

There he stood, commander of the Free Siberian Navy, a single ship at sea now, with four or five destroyers huddled in the icy waters of Magadan back home. Unlike Admiral Decoux, however, he knew exactly how to command his ship, when to turn, when to fire, and his particular competence when it came to the violence of war was also layered with a flair for drama. Karpov had made his statement to Japan, one the ministers in Tokyo literally laughed off when they first received the messages. Japan had stepped boldly onto Siberian territory in 1908, and had kept it under foot ever since. Their Kwantung Army was between the Siberians and the object of their demands, Urajio, old Vladivostok, the war prize they had taken because of Karpov's last unfortunate sortie in the Sea of Japan.

Back then, he had faced an experienced and determined Admiral Togo, but the Japanese Navy that now graced the shores of Kure, Sasebo and Yokohama was an enormously enhanced force compared to Togo's fleet. As reports came in flurries concerning the outcome of the attack on Pearl Harbor, and the progress of the Japanese offensive into Southeast Asia, Karpov's ultimatum was largely ignored. Fedorov's assessment had been spot on. There was simply no way they would ever consider handing over Vladivostok as Karpov wanted, nor would they give his demands even passing consideration.

On one level, Karpov knew that would be the case, but he also knew exactly how he would shake the lapels of the Japanese diplomats and get their attention. Japan's naval fortunes rested with her carriers. They were her real battle sword in the Pacific, clear and convincing proof that a sea change had swept through naval strategy, and the era of the great battleships was now over. The attack made by the *Kido Butai* had been largely symbolic of that fact. The loss of those fleet carriers at Midway was the great turning point in the war, one that would have eventually come at some place, with an inevitability that was almost certain, but it came at Midway when four fleet carriers went to the bottom of the sea.

Now Karpov was considering how to proceed. Fedorov's course plot had been true, and on the 16th of December, *Kirov* found itself in a good position to launch helos and hone in on the location of the *Kido Butai*. It was not long before the *Oko* panels on the KA-40s found their quarry, about 300 miles north of Wake Island, half way home. The helos had approached to within 300 kilometers using their extended range panels to find the Japanese. While Admiral Nagumo had search planes up, he was not expecting a threat where he was, and even had minimal CAP up over the task force, giving his hard working pilots a good long rest on the journey home.

Karpov ordered the ship to continue to close, and it wasn't until late on the 17th of December that his prey was brought within missile range. In many ways, *Kirov* was like another battlecarrier as it crept up on the *Kido Butai*. Its missiles were like kamikaze planes to be sent out, sure to hit their targets, but never to return. Yet the longest range missile he had was the P-900, which could get to targets at a maximum range of 370 kilometers, or about 200 nautical miles. The ship had received better ranged weapons transferred from *Kazan* at one point in this long saga—but not this ship. Karpov was standing with the hand the ship was dealt when it first arrived, a royal flush in his mind, but it nonetheless had real limitations.

First off, there were only ten P-900s aboard. His real ship killers, of which he had a generous double order on hand, were the *Moskit-II* missiles, fast, heavy, but with a maximum strike range of only 222 kilometers, or about 120 nautical miles. Those Japanese carriers had strike planes aboard that could deliver ordnance at better than twice that range, and this meant that *Kirov* would have to come well within the strike radius of the *Kido Butai* if it wanted to engage. *Kirov's* initial advantage was the sheer shock of a missile attack as it first struck home on his enemy, but both Karpov and Fedorov knew that it would not end there. The Japanese would fight, with a ferocity and tenacity that was unlike any other foe the ship had faced in its long sojourn through time.

That brought up the question of how to attack, as it was already clear that Karpov was taking the ship to war. He had declared all Japanese shipping found at sea would be deemed hostile, and treated accordingly.

"You know the drill," said Karpov. "It's the old struggle to obtain the first salvo, only in our case, that is now our easy prerogative. The question is how hard to hit them. A heavy salvo could rain hell upon them, just as they did with the American battleships at Pearl Harbor. But there are other ways to humble an enemy, the slow, measured cut."

"I'm not sure what you mean," said Fedorov.

"Perhaps it is something I'll have to demonstrate rather than explain," said Karpov. "I suppose I could just get in close and give them the *Moskit-IIs*. A salvo of six or eight missiles would wreak havoc, would it not?"

"Given that none of those carriers are heavily armored, I would have to agree," said Fedorov. "But what about a possible counterstrike? Remember what happened to the battle bridge the last time we faced the Japanese."

"That isn't going to repeat itself," said Karpov. "First off, I will not be so squeamish in plucking out my enemy's eyes if he comes looking for us. They aren't using naval search radar, am I correct?"

"That was very limited technology at this point in the war," said Fedorov. "No, they'll rely on visual search from aircraft."

"Exactly, which means I can see those search planes on the Fregat system long before they get anywhere near enough to spot us, and I can shoot them down with our long range S-300s. They'll hit targets 150 nautical miles out."

"We can do that 64 times," said Fedorov.

"Yes, I'm well aware of the inventory, and our limitations. This is why I believe I'll try something a little different here. I could smash them, obliterate them in fact, and that without even thinking about the special warheads we have. The shock of that would be quite daunting."

"Yet they endured that at Midway, and still fought on for another three years," Fedorov warned.

"Precisely." Karpov clasped his hands behind his back, thinking. "How to break them psychologically, that is the question."

"That won't be easy, sir."

"Nothing about war is ever easy, but I can show them what I'm capable of, and how powerless their vaunted *Kido Butai* really is, and I think that will be the first lesson here. I addressed the crew this morning, and they are ready. The ship is ready, and so am I."

Fedorov noted that Karpov did not ask him to second the decision he was making now. He listened to his *Starpom*, considered everything Fedorov said, but when it came time to take action, the orders came from Karpov.

"Mister Samsonov."

"Sir?"

"Please sound battle stations and make two P-900 cruise missiles ready for immediate action. I will want to see your target plot board before we fire."

The warning claxon sounded, and everyone on the bridge stiffened, sitting just a little taller in their chairs, eyes fixed on their equipment.

"Air threat report," said Karpov, as if running down a checklist in his mind.

"The screen is clear out to 150 kilometers on the Fregat system," said Rodenko.

"Good." Karpov drifted over to the CIC, his eyes on Samsonov, seeing the big man hunched over his board. His fire control officer had been eager to conduct live fire exercises, though the ship never got that chance before this impossible accident sent them here. He had heard all the rumors at first, then the endless discussions among the junior officers, but Victor Samsonov was a simple man. His world was the ship, which seemed largely unchanged aside from the absence of the Admiral. His universe of understanding was in that CIC, and the weapons and systems at his command there. All he felt now was the jubilation of a warrior about to exercise his deadly craft.

"Missiles up and target board ready sir!"

Karpov was hovering over his broad right shoulder now. "filter your data and show me primes."

With a flick of a switch, Samsonov told his computers to display the strongest signal returns in the clustered group of some twenty contacts. The structure of the enemy cruising formation was clearly evident when the system processed the data, and then drew out the equivalent of a map on another screen. By analyzing that data over time, noting air blips rising from signal points, it was possible to determine which contact was a carrier. One strong signal was well out in front, surrounded by a cluster of smaller contacts. Karpov took it to be one of the fast battleships that had accompanied the force, and immediately discarded it as a first strike target.

"This is interesting," he said, looking Fedorov's way. "I thought there were six Japanese carriers in this operation."

"Remember that Nikolin picked up orders for the *Kaga* to detach to Kwajalein," said Fedorov.

"Yes, but that should leave five here. I see only three primary contacts, if I'm correct in assuming this one here is a battleship."

Fedorov came over, noting the target board with a knowing glance. "Wake Island," he said quietly. "It's amazing how the history rings so true in places, in spite of all the changes. In our history, the Japanese detached Carrier Division 2 to support the attack on the American outpost at Wake, along with the heavy cruisers *Tone* and *Chikuma*. If this remains true, then those three contacts would be the *Akagi*, the fleet flagship, and then the two newest carriers, *Zuikaku* and *Shokaku* in Carrier Division 5 following."

"Excellent," said Karpov. "Here," he pointed to the carrier leading this group of three. I want a P-900 right there. Mister Samsonov."

"You're going to hit the *Akagi*?"

Karpov looked at him. "You would prefer another target, Mister Fedorov?"

"It's not a question of ships in my mind now sir. It's the men aboard them. That is Admiral Nagumo's flagship, and he is a very significant player in the opening game of this war. After replenishing in our history, he attacked the Australian Port Darwin, mounted a daring Indian Ocean raid, and then moved on to meet his doom at Midway. Suppose he were wounded or killed? That could have a significant effect."

"Of course it would, but I am not ready to try and sort out all the possible consequences each time I fire. You are still looking over your shoulder, Fedorov. We are not sifting through the old history now, except as a possible intelligence source. Here we write all new history. Nagumo went to war taking the same risk any man does when he picks up a weapon. So fate will just have to throw the dice in his regard. That is not my concern. Mister Samsonov?"

"Keying target sir…. Missiles 09 and 08 ready to fire." Karpov noted that Samsonov carefully started with missile nine, as number ten was in a special silo used for the mounting of an equally special warhead. He had not given that order, and all those weapons were stowed in Martinov's larders below in the armory, but that missile would be the last to fire in the event it was ever tapped for special duty.

"I like that," said Karpov. "Yes, always affix a numerical suffix to each missile we fire. It will help me track our inventory. Very well, Mister Samsonov, sound your missile fire warning, and commence."

* * *

Admiral Nagumo did not yet know it, but a large and powerful wolf was stalking his fold. He was standing on the bridge of *Akagi*, just having finished a discussion with Captain Kiichi Hasegawa concerning the Wake Island detachment. The two carriers they had sent south to bolster the attack on the American held Wake Island were well on their way, and should be reporting in soon. The history had indeed reflected back with great integrity here, with one small change. This time Nagumo had sent Carrier Division 5 south, largely because it had been at the back of his cruising order, and was easier to move. That meant he had Carrier Division 2 in tow now, with *Hiryu* and *Soryu*.

From all reports the enemy garrison on Wake was putting up a stubborn fight. The initial landings had been repulsed, with the loss of a destroyer, and a little more air power was needed to soften the island defenses up, along with a promise that the Japanese would be back soon to knock a little harder on Wake's door.

It was a little after 15:00 when the radio man came in with a report from a search plane of a strange contrail in the sky, aimed directly at the task force.

"What is this supposed to mean?" he handed the report to the Captain. "A fast moving vapor trail?"

The Captain frowned at the paper, but at that moment a bell rang and the upper watch was reporting verbally that something was in the sky to the north. Nagumo considered the possibilities quickly. The only land mass that could have launched an aircraft was Wake Island to the south. What would be coming out of the north? Could one of the American carriers have been so bold as to follow them? Surely his search planes would have spotted such a task force creeping up, but he had not paid much attention to the northern flank. He had three fighters up on cap, with three more on the decks of his three carriers ready for immediate launch. He had it in mind to have his Air Commander, Masudo Shogo, vector in one of those fighters for a look, until he saw what the watchmen were reporting with his own eyes.

The meaning of 'fast moving vapor trail' was now immediately apparent. Something was soaring towards his position, high in the sky, but now it began to descend, like some demigod or demon swooping down. It had to be a plane on fire, he thought, raising his field glasses, and thinking he could even see the faint gleam of fire there. Some ill-fated pilot was falling to his doom, but impossibly fast in the descent. Who could it be?

Then, to his utter amazement, the falling aircraft leveled off just before it would have crashed into the sea. All the men on the bridge who saw it reacted, some pointing in awe. The Admiral's eyes narrowed as he watched. It was coming, still burning from what he could see, low and fast over the water, and the fire from its tail glowed upon the sea. That such a descent could have been corrected at the last moment like that seemed an impossible feat of flying to his mind, but now he would see more than he ever thought possible. The aircraft suddenly veered left, then right again, dancing over the water like a mad kami from hell. The pilot must have finally lost control, he thought, but the longer he looked, the more those first moments of surprise extended into shock.

The maneuvers that aircraft was making could not be accomplished by any plane he had ever known, and yet there was something about the snap of its course corrections that led his mind to conclude they were carefully controlled. And the speed… *The speed!*

Chapter 17

The thing in the sky flashed in at them now, coming even faster, though he could hear no sound at all. It was well ahead of the roar of its own engine noise in this final approach, at almost Mach 2, though its high altitude flight path had been sub-sonic at Mach 0.8. The missile had completed its mind boggling evasive maneuver run, intended to defeat weapons that were not even aimed at it, weapons that simply did not exist, except on the ship it had been fired from. No radars were looking for it, no SAMs taking aim, and no fast firing Gatling guns waited on the final line of defense. *Akagi*, the fleet flagship, and one of Japan's most venerable carriers, was now no more than a fish in the barrel, about to be harpooned.

The P-900 carried a powerful 400 kilogram warhead, and only the *Moskit-II* was heavier. It was an optimized heavy HE blast-fragmentation penetrator, and it was going to strike *Akagi* right amidships. Even though the ship had not fully completed its 1935 refit to extend the upper flight deck all the way to the bow, *Akagi* did have her island installed in that work, and a slightly longer top deck than the original design. That island was on the port side of the ship, opposite the odd downward facing exhaust stack on the starboard side so that the smoke would not interfere with bridge operations.

The P-900 would strike directly on that strangely curved stack. obliterating it, and penetrating deep into the ship's lower decks. There were hangers crowded with aircraft on both sides of that compartment, but the bulkheads would not contain the blast. The explosion was even enough to rupture the flight deck above, rendering the carrier all but inoperable when it came to flight operations. A Zero sitting in that spot on the flight deck was broken and flung up and off the carrier. The heavy black smoke billowed from the gaping hole, and the bridge crew stared, aghast.

Nagumo saw the deck and plane heave upward, felt the jarring impact, still stunned and not yet even knowing what could have possibly hit the ship. Yet he had seen it with his own eyes, and now the roar of chaos and fire was all about him. It was as if some demonic spirit had simply reached down and hammered his fist against the side of the carrier, breaking its hard metal hull and shattering all within.

The ship had six-inch belt armor, a legacy of her origins as a battlecruiser, but it had been slimmed down from ten inches and lowered during her conversion to a carrier. So the missile had hit just above that hard shield, right on the vulnerable external side mounted stack. The ship had already taken some damage there in the American air raid near Pearl Harbor, but this was complete destruction. The side ventilation stack was completely gone.

The shock of that hit weighed heavily on the entire bridge crew, but they would soon learn that the entire center of the upper hanger deck was involved with fire. Had the range been shorter, those fires would have been much more severe. As it was, the missile had expended almost all its fuel before striking, and so it was the warhead, and sheer kinetic force, that did most of the damage, the explosion igniting any fuel in the planes stored in that portion of the hanger.

There were six more planes on the aft flight deck, three aloft, five that were downed in the raid on Pearl Harbor, but all the rest, some 58 aircraft, were below in the hangers. About half were fueled, but there was no ordnance installed, and that had also been a saving grace. The ship had therefore taken a severe blow, but not a fatal one. Had her decks and hangers been crowded with fully fueled and armed aircraft, she would have faced uncontrollable fires from that single hit.

Nagumo was shaken by the sudden and unexpected attack. With *Kaga* already damaged in the carrier duel off Hawaii, the thunder that had struck *Akagi* had now effectively removed the entire 1st Carrier Division from the navy's order of battle for months. Reacting in the heat and shock of the moment, it was soon clear that this attack had been made by a single aircraft, deliberately crashed into his carrier to achieve maximum damage. But what could it have been? How could it move as it did, with such speed? There was no plane he had ever seen that could do what he had just witnessed. It was as if *Raijin*, the god of thunder, had just hurled his lightning down from above.

As the next minutes passed, and damage control parties reported, it was clear that the ship was badly hurt. Now he met with Captain Kiichi Hasegawa, Air Officer Masuda Shogo, Strike Leader Mitsuo Fuchida and one of the chief planners of the operation just concluded, Minoru Genda. No man among them could explain what just happened.

"It was clearly a single plane," said Fuchida. "I was well aft when it came, seeing to the three Zeroes we have spotted on ready alert. The impact knocked me from my feet."

"One plane?" said Shogo. "Its speed was fantastic! Could it have been the rocket weapons we were warned about?"

"The tales told by the Prophet?" said Hasegawa. "You might just as easily tell me it was a sky demon"

"That is not far from the truth," said Genda. "Plane, rocket, it does not matter. We have seen what it can do, how it can move and strike us with such precision."

"It must have been piloted," said Shogo. "No rocket fired from over the horizon could hit with such accuracy. So if it was piloted, then it must have been launched from a carrier. We must find it and destroy it at once!"

"*Hiryu* and *Soryu* are already scrambling fighters," said Admiral Nagumo, glancing at Genda as he spoke. "We can clearly see the direction it came from. It has left that high white vapor trail in its wake."

"That plane could have maneuvered to that heading prior to attacking us, simply to hide the real location of the ship."

"Perhaps," said Nagumo, but I will order a search to the north in any case. The only question I have is this. We sunk one American carrier off Hawaii. How could there be another here, this far west, without our knowing it.?"

"Nothing followed us," said Fuchida. "I have had searches mounted to the east for the last three days."

"But not to the north," said Nagumo. "This enemy carrier may have been lurking there, which means the Americans may have known about this operation from the very first."

"You are suggesting this was a deliberate ambush?" Shogo had a difficult time believing that. "All our intelligence found nothing to suggest that could be possible."

"Nor did we know where the American carriers were," said Nagumo. "Do you not find it strange that none were at Pearl Harbor—that they all left that place just prior to our attack?"

"Then *Hiryu* and *Soryu* will have to deal with this threat," said Fuchida. "The 5th Carrier Division is now approaching Wake Island to support our landing operation there."

Nagumo shook his head. "A third of our carriers off to the south. *Kaga* has limped to Kwajalein, and now we will be lucky to put that fire out and return *Akagi* safely to Japan."

"Sir," said Captain Hasegawa. "The loss of our ventilation shaft and the damage to the boilers from that attack has reduced our speed to a maximum 18 knots. You should consider transferring your flag to one of the other carriers."

Nagumo looked at him, realizing the deep shame he must feel, and the difficulty in making such a suggestion, his ship to be gelded and sent home alone. He then looked at the others, one by one, seeing a silent accord in their eyes that Fuchida eventually vocalized.

"*Hiryu* and *Soryu* are fast, and now we must fly like the wind to find and attack this unexpected enemy. *Kirishima* is still with us. May I suggest that ship position itself right off our starboard side. It has good armor, and better guns to repel another attack like this. It can serve as a strong shield for *Akagi* while the other carriers strike out to the north to find and kill our enemy."

"Should we recall the 5th Carrier Division?" asked Shogo.

"Two carriers should be sufficient here," said Genda. "Leave *Zuikaku* and *Shokaku* where they are."

"I agree," said Nagumo. "Signal Rear Admiral Tamon of the 2nd Carrier Division. I will transfer my flag to *Soryu* at once. The destroyer

Akigumo will come alongside *Akagi* to assist. Captain Hasegawa, you have fought well, and there is no shame to be laid upon your shoulders as I leave you now. Your orders are to break off here, move south to effect an eventual linkup with Carrier Division 5. You must do everything in your power to get *Akagi* safely back to Japan."

"Sir," said Fuchida. "That hit was right between the forward and 'midships elevators. We have lost many planes on the hanger deck, and the crews have fought like demons to move as many aircraft as possible forward and aft, away from the fires. As for the pilots, they are a precious asset. It may be wise to send them along with you to the *Soryu*. We can always replace those planes, but the men who can fly them are rare jewels."

Nagumo looked first at Hasegawa, seeing him nod agreement with a bow. "Very well," he said. "Leave Captain Hasegawa enough to get a fighter squadron into the air for self-defense. If the damage can be controlled and the deck patched, he can use them to mount combat air patrols on the way home. I will transfer my flag at 11:00. Pilots selected by Fuchida and all members of the Fleet Air Planning Staff will accompany me to *Soryu*. Yet, as this ship is in no immediate danger of sinking, the Emperor's portrait will remain here in the capable hands of Captain Hasegawa."

The next hour, all was quiet. The fleet was at the highest state of readiness, and the four ships of the 18th Destroyer Division were attached to the last mobile element of the once vaunted *Kido Butai*. Only two destroyers remained to escort *Akagi* and *Kirishima* south. The two carriers that now made up Nagumo's hunting party had fared very well at Pearl Harbor. *Hiryu* had only lost three planes, and five were lost from *Soryu*. So their air wings were all at full strength, given the fact that many of *Kaga*'s planes had landed on the other carriers before she was detached. Each of the two carriers had 62 planes, with eight or nine spares from *Kaga* and some even remaining in crates.

Aboard *Kirov*, Karpov had not followed up his first missile strike with a second P-900. Instead he waited, wanting to see the reaction in the enemy formation, and launching a diplomatic missile at Tokyo instead. He signaled that he had just initiated hostilities against the *Kido Butai*, giving the formation's exact position, and stating that he had deliberately struck the carrier *Akagi*, Fleet Flagship, as a final warning. He knew that the Japanese had a small destroyer flotilla anchored at Urajio, Vladivostok. So he demanded that flotilla make steam by 24:00 that night, and leave the port as a sign that the Japanese Government would initiate talks on the repatriation of Siberian territories. The message also indicated that any ground troops present in the Harbor were to be embarked and returned to Japan.

This was, of course, an impossible demand from the Japanese perspective. Urajio was now their principal supply port for the Kwantung Army. The rail line from there to Harbin in Manchuria, to occupied Chita, was now the quickest overland route to move those supplies up to the Baikal front. To lose Urajio would force them to completely restructure their logistics plan, moving the bulk of supplies to Dalian, the old Port Arthur they had also won in wars of the early part of the century.

"They won't concede such a strategic port simply because you have struck a single carrier," said Fedorov.

"Of course not," said Karpov. "But I now give them every warning that further attacks will follow should they fail to comply with my demands."

"What is the point in that?" said Fedorov.

Karpov responded with a single word. "Drama."

"This isn't theater, Admiral."

"Oh, but it is, Fedorov. I'm going to literally telegraph my punches here. I intend to show them just how powerless they are against us, and then the real demands will be made. I've just nicked their cheek with the tip of my sword, but that was only the first cut. I intend to bleed them, hobble them, humiliate them."

Rodenko looked over, a warning in his eyes. "The two remaining carriers have now moved away and they are turning north. They appear to be splitting their battlegroup. The original target has reduced speed, and it is now moving off to the south."

"Mister Fedorov? Your assessment?"

"No mystery here," said Fedorov. "If he wasn't killed in that missile strike, I believe Nagumo has just transferred his flag and sent *Akagi* south with orders to try and limp home. The remaining carriers should be moving at close to 30 knots soon."

"Correct," said Rodenko.

"And they are looking for us," Fedorov continued. "They should turn into the wind in a few minutes, so I expect them to assume a heading of about 350. Then they'll launch a search detail covering this entire northern arc out to at least 300 nautical miles. If my navigation plot is correct, we are now 210 nautical miles north of their position, which is just an hour's flying time at the normal cruising speed of a D3A Val. They'll be about twenty minutes launching and then form up before dispersing on their assigned search path. So I expect they will have planes in visual range of us in about ninety minutes. Their D5A Vals could range out to nearly 800 nautical miles, and the Kate torpedo bombers close to 1100. Those planes are likely to be used in the search, and they will be armed."

"Fair game then," said Karpov. "It won't be like Volsky's equivocation over taking down an unarmed search plane. Then again, with me it would never be like that. How many planes do those ships carry, Fedorov?"

"Over 60 aircraft each. That's a good chunk of our SAM inventory."

"Indeed," said Karpov. "Mister Samsonov, let us show them the futility of what they are now attempting to do. Mister Rodenko will closely track all those search planes, and we will take out any who come anywhere close to a sighting position on this vessel. Ready one silo of our S-300 SAMs."

"Aye sir. Activating missiles 63 thru 61. Missile 64 has already been fired."

Karpov moved to the radar screen, watching over Rodenko's shoulder for some time. Fedorov's prediction was right on. They could soon clearly see the planes dispersing into a wide search pattern that would cover everything through a 180 degree arc north of the carriers.

"Those three planes there," said Karpov. "Feed targeting data to Samsonov."

Rodenko tapped the three contacts on his screen, then pressed a button to feed the data to the CIC. In a matter of seconds, they were on Samsonov's board as red targets, and he quickly assigned the three S-300s he had readied.

"You realize shooting those planes down will clearly reveal our position," said Fedorov. "They'll know exactly where our jab hit them, and the missing teeth will tell them where we are—that and the contrails of those S-300s."

"Yet you just said those planes would be armed," said Karpov. "So they will be treated as the threats they are, and destroyed. Mister Samsonov. Fire on designated targets."

"Aye sir."

Chapter 18

The warning claxon, the snap of the hatch opening, the hiss of the first missile out of the underdeck silo—it was all par for the course they had been on these many long months. And sure as the moon would rise later that night, those three planes were going to die. Karpov watched the blistering speed of his missile tracks to the targets, one by one. When it was over he lingered, noting the reaction time of his enemy. It was as if they were fighting a modern carrier battlegroup that was moving in slow motion. The lightning fast reflexes of the Russian ship were now further amplified by the plodding, groping slowness of the enemy.

"Give them another twenty minutes, and you will see their strike wave forming up," said Fedorov.

As before, he was correct.

Rodenko notified Karpov that the first of the enemy planes were now starting to emerge from the contact blips of the carriers. This now presented one more decision.

"Am I correct in assuming the decks of those ships will be full of strike planes, with more in the hangers below, all armed and fueled?"

"That is very likely." Fedorov knew exactly where this was going.

"Then those carriers are now at their moment of maximum vulnerability. A pair of SSMs will do the work that a hundred SAMs might have to do in another ten or fifteen minutes. This is not a matter for further deliberation. I've been watching to see how they operate, and now the theater is over. Mister Nikolin. Send coded message three. Mister Samsonov. Range to primary targets?"

"Sir, 190 nautical miles. Just within range."

"Two more P-900s please, as before. Assign one to each carrier. You may fire immediately."

"Aye sir. Firing Missiles 8 and 7."

Raijin the God of Lightning and Thunder would soon be beating his war drums, and right at his side would go *Raiju*, his demon friend, called "thunderbeast" by the Japanese, and depicted as a white and blue wolf surrounded by lightning. It was said that buildings and trees would be clawed by this demon in a storm, and now those claws were out to score the hard metal hulls of two dragons at sea. *Hiryu*, the Flying Dragon, would be the first to feel their bite.

The approaching missiles, with the long vapor trails, would again confound the Japanese, to the utter amazement of the officers and crew who saw them dancing above the sea in that final dizzying run to their targets. Zero fighters had tried to climb up after them before they dove for the sea, but when they did so, accelerating through Mach 1.5, the pilots were astounded to see them streak away. They were unearthly in their movement, a computer controlled dance no more than 20 meters above the ocean.

Every ship in the division opened up on them, but it was simply impossible for the gunners to track and aim at a target moving at that speed. One of the escorting destroyers had maneuvered just off the stern of *Soryu*, and when Commander Ogata saw the missile aiming for that ship, he ordered all ahead full, in a desperate effort to interpose his vessel and take the enemy lance upon himself.

Nagumo watched from the bridge of *Soryu*, the Blue Dragon, dumfounded to think these two planes could move and strike his ships again, but they did. He saw the first missile bolt into *Hiryu*, and the massive orange fireball that soon became a series of powerful explosions, one after another, as the planes in the stricken hanger deck began to blow up.

Yet his own ship was spared the same fate by the sacrifice of destroyer *Arare*, which had not hesitated a second to answer the question posed by Rooks' Gambit. It raced in just as the missile was about to hit, taking the blow about 50 feet from her bow. Her Commander had instinctively employed the only tactic that could stand as a defense against such attacks. Tovey had used it with his own cruisers and destroyers, then the German fleet when *Siegfried* and *Loki* had been sacrificed in the same way. Now *Arare* would endure the agonizing death, for 400 kilograms of high explosives, thundering in at nearly Mach 2 on a missile weighing over two tons, was enough to literally break the destroyer in two.

Half of the carriers that had left Japan to make their daring attack at Pearl Harbor were now casualties of war, two stricken by an enemy they had not even seen. The damage to the Flying Dragon was much more serious than that inflicted on *Akagi*. The P-900 was a perfect carrier killer, easily penetrating the thin side armor of those ships, and exploding right in the interior spaces of the hanger deck. There it would detonate armed and fueled planes, and start raging fires that the Japanese damage control teams were often unable to suppress. In the case of *Hiryu*, the ship was so badly ravaged by all the secondary explosions that it would not survive. The fires would spread unchecked, eventually reaching her boiler spaces, until the loss of engineering capacity there saw the ship fall off to only 12 knots.

Nagumo was staggered by the loss, his eyes fearfully scanning the northern horizon for any sign of this amazing enemy weapon. This time, many who had seen the attack claimed it was clearly some kind of aerial torpedo, a rocket that made all the rumors and half formed intelligence concerning events in the Atlantic real. With great regret, he coded a message to Tokyo to inform them of the damage to all three carriers. At the same time, he ordered the 5th Carrier Division to abandon *Akagi*, and steam at their best practical speed for home waters, determined to salvage Japan's two newest carriers unscathed.

No further attack came in that long hour after *Hiryu* was hit. The three destroyers remaining in the task force huddled around the stricken carrier, while Nagumo was now forced to make a most difficult decision.

"We must continue our launch at once," Air Commander Shogo argued. "You have seen what has happened to *Hiryu*. If we are also hit with all these planes armed and fueled, then that will be our fate as well. It was only the bravery of Commander Ogata on *Arare* that now gives us this moment to attack. We must find the ship launching these weapons and destroy it."

"Yet to do so we will have to abandon *Hiryu*," said Nagumo, "With the destroyers taking on her surviving crew, we will be completely exposed if we launch now. And supposing we do get all our planes off? The danger still exists. If we are struck, and unable to recover planes, then we lose them all, every plane, every pilot. We become nothing more than an empty shell." He looked to Fuchida now, knowing he would appreciate the value of those planes and pilots.

"*Kaga* has already suffered that fate, and now *Akagi* and *Hiryu*. We managed to save 48 pilots, but some of those were on *Hiryu*, and who knows how many remain alive. I have 126 trained pilots aboard this ship. If we lose *Soryu*, as Admiral Nagumo fears, then we lose them all. Two thirds of the *Kido Butai* will have been effectively destroyed. Even if *Akagi* and *Kaga* return to safe waters, they, too, will be empty shells. And yet… How can we not at least strike at our enemy? If we do nothing, we may lose all. Better that these men die in battle. That was what they trained for, and it would at least be an honorable death."

"Agreed," said Shogo. "We must order the strike to proceed. *Hiryu* already had twelve planes up before it was hit. We must continue the launch immediately. We are losing daylight in another hour!"

Nagumo hesitated, thinking, until he realized there was really no option. What else could he do? To turn away now was not only a supreme loss of face, but it would also offer no guarantee that *Soryu* could escape harm. Fuchida, more than any other man here, knew the value of the men that would fly this strike, but they simply had to go. There was no other choice.

"*Soryu* will turn into the wind again and proceed to launch with all possible speed. All destroyers will move to a position off our starboard side and provide close escort. They will take a lesson from the bravery of Commander Ogata."

The fire in Shogo's eyes was far better than the shame he might see there had the Admiral decided otherwise. Now Fuchida saluted stiffly, and smiled. He was soon off at a run, heading for the flight deck to join and lead the strike.

Aboard *Kirov*, Rodenko reported the close clustering of four contacts, all moving at 30 knots, and the slow appearance of additional airborne contacts. They could visually see the launch proceeding on the super enhanced radar screens.

"They persist," said Karpov with a shake of his head.

"It is clear that one of the destroyers was hit by our second P-900," said Fedorov. "Now look at them, they are quick studies. Those three remaining escorts are in close to form a missile shield for the carrier."

"You know how we corrected that problem earlier," said Karpov. "We need to re-program some of our missiles for plunging descent instead of a low level attack over the water. At the moment, they approach like torpedo bombers, and we must convert them to dive bombers. That will frustrate this defense based on the sacrifice of screening ships. I could simply fire a barrage salvo, but the range is still almost 200 nautical miles, and the only missile we have that can go that distance is the P-900. Fedorov?"

"Well sir, We have only seven more P-900s, and one of them is in silo number 10, so let us presume we might wish to withhold that missile. That limits your salvo now to six, and effectively expends all our longer range missile strike capability. If we turn right at them, and make our best speed, it would be another hour before we get inside 120 nautical miles for the *Moskit-IIs* to fire. In that interval, we can expect that strike wave forming up will find us and attack."

"How many planes?"

"Depending on what ship that is, somewhere between 60 and 80 aircraft."

Now it was Karpov's turn to ponder the difficult decision. Should he expend the precious P-900s, or close the range to bring his best ship killers into the battle? While he had every confidence that the ship could meet and defeat the enemy strike wave, that would come at a cost. He remembered how he fought those earlier battles against the Japanese, though that seemed like it had happened in another life; another world. Then, the ship had only 72 SAMs when the first really big strike wave came in at them, 67 planes strong. They got all but seven, but one plane got through, and came right down on the ship in a deadly kamikaze dive. It struck the battle bridge, and that was the only thing that saved them, the 200mm roof and deck of that armored box was enough to take the hit, but had that plane struck them anywhere else… That could not happen here.

Something always gets through in an attack of this size, thought Karpov, but we have to be letter perfect. We've got to stop them all. I have more than twice as many SAMs as we had when I first defended the ship against a major air strike like this. Between the S-300s and Klinoks I have 188 missiles that can fire at ranges from 45 to 150 nautical miles. Suppose it takes 60 to 80 here, as Fedorov suggests. That is more firepower than I wanted to expend….

He looked at his watch, seeing it was 17:40. The sun was already low, and then an idea came to him. "Mister Fedorov," he said. "When will that sun set?"

"In about forty minutes sir, at 18:18."

"Excellent. Ready the KA-226. I want it armed with air to air missiles."

"Sir? You want to engage the strike wave with a single helicopter?"

Karpov just looked at him, a look that spoke volumes without vocalizing any admonishment there in front of the men. Fedorov read it well enough, and decided to keep to his bargain and follow protocols. "Mister Nikolin," he said. "Order the Helo Bay to make ready on the KA-226 for immediate launch—full air defense loadout with the best missiles we have."

Karpov said nothing, but was pleased Fedorov had withheld any further objection before seconding his order. He knew he owed the man an explanation, and drifted over, his eyes on Rodenko's radar screen. "The ship will come about and assume a heading of 350 degrees," he said. "All ahead full!"

The helm responded smartly, and *Kirov* surged ahead to her full battle speed of 32 knots. Now Karpov looked at Fedorov. "The KA-226 will launch and maneuver here," he said pointing to the Navigation Plexiglas board that denoted the position of all these contacts. "I want it well east of our new heading. Those enemy planes are losing daylight. It will take them at least forty minutes to get out here, and as they come, I want the KA-226 to engage them with a few missiles."

"Saving our SAMs?" asked Fedorov. "It will only be a pin prick, sir. The strike will not be impeded."

"Perhaps, but it may be diverted. Those planes will not be using radar, correct? They will rely on visual sightings. So I want the helo to lay a nice prominent trail back to its position with those missile fires. The vapor trails should glow nicely as the sun goes down. In the meantime, the ship will rig for black, and we will run northwest. If they take the bait, there will be no further action tonight. I want to see what the Japanese government does with my midnight ultimatum before I proceed here."

Fedorov raised his eyebrows, nodding his head. "A clever ploy," he said. "It just might work."

And it did work. Nagumo's strike wave was formed up and on its way north at that very moment. With *Kirov* still 200 nautical miles out, that was about an hour's flying time at normal cruising speeds. That meant the planes would not really get into visual sighting range until 18:40, in that long gloaming hour after sunset. In that fading ocher light, they would see a pair of R-75 air-to-air missiles coming right at them at about two o'clock. Originally developed for high performance fighters as the R-73, this missile was adapted for use on helicopters to give then some long range air defense. The KA-226 could carry them, and they would range out 50 kilometers and move at Mach 2.5.

Two planes would die that evening, one an escorting Zero and the second a D3A Val dive bomber. The contrails clearly marked the direction of the attack, which prompted the entire strike wave to turn and follow it, thinking to find the ship that fired the weapons. The military version of the KA-226 was just fast enough to disappear into the light cloud cover, all running lights off. When the planes reached their expected target area, they found nothing but empty sea, for *Kirov* had also raced away to the northeast and was now well over their horizon, which was considerably shortened with the setting sun.

The frustrated strike wave was ordered home, as it would be difficult enough to conduct a night landing on *Soryu*. They had hoped to find their enemy, and get retribution for the loss of *Hiryu*, which was now so badly burned that Nagumo ordered one of his three destroyers back to put four torpedoes into her side.

Flying Dragon slipped beneath the waves at 21:30 that night, never to rise again. Virtually alone on the wide Pacific now, the Admiral ordered his Blue Dragon to turn away south, and run at 34 knots after the recovery. No man on that bridge said a word, though rumors were now already circulating. Some said that all this misfortune was the work of the *Ayakashi*, spirits and ghosts that were seen to appear above the water. It was said they were the souls of those who died at sea, intent on dragging the living in passing ships to their watery death to join them. Some said the *Ayakashi* would take the form of a sea serpent, others that they were only spirits that haunted that thin boundary between water and air.

No matter what they were called, they carried with them the yawning danger of the unknown. The fleet had been hunted by the boat ghosts, by the oily serpent *Ikuchi*, which could only be appeased by receiving a tribute of coins. Some crewmen actually tossed coins overboard that night, whispering a silent prayer that the beast leave them in peace. But down on the lower deck of *Soryu*, as the maintenance crews worked to service the last of the recovered aircraft, one man spoke another name—*Mizuchi*—a legendary sea dragon. The pilot heard it, feeling very strange after that, and sleeping fitfully all that night.

He was not a believer when it came to ghosts and demons, but for some reason, this beast continued to plague him. He looked around him in the dark, wishing he was back aboard his own ship, *Zuikaku*, the Auspicious Crane. He had been out after the American carriers at Pearl Harbor, one of the men in on the battle that sunk the *Lexington*. But when his plane straggled home, the only carrier he could find was *Soryu*. His Val was damaged enough to keep him there for many days, and by the time it was finally repaired, his 5th Carrier Division had been detached for the Wake Island operation.

So there he was, marooned on the Blue Dragon, and spending a sleepless night fearing yet another dragon that was said to haunt the oceans and even rivers where the wary feared to go—*Mizuchi*. He could not shake the harrowing feeling that he knew what was out there on the edge of the night, silently stalking them in the darkness. Yet he chided himself, trying to chase his fear with the cold logic of reason.

All that night, he had strange dreams, of a dark ship, with tall battlements, bristling with dragon horns, its long white wake the tail of a sea beast, its claws a sharp death that could streak through the air like fiery demons. Lieutenant Commander Hayashi did not know why he was so troubled that night, but he could not shake the feeling that he had seen this hidden enemy once before, in a dream, in a nightmare, in another life….

He had seen it, yes, in another life, for he was the same man who had sacrificed his life for honor and vengeance, making his plane a human guided missile, and striking *Kirov* to destroy the aft battle bridge. And now Fate rustled the willow fronds of his recollection like a darksome wind, and whispered in a dry voice to him, speaking a single word.

Remember….

Author's note: Readers new to the series, or perhaps wading in for the first time with this very book, should know that LtC. Hayashi figured prominently in events taking place in Season 1 of the series, particularly in Book 3, Pacific Storm. The earlier action Karpov contemplates, and Hayashi's fitful dreams, were all lived events from that book.

Part VII

Aftermath

"*All was deadly still. There was no call and no echo of a song. Sorrow seemed to be in the air. 'Victory after all I suppose!' said Bilbo, feeling his aching head. 'Well it seems a very gloomy business.'*"

—**J.R.R. Tolkien**, *The Hobbit*

Chapter 19

That night Nagumo changed his heading, taking the Blue Dragon due south at 32 Knots for some time before signaling Carrier Division 5 off Wake Island to rendezvous. Some inner sense warned him of grave danger, the presence of that unseen wolf that had been stalking his fold. *Akagi* followed as best she could, her speed off to no more than 18 knots, and with orders now to proceed to the big Japanese naval base at Truk, some 1100 miles to the south. The Home Islands were still 2000 miles away, and so Nagumo looked for the best friendly anchorage he could find for that precious ship.

As for *Kirov*, Karpov lingered north, deciding to wait for the stroke of midnight for news from his intelligence unit at Vladivostok. The Japanese destroyer flotilla, and all the garrison troops there, had not made a move. By this time, after recalling his helicopters to refuel, the Japanese had slipped away. *Akagi* was already 300 nautical miles to the south, and the faster carriers were linking up and turning for home, now over 420 miles away.

"We won't catch them now," said Fedorov. "Those carriers are very fast. You might get south and find *Akagi*."

Karpov considered that, then decided to wait. He had received the news from Tyrenkov via a secret code message sent to Nikolin. The words there struck him: Plan 7. He was suddenly anxious, pacing on the bridge as he waited for more news, but no word came.

"Something amiss?" Fedorov was at his side, and Karpov gave him a strange look, then simply waved him to the plot room, shutting the door when they had entered.

"It's time you knew all this," said the Captain. "My Plan 7 is scheduled to begin immediately. I've jousted with their fleet carriers on the way here, but now is the time to make our move for Kamchatka and Sakhalin Island. It is the last thing they would expect, and if we can get a substantial force moved, we'll catch them before they have time to build up strength. Tyrenkov says the garrisons are quite slim, particularly on Kamchatka."

"How will we proceed?" asked Fedorov.

"We'll move the Air Mobile Brigade first, and we'll need most of the fleet for that. The terrain we'll be facing is rather formidable, and there are very few ports or other landing sites favorable for a seaborne attack. Yet most of the heavy equipment for the troops must move by sea, which means control of the few ports available is a necessity. I plan on setting up a forward depot at Nikolaevsk at the mouth of the Amur River. We'll need to secure Vanino-Gavan soon after that. I have already deployed the 40th Division to Chumikan and Torum near the mouth of the Maya River before the winter months set in. Airships did most of the work, and though it took some time, that division now has forward supplies for a move inland. 3rd Air Guard Brigade has been added to lead this movement by air. Its objective is to get down through Tyr to the mouth of the Amur, and get control of Lazarev on the Tatar Strait. That port is our land bridge to Northern Sakhalin Island, and that is where all the key oil fields are."

"Oil? In 1942?"

"Well, it hasn't been developed here yet, but we know where the oil is, and it will become an important resource in the future. The Japanese have set off to Borneo to secure oil, not knowing it was right under their feet. They have an engineer regiment in that area snooping around with heavy equipment and drilling rigs, but they haven't found anything yet, as most of the really good fields are just off shore. They have a battalion at Lazarev, another at Alexandrovsk. The rest of their forces will be south of the old treaty demarcation line, in Karafuto, as they call it now. Yes, they're fond of renaming things. That is all of southern Sakhalin Island, and now it's time we restored its original name."

"What about Kamchatka?"

"Again, they deployed no more than a single brigade, five battalions, all still south of the treaty line. That will be the first step. I will land the 92nd Division on the west coast, all well trained ski troops. They'll be supported by a Naval Marine Brigade, and my air mobile troops with a division of airships. It is only about 100 miles east from my chosen landing site to Petropavlovsk. That's where the main airfield is, and the best protected bay and harbor on the peninsula."

"And what good does all this empty territory do us, aside from assuaging our damaged pride?"

"It is more than that," said Karpov. "Those two airfields on Kamchatka will be quite tantalizing for the Americans."

"The Americans?"

"Of course. No one else can supply us with the necessary aircraft. I'm trying to demonstrate that this whole plan can be developed into a viable axis of attack against Japan. The idea is to offer the Americans basing rights to prosecute their bombing campaign against Japan. They'll fight for years, hopping from one island to the next before they can get bases close enough for strategic bombing. I can give them that this year, within months."

"But they aren't ready. They haven't got the planes with the range to reach Japan from Kamchatka. They won't have them for a year. We went over all of this."

"Yes, the airfields on Sakhalin are the real prize. They are much closer to Japan, and if I can secure those, and then offer them to the Americans, I will have a real lever on the Japanese. I'll have troops that could advance along the frozen Amur river towards Khabarovsk, bases, airfields, new ports, all slowly closing in on the plum—Vladivostok. If they try to reinforce by sea, *Kirov* can stop them easily enough."

"They don't all have to come by sea," said Fedorov. "Though I'm willing to bet they could get something from Hokkaido onto southern Sakhalin without much trouble, and very quickly, before you could get there to intervene. But don't forget the Trans-Siberian Rail. They can move forces to Vladivostok from all over Manchuko, and from there to Khabarovsk. That is not very far overland to Vanino-Gavan. They'll certainly do this if you try to come down from the mouth of the Amur River."

"That rail line can be interdicted very easily," said Karpov. "I have partisan cadres all over Primorskiy Province when this operation starts. We're even planning major uprisings in the big cities, including Vladivostok."

"That's what is so troubling," said Fedorov. "The scope of your plan makes it into a substantial threat to Japanese security. Why, it would put enemy bombers in range of their homeland, and cut off the entire Kwantung Army if you actually took Vladivostok. That is their primary supply port."

Karpov raised a finger. "If I am to ever win back the territory they seized in 1908, then I must certainly pose a significant threat. They received my ultimatum, and yet took no action. In fact, they did not even give me the courtesy of a reply. So I must show them I mean business."

Fedorov nodded. "This is why I believe your operation will provoke the Japanese into a major reaction. The security of their entire war effort in China would also be at stake, so I would not be at all surprised to see big troop redeployments to stop what you are planning. You may believe they have ignored you, but I expect your man Tyrenkov will soon learn that they have, in fact, begun to make preparations for renewed hostilities all along your border. That front has been stagnant for years now. You've maintained an army at Irkutsk, and they've sat on the other side of Lake Baikal on their border outposts, quietly facing you down. You can bet those troops will soon be on alert, and supplies also moving on their side of the board. Make no mistake—if they do take you seriously, you should expect to be attacked."

"Let them try," said Karpov.

"Just a moment," Fedorov countered. "You say that with such confidence, but how many divisions are you committing to this operation?"

"I'll have two veteran units, the 32nd and 92nd, and then a good line unit in the 40th Division, with one reserve division. Considering that I've sent so many troops to Sergei Kirov, that was all I could spare from the Far East Sector. All the rest is with the Irkutsk Army Group. I will also add three Air Guard Brigades that have been raised to operate with my airship fleet, and the Magadan Marine Brigade. So the force I have available amounts to five divisions."

"And did this Tyrenkov fill you in on what you'll be facing? The Kwantung Army Group has five *armies*, and over 20 divisions."

"Most will have to stay on their frontier positions," Karpov waved his hand. "They are scattered from Outer Mongolia all the way to the Amur River sector near Chita."

"And what about their armies in Manchuria? They could easily re-deploy two or three divisions from those forces to augment anything the Kwantung Army Group sends. How much force will it take to stop you? I'm guessing not much. You have good troops, well acclimated to winter warfare, and hardy men, but could one of your divisions push easily through a decent Japanese division? Could they push through two? Three? Considering the terrain, I find that unlikely. Just keeping your forward units supplied overland from the mouth of the Amur will be a very difficult task. There is no question of your ability to contest or control the sea, but on land, you may find out it's a different game entirely. There is very little *Kirov* can do to help you there."

"Don't forget my airships. They can move supplies for a full brigade to virtually any point I desire."

"That may be so, but if you push forward with an offensive of this scale, you will get a very strong reaction from the Japanese. Of this I have no doubt. You could find yourself in another bloody Russo-Japanese war if you aren't careful."

"That is the general idea here, Mister Fedorov. Why are you so squeamish?"

"Don't misunderstand me," said Fedorov. "My reservations are based on a good knowledge of the Japanese military. You forget that their troops have been fighting in Manchuria for years now. They are all veteran divisions."

"Yet you said yourself that most of the really good units were combed off to strike south."

"True, but that does not mean the forces remaining there are without capability. The Japanese Army was practically unbeatable at this stage of the war. If you want my real opinion, I believe this operation will fail. You'll have the best chance at Kamchatka, as that will be their least defended frontier, with second line garrison troops, and it will be difficult for them to support or reinforce. Sakhalin Island may also be feasible, at least the northern sector, but they'll fight hard for the south, and I don't think you can push all the way up the Amur River from the coast as you have planned either."

"We shall have to see, Mister Fedorov. War is not a certain enterprise. I realize there are risks in this operation, or any other. The Japanese may believe they can easily stop me, but I may show them otherwise. It is all a question of will, Fedorov, fortitude, perseverance, and determination."

"You may soon find your enemy has all of those qualities as well. And if they do stop you, Admiral, what then? Are you going to reach for a hammer?"

There was a moment of silence, for both men knew that Fedorov was referring to the one weapon Karpov possessed that could trump any army deployed against him, the nuclear warheads he still had on *Kirov*.

"Well Mister Fedorov, I will tell you that I have no intention of being the nail in this endeavor. They may be asking themselves just what exactly happened to that aircraft carrier I sunk. Well yes, I can make them wonder about so very much more if I so desire. I am not saying I have this in mind, but do not think I will hesitate to deliver a decisive stroke where one is needed. Now, in the beginning, I have exercised great restraint. It will be small moves, a pawn here, a knight there. Yet there is always an endgame in anything I do, and I intend to obtain one thing, and that without fail—checkmate."

Karpov said nothing more, but Fedorov thought he saw something in his eyes that he did not quite expect. It wasn't the gleam of satisfaction, or the pride of triumph. It was sadness, a quiet lonesome feeling that seemed to fall over the man like a shroud draped on his rounded shoulders.

Chapter 20

So *Kirov* turned away, leaving *Akagi* to limp on to Truk. As for Nagumo, his sword had been shattered, and now he would return home with only three operational fleet carriers from the six he was entrusted. It was only then, in a meeting with Yamamoto at Tokyo, that he learned of the demands being made by the Siberians.

"You mean to say we were attacked by a Siberian warship? This is outrageous!"

"You heard the rumors last year when I did," said Yamamoto, "and I trust you have also read the intelligence reports. We believe this is the same ship that has confounded the Germans in the Atlantic—the one that also sank their aircraft carrier. It has a rocket weapon of great range and accuracy."

"I have seen it with my own eyes," said Nagumo, "but I would not have believed it possible had that not been the case. Reading reports and listening to rumors is one thing, watching that weapon strike our ships quite another. I can understand why the lower ranks now whisper of *Raiju* and *Mizuchi*. The weapon is deadly, and terribly accurate. It must be piloted to strike us with such unfailing accuracy, and its speed was beyond belief. The gunners could not even take aim before it danced away, with maneuvers that would be impossible for any plane we have. *Akagi* was lucky that none of her planes were armed and fueled when the first attack came in. *Hiryu* was not so fortunate. It was just beginning launch operations."

"And yet you brought the rest of your forces home safely."

"Only by turning and running south," said Nagumo with the shame obvious in his voice. "Masuda Shogo and Fuchida wanted me to strike, and I did so, even with daylight fading. Something tells me that it was fortunate our planes did not find the enemy that day. I have also read the reports concerning the smaller rocket weapons used against aircraft. We lost three planes in that manner during our initial search, and then more from the strike wave. The only caveat we have is that when the enemy uses these weapons, the contrails in the sky lead us directly to the firing ship. In this case, darkness frustrated our search effort, and I ordered Fuchida to bring the planes home. Now the men speak of ghosts and demons. We were humbled by a ship we could not even sight, let alone attack. Yet somehow, they knew exactly where we were—exactly. It was a most difficult time. When I turned south, and at high speed, no man on the bridge said anything, but I could feel what they all felt. We were running."

"Every good commander must know how and when to make a skillful retreat," said Yamamoto, trying to give his fighting Admiral back some face. "I would have done the same in your situation, in fact, had the matter been before me, I would have ordered it. We may have lost the Flying Dragon, but you brought home three fleet carriers in good shape, and two others will be repaired. It is high time we extend that flight deck all the way to *Akagi*'s bow. I will order her home from Truk to Hashirajima. *Kaga* as well. Both of those old ladies can use a good refit. In fact, the work on *Akagi* was already scheduled right after this operation, so things are not as bad as they seem. In the meantime, *Tosa* will be assigned to Carrier Division 2 in place of *Hiryu*."

"You are too kind, Admiral. I bear the full responsibility for the losses we have suffered. The presence of those enemy battleships and carriers at sea should have been discovered, but we were too single-mindedly focused on Pearl Harbor."

"One must always expect the unexpected," said Yamamoto. "In this case, who could have expected the Siberians to intervene as they did? They had no navy to speak of."

"What about the demands they have made?"

"What about them?" Yamamoto folded his hands. "Neither Tojo nor the Emperor is about to simply hand them back all the territories we have been sitting on for thirty years. So it is war, with Siberia and the United States. We knew this would be the likely outcome of our attack. In this event, Urajio is now more important than ever. The Army has made it their primary port for supporting the Kwangtung Group. The Siberians used the element of surprise to attack us as they did. We know the advantage of that, but there is little else they can do on land. Yet one thing was disturbing about the action off Hawaii. We have learned the Siberians radioed a warning to the Americans, giving them the exact position of the *Kido Butai* on the morning of December 7th. This was most likely how the Americans were able to move their carriers and some of those battleships out of the harbor and operate against you."

"If that was the case," said Nagumo, "then why were they so ill prepared when our first strike wave came in?"

"Yes, that seems odd, but you nonetheless achieved surprise over the harbor, in spite of the intelligence failure that led to that warning. We failed to properly conceal our plans from every potential enemy. Who can say how the Siberians learned of our movements, but they did. That must be addressed before our next planned offensive operation."

"None of that excuses my failure to find those enemy ships at sea," said Nagumo. "For that lapse, both *Kaga* and *Hiei* have limped off to Kwajalein."

"Yet you sunk the *Lexington*, and also put hits on at least two of their battleships at sea."

"I should have sunk them all, but, having achieved our objective at Pearl Harbor, my mind was set on a safe withdrawal. It was shameful, particularly after we were attacked again, and this time by a third rate power that has been our serving boy for thirty years."

"You are too hard on yourself," said Yamamoto. "Things happen in battle that can foil the best laid plans. Take a lesson from this and hold your head high. I cannot tolerate gloom and doom just now. This is our hour. We have achieved a good victory, but there will be much more to accomplish in the months ahead. For now, with most of our amphibious landings completed, the offensive lies with the Army on the ground."

"I have heard there was trouble in the New Hebrides," said Nagumo.

"The French tried to intercept an American convoy bound for Australia." Yamamoto indicated the position on the table map.

"Apparently the Americans used those two light battle carriers we spotted at Mindanao to good effect. They fled south, possibly to cover the movement of this supply convoy. The French went after them, and lost their only carrier."

"And *Hiyo?*"

"It is back at Noumea, with engine damage, but that will also be repaired. Yet that action brings the entire question of Australia into sharp focus. The Ichiki Regiment was safely delivered to Noumea, which will now be a knife at the enemy's throat. It is right astride their lines of communications to Australia, but between that place and Truk, we have no secure positions. The offensive into Southeast Asia and the Solomons will now become the top priority for the Navy."

"You wish to move to the second operational phase soon?"

"Immediately. As a result of the smooth progress of the first-phase operations, we have established an invincible strategic position that cannot be maintained if we go on the defensive now. The Operations in Borneo and the Dutch East Indies will proceed as planned, but we must also look to our outer perimeter. In order to secure it tenaciously, we must keep on striking offensively at the enemy's weak points one after another."

"How will we proceed?" Nagumo leaned over the map.

"The first step will be Rabaul as planned, but I am canceling your Indian Ocean operation. We need to use Carrier Division 5 now in the Solomons. *Gozo* and *Mezu* are at Truk, but they carry only 24 planes each. I wish to occupy New Britain and Bougainville as soon as possible. Then we must push on to New Georgia, the lower Solomons, and possibly even as far as the Santa Cruz Islands. That operation will allow us to build a land bridge of good airfields and anchorages to Noumea on New Caledonia, but it will need substantial carrier based air support at the outset."

"Can we conclude all these operations before May? What about the plan for Midway?"

"At the moment, it is of secondary importance. It was only intended to challenge the Americans so we could complete the destruction of their fleet. We must isolate Australia before considering the Midway operation, or any significant move into the Aleutians. Your pilots performed bravely, and the sinking of the carrier *Lexington* was perhaps the strongest blow we landed at Hawaii. However, we have learned that their carrier *Saratoga* is now moving to Pearl Harbor. We can also anticipate that they will send reinforcements from their Atlantic fleet. So I expect our moves into the Solomons will be opposed. Ready yourself for that. But first, I want you to take the 5th Carrier Division back out again to support Operation R against Rabaul."

"Has there been any change in enemy dispositions?"

"Not much to speak of. The Australians dispatched a single battalion, apparently to defend their air base at Vunakanau near Rabaul. They also have a few flying boats at the nearby Simpson Harbor, and those should be destroyed immediately. There will be little air opposition. We have identified only a small squadron of perhaps ten obsolete fighters at that airfield, and four old twin engine bombers. Guam is now secure, so we will utilize General Tomitaro Horii's troops for the follow up landings at Rabaul. The 144th Regiment was retained with 55th Division for the Burma operation."

"Then what will we use for the initial landing at Rabaul?"

"I still have forces equivalent to a full brigade at Truk," said Yamamoto. "The 2nd and 5th Sasebo SNLF and two *Teishin* airborne battalions."

"*Teishin?* Those are air force troops."

"Yes, but Yamashita tells me our own Yokosuka Para Battalion was very useful in his Malaya operation. The air force has offered them to replace the 144th Regiment, and we will have 60 Ki-56 light transport planes to carry them. They have been ferrying additional supplies to Truk, and will soon be available for operations."

"Very well," said Nagumo. "I foresee no difficulty in completing Operation R successfully. Yet we should also clear enemy resistance in New Guinea. There are good sites for airfields there, and we must not allow the Australians to retain their position at Port Moresby."

"Agreed," said Yamamoto. "I will watch the progress of our thrust into the Dutch colonies very closely. The Island of Java will be the end point of those operations, and set the lower boundary of our defensive perimeter there. Yamashita must also occupy Singapore as planned. Then, once we are well established on Java, we can consider an expanded attack on both Port Moresby, and perhaps even Port Darwin. For now, Rabaul and New Britain will be your next objective."

"When am I to leave?"

"As soon as 5th Carrier Division can replenish. I will depart for Truk myself in a few days, and *Yamato* will be moved there as the new Fleet headquarters at sea."

"That will be a most welcome addition," said Nagumo.

"Considering that we have just shown how easy it is to sink battleships with aircraft, I sometimes wonder." Yamamoto hedged his bet, but Nagumo disagreed.

"Those old American battleships at Pearl Harbor were nothing more than nice fat targets. They are nothing like *Yamato*, and at sea, under a full head of steam, she would not be so vulnerable."

"I suppose this war will answer that question one day," said Yamamoto. "As long as our carrier based aircraft can rule the skies over the sea, then our battleships may move about with impunity. One day, however, that may change. At the moment, I want you to light a fire in the Solomons. Run wild, Nagumo. Hit hard, and always keep moving."

"What if the Americans do oppose me with their fleet carriers?"

"Then fight. We have the best ships, planes and pilots in the world. 5th Carrier Division has *Zuikaku* and *Shokaku*, our newest and most advance carriers. I know you will be eager to redress what you perceive as a failure in that last battle. But now is not the time to look over your shoulder with any regret. The next battle awaits you. That is where you must focus your thoughts."

Nagumo nodded, and there was silence between the two men for some time before he spoke again. "Admiral Yamamoto… Siberia is a beaten and backward nation. We have had them under our foot since

1908. How in the world did they produce such advanced rocket weapons, when our own programs are so far behind? And this ship? They have no major ports, no dry docks. Where did it come from?"

"We believe it was built by the Soviets. It was at Murmansk in September, then it moved east through the Arctic passage before the ice closed in. This is how we believe it came to the Pacific."

"The Soviets? Then they have these rocket weapons? They are responsible?"

"We believe so."

"And if they give this technology to the Americans?"

Yamamoto reached up, rubbing his chin, but said nothing more. He would take to the high seas aboard Japan's mightiest battleship, ordering that *Akagi* was to wait in the lagoon at Truk until his arrival. Once there, he boarded the venerable carrier to survey the damage, and discuss repairs and the upcoming refit with the engineers.

Before he left, he produced a list of all men lost in the sortie he had so long advocated against the Americans at Pearl Harbor. There were the names of the pilots and crews, men of the fabled Misty Lagoon. Some had died on this very ship, others on *Kaga*, and a great many more aboard *Hiryu*. True to his word, he ordered that all their names should be engraved on a brass plate and affixed to the wall, and that if ever this ship were in jeopardy of sinking, it was to be unbolted and removed, along with the portrait of the Emperor. Then he ordered the men out, and for a long time, he sat alone, silently reading the names upon that list, seeing their faces in his mind, hearing their voices, and taking upon himself the responsibility for each and every lost soul.

Chapter 21

While Yamamoto kept his silent vigil, half a world away, the Americans were also making plans of their own. Admiral Halsey's lonesome watch with the *Enterprise* was relieved with the arrival of the *Saratoga*, another big *Lexington* class carrier that had once been designed as a battlecruiser. He was also heartened by the news that *Yorktown* was arriving on December 20th, escorted by the destroyers *Russel*, *Walke* and *Simms*. Trailing in her wake was yet another ship, the *Kitty Hawk*, one of many logistical support vessels that would make the United States Navy such an efficient and formidable foe in the years to come.

The *Kitty Hawk* class was a special breed, over 16,000 tons fully loaded, and originally designed to transport commercial railway cars. The Navy saw them as perfect transports for crated aircraft and other equipment, and they could carry up to 120 planes in that capacity, and make a respectable 17 knots. They threw on a single 5-inch gun, four .50 caliber machineguns, and stuffed the ship full of planes for the carrier division. Two such ships were in the Pacific, the *Kitty Hawk* and *Hammondsport*.

Rear Admiral Frank Jack Fletcher brought the *Yorktown* in, and now he was meeting with Halsey to discuss the situation they faced in the aftermath of Pearl Harbor. An Iowa man from a Navy family, Fletcher graduated near the top of his academy class in 1906. He commanded a destroyer in the first war, won a medal of Honor at Vera Cruz, Mexico, and then was given the battleship *New Mexico* for a time before he moved on to command a Cruiser Division.

"Hell of a situation here," said Halsey. They were meeting aboard the *Enterprise*, berthed that night to replenish at Pearl. There was really no other suitable office ashore, for the entirety of CINCPAC headquarters had been destroyed in the awful fire resulting from the catastrophic explosion of the tanker *Neosho*. Fletcher had been shocked when he finally saw the damage.

"Couldn't believe my eyes," he said. "Thank God Battleship Division 1 was out to sea with your operation."

"We might have been sitting right here had it not been for Newton wanting that fleet exercise," said Halsey. "It put both our carriers right in the ring. Van Falkenburgh's old ladies too."

"I heard they gave the Japs a bloody nose," said Fletcher.

"Out gunned them and set two of their battlewagons on fire," said Halsey. "But they were too damn slow to close in and finish the job, and we had our hands full tangling with all those enemy carriers."

"Damn shame we lost *Lexington*," said Fletcher.

"That and the mess out there near Merry Point is where they really hurt us. I just heard the Navy is sending us Battleship Division 3 from the Atlantic. I asked for cruisers—I get more fat slow battleships instead."

"Pye should be happy."

Halsey gave him a look. "Haven't you heard? Pye was at CINCPAC headquarters when the *Neosho* blew up. He didn't make it out of there."

"Sorry to hear that, sir."

"Right… Well, when they get here we'll have more battleships than we did before the Japs bombed the place, but with one catch. I just can't use them now. They're too slow, and they'll need too much fuel to operate. That's a commodity we may soon find in short supply. That fire ate up 42% of everything we had bunkered. So we're going to have to be stingy. In fact, I'm having the fuel on the battleships siphoned out for the cruisers and destroyers."

"It won't be your problem long, Bull," said Fletcher. "Nimitz is flying in to take over out here."

"Good," said Halsey. "The last place I'd want to be is sitting in that pile of rubble over there behind the one desk they manage to dig up for me. There's work to be done at sea, and that's where I belong. The effort now is to support Wake and Midway as long as we can. Everything was destroyed at CINCPAC, including all those nice little war plans filed away. You've read them. One was supposed to have us out there trying to lay an ambush for the Japs at Wake. Well, we haven't the luxury of that kind of thinking right now. The time will come for that kind of finesse, but for now, we're playing defense. The only problem we have is logistics. We'll need to build forward bases out here, and I've just returned from the operation at Bora Bora. The French didn't like it, but the place is now ours. We'll make it a forward depot for operations into the South Pacific, assuming we can find the fuel, and ships to carry it. I requested tanker support, but it may be a while getting here."

"They're sending another *Cimarron* class ship," said Fletcher. "The *Guadalupe* should be here by New Year's Day."

"I hope they pumped in oil and not Champagne."

"That they did, sir."

"Fair enough. I could use a good stiff drink right about now, but first things first. I've got a job for you—Wake Island. Our boys repulsed a Japanese landing attempt last week, but they won't give it up. So we need to get out there with a relief mission. We've got one tanker available to support operations, the *Netches*. Lucky for us that ship was en-route to Pearl when they hit us. She'll only make 14 knots, so you'll have to leave her in your wake most of the time with a couple destroyers, but keep an eye on her. We can't afford to lose another tanker."

"But sir," said Fletcher haltingly. "You can see these nice black shoes I'm wearing here. I'm a cruiser man. I haven't any experience driving carriers. In fact, I thought they just stuck me on *Yorktown* for the ride."

"Look Jack, we also lost Will Brown in that fire, so they sent you out here for a reason. Yes, I know the navy aviators get a hair up their ass whenever they don't see an Admiral with gold wings on his chest commanding a carrier. Fitch can handle *Saratoga* with TF 11. I get the *Enterprise* with TF 8, and I want you to stay with *Yorktown* and TF 17. Nimitz recommended you, and the job is yours. Between the three of us, we'll have enough clout to at least enforce security here in the Central Pacific."

"Alright sir. If you and Nimitz want me, I'm happy to serve."

"Good. I was going to give you *Indianapolis, Chicago* and *Portland*, but the last two got roughed up a bit and repairs are still underway. Don't worry. I'll find something for you. If you want the truth, I knew that Nimitz was flying in, and actually spoke with him just last week. In fact, I asked for you directly—and for more cruisers so I can keep you happy. *Richmond* pulled into Pearl on the 10th, and they're sending us a new air defense cruiser, the *Atlanta*. God only knows when. Until then I'll see what else I can find. That said, job one for us now is to lend a hand at Wake, and cover Midway. But there's one other thing we need to discuss."

"I'm all ears," said Fletcher.

"Code and Signals section says they got an earful the other day. Apparently there was some kind of ruckus northwest of Wake."

"Northwest? Nothing much out there, except Marcus Island."

"It was much closer in. In fact, the boys on Wake picked it up too. There was a fight underway, that much was clear, but we didn't get an invitation. It wasn't any of our subs either, so this is a bit of a mystery. All we know is that the code crowd thinks it was the Japanese main body, the same group that hit us at Pearl, and after this engagement, they hightailed it for Japan. One of our subs spotted them on the way. There were only three carriers."

"Three? The reports I read said they hit us with six."

"We know they sent one carrier to Kwajalein, and now they've sent another to Truk, but that still leaves one carrier unaccounted for."

"Then you think they took damage in that engagement?"

"Seems that way, though I'd like to think they're still shaking off the punches we landed on them when they hit Pearl. But the signals troop thinks something else happened. They think there was a scrap up there northwest of Wake, and I'll be damned if I can figure out who might have had the balls to tangle with them—or the ships! It certainly wasn't a commonwealth battlegroup."

"It does smell fishy," said Fletcher.

"Well, I just wanted you to know about it. Keep your eyes open, and run good search routines. That carrier might still be out there somewhere. We can't write it off just yet."

"That would be a good assumption," said Fletcher. "So what happened with the *Pensacola?*"

"The damn French got in on the game, that's what happened," said Halsey, "and we gave them a black eye. *Antietam* and *Shiloh* were at Mindanao, and someone had the good sense to order them out of there when this thing started. That someone was me, of course. Well, they were headed for Fiji, and showed up just in time to head off that French task force, and the Frogs had a carrier. Jimmy Hansen was out the on the *Antietam*, and damn if they didn't stick it to that French flattop."

"Good for them."

"Unfortunately, the Japanese showed up soon after. We've got more trouble than we realize now. They were running a troop convoy down to New Caledonia, and the escort carriers tagging along mixed it up with Hansen's group. *Antietam* got hit, but she's still haze grey and underway. I'm calling that group home to Pearl. They can patch up and then escort the Marines out to Samoa and Fiji. That'll leave our three fleet carriers free for independent operations. The thing is this. If the Japs moved troops to Noumea, you know damn well they can't just leave it at that. They'd be out there like ripe fruit—really out on a limb. So I'm thinking they'll need to move into the Solomons soon to support that forward base. Nimitz agrees."

"Sounds logical," said Fletcher.

"And also dangerous," said Halsey. "Jack…. That's where we'll have to meet them, right there in the Solomons. There's a whole string of islands out there up for grabs, and we need to get in on the action before they take all that prime real estate and set up shop. Something tells me that if we can stop them there, then we can turn this mess around and get moving again."

"The Aussies will be happy to hear that," said Fletcher.

"Yes they will," Halsey nodded. "Because if we don't stop them there, then Australia is next. We can't lose them, they're too damn valuable. The Aussies are the only thing stalling the Japanese drive on Singapore now. So once we get thing squared away, our primary strategic mission is to keep the lines of communication open to Australia. If we lose Australia, then this thing just might get out of hand. Believe me, if someone as dumb as me knows that, then the Japanese certainly know it too. So we can't drop the ball. If we do, who's going to spank Tojo? Certainly not the Siberians."

The two men had a good laugh at that, but for another man, it would soon be no laughing matter. He was determined to make a difference in this affair, and had the means of doing so, along with a plan.

* * *

"**Alright**," said Karpov. "Plot me a course for the Sea of Okhotsk. We're going to begin operations on Kamchatka and Sakhalin Island. Those territories will be the first to be liberated, and if the Japanese want to try and reinforce them, they'll pay the price."

"How can you possibly operate against those places?" asked Fedorov. "It is nearly 2000 kilometers from Magadan to Yakutsk, and that's on an unpaved road that can only be used when it is frozen in winter."

"Correct," said Karpov, "but you forget my airship fleet. I've had the Far East Airship Division moving troops to Magadan for some time. The transport ships from Magadan can move the rest."

"But those airships can only provide limited air support against the Japanese. What if they move squadrons of fighters to oppose you?"

"They can try, but with *Kirov* at hand, I can project a lethal air defense umbrella over any chosen landing zone. And do not write off my airships so quickly. They are vulnerable to heavier guns, but not the typical machineguns most fighters carry. We have amazing self-sealing gas bag linings. I've assembled a nice little fleet at Magadan—

five destroyers, over 20 transport ships, icebreakers, and a full division in reserve. Another will be raised shortly."

"Then you are planning an offensive against Japanese held territories?"

"Where else? I have opened negotiations with the Americans, and I am trying to persuade them to support me as they did with the British in those lend-lease convoys. I have the gold to pay for anything they will sell me. The gold mines near Magadan will provide anything I need. At the moment, the Japanese presence in Kamchatka is very weak, and they don't have much more than a few battalions on Sakhalin Island. They simply do not think we pose any threat, which is why they ignore me now, though they may think twice after they see their flagship limp home. I have an operation all ready to go, under the code name Plan 7. It was triggered the moment Volkov decided to strike at Ilanskiy again. We've been preparing an offensive for a good long while, in spite of all the troops I've sent Sergei Kirov. We're going to hit them, and let them know we mean business. Once I show the Americans I can take and hold territory, and then offer them airfields for their bombers on Kamchatka and Sakhalin Island, you will see how things change."

Fedorov nodded, seeing Karpov with new eyes now. The man had a strategic plan. He had been husbanding resources, troops, weapons, supplies, transport shipping, and he was planning to stage a daring attack somewhere that was very likely to succeed, unless the Japanese got wind of it.

"So this is why you are not dead set on pursuing the *Kido Butai*."

"Correct. I've done what I intended here. I've declared war, made my demands, initiated hostilities, and shown them just how powerless they are against *Kirov*. I don't suppose they even know what they are up against, but they will certainly know *who* they are facing in battle soon enough. Once I establish a secure lodgment, clear Kamchatka and Sakhalin, then they will sit up and take real notice. That's when my little war with the Japanese really starts.

Part VIII

Banzai!

"Speed is the essence of war. Take advantage of the enemy's unpreparedness; travel by unexpected routes and strike him where he has taken no precautions."

— **Sun Tsu:** *The Art of War*

Chapter 22

General Yamashita was on the move, his single minded obsession—the British bastion at Singapore. The Jewel of the East was the symbol of British power in the Pacific, just as Gibraltar had been in the Mediterranean. Like the Rock, it also had a reputation as being unassailable, at least from the sea, and no commander alive had ever seriously considered it would fall to an army that would first have to seize the entire Malay Peninsula before it could deliver the coup de grace. There on the edge of the great trans-Pacific trade routes, a thriving, exotic yet modern metropolis had grown up out of the jungle, and it was now a waystation and trade center for nations all through the resource rich Southeast Asia.

This enormously valuable bastion of British power had enough sea room in its harbor to hold most of the British fleet, with a pair of 50,000 ton dry docks for repairs. The island alone had four airfields, a naval base, stores and munitions to support 100,000 men. It simply had to be taken, and then made into Japan's principle supply base for this segment of the new Co-Prosperity Sphere. But how?

There were imposing fortifications on the southern shore, five 15-inch guns, two in the Buona Vista Battery and three in the Johore Battery. One of the latter three had started its life as a 14-inch gun, but was re-bored to a 15-incher. The other two were the last remnants of guns taken from British battleships during refits, like teeth pulled from a steel shark. One was taken from *Barham* and another from the ship that had only just met her fate in the Atlantic, the battleship *Valiant*. The battleships were dead, but their old guns would still fire in anger, a last hollow roar from the bygone era in which they were forged and rifled. Alas they had only armor piercing shells, which would be of little use if they could be turned around.

To these the British also added six 9.2-inch guns, and eighteen more 6-inch naval guns, not to mention the five additional twin 6 pounder batteries around the harbor. To service those guns, there were hundreds of gunlayers, spotters, magazine crews, and an enormous stockpile of 10,700 shells of all calibers. Yet in Fedorov's history, no more than 10% of that ammo stockpile would ever be fired in defense of this highly prized and invaluable outpost.

The question to be asked now was why weren't the guns turned around by this time in the war, and why were the fortifications there so unprepared for an attack from the landward side? Fedorov had warned Churchill how Singapore would fall many long months ago in their desert meeting, but nothing had been done. Churchill did, in fact, send communications that the batteries should be prepared to turn about and be used in defense of the city. Many had the ability to traverse 360 degrees, and even those that could not manage that could still range on many targets to the north. Yet no one took the matter seriously. Defense against what, they thought? They had all of III Indian Corps watching their back, and 700 miles of impregnable jungle, or so they believed.

Before they entered the war, Japan sent agents posing as visiting businessmen to wander through the city, and then take small boats into the harbor to study it all from the sea. They quickly concluded the same thing the British believed, that it was simply unassailable from the sea. So the only way to take Singapore was from the landward side, by first doing another thing the British deemed impossible, seizing all of the Malay Peninsula.

When the Japanese proved how porous Percival's defense really was, the shock was lasting and profound. No matter how 'unsporting' their tactics were, they worked, and that was all that mattered in war. A good General had to know that, and there had to be in him a measure of ruthlessness that real warfare demands of its true practitioners. Unfortunately, the man commanding Fortress Singapore was not ruthless, nor was he up to the task that was now before him.

On the other hand, General Yamashita had something to prove in this campaign. He had fallen out of the Emperor's favor during the unfortunate "February 26th Incident," where a group of Army rebels planned high level assassinations in a self-styled coup. At first Yamashita was sympathetic, but later he ended up as an intermediary attempting to resolve the crisis. In any case, the Emperor, and Tojo, had turned a cold shoulder to him ever since. So he had set his mind on capturing Singapore and handing it to Hirohito like a gift on February 11th, the anniversary of the founding of Japan by the Emperor Jimmu in 660 BC.

The first phase of his landing in the north had gone off without a hitch. He had stormed ashore, seized the vital British airfields at Alor Star and Khota Baru. To do so, he had taken his 25th Army right through neutral Thailand, some parts coming overland, and most others landing by sea. Speed was of the essence, so much so that one of the chief planners in this campaign, Masanobu Tsuji, personally went forward with a small detachment of 300 men and a few light tanks to keep the spearheads of the Japanese columns moving.

A man with a brilliant tactical mind, Tsuji had been nicknamed "the God of Operations" for his skill in planning. He had a unique ability of cutting through red tape, and was also a strong believer of taking matters into his own hands when necessary, the peculiar brand of Japanese initiative that was called *gekokujō*, "leading from below," a kind of loyal insubordination that had led to numerous incidents of rebellious behavior in the past. It was the mentality that had triggered the war in China at more than one place, where enterprising young officers deliberately sabotaged a Japanese controlled railway as a pretext to blame the act on the Chinese and begin reprisals.

Tsuji had also instigated several "incidents" along the Siberian border, one provoking a combined Soviet-Siberian force that had been deployed along the Khalkhyn Gol River. That sparked a major battle, which backfired on Tsuji when another master strategist took charge of the fight, a man named Georgie Zhukov. The Japanese were taught a valuable lesson in that battle, and learned a healthy respect for the fighting ability of their northern neighbors.

Now, however, Tsuji's fortunes would be found here on the so called "Southern Road," and the segment he was walking now would lead through Malaya to Singapore. Nor would he be facing a brilliant mind like Zhukov. Instead, the chief opponent for Yamashita and Tsuji would be Lieutenant General Arthur Ernest Percival. No stranger to war, Percival had fought at the dreadful Battle of the Somme where he earned a Military Cross, and later, a Distinguished Service Order that specifically noted his "power of command and knowledge of tactics."

No matter how well schooled he was, the Lieutenant General was about to meet his match, and then some, when Yamashita and Tsuji brewed up their own styled brand of Banzai Blitzkrieg. Percival had studied his situation and came to conclude that the enemy might do exactly what Tsuji had planned one day—land in Thailand and "burgle Malaya by the backdoor." He noted that the fortress of Singapore might be impregnable from the south seaward approach, but that vulnerabilities presented an enemy with opportunities to attack from the north, through Malaya. He had laid out the plan his enemies might follow, almost chapter and verse, yet when it finally came at him, he seemed entirely powerless to stop it.

A kind of lassitude born of overconfidence had settled on him, a complacency born of misapprehension. If the enemy came, he thought he would simply meet and defeat them in Northern Malaya, and his faith in the invincibility of Western arms and military forces would be rudely abused.

At one point the British sent up a small mechanized column, with armored cars and Bren carriers. Tsuji was at the point of contact, quickly ordering the British defensive line to be enfiladed through an abandoned rubber plantation, where he personally captured a valuable map of the peninsula, detailing all the key British positions. He went to Yamashita, jubilant with his find, and the two men decided the strategy they hoped that would bring them victory.

"They will defend here, along the Jitra River," said Tsuji, his balding head and round eyeglasses catching the light. "The British were kind enough to build us those airfields, and also that lovely coastal road. Now we will use both against them. They hope to block our advance down that one good road along the west coast, but we will foil them. Our tanks will punch through, but the main attack will be a flanking maneuver by our infantry through the plantations to the east."

"Can they move fast enough through the jungle?"

"They will with these…" Tsuji had shown Yamashita the special bicycles that the troops would take to battle, assembled in the field and used to literally ride right through the jungle, over terrain no one thought any force could easily penetrate. Forsaking trucks in his plan, he would bring 6000 bicycles for each division instead, and use man portable mortars instead of heavier artillery.

"The British have plenty of trucks there for us to use," he boasted. "Why bring our own when we can simply capture theirs?"

"What about the rivers?" Yamashita had asked. "What if they blow all the bridges?"

"The infantry will not need bridges to cross those rivers. And there are plenty of saw mills along that road, with good lumber to rebuild anything the British destroy."

It was a masterful economy of thinking—why burden the army with things the enemy would provide? The bicycles would allow his men to stay right on the heels of the British as they withdrew, giving them no rest or means of consolidating in a new defensive position. And since Japan had exported this same model to other Asian nations for years, Tsuji said there would be no problem finding spare parts for the bikes. Everything they needed for their advance was already there. All they had to do was make use of it.

When the Japanese landed in the north, the Governor of Singapore, Sir Shenton Thomas, simply shrugged his shoulders and remarked to Percival: "Well, I suppose you'll shove the little men off."

It was typical of the attitude the British held towards the Japanese, a grave underestimation of their war fighting prowess. The little men would soon show the British Army what they were made of, moving with such speed, ferocity, and determination that plodding Percival, who stated the enemy has "rather less than a division ashore," was soon seeing his Indian Brigades breaking and being swept south before the rapid tsunami of the Japanese advance.

In truth, the Japanese had rather more than two divisions, the elite

5th, which had led the Siberian Intervention years ago, and 18th Division, one of the units that had been part of the murderous rampage through Nanking. Behind these the Imperial Guards would come, though their name belied their real inexperience when it came to battle. The real fighting troops were in those first two divisions, and they would get the job done easily enough against the 9th and 11th Indian Divisions. Only the tough Australian 8th Division would give them a fight, but without the Indians to hold on their flanks, they became a rock in the stream.

The tactic the Japanese would use was called *Kirimoni Sakusen*, a driving charge with the armor leading in the vanguard, and the light footed infantry on either flank to infiltrate and encircle points of resistance. It was the charging bull that Percival thought his men would parry in his Operation Matador, but in this case it was the matador that was skewered and gored, his cape trampled and lances broken and scattered.

"They boasted they could hold their vaunted Jitra line for three months," said Tsuji. "We went through it in 15 hours, and with no more than 500 men! And we are advancing so quickly that we capture the British forward supply dumps before they can even evacuate them. As I said earlier, the enemy will provide us with everything we need, trucks, fuel, food. We can even use their rail road and captured rolling stock. It is all there. We have merely to take it from them."

And that they did. The Japanese advance outpaced the British withdrawal in places. At the Slim River defensive line, Yamashita executed a daring flanking maneuver using landing barges along the coast that Tsuji thought would end with disaster. If caught by British planes, the troops would be sitting ducks, but only a few came and made one ineffective strafing run. The maneuver was a resounding success, and it was followed by an equally bold armored thrust.

The Japanese call their tanks *sensha*, or "battle wagon," and it was their doctrine to assign small battalion sized units to operate with the infantry. A column of 20 Type 97 medium tanks, with 57mm main guns and two 7.2mm machineguns, was led by the intrepid Major

Toyosaku Shimada. He decided to attack at night, which caught the British defenders completely by surprise.

The scattered defenders of 5/2nd Punjab Regiment managed to knock out four tanks, one from artillery fire, two others to a Boys AT rifle, and one to mines, but the remainder pushed around them and on through the Indian troops. A survivor ran with a breathless warning to perhaps the best unit on the position, the British 2nd Battalion, Argyll & Sutherland Highlanders. They had just arrived to put some backbone into the defense, but hardly had time to look over the ground when they saw four Bren carriers approaching along the main road.

"Look here," said a Lieutenant. "Who's that rushing about like this after dark?" He collared a Sergeant and sent him off. "Kindly get hold of that lot and tell them to quiet down. The enemy will hear that racket for miles."

The Sergeant would soon learn the supposed Brens were actually Japanese tanks, which barreled right on through the British position, leaving astonished Majors and Lieutenants holding evening tea in unsteady hands and looking at one another as if someone had just committed an unpardonable breach of decorum.

That was the attitude that sunk the British in Malaya, from Percival's initial underestimation of the enemy strength, and right on down through the ranks. Officers were too regimented in their thinking, and adhered too often to the rules of war where each side would line up and "have a go" at the other. One did not ride off around and behind his opponent's lines on bicycles, and one did not attack up a road with armor after dark… except Yamashita.

The "Tiger of Malaya" was teaching his stodgy rivals that war was not a game of cricket. The unorthodox tactics Tsuji and Yamashita devised would unhinge one defensive position after another. Those four tanks would soon be backed up by the rest of the column, and the infantry of Colonel Ando's regiment of the 5th Infantry Division. They would race ahead to the vital railway bridge, and Major Shimada would have the satisfaction of personally leaping from his tank, drawing his samurai sword, and cutting the carefully laid demolition cables.

"Not very sporting," would come the British reply from a captured officer in the 2nd Argylls. "I mean what do you mean by attacking us at night like this when we weren't prepared to meet you? And what do you mean by using tanks on a narrow road and all? It's really quite frustrating. When we hold the coast, you come at us out of the jungle. When we dig in on good ground, you come at us from the sea. If you take a position, you don't consolidate it and wait to bring up reserves, but just rush about like madmen on those bicycles. One can't sort out exactly what you seem to be doing here, which is most disconcerting. If you had made a proper attack after sunrise, I'm certain we'd have stopped you."

The only thing certain for the man now was a long, arduous and often brutal stint as a P.O.W. The Japanese were already shooting and bayoneting any captured prisoners who could not walk. They were not about to nursemaid them along under the rules of the Geneva Convention. Theirs was not the cautious and plodding position game of chess that the British expected. Instead it was a daring leap by a knight, bypassing the carefully placed pawns and appearing right in the heart of the enemy camp. Yes, it was a Knight's move….

As the last of the defenders to escape boarded trains in Kuala Lumpur, about 50 miles to the south, a railway manager looked sheepishly at a group of eight rail cars that had just been loaded with supplies.

"What will I do with them?" he asked an officer. "There's too much traffic on the line south to Singapore. They won't be able to move for hours."

"Well what did you load on them?"

"Just the usual, sir, beef tins, biscuits and boxes."

"Then just leave them here and don't bother with them. We've plenty of beef and biscuits in Singapore as it stands."

The Japanese would be very pleased when they arrived and found those eight abandoned rail cars loaded with supplies. One little windfall was in the "boxes," a stack of detailed printed maps of the city of Singapore that were a dream come true for Yamashita and Tsuji. As late as October of 1941, Japanese "tourists" had been visiting Malaya trying to find decent maps, and Yamashita had nothing he ever deemed adequate, until that lucky find, just another of many oversights on the part of the British, who were too flustered by these unorthodox moves, and found the whole Japanese attack simply too untidy for their liking.

Chapter 23

Percival had conceived his defensive plan, and gave it the flamboyant name of Operation Matador, as if the British defenders would swirl their capes at the boldly charging Japanese bulls, never giving an inch and sticking them with a lance as they rumbled by. Yet the troops he sent north to hold a territory as big as England itself were two under strength Indian divisions from III Corps, each missing one of its three brigades. They were not the toughened troops that had fought for Britain in North Africa, but illiterate cast offs, pressed into the service, shipped off to a foreign land with little training, and even less equipment. It was a British practice to stiffen these brigades by always including a battalion of British regulars, but of the six available in Malaya, only three were sent north to backstop this thin defense. It was no more substantial than the Matador's cape, and just as fleeting. So the bull leapt right over this hapless toreador, then turned and gored him in the back.

Yes, it wasn't very sporting, but it was a tactic of war that was quite effective. A defense that might have held for months if properly established was rolled up in a matter of a few weeks, and soon Yamashita's men would be approaching the next bridge they needed near the Muar River. This time it was the men of the 8th Australian Division on the line, 2/30th Battalion commanded by Colonel "Black Jack" Gelleghan.

"They've taken positions by storm so often that I think we can hoodwink them here," he said. "We'll set up south of the bridge, and then let them come trundling right over the bloody thing. Once they get here, have the engineers blow the bridge behind them."

Black Jack's battalion would hold up the Japanese for two days, inflicting a thousand casualties in the process, as they fell back from one stubbornly defended position to the next. They would prompt Yamashita to order a major attack by the air force to pave the way for his renewed advance. The Diggers showed what could be done by disciplined troops willing to roll up their sleeves and start thinking like their enemy. They anticipated many planned Japanese countermoves, and laid some very skillful ambushes, but there just were not enough of them to matter in the end. In spite of their valor, Yamashita would continue to drive relentlessly towards the last obstacle between his rampaging 25th Army and Singapore, the Strait of Johor.

In what seemed like desperation, Churchill had wanted to send *Prince of Wales* and *Repulse* to the aid of this most valuable jewel in the crown. But those two ships would meet another doom off the coast of Northwest Africa. Dissuaded by Admiral Tovey, he instead sent two aircraft carriers, *Indomitable* and *Illustrious*, their decks laden with Hurricane fighters to be flown off for operations from airfields on Singapore.

Yet that was not all that Churchill sent. He hoped he could reverse the inexorable momentum of the war by sending a secret weapon—a single man in fact, one of his closest advisors, Brendon Bracken. A financier and businessman, and a longtime supporter of Churchill, it was Bracken who advised Churchill not to say a word if Lord Halifax was named as a possible successor to Neville Chamberlain. In fact, he held Churchill to a promise that he would remain silent. As Bracken predicted, Halifax had his name put forward, and Churchill said nothing, a long two-minute silence that was eventually broken by Halifax himself, stating he did not think he was in the best position to form a government. Lord Beaverbrook would later claim that was "the great silence that saved England."

So Bracken was delighted when Churchill became Prime Minister, and was soon a member of the Privy Council, and Churchill's Parliamentary Private Secretary. He would also serve as the Minister of Information, and it was this commodity that he was carrying with him to Percival on Churchill's behalf that day—information.

In an effort to stiffen Percival's resolve, Churchill dispatched his trusted associate and confidant to Singapore on the eve of the final battle, hoping to put into his mind that the attack that would soon come must certainly fail, if only he could maintain his resolve and stand fast.

* * *

"**What** do you mean by this?" said Percival. "You say the Japanese are bluffing? Then how did they manage to chase my entire army 700 miles in the last two months? That was no bluff, Mister Bracken, no matter what the Prime Minister might think. It was a shameful performance on our part, and I'm fully prepared to shoulder the responsibility for that. If I had it all to do over, I would have held the line much closer to Singapore, as General Heath of III Indian Corps suggested. We were trying to protect the airfields up north for the RAF. Without their air cover, how could we expect to receive reinforcements here by sea? Yet my Operation Matador was the wrong plan at the wrong time. I'll admit that much."

"General," said Bracken, running a big hand through his wavy hair. "What I am now going to suggest is that you do indeed have a second chance here. As Minister of Information, I come by a few tidbits that may prove interesting from time to time. Mister Blair?"

He turned to an aide, a man who worked as a clerk which he brought along to manage the files and papers he would now present. He had fished him out of the imposing stone edifice of the Ministry building, a humdrum clerk doing a little war time work there. Unbeknownst to him, Clerk Blair was much more than he seemed, a prolific writer with a political edge, and an eye for things that would soon come to pass in the shadow of the war.

"Mister Blair here will present you with some rather detailed information as to the real force the enemy now has outside your keep. As you will soon see, it is hardly the invincible host you may think it to be. The Japanese 25th Army, if it could be called that, is actually a force of no more than 30,000 men—less than three divisions. That was what he started with, and his forces may be whittled down considerably by now. Why, you have 33,000 British troops at your disposal here, and another 17,000 Australians. Along with the Indian units, your force totals at least 100,000 men. Am I correct?"

"30,000 men?" Percival could not agree. "My good man, the

Japanese must have at least 150,000 out there by now. As to our own forces, I have more like 85,000 men, and of those I would deem 15,000 to be non-combatants. No offense to you or your ministry, but you have been out of the picture as I've seen it here, and your information is simply wrong."

"But surely you have enough with that to throw the enemy back should they attempt to cross the strait."

Percival was quick to reply. "Yet I have to cover 70 miles of coastline. The Japanese can pick and choose their points of crossing, and hit us there with everything they have."

The big Irishman sighed, pursing his lips and extending an open hand to his clerk again. "Mister Blair, the letter. I probably should have presented it first. It is the Prime Minister's own hand and mind, and I urge you to heed it in the strongest possible way."

Blair fished out an envelope, and Bracken handed it to the General stiffly. "I must say, General, that I have spent more than a good amount of time burning the proverbial midnight oil with Mister Churchill. I am, you see, one of the few men in the government who sees him after that hour."

Percival opened the envelope and read the note: *General Percival, I am sending you this letter to reveal the full scope of what British Intelligence has now come to know concerning the forces arrayed against you. Take it on faith, in spite of your own setbacks in recent weeks, that the Japanese will not have 30,000 men to put against you in this fateful hour, and your own troops certainly number many times that. This is not conjecture or speculation. We have this information from a most reliable source, which for reasons of national security, cannot be revealed in this letter.*

Beyond that, the condition of the enemy is precarious. They are presently at the end of a very long rope, low on food, supplies, and certainly ammunition. You simply must oppose them now with every sinew of war you can muster. The battle must be fought to the bitter end at all costs… Commanders and senior officers should die with their troops. The honor of the British Empire and the British Army is at stake.'

Percival raised an eyebrow at that, slowly folding the letter. Later he would write back to the Prime Minister: *'In some units the troops have not shown the fighting spirit expected of men of the British Empire. … It will be a lasting disgrace if we are defeated by an army of clever gangsters many times inferior in numbers to our men.'*

"I trust you will accept what I say now, sir," said Bracken, his hand again in the thick hair that seemed plastered on his wide round head. "You must do as the Prime Minister urges. Do you realize that if Singapore falls, it will be the most disastrous military setback in all British history? We thought losing Gibraltar was bad enough, then Hong Kong, but this is the Gibraltar of the East, and we simply must hold on here. I do not also have to tell you that capitulation will be forever associated with your name if you don't stand up now, something I am sure you might prefer to avoid. Why, it would be the most ignominious surrender of British forces since Cornwallis. Now then, in light of that letter, what is this business I hear about your not wanting fortifications built on the northern borders of the city?"

"Bad for morale," said Percival, a tall, thin man, beady eyed and with a tiny wisp of a mustache above prominent rabbit like teeth that protruded whenever he spoke. He looked more the office clerk than the man Bracken had with him. "Fixed fortifications send the wrong message—bad for both the troops and civilians alike."

Bracken shrugged his heavy shoulders. "Well what in god's name do you call all those heavy naval batteries facing south, if not fixed fortifications! That is what makes this island impossible to assault from the sea. You must build an equally tough defensive line to the north, facing the Strait of Johor."

"And you must mind your manners, sir, notwithstanding your close association with the Prime Minister, you are certainly not a military man, or in any position to understand what we're facing here."

"General, I understand you quite plainly. The Prime Minister might have sent General Wavell, but he's tied down with some big decisions in North Africa. So I've been sent in his place, and I've just told you what you are facing—less than 30,000 hungry, tired Japanese troops, who have little ammunition to prosecute a long siege. If you hold out, stand firm, then your name will forever be associated with something much more palatable—the defense and salvation of Singapore. The Japanese will propose your surrender, but you must not listen to them, or even treat with them seriously. This is an order, not from me of course, but from your government. No consideration must be given to surrender here."

Percival was quiet, a manner he had lately come to adopt at strategy sessions with his subordinate division and corps commanders. A shroud of gloom seemed to hang over his thin shoulders, and if anything could be said to be in his eyes now, it was not the light of determination to stand and fight. Rather, a look approaching desperation seemed to haunt him, an indecisiveness that Churchill's messenger could clearly perceive.

"Remember," said Bracken, "you are the Rock of the East."

"The Germans took the other one easily enough," said Percival.

"Only after they threatened to pour gasoline into the tunnels from above and set the whole bloody place to an inferno," Bracken shook his finger. "I hardly think the Japanese are capable of such depravity."

That was to be an understatement, for at that very moment, the Japanese had come across a group of Aussies on the other side of the Strait, cut off, all wounded, and quietly waiting for their war to end, thinking the hardship of a prison camp might not be half as bad as the jungle. The Japanese officers who came across them decided to spare them that fate. Thinking it was time for their samurai swords to be blooded, they summarily beheaded each and every man. Atrocity and depravity lay dead ahead, and Percival stood there, completely unknowing, and oblivious to the fate that might soon overtake his island fortress.

The history books Fedorov read had pointed out the bayoneting of patients and hospital staff in Hong Kong, and the ravaging of nurses on their bloodied bodies, but the real atrocity would be the slaughter of 50,000 to 70,000 Chinese civilians in Singapore, and up country in Malaya, all summarily executed for being 'anti-Japanese.'

They would call it the *Shingapōru Daikenshō*, or "great inspection of Singapore," but Western historians would name it the Sook Ching Massacre. Their troops would swarm into the steamy warrens of Chinatown, smashing the carts of the street vendors, overturning the fleets of rickshaws, breaking into the small family owned shops, putting the torch to lavish silks, exotic teas, ransacking the pearl and jade markets, looting, raping, and dragging out all the young men for "inspection." Those from wealthy families thought to be financing resistance movements were of special interest, as were communists, civil servants, and any who might have been in a militia group. Those with tattoos were also selected out, for they may have been members of the Chinese "triad" gangs. Simple possession of any weapon could result in summary execution.

The old Amahs, grandmothers, and wizened old grandfathers would watch like shadows from the shrouded windows of the tenements. The mothers screamed and wailed as their young sons were dragged off, many never to be seen again. Those that managed to "pass" inspection had the word "Inspected" stamped onto their foreheads or clothing.

Out on the water, the sampans clustered there like birds on a pond would be put to the fire, and on Nankin Street, hundreds of squalid families would be rousted out of their tiny stalls, herded like animals as the troops gave them a liberal treatment of rifle butts, bayonets, and then simply began shooting them. But most "selectees" were herded out to designated sites, like Changi Beach, where the *Kempetai* would line them up and gun them down. It would be a death toll that would exceed the total number lost to US forces over 10 years of fighting in Vietnam, and it was all put to the sword and fire in a two to three week period after the fall of Singapore.

But none of that had happened yet… There was still the Strait of Johor, 100,000 men, and General Percival between Yamashita and his prize, and Brendon Bracken was there to see that they held the line.

"Mister Bracken," said the General. "You can go back to London with every assurance that I will do my level best here to hold on. And while you're there, you might ask around as to when we might expect relief."

Bracken smiled, realizing now that Percival would have to say as much in this situation, but still not seeing any real resolve in the other man. He realized he had to offer the General something to bolster his morale, and was authorized to do so by Churchill. So he lowered his voice, stepping closer, as if to confide something of a sensitive nature.

"My good general," he began. "You didn't think I've come all this way merely to give you a pep talk, did you? What I will tell you now is to be kept secret, a matter for discussion between you and your senior division commanders only."

"Of course," said Percival, waiting, with just the barest light of expectancy in his eyes.

"You should know that the Prime Minister was dead set on sending a strong naval force to your aid, but his battleships have been seeing to another problem with the French and German fleet in the Atlantic. In their place, I can tell you that a powerful naval squadron is presently in the Indian Ocean, and with every intention of intervening here at the eleventh hour. The aircraft carriers *Illustrious* and *Indomitable* have been dispatched, and with another 45 Hurricanes each to send to your immediate aid. Now, you said yourself that much of your thinking involved protection of those airfields to insure relief by sea would remain possible. This is the aim of this flotilla, and you can expect support directly."

There, that was his bait, and now the artful Bracken had only to hope the General would take it, and allow him to reel this fish in and get a net on him.

Chapter 24

"I see," said Percival, looking a bit more hopeful. "The RAF boys will certainly be glad to hear that. As it stands, the only thing they can do in those unwieldy Buffaloes is out dive the Japanese fighters to escape from having to dog fight with them. They can't get up after the Japanese bombers. It takes them all of 30 minutes to climb to 30,000 feet, and by the time they get up there, it's usually too late. Needless to say, that is of little help to our cause."

"Well sir, the Hurricanes do a little better." Bracken needed to reinforce his point here.

"They do, if we can get them in action soon. Of the 51 in the first lot we received in January, only 21 remain available for operations."

"If you are to make good use of these planes," said Bracken, "then you'll certainly have to hold the airfields on this island, and rather tenaciously. Kallang is well in hand, but the fields at Tengan, Sembawang and Seletam are all in jeopardy should you fail to stop the enemy from obtaining a secure lodgment here."

Percival shook his head. "My good man, once the Japanese bring up their artillery, those fields will be under the gun and impossible to use. We'll only have the old civilian field at Kallang, and they've been bombing it daily. The damn place was built on reclaimed land, and the bombs kick up the mud from below. The planes have to dodge mud craters just to get into position to try and take off, which makes getting them up after the bombers a bit of a task."

Percival's subordinates always said he would see five difficulties for every opportunity he was presented, and Bracken was beginning to take the measure of the man.

"Frankly," the General concluded, "I'm not sure what good these 90 Hurricanes will do here now. I'm not even sure we'll be able to find a place to park them at Kallang, and if we do, they will most likely make good targets for the Japanese bombers."

"My, my," said Bracken. "Yes, I'm not a military man, but I believe I'm beginning to see the difficulty here, and it starts with you, sir, though I mean you no disrespect. You tell me you disposed your troops to fight for those airfields, and now, when I come with news of fresh fighter reserves, you make it seem as if they'll be more of a bother than any help!"

"What about additional troops and supplies?" said Percival. "I was only sent one Brigade of the 18th Division, and I could use more along those lines if you have them handy."

"They'll be coming," said Bracken. "The rest of the 18th Division is already at sea and should arrive shortly. But the first step is to get your existing troops ready to repel the attack that will inevitably come. I wish I could give you specifics on troop arrivals, but this was all I've been authorized to disclose at the moment. Yet I can tell you one thing…" he leaned in, lowering his voice again with a wink. "Something is in the works, old boy. Something big."

"Indeed…" The light shone a little brighter in Percival's eyes. "Well then, I appreciate everything you've said here. We won't let the Prime Minister down, I can assure you."

The two men shook hands, and hours later Bracken and his aide were on a plane, flying off to the nearest British base at Colombo. Blair felt privileged to have been in on the whole scene, even though he was no more than a mute attendant to the discussion.

"Good to hear there's a big relief effort in the offing," he ventured when they had settled in for the flight.

Bracken gave him a sideways glance. "Yes, good to hear it, yet it would be so much better if there actually was something big in the works, wouldn't it?"

"I'm sorry? You mean to say there will be no relief operation?"

"Mister Blair," said Bracken, "the Empire couldn't find another division to stand up on the cliffs of Dover if the Germans were about to cross tomorrow, and they certainly can't find one to send all the way around the cape and through the Indian Ocean to Singapore!"

"Oh… I was rather thinking it might be another Aussie unit."

"Australian troops? Percival is damn lucky he's got the two brigades of the 8th Division there. The rest have all been recalled home.

So you see, my little disclosure there was meant entirely to give the man hope. If Percival thinks there's a big push on to relieve him, he'll act as if it was actually going to happen. That was the only reason I was sent here. You see, appearances make truth, irrespective of the reality in any situation. Truth is what we decide it to be, understand? Now then… You're not to breathe a word of this to anyone, or you'll find yourself sitting in a most uncomfortable room."

"I understand, sir."

Blair never liked his superior, and after that little incident his contempt for the man deepened considerably. He would later come to call him B.B., using his initials instead of the man's name. The imposing edifice of the Ministry of Information in the Senate House of Bloomsbury would also come to seem a hopeless tomb to him, and all these experiences would figure prominently in his future writing. He never forgot what Bracken said to him about truth and appearances.

Blair adopted a pen name for his work, something he just made up one day. He changed his given name to George, the name of the monarch, or perhaps old St. George himself, the slayer of dragons. His sharp pen would be his lance ever thereafter, and he would joust with demons in many famous works, one day named as one of the most significant English writers of his era. For the surname he chose was Orwell, the name of a river in Suffolk, though some say it was a village in Cambridge that he fancied.

The book he would write one day after the war was, of course, *1984*, a dark vision of the future world he thought men like Brendon Bracken would give rise to. For old B.B. was his analog for Big Brother, and the Ministry of Information in Bloomsbury his analog for the Ministry of Truth. Mister Bracken had told him just now, a simple maxim that he would put at the heart of that novel. "Reality exists in the human mind, and nowhere else." If Percival thought relief was imminent, he would perhaps become more of a man than he could by thinking otherwise.

"In wartime," Churchill would quip one day, "truth is so precious that she should always be attended by a bodyguard of lies."

* * *

Whether he was the image of Big Brother or not in Orwell's mind, Brenden Bracken had come to one inescapable conclusion during his talk with Percival—the man was not capable of properly defending Singapore, and under his watch it would certainly be lost. He reported this directly to General Wavell, who had flown from Alexandria to Colombo to take his report at Churchill's urging.

"Rotten from the top down," he said. "Any fight left in the division commanders will be leached right out of them under that man. Percival may be stolid and obey orders to hold on, but he won't conduct a spirited defense. I fear we're looking at the same disaster foretold to us earlier by the Russian Captain. We need someone else, and quickly."

Wavell nodded, his expression dark and grave. His unique position as one of the very few men 'in the know' concerning the Russians had kept him in his post as overall Theater Commander, and now he was feeling the weight of that command.

"I agree completely," he said at last, "and I believe I have just the man for the job, our own General Montgomery. He's a particular genius for a situation like this—cut his teeth organizing the defenses along the coast of Kent and Sussex when we thought the Germans might try to kick in the door. He held Tobruk, and to the point of taking up a rifle himself in that fight when we stopped Rommel. I'd say he's the perfect man of the hour for Singapore."

"Then get him there, and as quickly as you possibly can. And if you have anything at all you can spare by way of additional troops, even a single battalion, by all means, send it with him."

That was Wavell's order, and the troops he found to send along with Montgomery were the 6th Infantry Brigade of the 2nd New Zealand Division. Along with those three battalions, he added the crack 28th Maori Battalion, a company from the 22nd Machinegun Battalion, and another from the Recon Battalion and Royal Engineers.

The troops would have to make a long sea journey, all of 7000 miles from Alexandria, but they were dispatched that day, the 15th of January, on the fastest transports available, and would get there inside two weeks. RMS *Empress of Asia* was also dispatched from Cape Town, a steam liner that had once served as an auxiliary cruiser hunting WWI German raiders in the Indian Ocean. Her holds were packed with machineguns, rifles, mortars and other military supplies, and she was leading a little convoy comprised of *Félix Roussel* and *City of Canterburyn*, escorted by HMAS *Yarra* and HMS *Danae*.

General Montgomery arrived by air on the 24th of January, stepping in with the rest of the fresh 18th British Infantry Division, which was there a little earlier than it arrived in the old history. He wanted to make it seem that they were here at his behest, a proud new General leading in fresh troops to buck up morale. He met Percival in the "battlebox" beneath Fort Canning, a warren of narrow halls and rooms where the General held forth with his staff. There were offices and conference rooms, a gun operations room to control the shore batteries, a signals control room for communications back to Wavell. To Monty it all seemed a stench ridden, oppressive Ostrich hole, and he resolved to move his own headquarters much closer to the front lines he had in mind.

It was only then that Percival learned what was 'in the works,' as Bracken had put it to him. Monty handed Percival yet another letter, signed by Wavell, and formally relieving the lanky General of command. Percival would stay on in a secondary role as Chief of Staff, for Wavell believed his knowledge of the local scene would be of considerable use to Montgomery.

"Well then," said Monty. "I can say I'm accustomed to the heat, but certainly not this humidity. It's been a bit dry where I hail from. That aside, I shall want to review all your dispositions for the defense of this island immediately, and tomorrow morning, we will hold a meeting with all the senior division commanders. Am I to understand that you're planning to pack all the fighters off our carriers into one small civilian airfield near the city?"

"We certainly can't use the forward air fields," said Percival. They'll all be under the Japanese artillery soon."

"Quite so, but this single airfield, what is it, Kallang? Well it simply won't do. So I propose those fighters operate from Pakanbharu on Sumatra. It's only 170 miles from Singapore, and our Hurricanes can manage that, with plenty of fuel left for combat air patrols over the city. The Fairey Fulmars on the carriers have even better range, but I'll leave their disposition up to the Commanding Officer, Carrier Force. The Blenheims in theater can operate from Padang on the west coast of Sumatra, and Palembang."

It was amazing how this single change suddenly imparted a whole new attitude. Unlike Percival, Monty was all business, quick minded, obstinate, decisive, and with a keen eye for defense. He soon looked over Percival's plan, having discussed it all with Wavell earlier.

"It seems you wanted the Australians in the Western sector. Wavell believes that will be the most likely point of attack, and I tend to agree. Therefore, British regulars should be defending there."

"But I've posted them in the Eastern sector, around the naval base," said Percival. "Surely the Japanese will make that one of their initial objectives. They've already put troops on the islands nearby. They'll want the oil fuel stocks."

"Then we'll give it to them, but not in any way they might like. As for the Australians, they only have two brigades, and you've split them in two, on either side of the Kranji river inlet. That' won't do at all. How will they communicate and support one another? Instead, I'll put them side by side, near the village of Kranji and the Causeway sector. I'll move one of the Indian brigades to the Naval Base, and they can watch the northeast section. As for those oil stocks, I'm afraid they can't be defended—simply too vulnerable. So what I propose to do is spill the tanks into this slough and simply set it all on fire at an opportune moment. We've got to get positively medieval here. This is a castle, and the Strait of Johor is our moat. We've blown the

Causeway, but they'll try to rebuild it, as it is the only real road they can use to move in any heavy weapons or armor they may have. Think of it as the main gate, and this is why I want both Australian Brigades to stand the line there."

"And if they come over these islands east of the naval base?" said Percival. "They'll have the Aussies cut off."

"I very much doubt that. If they do put in an attack there, it would only be a feint. No, they must take that Causeway. As for the British troops, I think I'll post the 18th Division here." He was pointing to a spot in the center of the island near Tengah airfield.

"Well they certainly can't cover the Northwest coast from that position," Percival protested.

"I have no intention of trying to man the entire coastline. If we try to hold everywhere, we'll be spread thin, like too little butter on bread. We need to mass our troops, and for two good reasons. Firstly, their numbers when massed are mutually supporting and good for morale. Secondly, they'll be much easier to control on the field, particularly in an attack. From this map, the northwest looks to be nothing more than a mangrove swamp. You've placed the entire Australian 22nd Brigade there, but the river near Kranji forms a natural barrier to the east, and any troops posted there will be cut off immediately if the Japanese land to their south. So I'll cede that ground to the enemy, if he wants it. In fact, I'll position my artillery so as to make it a nice killing field. They'll be tangled up in the mangrove swamps, and make good targets. We'll defend here, on a line from Kranji, along the river, and down to the airfield at Tengah. Leave the 27th Australian Brigade where you've placed it at Kranji. We'll move the 22nd Brigade east and have them take over the positions you've assigned to the 11th Indian Division, and then send those troops to the Naval Base. That should do."

"Then nothing will defend the northwest sector?"

"We'll post forward detachments to watch the coast, and they'll all have radios."

"You'll break radio silence?"

"And why not? The Japanese will know exactly where we are. It's not like we have anything to hide here. Besides all they will hear is my order for our guns to fire. So the main job of these forward spotters will be to alert the 18th Division as to the enemy landings, and to call in our artillery."

"Then you plan to hold that far inland, behind the airfield at Tengah?"

"No, my good man, I plan to counterattack from that location. That is the whole point of massing the division there. We can't cover the entire coast in any real strength, so we'll hold in key positions to the rear, and when we've identified their main effort, that's when we hit them. It's what I recommended at Dover when the Germans were looking at us across the Channel. That's what we'll do here. The Indian Brigades are worn out, so I'll post them to the rear as a reserve, along with the Malay Brigade, Dalforce irregulars, and the Fortress Troops. Now then, I shall want to tour the entire sector today to look over the ground."

Montgomery had immediately seen the flaws in Percival's deployments and corrected them. Where Percival had his freshest unit, the 18th British Division, spread all along the northeast coast, Monty Moved it to Tengah Airfield in one concentrated force. Where Percival had split his next best force by separating the two Australian brigades, Monty combined them to reinforce the Causeway Sector. He then used the Indian troops to fill in here and there, and left the Malay Brigades and Fortress Troops to watch the south and stand as his reserve.

So Monty was off, baton in hand, visiting one unit after another and already issuing orders to get them moving where he wanted them. Some of the Australians muttered that they had only just settled in and now they were looking at yet another withdrawal.

"How big do they think this bloody island is?" they said. "How do we stop the Japs from crossing if we aren't in good positions on the shore?"

"Beats me," said a Corporal, "but this ain't a retreat, mate. He wants us over on the other side of the island. This one seems to know what he's about. He's got that look about him—stiff upper lip and all."

"Better him than Percy, I suppose, and better by the Causeway then in this bloody Mangrove swamp. But I've had enough of running from the Japs. When we get to Kranji, I'm staying put."

"The general will certainly be glad to hear that Bob. Can't say the Japs will fancy it. They'll want that Causeway, and to get at it, they'll have to cross one side or another, right in our laps."

* * *

The Japanese continued to push, closing inexorably on the island, and forcing the defenders back over the long stone Causeway to Johore, their last connection to the mainland that had been taken from them in just fifty days. The last of Brigadier Bennett's Australians tramped in, moving into positions near the Causeway where Monty wanted them. The engineers were soon busy tending to the demolition charges, and they blew a 70-foot gap in the Causeway, sending the steel of the rail line and water pipe into the murky waters of the Strait of Johor.

"That ought to stop the little bastards," said a big Scotsman as he watched the smoke and dust rise from the explosion.

"Right," said a Sergeant of Engineers. "And that's also stopped all the water coming in from the mainland. Now we're just down to what we have in the reservoirs here, and the city has swollen with refugees from up-country."

It was an observation worthy of Percival himself, yet water would definitely be a factor in any protracted siege. The weary, disheartened troops filed back to their newly assigned positions on the island, the draw bridge was blown, and there they sat behind their moat—only this castle had no walls. Very little in the way of fortifications had been built in the north… bad for morale….

Montgomery would soon get busy recruiting volunteers from the city's swollen population to dig new defensive positions and trench lines. In this, the Chinese provided stalwart and eager workers. He was already picking out his secondary defensive lines, pouring over the maps day and night. The time he would spend in his temple with all this planning would serve him very well.

Part IX

Rock of the East

*"Invincibility lies in the defense;
the possibility of victory in the attack."*

— **Sun Tsu:** *The Art of War*

Chapter 25

The wild, exotic, prosperous city of Singapore was a much different place now under the impending shadow of war. While the fighting was still up country, far off and beyond the range of the gunfire, people could still go about their lives with some sense of normalcy. The street vendors were still out, the shops still open, the smell of scrumptious foods, cigarettes and fresh roasted coffee, wafting on the city airs, with people eating late in the restaurants, coming and going in the night, until the bombers came that first dark hour.

The city was never the same after that. The whining fall of the bombs, the shock of the explosions, the muffled mutter of the 40mm Bofors lighting up the night sky in a vain effort to fend off the attack—these were things that are seared on the memories of anyone who ever endures them. War had come to city after city like this, to France, the Low Countries, Denmark, England, and all across Russia. It wasn't half as bad as the things that had already happened in places like Moscow, but to those experiencing that slow, steady transition from a normal life for the first time, seeing and feeling it sliding into the inexorable decline of order that builds with a restrained sense of terror towards chaos, it was always a heartrending and tragic affair.

Moscow was burned and ravaged, like the dead nurses in Hong Kong, but just knowing about the fate that befell that city on Christmas Day when the Japanese finally burst in, was enough to build that palpable sense of fear and dread in the swelling population of the city. People saw the streets slowly filling up with strange, haggard faces, a vagrant wave of riff raff refugees from up country, sweeping into the streets like muddy rain water, running down the alleyways where they huddled in the night beneath old boxes and tattered blankets. The refugees brought the infection of terror with them, and the fear redoubled. Then the troops began to arrive in the harbor, the 45th Indian Brigade the first reinforcements since the beginning of the war, and the bombs came after them.

The Buffaloes lumbered up to try and find the bombers, and

found the dreadful artistry of the A6-M2 *Reisen* Zero instead. It was only their heavy, unwieldy design that kept many of them flying, with wings and tails scraped and riddled with patched over bullet holes. They couldn't stop the bombers, and day by day, the rubble mounted up, and the civilian death toll with it. Roads were blocked by abandoned vehicles, many set on fire when the bombs fell, and lighting up the long, empty streets at night with their eerie glow of terror until the weary fire brigades could get to them.

Fresh water was at a premium now, and so they were hauling seawater in barrels and rigging up makeshift water pumps to fight the fires that never seemed to be under control. The posh restaurants soon closed, the city dark each night, and a heavy, thick shadow of smoke and burning oil obscured every dawn. Looters and some deserters picked about the edges of the main town, breaking into houses and stores that seemed unguarded; taking what they couldn't buy or find by any other means. After dark, the mournful wail of air raid sirens would come, the distant rumble of the planes, and then the whistle of the bombs. The airfields were hit every day, the city every night, a campaign that became more and more indiscriminate, as war had a way of removing every vestige of civility and restraint, and killing compassion first and foremost with its cruel bayonet.

It would not be the worst fate a great city would suffer in the war. London had it worse, Hamburg, Dresden, and so many others. It was just the early autumn of war here, as its dreadful seasons turn. It wasn't the stark opposition of fire and frost that had blighted Moscow, but it was still death coming, and everyone in the city could feel it, sense it, fear it.

Soon the crews could not get to all the fallen after the night raids, and the morning would see the streets stained with the fresh blood of those who were killed, their corpses lying on the pavement, some headless from the awful concussion of the high explosive bombs. The heavy tropic airs carried the scent of their death, and dismembered arms and feet that washed into the sewers would fester and rot quickly in the muggy humidity.

Streetlamps tilted at odd angles, store windows were shattered, with the shards of glass gleaming with any sunlight that could penetrate the gloom. Dogs wandered through the streets at night, feeding on the dead. By day, the only energy in the city was clustered in a mad impulsive rush about the harbor and docks. There the quays were overrun with panicked citizens, those well off enough to think they could gain easy passage on a steamer out to points unknown, the white and wealthy first, the rabble after, or so they saw things. Many that took to those boats would die on the sea, the ships strafed by Japanese aircraft, which growled and wheeled with impudence over the city, for they had been masters of the sky for the last three weeks.

And then the Hurricanes came.

The last had fled the civilian field at Kellang three days ago, which did little to still the slowly rising panic in the city, but then they returned. The Japanese had been so emboldened that they came with fewer fighters that day, and well after dawn. On the 26th of January, the drone and thrum of engines craned necks upwards again, sending people running for any shelter they could find, until they saw what was happening through the wind rifted clouds of smoke. Dark blue fighters came wheeling in, their wings bright with fire, and people suddenly realized they were not the enemy.

"By God, those are our boys up there!" a man shouted. He pointed, seeing the bright fire at the tail of an enemy bomber, watching it fall.

Miles away, on the other side of the vast steamy bulwark island of Sumatra, the carriers *Illustrious* and *Indomitable* had flown off their Hurricanes to airfields designated by Montgomery. They landed just after dark, refueled, and were up at the break of dawn to make a sweeping show of strength over the embattled city. They brought the wrath of vengeance in the machineguns as they wheeled and dueled with the Zeroes, some losing that fight, others getting hits and even downing two enemy fighters. Yet more than that, they brought hope, a commodity that had been in very short supply, rationed in the hearts of only the most stalwart souls. And they were there for yet another reason that morning. *Empress of Asia* and a convoy of relief ships were bringing in the New Zealanders. It was a ship that had been fated to die there, bombed by the Japanese, run aground, and ravaged by merciless fire, but that would not happen today with all that air cover swarming over the city and harbor. The ship would get through to safely deliver her charge, and the considerable stores of weapons and ammunition within her holds.

Soon the crowds parted on the quays to make way for the tall, suntanned men marching briskly off the boats, easily carrying their heavy kit and packs, rifles slung over broad shoulders. With smiles and grins, "good-day" was on the morning air instead of the whine of enemy bombs. Monty knew they would be in that morning, for he had arranged the whole affair, and when they came he was there to greet them, standing proudly with their newly promoted Brigadier, William Gentry, grinning broadly himself as the troops marched by.

The last battalion off the boat, following the Maori troops, turned quite a few heads, the men were shorter, yet well-built and stocky in stature. They moved with a precision that spoke of thorough military training and ironclad discipline. Their kit, backpacks and rifles seemed unfamiliar, and each man carried what looked like a machete at the back of his belt, a long curved knife. In fact, they were the last gift Wavell had sent, Kinlan's elite Gurkha Battalion, armed to the teeth with modern assault rifles, ATGMs and even Swingfire anti-air missile teams. No one on that island would ever know the real secret of how they came to be there, which is another long tale, except Montgomery.

Someone got hold of a bagpipe, and the squeal of the pipes welcomed the boys ashore. For the first time in many weeks, people smiled. They shook their fists and shouted to the lads to go and give it to the Japs—stick it to them, give them the boot and brawn. And that was exactly what Bernard Law Montgomery had set his mind to do—and then some.

* * *

To prepare for his attack, Yamashita and his God of Operations, Tsuji, would occupy the opulent palace of the Sultan of Johor, Ibrahim II. When the British were there, he coddled to them with gifts and favors. Now that the Japanese had come, he wisely had a Japanese flag raised from his high palace tower, overlooking the straits and presenting a splendid view of the city of Singapore beyond. The 25th Army had come over 700 miles in just 54 days, through forbidding jungle, and over countless rivers which they crossed by storm or the sweat of their troops and engineers, building well over 200 new bridges.

It had all been done exactly as Tsuji said it would, by using the materials and supplies, and the physical assets the British already had in place there, and with a little dash, fervor, and abundant imagination and courage. When news came to Churchill that his Malaya defenders were now bottled up in Singapore, he seemed listless and worried. He had been told, long ago by Fedorov, that this would happen. It seemed that in spite of his constant urging, nothing could be done to stem the flood of the Japanese offensive. The British Generals thought they would hold Malaya for a year to eighteen months. They lost it in six weeks.

The night of February 1st, a week earlier than in Fedorov's history, Colonel Ikatani, Yamashita's Quartermaster, reported that the shortages of petrol and ammunition were very serious.

"We have come a long way, fighting the whole distance, and stores are very low. If we have to fight a long siege here, I believe we will fail. It may be better to wait until we have time to bring up more fuel and ammunition."

"Impossible," said Yamashita. "We must be in the city by the 11th of February. This is imperative."

"Very well, then shall I order the artillery officers to ration their fires?"

Yamashita thought for a moment. "No. Have them make a powerful opening barrage. I want the enemy to think we are stronger than we truly are. We must make them believe what they already fear—that we are invincible."

Yamashita left the opulent palace and moved to an abandoned bungalow near the village of Kulang, summoning his officers for a final briefing. "We have lost nearly 1800 men since we landed, but here we stand, victorious, inflicting many times our losses on the enemy. Now the spirits and ghosts of those men who sacrificed themselves are watching us. The final victory lies ahead, on that island, where we will humble our enemy once and for all, and deliver a prize of great value to the Empire. But this must be done before the anniversary of the 11th of February. Never forget that. The division who reaches Singapore first will gain lasting glory."

The men assembled all cheered at that, pledging they would be the first to enter the city. "And so we strike the northwest shoreline tonight," said Yamashita, "but we will also bombard in the north, where the Guards Division will demonstrate to confuse the enemy as to our real intentions. The 5th and 18th Divisions will begin their crossing to assault the island a few hours after sunset, and be well ashore on the other side of the strait by dawn. Our first task is to secure the airfield at Tengah. After that we will drive up the road to this village, Bukit Panjang. Then phase two of the assault begins, with the Imperial Guards Division crossing to seize the Causeway and push south to the village of Mandai. They will then drive east, and cut off any forces defending the British Naval Base. After that, we move south to Bukit Tamah, and the water reservoirs. When we capture those, their surrender must surely follow soon after."

Lieutenant General Takuma Nishimura, commander of the Imperial Guards Division, had been most unhappy to hear these orders. He had already been asked to make a demonstration against the eastern defenses of the island, sending a battalion to occupy a small islet there, and to threaten the naval base. Yet such an assignment seemed demeaning to him, while the two regular army divisions were both massing to attack the other side of the island.

"This is an insult to my division, and to me personally," He steamed, saying his men were not shadow puppets, but the elite guards of the Konoye Regiments, and he was eager to bloody his samurai sword.

In truth, the "elite" troops were in both those regular army divisions, the 5th and 18th. In spite of its impressive name, the Imperial Guards here had little military experience, though they fought well against the 45th Indian Brigade on the Muar River earlier. Nishimura was eager to win more laurels for his men, and was bitterly disappointed that his troops would be used as a feint in the initial attack, and as a follow up force in subsequent operations.

He had been so eager to bloody his sword, that he ordered the massacre of 155 prisoners after that first battle on the Muar River, and would later be tried and executed for war crimes, which included his participation in the massacre of Chinese civilians.

Yamashita heard his complaint, but said nothing more, offering the officers a toast of sake. When he offered a cup to Nishimura, the Lieutenant General turned his back and strode away. He would hold a grudge against Yamashita ever thereafter for the slight he thought he had received here, fuming that he would get his men into the battle one way or another. It would be his wounded pride that would have an unexpected effect on the battle, just one of the many instances where the will of a single man could strongly influence the course of events.

That night, the Japanese sent three swimmers across the strait to reconnoiter the position. They reported back that most of the north coast west of Kanji was simply undefended, though they found signs of positions that had been abandoned there in recent days. The morning of the 4th of February, observation balloons were seen floating over Johore Bahru, with a single observer in each to spy on what the British were up to. Later that day, Nishimura penned a formal demand to General Yamashita. "My troops must be given the chance to demonstrate their bravery," he wrote.

Though he was inclined to ignore the letter, Yamashita began to have second thoughts when the balloon observers reported a buildup near the Causeway. So he went to Nishimura and gave him permission to attack directly against this position, thinking it would still be a good diversion from his main landings to the west. Only he ordered him to begin the assault at noon the following day.

Having other ideas, Nishimura planned an immediate seizure of the Causeway bridge, ordering his engineers to make ready for repair work as soon as his men gained the far shore.

Colonel Iwaguro's 5th Konoye Imperial Guards Regiment was chosen for the attack, a formation of three battalions supported by the engineers. "Attack at noon?" Nishimura said to the Colonel. "Ridiculous! We will begin the operation immediately, taking every advantage of the cover of night." He also disobeyed his orders to concentrate his artillery fire on inland targets, redirecting it to fire right on the Australian battalions of Taylor's 22nd Brigade. At dawn, his initial attack would fall on II/20 Battalion and C Company, Royal Engineers, just east of the Causeway.

That night, the crossings in the northwest were made in wood and canvass boats, 100 for each of the two primary assault divisions, and a few heavier rafts that could support the weight of light artillery pieces. They formed up in the estuaries of rivers flowing into the strait, and slowly edged out into the open waters, the first wave being 4000 strong. They were expecting a tough defense on the opposite shore, but would find it completely abandoned, the darkness and quiet heavy on the water, with the moon the barest morning crescent, casting thin pale light on the water.

Yamashita had returned to the high tower of the Sultan's palace, watching and waiting with his staff. There would be no radio communications established to his two assault divisions, but as midnight passed, he saw the first sign of success rise in a red star shell over the beaches closest to his position. 5th Division had made a safe crossing, securing a beachhead and pushing inland unopposed. They heard the boom of a distant gun, the shore battery at Pasir Laba to the south, which scored a lucky hit on one of the engineering barges. Then, minutes later, a white star shell rose, brighter than the thin moon, and

Yamashita knew 18th Division was ashore. What he did not know is that Nishimura's Imperial Guards were also nosing their rafts into the black waters of the strait, paddling towards the far edge of the Causeway, and hoping to take it by surprise and storm. It wasn't until he heard the small arms fire coming from that direction that he realized something was happening at the Causeway.

"What is going on there?" he said sternly to a staff officer. "Nishimura was not to attack there until noon!"

Unfortunately, it was already high noon in Nishimura's mind, and he was going to do everything possible to show Yamashita what he and his men could accomplish.

Chapter 26

Major General Gordon Bennett finally got his troops redeployed, and he was down in the ranks with the men at Kanji village, a small town just west of the Causeway. He was feeling a good deal better about his situation, glad to have his two brigades under Taylor and Maxwell, side by side.

"Much better ground here sir," said a Sergeant. "I've got decent fields of fire for my machineguns. Out west we couldn't see anything but the bloody Mangroves and rubber trees."

"Glad to hear it," said Bennett, removing his hat. "Good to feel the sun on this old bald head of mine, but stay alert, because the Japs will want that bridge, and this village with it."

Bennett had fought in the ill-fated landings at Gallipoli, a battalion commander then, where he was wounded when his troops were cut off by the Turks, and literally wiped out. That experience, and the long retreat he had just made down the Malay Peninsula, left him in a state of mind to always keep a wary eye over his shoulder. Later he would move up to command 3rd Infantry Brigade, fighting at Passchendaele and the Hindenburg Line with distinction. He had already been admitted to the Order of the Bath, and had his DSO by 1919. An opinionated man, some believed he did not think much of British commanders, particularly Percival, but he had been willing to give Montgomery the benefit of the doubt.

"What do you make of him?" asked the Sergeant.

"Haven't heard or seen much," said Bennett. "He's a teetotaler, and any man who can't stomach a good whiskey is questionable, but there's nothing wrong with his orders. I agree, we're in a much better position here. That said, have your men write any letters they may want to send home."

Bennett had become a controversial figure in this battle when he refused to become a prisoner and commandeered a sampan to escape the island. Some said he should not have abandoned his troops, others that he had done the right and expedient thing, though he had not yet been tested in this 11th hour.

* * *

The action started a little after midnight, when the restless sentries thought they heard movement near the water by the Causeway. A sentry team of two men slipped out of their slit trench, and scrambled down towards the embankment, and minutes later the sound of sporadic rifle file alerted the whole battalion that the enemy was there. It could have been a probing attack, a feint as had been initially ordered, but something told Bennett otherwise. He had seen those flares to the west, and knew the enemy was signaling something of importance. As those first shots were fired, the battle of Singapore would begin on the island itself, and his battalions would have a front row seat.

It was hot action all that night, with the Australians holding their ground in the face of Iwaguro's initial attack. Machineguns chattered and fired at anything that moved in the shadows hovering near the dark waters, then, on Bennett's command, the Aussies switched on three search lights that had been rigged up with portable generators. As the glare of the beams illuminated the scene, they could see about twenty assault boats still in the water, and the shoreline dotted with enemy infantry.

Now mortar shells fell down the short metal tubes and hissed up with a pop, exploding around the Causeway seconds later. The Japanese had a heavy machinegun team deployed, and it began to growl at the heights above, the bright tracers scoring the night. Deep throated shouts from officers were urging the guardsmen forward, and several platoon sized rushes were made, one led by a lieutenant brandishing his samurai sword. The Australians opened up with everything they had, and the casualties were heavy for the Japanese in those first hours.

The action was bitter all night as Iwaguro's three battalions built up on the shoreline. They soon perceived that the weak link in the Australian defense was the company of Royal Engineers, and 1st Battalion of the 5th Imperial Guards led the attack there. Unfortunately, the engineers had sewn mines and laid wire, and they had three Vickers machineguns with them. A scene that might have occurred in the last war resulted, with the Japanese infantry flinging themselves onto the wire to depress it for following troops, the mines detonating, sending bodies flying into the air, and then the Vickers guns rumbling away at the onrushing infantry. All that was missing was the artillery, but it wasn't missing long.

Taylor's 2nd Field Artillery was on the high ground near Bennett's headquarters, and they had fifteen 25-pounders. Soon the crack of those guns entered the rising swell of the battle noise, and their heavy shells began to fall with pre-registered fire.

By dawn, with the position still holding, the Japanese were clinging to a narrow strip of land on the shoreline. Bennett ordered up the one reserve battalion in his sector, and directed his artillery to begin shelling the Causeway itself. Unaware that enemy engineers had been working all night to rig up a section of bridge reinforced by steel rails they had discovered in Johore, he nonetheless suspected the Japanese had been using the bridge to get half way over the strait before lowering light rafts and rubber boats to complete their crossing. To his great surprise, after working all night and through the entire morning, the dogged engineers had been able to set the rails in closely spaced bundles, covering them with cross planks of timber.

They were already placing heavier wood beams to reinforce the structure from below when the first light broke and the Australian artillery began to fall. This soon prompted a vigorous round of counter battery fire on and around Bennett's HQ, which was so disruptive that he decided to move his staff elsewhere. He got to a car and was moving to the Mandai road when a Sergeant flagged him down with some alarming news.

"It's tanks, sir. Japanese got three over the Causeway bridge late today, and Brigadier Taylor says there'll be more."

"Damn!" Bennett swore. "How in bloody hell did they manage that? Alright, the Indian Division has a couple companies of 2-pounders at Nee Soon. Find a radio and get them moving on this road to Mandai. If the Japs get there with tanks, they can run right down the main road and rail line to the center of the island!"

Get to a radio… Why in god's name didn't he have one with him? There simply weren't enough to go around, and the two sets he had been allocated were somewhere on the road behind him. He saw a man on a small motorbike and collared him immediately.

"Get to General Montgomery. Tell him the Japanese have managed to rig out a bridge over the Causeway gap. They're moving in armor—tanks!" Then he was off to Mandai, for that was where he most feared the enemy might come, a small village just down the road south of Kranji. The man started to say something, but Bennett was off, tapping his driver's shoulder. As the car sped away, the man made a half-hearted salute, then scratched his head. He had no idea where Montgomery was, and no intention of looking for him. Instead he started down the road towards Singapore, his mind set on getting to the harbor.

Further west, the landing of the Japanese 5th Infantry Division had gone off without a hitch, but as the troops pushed inland, they were suddenly ambushed by a company of Chinese volunteers from Dalforce. The Chinese had been ready to go into these positions as a forward screen, even though only half of them had rifles, and only 24 rounds each. They didn't even have proper uniforms, and the men had tied red bandanas on their foreheads and white armbands to identify them as friendly troops to the British.

That was how they would have fought, but the *Empress of China* had been saved by those Hurricanes, and so all the arms and stores had made it safely ashore. This time, all the men without rifles were issued combat shotguns, because the British doubted their marksmanship. They put them to good use, catching the Japanese unawares and popping up to blast them with shotgun fire at very close range. Their gallant stand was so effective, that two other Japanese battalions had to be deployed to make a prepared assault on their cleverly hidden positions. These men would fight so well that they would come to be known as "Dalley's Desperados," but 1st Company would soon be enfiladed, overrun and killed to the last man. The death they had there in the Mangroves was infinitely better than the one they might have otherwise suffered. Yet in all this early action, word filtered back to Yamashita, and left him with one salient question. Where were the British regulars?

* * *

The miracle performed by those intrepid engineers was going to have a major impact on the battle Montgomery had planned to fight. He still had all of the British 18th Division concentrated in and around the village of Bulim, just east of the Tengah airfield. There he had set up a line of good defensive positions. Brigadier Blackhouse had 54th Brigade on his right, and Brigadier Massy-Beresford had the 55th Brigade on his left.

Both were dug in, and with good fields of fire across the open ground of Tengah airfield. Behind them Monty had positioned his tactical reserve, the newly arrived 6th New Zealand Brigade under Brigadier Clifton, with four good battalions, including the 28th Maori. The 53rd British Brigade had arrived first, thrown into the battle north of the Causeway, and their numbers were reduced by casualties from that action. So he placed those troops astride the road north through Mandai to Kranji and the Causeway.

It was to these forces that Bennett came, looking for some way to get a blocking force in position on the main road. There he found Brigadier Duke, and asked him to move a battalion to the village of Mandai as quickly as possible.

"But our orders are to stand here on reserve," said Duke. "And I have the feeling this new General Montgomery won't like his dispositions fooled with."

"Well let me put it to you this way," said Bennett. "You can either sit here and wait for a column of Japanese tanks to come barreling down that road, or you can get some men up into the village in good positions where they might stop them. That should be clear enough."

Duke relented, and sent an order to the 2nd Cambridgeshire Battalion, which was still at about 80% of nominal strength. He was only a couple miles south of Mandai, so the men started off, marching up the road, with Bennett right behind them. When they got to the village, they found a company of Indian 2-pounders already there, for Bennett's other messenger had been a man on his own HQ staff, and completely reliable.

It was at this point that they heard the distinctive rumble of field artillery to the south and west. Bennett looked over his shoulder, wondering what was going on. It sounded like the British 18th division was finally being engaged, and now he began to wonder what would happen if the Japanese got through.

If they overrun the airfield, then they can push right along King's Road to Bukit Panjang. That's five miles behind me, and my boys are all up there in the Causeway sector. There won't be any way for them to get south. They'd be cut off, pawns on the front row, and with a knight leaping right into the center of the board behind them.

That had been Monty's plan. If the island had been a chess board, he was a strong rook, developed after a deft castling move, and that main road was an open file right back to Singapore—checkmate…. That rook had to stand, and by god, this file had to be closed and well guarded. Otherwise this whole bloody plan could come unraveled in a matter of hours.

* * *

The guns that had turned Bennett's head were indeed the three regiments of field artillery with the 18th Division. They were more like battalions, for there was simply not enough transport available to send their whole allotment of guns. All the rest were out in convoy WS-15, still enroute. 155th Regiment had 21 guns, the 88th Regiment had 18, the 118th had 14 guns and there were 13 more in the 148th Regiment. Altogether, he had 66 guns, mostly 25-pounders, enough to tear up some turf when fired together, and that was what they were doing now.

Montgomery's screening units in the Recon Battalion, engineers rigging minefields, and another company from Dalforce had been slowly falling back towards the airfield. The enemy was massing in front of them, and Monty decided to try and break them up a bit with his artillery. At this point, he still had no idea what was happening at the Causeway. Bennett might have motored over to find him, but he was too set on minding the defense of that open file.

Reports Monty had received were mostly from those screening units to the west, where he learned the Japanese had landed their main force right where he expected them. Thus far, his outlying units had fallen back in good order, for it took the enemy some time to get sorted out, ferry their artillery across the strait, and work their battalions through the mangroves and rubber plantations to approach Tengah airfield. That was where Montgomery thought to fight his decisive battle here, but reports of enemy forces taking the shore battery at Pasil Laba to his southwest made him nervous.

"I can't very well fight my battle here if the enemy is going to creep down along that coastline," he said to General Smith of the 18th Division. "I believe this warrants some investigation."

"How about that Gurkha unit?" Smith suggested. "They're down at that end of the line. A damn fine looking bunch, that battalion."

"Indeed," said Monty. "I had them at Tobruk, and I put them to very good use there. I should like to keep them in hand, but under the circumstances, your suggestion makes sense. See to it, will you?"

So the Gurkhas were off, and Colonel Rana Gandar briefed his Company Subedars and Halvidars that this was to be a search and destroy mission. Many of these men had served overseas in their own day, and in every terrain imaginable. So they had no difficulty managing the heat and mangroves, and soon the lead teams of scouts and snipers were moving forward.

They were going to find the 3rd Battalion, 56th Regiment of Lieutenant General Renya Mutaguchi's 18th Division. He was a veteran of the Siberian Intervention, and had fought for years in China before his division had been handpicked to join the 25th Army. Earlier that day, 3rd Battalion had landed to take out that shore battery, finding it already destroyed by the crews when they got there. In spite, they herded the entire gun crew into the enclosed concrete housing, and then set the bunker on fire, laughing with one another at the screams of the tortured men. Then they were off, intending a wide envelopment to the south of the airfield.

But they were about to have a very bad day.

Chapter 27

3/56 Battalion came out of a thicket of mangroves when the lead Sergeant suddenly stumbled and fell. A private ran up to help him, thinking he had stumbled on a hidden tree root in the undergrowth, but then he, too, keeled over and fell. The third man in the column knew enough to realize they were under attack, and he shouted, turning to look back down the line, when a bullet came whizzing in to cut him down as well.

Gurkha Sniper Rana Sunil was well concealed in his camouflaged gillie suit, peering through the powerful optical sight on his L1115A3 Long Range Rifle. He reached up to his collar, pinching a button there three times. A quarter mile away, his Company Sergeant, Halvidar Druna Rai, got the message on his helmet microphone—contact! He, in turn, passed the message back to Battalion CO, and soon the other two companies were stealthily moving to the south, around the reported point of contact.

The Japanese reaction to the sniper was not to go to ground. They immediately organized a full platoon with fixed bayonets, and then set up two light machineguns, with another squad of riflemen scanning the trees. The platoon was going to make an attack in the presumed direction of the enemy, intending and hoping to draw their fire. They would head directly for Sniper Sunil's hidden squad, a blocking force, yet with more equivalent firepower than ten machineguns.

The Japanese made a brave charge, until the tree line opened up on them with that withering assault rifle fire. Colonel Yoshio Nasu soon realized that he must be up against a strong enemy bunker. He blew his whistle, intending to order up a section of demolition engineers, when the low tree sewn ridge to his right erupted with fire. The crump of mortar rounds was heard, and their whistling fall soon began to explode all around his battalion CP.

The Gurkhas were attacking, and before it was over, 3/56 battalion would lose half its squads, driven relentlessly back on the supporting 2/56 Battalion to the north. The Gurkhas had found the enemy's southernmost flank, and they were slowly rolling it up.

Farther north, the line of screening forces finally gave way, and began to rush to the rear across the Tengah airfield while Monty's 25-pounders provided that covering fire. Here the bulk of the Japanese 18th division thought it was about to seize its first objective, the leading battalions hotly pursuing the retreating engineers and scout teams, and some pushing out onto the airfield itself. It was a single wide central strip, with two other strips making an X right in the middle. The administration buildings and hangers were to the east, all occupied by outliers of Montgomery's main line. Those positions concentrated in and around the village of Bulim, and on a line to the south and north, right astride King's Road.

Monty's plan was to receive the enemy attack as it came over that airfield, a perfect killing field as he called it. He had every Vickers the division possessed in small dugouts, backed by his infantry, with the New Zealanders right behind. In effect, he had built a stone wall with the best two brigades of the British Division, and he intended to hold it, break the enemy charge across that airfield, and then send in his 6th New Zealand Brigade for his counterattack.

By the time the Japanese reached the airfield they had already been fighting for nearly 36 consecutive hours. In spite of that, both Brigades of the division sent battalions across, each vying with the other to be the first to storm the enemy position. On they came, the lead companies running right into those Vickers MGs and taking fearful losses. To the north, the first units of Lieutenant General Takuro Matsui's 5th Division were arriving on the scene, having cleared the entire northwest corner of the island around Sarimbun. They had engineers setting up a small bridge over a deep tributary to the Kranji river, but their main force was concentrated to attack that airfield.

Now Monty would face not one, but two enemy divisions, the real strength of the Japanese forces ashore. At the moment, only a portion of each division was forward to make the attack. In fact, Yamashita had retained one full regiment from his 5th Division as a reserve, and it was still in Johore Bahru near the Sultan's Palace. Yet between both units, there would still be at least 12,000 men to make this assault.

The initial casualties were so sharp that the regimental commanders were wise enough to stop the mad rush, get hold of their men and consolidate. The sun was already low, and the new plan would be to make this attack that night, with darkness providing cover for the movement over that airfield.

Both these units were "Square" divisions. They therefore had a unique structure, being composed of two brigades, which each had two regiments of three battalions. By comparison, they were facing a triangular British division, composed of three brigades containing three battalions each. The New Zealanders would make this force "Square," standing in for Monty's fourth Brigade element. That said, he would have only 54th and 55th brigades on the line to receive the attack. The 53rd had already sent one battalion north to Mandai, and then a second, the 5th Battalion, Royal Norfolk, had been sent to defend the Kranji River line and stop the work of those Japanese engineers.

As darkness fell, Montgomery finally learned what had happened up north. The Japanese had managed to get enough Type 95 light tanks over the makeshift Causeway bridge, that they had stormed the village of Kranji, and were already pushing south down the main road to Mandai. They had cleared the southern end of the Causeway, still improving their bridge, and now controlled the area known as Woodlands. In these actions, Taylor's Brigade had taken the worst of the harm. Maxwell's was still holding firm to the right, but this was largely because General Nishimura was concentrating his attack down that main road.

Realizing that he now would no longer have the services of 53rd British Brigade to oppose the attack that was surely coming soon, Monty remained stalwart. He would receive the enemy as planned, and counterattack as planned. His intention here was to hurt them so badly that they would not have sufficient strength and ammunition to carry on. To do so, he was prepared to sacrifice the entire British Division, for behind him he still had the Malay Brigade, and fortress troops, though they were not as reliable as his regulars. His strategy was well informed, for Brigadier Kinlan had sent over two staff officers to brief him before he set off to his new post. They had told him where the Japanese might land, in what strength, and what their initial objective would be. Being forewarned, he was also forearmed. This was his battle, and he was determined the night would remain his as well.

* * *

When Yamashita learned what the disgruntled Nishimura had done he was initially very angry, resolving to go and find the man at once and berate him for disobeying his orders. Yet as reports came in, he realized that he now had this strong force to the north, controlling the Causeway, Woodlands, and Kranji. Yet this force had been meant to make that crossing only after he had the enemy well engaged, and possibly retreating further south. In effect, his reserve had been prematurely committed by the steamy Nishimura, and this was going to weigh heavily on his mind.

I was wise to hold back the 11th Regiment of my 5th Division, he thought. And Nishimura still has one regiment uncommitted. That may be enough. I must break the enemy in the center, and the Imperial Guards are now in a good position to provide a strong flanking attack. But can Nishimura break through?

"What you have achieved is laudable," he said to the Guard's commander, "yet you clearly disobeyed my orders. Do so again, and I will relieve you of command."

The two men locked eyes, a contest of wills, but Nishimura knew he could not blatantly oppose his commanding officer again, and slowly nodded, saying nothing.

"Now that you have the Causeway, get all your remaining tanks across. Form them into one strong group and be ready to attack tonight down the main road. The British do not like to fight after dark.

Lead with Kita's light tanks, and Colonel Komoto should follow with the medium tanks. Your objective is here—Bukit Panjang. Once we have it, fire off a red flare signal. That will mean the main route for the British to withdraw is in our hands. At that moment, I will seek to send the whole of my strength against them, and annihilate them."

"They will turn and run, just as they have for the last two months," said Nishimura. "And once we force them to surrender, I will personally see that they suffer for their cowardice."

"First things first," said Yamashita. "Our men are tired. It is difficult to get what little supplies we have left over the strait. Your division is isolated from the others, and our artillery is running low. My plan is to make a strong attack, and if the enemy does not rout as you say, then I will send them an ultimatum, demanding their surrender. The 11th of February is drawing nigh. We have very little time, and very little ammunition. So collect your last three reserve battalions, and get them into position to cross at the Causeway and follow your tanks. Because of the favorable position your men have given us, I have decided to commit Colonel Watanabe's 11th Regiment to support your attack."

At this, Nishimura stood taller, taking a deep breath, his jaw set. This was the way it should have been all along, he thought. The Imperial Guards will lead, the others follow. He had disobeyed orders to force Yamashita to see this, and his men had fought well. Now, with these last two regiments to support them, their attack must certainly bring him the glory in battle that he so coveted. He would lead the assault, trapping the main enemy force by so doing.

"This is wise," he said. "We will not fail."

So just after sunset, Watanabe's 11th Regiment started marching through the streets of the squalid neighborhoods of Johore Bahru, intending to be in position on the other side of the straits by dawn. They were Yamashita's last reserve, and Nishimura's attack must not fail.

Am I a fool to entrust such an important mission to that man, he thought. He will certainly cluck and strut if he wins through, but I cannot consider such things now. I must break the enemy tomorrow to have any chance of forcing their surrender by the 11th. Yet when I send them my ultimatum, it will be a complete bluff. I will not really have the strength and ammunition to prosecute the battle here very much longer. So we win or lose tomorrow. After that, it is all theater.

* * *

When the attack came on the Mandai road, Taylor's 2/19th Battalion had only ten of 36 rifle squads left. The shattered companies fell back down the road, stumbling in the near pitch black darkness, and there was a tense moment when the men of the Cambridgeshire Battalion almost gunned them down. They reached the village, reporting a strong column of Japanese tanks and infantry was right behind them.

The Indian 80th AT Regiment had brought up eighteen 2-pounders, and they had worked the light guns into houses and behind low stone walls, and any other covering terrain they could find. The rifle squads of the Cambridgeshire Battalion, and those 18 guns, were now all that stood to guard that vital road. Major General Gordon Bennett was right behind them, the four squads of his HQ section, a few light AA guns and one 75mm howitzer now standing as tactical reserve.

The Japanese tanks rattled up, as it was impossible to achieve surprise on that road, and soon the firefight was joined. The Type 95 light tank had a 37mm main gun, and two 7.2mm machineguns. The medium tanks behind them had a bigger 57mm gun, and they were coming in good numbers in spite of losses sustained in the storming of Kranji against that dogged Australian battalion. The 2-pounder was, by comparison, a 40mm gun, largely obsolete by this time in the war—but so were those Japanese tanks.

"Steady boys," said Lt. Colonel Gordon Thorne. "Hold your fire now until they come up. The closer they get, the more holes we can drill into them."

In that he was completely correct, a maxim that would hold true for any similar confrontation between AT positions and armor. The QF 2-pounder could penetrate only 17mm of armor at 1500 yards, 27mm at a thousand yards, 37mm at 500 and a very respectable 49mm inside 100 yards. That was where the British opened their fire, what would be considered near point blank range. They easily 'brewed up' the lead light tanks, for even the heavier Type 97s behind them had no more than 26mm of turret armor, and 33mm frontal armor. But tanks fire back, and three 2-pounders were also hit in that wild duel, with hot tracer A.P. rounds zipping back and forth, and the hard clink of hits and exploding ordnance breaking the hush of the dark night.

Machine guns chattered, tanks burned, and then the British riflemen began to fire as the enemy brought up supporting infantry. The Japanese pressed a determined assault, but the Cambridgeshire Battalion stood firm for two violent hours of hard fighting. Nishimura realized he would not easily get through that village, so he ordered up everything he had, assembling on the road behind his tanks.

"The honor of our division goes with you!" he shouted. "Take that village! Get up that road!"

Further east, a macabre scene was taking place at Tengah airfield. The Japanese mounted a well-coordinated attack, with all their artillery firing to soften the enemy line before the harsh throaty calls of the Sergeants and officers sent their infantry forward. At that moment, Monty had all the searchlights they could salvage from the airfield turned on, and the 25-pounders fired a salvo of star shells. There, swarming over the airfield in full battalion formations, came rank after rank of veteran Japanese infantry. It was a banzai charge of enormous proportions, with fully twelve Japanese battalions involved over a three mile front that stretched from the Kranji river to a mile south of Bulim.

The officers had drawn their swords and led the assault in with the cry, "*Tenno Heika Banzai!* — Long Live the Emperor!" They swept over the airfield towards the British lines, in a dreadful rush. Sergeant Dillmore saw one of his lads in the 1st Cambridgeshire start to turn and run, but he collared the man. The unit had been positioned at an angle in Monty's defense, and now faced charges on three sides.

"None of that," said the Sergeant. "Look to your mates and look to your front. If we go, the whole line goes with us, so here we stand."

The 25-pounders got in on the action, their hot barrels depressing to fire H.E. rounds as the enemy came on with a terrible din. Someone sounded a bugle, and then behind it came the pipes played by a big Scot from 1/5th Foresters further down the line. A whistle sounded, and the British infantry actually volley fired, then it was independent action, with every man firing for all he was worth.

The Japanese attack was strong and mercilessly brave, but also reckless. It was an attempt to storm the British lines by sheer will, determination, and ferocious numbers. Up country, their enemy had broken in the face of such attacks many times, but here Montgomery had his men in good defensive positions, weary from digging them, but glad the trenches and sand bags were there now that the bullets were flying.

And they held.

Both of the two Cambridgeshire battalions stood their ground, at Mandai and on the angle at Tengah, which would now go down as a decisive moment in the annuals of British infantry battles. They held, for two hours, then three, as the skies began to lighten over the terrible scene, where it was hand to hand at the sandbagged wall, bayonets on either side flashing with the early light.

A couple miles back, Monty was on the highest ground he could find, Hill 477 overlooking Koat Hong, King's Road, and the village of Bulim. He looked at his watch, then turned to Brigadier Clifton of the 6th New Zealanders. "Gurkhas should be back on the line by now. They'll watch things here. General, have at them, if you please. Take your men in, all four battalions, and give them bloody hell."

Montgomery's defense had stood like that strong Rook in the center of the board, and now he was sending in his Knights. It was a line that might have rolled off Wellington's tongue at Waterloo. It was a "Maitland, now's your time" moment. It was the very best that New

Zealand could have sent to the defense of the Commonwealth, tall, strong young soldiers that had been hardened like twisted rope in the desert fighting against the Germans.

The Rock of the East was crawling with enemy infantry, but Montgomery was determined that it would not fall.

Part X

Bitter Dregs

> "Masters, I have to tell a tale of woe,
> A tale of folly and wasted life,
> Hope against hope, the bitter dregs of strife,
> Ending, where all things end, in death at last."
>
> — **William Morris**

Chapter 28

Thus far the twisting cords of history had seen the British holding the line. The last minute arrival of Montgomery, and his complete redisposition of the forces on the ground, had dramatically changed the complexion of the battle. With foreknowledge of the likely enemy landing zones, Monty had concentrated his best units in the key area for defense. Instead of being spread out all along the northeast coast, from the Naval Base to Chanji, he had the British 18th Division well in hand, a strong bulwark astride King's road and the village of Bulim.

The timely arrival of those carriers transferring 90 Hurricane fighters, and the salvation of the *Empress of China* had all conspired to bolster the British defense. The planes were double shifting from their new airfields in Sumatra, with 36 to 40 going out for a combat air patrol sweep in the morning, dueling in the skies with the formations of Japanese bombers escorted by Zeroes. As their fuel ran out, the survivors would head home, tipping their wings to see the relief squadrons coming in the next wave to stand their watch. Losses had been heavy, with fully a third of the planes shot down in the ceaseless duels with the enemy fighters, but their dogged presence was both a bolster to the British morale, as well as a brake on the Japanese bombing effort.

The presence of the 6th New Zealanders, and the Gurkha Battalion also weighed heavily on the scales of this battle. They were troops that never should have been there, Monty's sword behind the shield of the British Division, which he had used to good effect.

Yet on the other side of the equation, the disgruntled disposition and wounded pride of General Nishimura had also changed the complexion of the battle considerably. He was facing the Australians at Kranji, as he had historically, but in Fedorov's history he had tried to slip up the estuary of the Kranji river to get behind that position, and his attack had become a disaster. His troops had become lost in the many sloughs and minor tributaries, bogged down in the mud flats and mangroves, and then caught in a sudden conflagration when the Aussies emptied the fuel bunker at Kanji into the river and set it on fire. This time, his daring attack had come right on the Causeway, and the open ground to the east. While his casualties were heavy, the herculean effort of his engineers had saved the day when they bridged that 70-foot gap and got those first few light tanks across onto the main road.

Seeing the opportunity this now presented him, and learning of the heavy fighting then underway near Bulim, Yamashita decided to risk everything by sending his last two fresh regiments into that battle. It was a gamble that looked like it might pay off, for on the morning of February 10th, Nishimura's tanks and infantry finally stormed the position at Mandai. Only six of the eighteen 2-pounders were left as the defenders fell back to the hamlet of Yew Tee, and a company of Japanese tanks was already pushing past the retreating defenders on the main road.

To make matters worse, the Japanese engineers had bridged one segment of the Kanji river, allowing a battalion of Sugiura's 42nd Regiment to cross. Supported by the engineer battalion behind them, they slowly overcame the resistance of the 5th Royal Norfolk Battalion, which was now retreating south, along with a battery of artillery that had been positioned in that sector. Monty had counted on the natural defense of that river estuary, but now it had been compromised. In effect, while his strong defense east of Tengah was holding as planned, the Japanese attack precipitated by General Nishimura was turning his right flank.

General Bennett's own HQ staff and support squads had been caught up in the fighting at Mandai, but seeing the desperate situation collapsing, he got to a radio and made a frantic call to Montgomery. With his battle at Tengah still underway, Monty received this news with some consternation. He had already committed the New Zealanders to counterattack, and they had just driven the Japanese off his forward lines, restoring many positions where they had made inroads. Yet now the only reserve he had in hand was the Gurkha battalion, and that suited him perfectly. He sent a signal to Colonel Rana Gandar, telling him he was to take his entire battalion up the main road, establish a blocking force, and delay the Japanese advance as long as possible.

"The loss of the Causeway has buggered me," he said to Percival where they were huddled in a small farmhouse at Koat Hong right on King's Road. "The Australians are still holding up there to the east, are they not?"

"Maxwell's Brigade is standing firm. Taylor took the worst of it."

"Well then Maxwell must attack. We've got to cut off that bridge. They'll rely on it for all their supplies now. Order all the Indian troops in the Naval Base to move west along the north shore and support Maxwell."

At that moment, a low flying formation of Japanese bombers came roaring in, dropping sticks of 250 pound bombs that fell right on Koat Hong. The concussion and explosions raised havoc, overturning carts, blasting the farm houses, and smashing three staff cars parked outside Monty's position. Percival dove right under the table as part of the roof collapsed, looking up to see Monty staring down at him, still standing, hands on his hips, his red beret askew, but otherwise unharmed.

"General Percival," he said. "I don't think you'll have a very good view of the map from under that table."

Those orders were relayed by radio, and late on the afternoon of the 10th, Maxwell threw 2/29th and 2/30th Battalions right down the coastal road towards the Causeway. Behind them came 5/14 Punjab of the 11th Indian Division, which had been holding in the fortified positions at the Naval Base dubbed "HMS Terror." While none of the three battalions were up to strength, they had enough in hand to make a strong attack down that road, driving back 1/5 Imperial Guards battalion, to Nishimura's outrage. The fiery General pulled one company of tanks off the tail of his assault column, and then personally led a counterattack with all the troops in his headquarters section, and those in Colonel Komoto's HQ. Seeing the dire threat to the bridge, many batteries of artillery across the strait on the shoreline of Johore Bahru depressed their barrels and began pouring fire onto that road.

The Japanese counterattack was furious, for their soldiers knew they were fighting directly under the eyes of their senior officers. They threw themselves at the Australians with complete ferocious rage, and the timely arrival of 16 Type 97 tanks made all the difference. With little more than a handful of Boys AT rifles, the Aussies could not stop them, and they were inexorably pushed back. At one point, Nishimura drew his samurai sword and personally beheaded two men of the Punjabs who were cowering on the ground, when the tanks overran their position. After Maxwell's men made it back to their original positions, there were no more than two companies left of the two battalions that he had sent on that desperate foray.

* * *

The sun was falling, and as dusk settled on the battlefield, both sides tried to pull themselves together. The night would see no end to the bitter struggle on the road to Mandai. With Yamashita's 11th Regiment now deploying through that blighted village, the Japanese paused briefly to bring those fresh troops up and plan a pre-dawn push down the road. In the battle for Tengah airfield and Bulim, both sides fell back to regroup. Monty was forced to pull his New Zealanders off the line to re-establish a reserve, but the other two British Brigades were still in good shape, and still manning their trenches and fox holes after that long day's fight.

Yamashita received word from his 5th Division commander, Lieutenant General Takuro Matsui, that casualties were very heavy. In like manner, the 18th Division had suffered serious losses, and supplies and artillery were very low. He had gambled on breaking the enemy there with that massive attack, but it had come close to becoming *gyokusai*, a 'shattered jewel' attack that was near suicidal. It was not the first time a battlefield would see a desperate and determined charge like that, and be left with a carpet of the dead lying in clustered heaps all along the line.

At this point, Yamashita decided to play one last card, realizing his enemy must have also suffered grievous harm. He had his staff draft twenty copies of a letter to Percival, not yet realizing that he had been relieved by another man. They were placed into communications tubes and fired off with light mortars at presumed enemy HQ positions, and also delivered under cover of a white flag to the bunkers near Bulim. Montgomery got the message at 22:00 that night, reading it with a wry grin.

"I call upon you to cease this meaningless fighting and instead discuss the issue of surrender," he said aloud. "It seems we've knocked the wind out of them."

He got hold of a staffer and told him to draft a reply to send back across the lines. "We are not prepared to discuss the terms of your surrender while your troops remain on this island. Should you lay down your arms and withdraw as you came, we will then consider suitable terms, and will promise you and your men fair treatment."

When Yamashita received that reply he was dumbfounded, staring at the signature there of a man named B.L. Montgomery. His surprise soon turned to anger, and then utter frustration. Who was this man? Could it be that General Percival had been killed in action, and this was a relief officer?

It was now the eve of the 11th of February, Japan's "National Day," the equivalent of the American 4th of July. It was the day he had hoped to deliver his prize to the Emperor, and the temerity of the British reply to his demands, presuming he would be the one to surrender, now enraged him. He left the high tower of the Sultan's Palace, drove through the hovels of Johore Bahru, and right over the Causeway bridge, intending to personally direct the attack down that road with Colonel Watanabe's 11th Regiment.

"You are the last regiment not yet engaged," he told the Colonel. "Nishimura's Guards have fought hard to get this far, but now the honor falls to you. It is the eve of *Kigensetsu*, the day our Empire was founded. Tomorrow the spirit of the Emperor Jimmu will be watching every last man. You must prevail! The people of Japan are waiting to hear of your victory here. The Emperor himself is waiting. Let every man do his utmost to see that it is delivered!" The men would advance that night, pushing the weary troops of the 2nd Cambridgeshire Battalion out of the village of Yew Tee in preparation for their morning assault.

That night, the men of Kinlan's Gurhka Battalion took up positions astride the road to Mandai. Two companies of the 6/14 Punjabs came up on their right, and half a mile behind them, Montgomery was busy reorganizing the men of Brigadier Clifton's 6th New Zealand Brigade. Each of those four battalions had lost a third of their strength, and the entire brigade now amounted to eight companies.

As the sun rose on the 11th, the Japanese tanks led the way, backed up by the fresh troops of the 11th Regiment of 5th Division. They came right down the road, where 2nd Company of the Gurkhas had set up a blocking position. Such an attack had always pushed unsupported infantry aside in the past, and their scouts had identified no enemy AT gun positions, yet the Gurkhas had just a little more than Boys AT rifles with them.

The hiss of Javelin ATGM missiles came as a complete shock, smashing into the lead tanks and blasting them to pieces. Colonel Komoto's tankers had never seen such utter destruction of their vehicles, and the Japanese were momentarily stunned by the sudden, unexpected blow. Yet this was February 11th, and if the tanks could not bull their way through, the infantry would now have to do the job. They advanced, utterly fearless, moving in determined rushes past the smoldering remains of the leading tanks—and then the Gurkhas opened fire with everything they had.

Every man in every squad had the equivalent firepower of a machinegun in his assault rifle, and these were also backed up by teams with heavier machineguns and a pair of German made L123A1 Grenade Machineguns. The hail of those 40mm grenades popping off at a high rate of fire that could reach 320 rounds per minute was devastating. The Japanese would lose the equivalent of a full company, yet the close terrain and sheer momentum of their charge would carry them into the defensive line, where it was soon hand to hand combat. Now the bright flash of the Kukri knives met the Japanese bayonets, and the Gurkhas fought like demons.

Then, coming up in support, the Maori battalion surged up the road, their brave companies charging in counterattack. They fell on the scene, and the fate of Singapore was riding in the whirlwind of their attack. Neither side broke, and the fighting was fierce until the weight of those Gurkha assault rifles at close quarters literally cut the Japanese squads to pieces. They staggered back, driven on by the Maoris, and the enemy attack was finally broken. Over a third lay dead on the field, but undaunted, the remaining men of the 11th Regiment were already reorganizing for another charge.

Further west near Bulim, the 5th Division troops had fought to the point of utter exhaustion, yet were unable to take that strongpoint. The village was a burned and blackened wreck after that battle, but Yamashita's great morning attack had failed. When he got the news he buried his forehead in his clenched fists, realizing that he would not have the resources to continue the fight for very much longer. His tanks lay blasted, broken on the main road. His assault battalions were shattered. In spite of that, the Japanese morale had not broken, and his hardened veterans would still fight if he ordered them to persevere.

Yet Yamashita realized he could destroy the fighting effectiveness of his entire force if he continued to press the attack under these circumstances. The ferocity of the enemy defense on that road had been completely unexpected. They had beaten back the very best troops he could throw at them, and all supported by armor that was good for nothing against a terrible new enemy anti-tank weapon. Who were these men? Surely they were demons from hell, sent to mock and berate him for his failure to break the enemy's will to resist.

By mid-day he could see the futility of pressing on, and ordered his men to consolidate and rest for a night attack. General Nishimura came to the headquarters, his face blackened, a haggard, harried look in his eyes. The two men said nothing, but shared the same cup of tea. Theirs was the bitter dregs of fortune's cup to drain that day, and the ghost of the Emperor Jimmu sat there with them.

Chapter 29

The line held, and on the road north to Mandai, the Gurkhas advanced with the Maori Battalion, pushing the Japanese back, and leaving wrecked tanks in their wake. It was only the artillery fire that forced them to halt, then slowly fall back to British lines. Both sides were exhausted by the three days fighting, and ammunition was low, especially for the Japanese. Now Yamashita's opening bravado, firing that powerful barrage to cow the British, came back to haunt him. He was shocked when his Quartermaster, Colonel Ikatani, reported the guns had perhaps an hour or two left, and would then go silent.

The question now was what to do? He knew he could not simply withdraw, and yet his position on the island was precarious, with the bulk of his force to the west, and the British occupying the only roads that linked the Causeway sector to those troops. Thus the Imperial Guards Division would remain unsupported, and Montgomery's position standing firm at Bulim was now a major problem. He considered one more attack, the 'Broken Jewel' massed charge as before, but the casualties were already too high. If he preserved these troops, replacements would eventually bring his divisions back up to full strength. But how to explain this to Tojo and the Army General Staff? How to bear the shame of having to ask for additional support here?

An idea occurred to him, and he looked at Nishimura with dark eyes. "This is what happens when orders are not obeyed," he said accusingly.

"What do you imply by such a remark?" Nishimura set down the teacup on the small wooden lap tray, the wan light a dull gleam on the sheen of perspiration on his balding head, his dark rimmed eyeglasses almost fogged over.

"What I mean should be obvious enough," said Yamashita. "Your premature attack expended not only your division, but also forced me to commit my last reserves before the situation in the west was clarified. I had to drop everything, leave my headquarters, and drive through that pig pen of a city on the north bank just to see what a shambles you have made of this operation!"

Nishimura stood up abruptly, his knee spilling the tea tray and sending the cup falling, shattered on the cobbled stone pavement of Kranji where they were meeting. The broken glass was the end of their tryst, and the long moments of sulking and mutual consolation that the silence provided each of them. Now it was back to the old enmity, the resentment and annoyance with one another, the suspicion that each man was trying to secretly undermine the other, wishing him nothing more than ruin.

"Do not attempt to blame me for the failure of your own troops." Nishimura's statement carried the unspoken rift between them, a wedge as wide and deep as the Kranji River inlet that now prevented those divisions from establishing communications.

"My own troops?" Yamashita almost laughed, then darkened with anger. "They are *all* my own troops! Do not presume to think your precious Imperial Guards are sent here from the heavenly realms at your bidding. I command here!"

"Then you must also shoulder the blame for this failure as a man. Only a coward would try to blame another. Where is your honor?"

Yamashita's hand went to the haft of his sword, and Nishimura's to the butt of his service pistol on his hip holster, but both men froze in that moment of terrible hostility, simply glaring at one another.

"Go!" said Yamashita. "Back to the front lines! Let us see how well you lead the next attack down that road. And do not come back if you should fail this time. Die on that road, Nishimura. Die there and go to smirk with your ancestors."

Nishimura spat to one side, but did not utter the curse that came to his mind. Then he turned his back and stormed out, his footfalls hard and sharp on the stone courtyard. That night he would send a secret message to Tojo and the General Staff, blaming Yamashita for interfering with his attack, and saying it was now impossible for his division to fight under Yamashita's command. He now contemplated pulling the Guards Division back over the Causeway, and all the supporting tanks, but knew he could not do this without losing face with his own men. They had fought hard to make that crossing. It was only the failure of Yamashita's suicidal banzai charge across Tengah airfield that had so depleted his divisions that they could not support his victorious guards. This was how his message read.

Back in Tokyo, Tojo received the message with mixed feelings. On the one hand, if Yamashita failed to take Singapore, the timetable for operations against the Dutch colonies, Sumatra, and Java, would now be in jeopardy. On the other hand, he had little love for Yamashita, and was secretly pleased on one level to see him fail. It would give him just the excuse he needed to get rid of the man, for he had watched his whirlwind advance down the Malay Peninsula with some consternation. What to do?

Soon he was handed yet another communication, this time from Yamashita himself. It noted that as the navy failed to prevent the arrival of carrier borne aircraft, the 3rd Air Group had also failed to prevent timely British reinforcements. Given the condition of his divisions at the end of a long six weeks of fighting, and the present depleted state of his munitions and supplies, a siege of Singapore was not practical, nor advisable, and any further attack would have to be delayed.

The Tiger of Malaya, thought Tojo, smiling. Listen to him growl now! It was the Navy's fault, and then the fault of the Air Force. Next he will tell me it was Nishimura's fault for disobeying his orders. Yes, Tojo already knew everything that had happened. He had many eyes and ears among the staff officers in every command of the Army.

Yet given Homma's difficulties in the Philippines, he thought, Yamashita's position is not anywhere near as grave. Manila is a port we simply must have, and the enemy has retreated to the Bataan Peninsula, stubbornly refusing to surrender.

Yet Singapore is but a bauble for the Emperor to faun over. We do not need it. We already have the airfields in Malaya, and all I need to do is transfer sufficient force to crush the remaining enemy air power. Without air support, the British will find out that trying to hold on to their 'Jewel of the East' may burn their own hand. They will have to find a way to keep that entire garrison supplied, not to mention nearly half a million civilians who will need food and fresh water. What to do?

For now, I think it best to suggest Yamashita pause his attack, in honor of the 11th of February, and make one last effort to secure the enemy's surrender. If they remain adamant, then I might recall the toothless tiger and send him up to the Siberian front. In fact, I could simply turn over command of the 25th Army to Tsuji and Nishimura. That would gall the tiger, would it not?

He considered that, realizing this news now arriving from the far north would be the perfect cover for such a move. My, who would have expected the Siberians to attempt what they were now doing—and on this day, of all days, the founding of our Empire? Their ultimatum was an insult, and their attack upon our ships at sea gives me every pretext to renew operations in that sector. Now they have the temerity to actually cross the treaty line in Kamchatka, and land troops on North Karafuto Island. They think they will soon be changing its name again, to Sakhalin Island. Well, something must be done about them. The Emperor will surely ask me about all of this at our next meeting. But what to do?

Should I recall Yamashita and tell him that because of his outstanding performance, he is now given the honor of punishing the Siberians. Yes, that is how I will shine that apple before I hand it to him, but when he takes the first bite, he will know the rotten truth. He will know how I am shaming him, sending him off to the land of ice and snow in the dead of winter, and with Nishimura given command of his old army.

Yes, he thought, that is exactly what I will do.

* * *

Karpov's "Plan 7" was as audacious and daring as it was impudent. Japan had sat in the "occupied territories for 30 years, with a strong military presence on the roads leading north, as far away as Outer Mongolia. They had stopped at the narrow mountain pass that edged around lake Baikal to the major Siberian city of the east, Irkutsk. There the line was held for decades, with troops on both sides patrolling the passes, and the cold rugged shoreline of Lake Baikal.

Yet on the 11th of February, as Yamashita drank his bitter cup of tea on the Island of Singapore, the night sky was lit up with the brazen sound of artillery firing over Lake Baikal. The guns rumbled through the pre-dawn hours, falling on Japanese border stations, guard posts and lakeside patrol boat ramps built over the years. With war declared weeks ago, Karpov had taken his battlecruiser up to the icy waters of Magadan, and then seemed to vanish into silence. The Japanese paid him no mind, being busy with their great 'Southern Offensive,' until those guns opened a new front in their war, as surprising as it was unexpected.

All along that front, Siberian troops were now on the move. Swarthy Tartar and Cossack Cavalry had crossed the Amur river in many places, emerging from hidden assembly areas in the thick, impenetrable forest of the taiga. Their first mission was to reinforce the work of Partisan cadres, who had placed explosives and obstacles all along the thin steel lifeline of the Trans-Siberian rail, effectively denying its use to the enemy as a means of moving troops and supplies. Then they moved out in small battalion sized formations, sweeping like a shadowy tide into Japanese controlled Primorskiy-Amur Province. They would be scouts and marauders, using lightning quick hit and run tactics to strike at border stations, garrisons, rail depots, key bridges.

Elsewhere, two of Karpov's three divisions were on the move. The 92nd had made the long, hazardous journey from Magadan through ice floes and heavy fogs to land on the western shores of Kamchatka. The 32nd would soon make the same journey by airship to land on the northern tip of Sakhalin Island. Their intention was to establish a

Siberian military presence in both places, and then move inexorably south to reclaim the territory that had been lost to them decades ago.

The scale and scope of the attack was completely unanticipated by the Japanese. On the massive Kamchatka Peninsula, a "Treaty Line" had been drawn at the 54th parallel, but Japanese occupation stayed well south of that on the 53rd, with their main operations base at the largest town, Petropavlovsk. They had renamed the place *Joyaku Kazantochi*, the land of volcanoes. There the tall brooding cones dominated the mountainous landscape to the north of Avacha Bay, which was the best sheltered anchorage and port in the region.

The previous month, the 4th Independent Mixed Brigade had been moved from duty in the southern Kuriles to beef up the garrison there. It consisted of five battalions of infantry, with an engineer battalion that was working on improving roads in the area, and establishing a secondary airstrip well inland at Nachiki, about 130 kilometers to the west of the port. There was only one good road that wound its way through the mountains and valleys to the west, eventually reaching the tundra and marshland near Apacha and Lenino, and then continuing on to Bolsheretsk near the western coast.

Here the land was flat and open, and the coast offered several good landing sites that were now frozen solid. Trying to make the journey by sea all the way to Petropavlovsk on the east coast would not be possible. To do so, the convoy would have to pass through the real bastion of Japanese power in the region, the fortified islands of Shumushu and Paramushir just off the southern tip of the peninsula. The risk of detection was almost certain, and the risk of attack from enemy aircraft, surface ships or submarines was deemed too high to contemplate such a move.

So instead, the plan was to land just north of what is now called Ust-Bolsheretsk, and then move along that one good road east, a little over 100 miles to secure the port of Petropavlovsk. All the airfields north of the southern tip would be along that road, and once secured, Karpov would also have a port directly on the Pacific.

Karpov planned to move the entire 92nd division, but his initial assault would be made by the Special Marine Landing Group. He had also assigned three airships carrying troops of his 22nd Airmobile force, and recruited three battalions of mountain cavalry from the local Koryak natives in Kamchatka's wild north.

All that artillery near lake Baikal was meant primarily as a feint and a distraction so Karpov could get his Marines ashore, and move the transports north again to Magadan, where the 92nd infantry waited. With surprise complete, those initial landings went off without opposition. The defensive eyes of *Kirov's* radar saw no threats on the horizon, and above, a division of three airships hovered over the landing zone for additional cover.

The planners knew they would easily get those Marines ashore, and now they began to move out, soon to be followed by the 92nd Division, which was comprised of three Ski Brigades. Local partisan groups, the Koryak Cavalry and Karpov's Airmobile units would be the advance scouting forces, preparing the way for the overland troop movement. Initially, they would make good time on the flat western reaches, but at Apacha, the ground would begin to rise into the rugged mountains that ran down the spine of Kamchatka, and the going would be slower.

While Karpov could lay claim to all the turf his men now occupied, it mattered very little to the Japanese as long as they held the key eastern port at *Kazantochi*, and the big islands off that southern tip that anchored the Kuriles to the peninsula. They stood like Singapore had in Yamashita's campaign, fortified islands at the end of that long peninsula. It was there that their real power base was established.

Known as the *Kita Chishima* Fortress Region, Shumshu Island had a seaplane base, and three other airfields defended by nine fortified areas and the 73rd Brigade of the 91st Infantry Division, including three tank companies of the 11th Regiment. There were numerous bunkers at all likely invasion sites, and underground facilities well protected from bombardment or attack.

The much bigger island of Paramushir had two more airfields in the north close to Shumushu, where the channel between the two islands provided all the good naval anchorages. There was also Suribachi Airfield along the southeast coast, and the Musashi Naval Base and airfield at Karabu Zaki on the southern tip of the island. Here was the 74th Brigade of the 91st Division, with numerous fortified positions and AA installations.

The campaign had many objectives. Karpov wanted to make good on the threats he had leveled earlier, re-occupy lost ground, secure that port and anchorage at Petropavlovsk, and all those vital airfields on the peninsula. If further developed, he hoped they would be a strong lure for the Americans, outflanking any Japanese move in to the Aleutians, threatening the Kuriles, and providing bases from which US Bombers could even strike Japan.

The first convoy loomed out of the ice fog like frozen grey shadows. *Anadyr* Class icebreakers *Saratov* and *Krasin* led the way, with 500 Marines on each ship to make the first landings. Behind them came the small convoy of Siberian "Timber Ships," *Komoles*, *Sevzaples*, *Klara Cetkin*, and *Maxim Gorky*. Next came the old refrigerator ships, *Rion*, *Mironych*, *Krasny Partisan*, and *Krestyanin*. Above them hovered three airships, *Novosibirsk*, *Abakan* and *Andarva*, and *Kirov* watched over the whole flock, with a pair of destroyers riding shotgun on either side of the convoy.

Of course, none of these grandiose scenarios ever entered the minds of the Japanese. The north had been theirs for so long that it seemed an endemic part of their empire, never to be lost again. Even as this first bold move was made in the game, with Karpov's Knights leaping from Magadan to the distant forgotten reaches of Kamchatka, the Japanese still never clearly saw or believed the attack was anything more than a nuisance. They would soon learn otherwise, or as Karpov would put things, they would soon learn who they were now dealing with.

Chapter 30

When word came of the landings the Japanese did not quite know what to make of it. A small security detachment at the Lenino airfield, about 80 kilometers east of the landing operation on the coast, radioed to report it was under attack. The Lieutenant who took the report thought it was just another instance of partisan activity. The vast up country region of Kamchatka was never securely held outside of Petropavlovsk. Disgruntled partisans would occasionally raid hamlets around the new Japanese airfields under development in the west. All the Japanese usually had to do was send up a *shotai* of planes from the southern or eastern fields, and a few strafing runs would be enough to settle the matter. Then, one plane would land at the air strip to refuel, while the other two waited above for their turn.

If the outpost garrison was lucky, the pilots would bring them rice wine or saké, and sometimes a call might come in just because the garrison wanted a visit like this. But Lenino, now called Suyako by the Japanese, would never call back. Then a second message came in that raised an eyebrow. A large airship had been spotted just east of Apacha, another 45 kilometers east of Suyako, the gateway to the road east through the mountain valleys.

"Airship?" said the Lieutenant. "What kind of plane is it?"

"Not a plane, sir, a giant airship. And there is something else in the sky—a very strange aircraft. It has no wings! It is low over the road about two kilometers east."

"Then go and see what it is doing." The Lieutenant shook his head, thinking the outpost security company had more than enough saké as things stood.

Karpov's opening moves were Knight's Moves, the daring attack of his 22nd Air Mobile Battalion aboard Airship Division 3. He was posting two companies to guard the road as it wound inland, following the winding course of the Platnikova River. With those lead elements, was a most unusual aircraft spotted by the Japanese at Apacha, a KA-

40 off the deck of *Kirov* carrying Sergeant Kandemir Troyak and a pathfinder squad of Marines.

They had set down in a clearing beyond a line of trees, prompting a squad of Japanese security men to come rushing to that area to see what all the commotion was. Those troops ran right into the automatic weapons fire of Troyak's Marines, and ten minutes later, as the officer in charge fussed irritably with his jammed radio set, the door to his shed was suddenly kicked open. He turned, wide eyed, to see a stocky man in a black beret and white camo fatigues. It was Troyak, and the outpost at Apacha would never call back again either.

The weather was heavy, with a thick overcast and frigid temperatures in the mountains. This precluded any Japanese aerial reconnaissance that day, which would allow the little invasion to get a secure footing on the coast, and begin moving inland on the only road available. The odd reports eventually found their way to the desk of Brigadier Kenji Ozawa of the 4th Independent Mixed Brigade at Petropavlovsk, and he pursed his lips, thinking.

He looked at his map, his finger tracing along the main road, which ran northwest from the harbor following the Avacha River through Yelzevo to the village of Koryaki. From there, it turned slightly southwest, winding around the massif of Mount Ostraya, and finding a tree-sewn river valley that led to the site of the new airfield at Nachiki. Then it jogged northwest again until it reached the Platnikova River, where it split. One branch went north through the tiny settlement of Malki, the other went south, down through the hunting settlement of Kostogor, following the river southwest to Apacha, and then Lenino Airfield.

A third report had just come in from the guard outpost at Malki. That incident involved the troublesome local native Koryak tribesmen, and the report indicated a large group of horsemen was coming down that northern branch of the road. Was that what all this fuss was this morning? Were the Koryak out raiding for food and supplies when the hunting went bad? Yet when he learned none of the other outposts had reported in, he grew more concerned. He turned to an adjutant on his staff, still wondering what was happening.

"What unit is stationed on the main road northwest of Nachiki?"

"Sir, we have posted the 67th Machine Canon Company at Dal'niy."

"There are trucks there?"

"Six halftracks, and three motorcycle squads."

"Send them to investigate this report at Malni."

The order was radioed, though a strange static was beginning to cloud the airwaves. The unit was unhappy to have to take to their vehicles that grey morning, the cold intense in the mountain valley, and a light snow on the ground. They tramped out, and the halftracks rattled down the road. Fifteen kilometers later, they came to a clearing where it bent towards the river, and Sergeant Kimmoura knew the fork was just ahead.

* * *

Zykov heard them first, for he always had good ears in the mountains. Cold as it was, the Russians were in their element now, and moved about with lighthearted energy, glad to be on home turf again. For Sergeant Troyak, the region was very near his birthplace, which was farther north on the coast of the Chukchi Peninsula.

"What is it?" said Troyak.

"Vehicles—on the road to the north. Four…. Maybe more. It sounds like tracks."

"Tanks?"

"Possibly, but the engines sound more like trucks. Maybe halftracks."

Troyak listened, looking over his shoulder. Most of the platoon was scattered down the road, looking for positions near the bridge. He looked at Zykov. "Bring them up."

The corporal nodded, and was off at a run. Thirty yards down the road he caught the eye of Private Gomel, and spun his finger in the air three times before pointing north. That was enough to get the message flashed from one man to another, all the way back to the bridge.

The men took little time getting up to the edge of the open ground, where Troyak now stood watching the road north, hands on his hips, eyes narrowed, a stony silence about him. The noise of vehicles was very evident now, and the Sergeant slowly turned to his men, a light platoon of five squads.

"Sniper team, pick your own ground. Koronet team, left to that notch. Mortar team a hundred yards back on the fallen log. Bullpups on either side of the road with a rifle section. Leave the Autogrenade MG stowed. Move!"

The men were all wearing their arctic whites, and now they moved like ghostly shadows, rushing to positions and swinging their assault rifles off shoulders as they went. Troyak had picked out a good position himself near a stump and boulder, and now he pinched off his collar microphone. His flak jacket was also a short range radio, and he sent a brief message on a secure channel.

"Grey Wolf One to KA-40. We have contact. Standby."

"*Affirmative Grey Wolf. Contact reported. We're ready if needed. Standing by.*"

They saw the first vehicle on the road ahead, and Zykov had been right. It was actually a Type 98 Ho-Hi flack gun chassis, designed to mount a 20mm AA gun. They were few in number, but the Japanese found the tracks gave them good traction on the mountain roads, and this particular vehicle was eventually going to be posted at the new Nachiki Airfield. A second vehicle, just a standard infantry truck, came round the bend about thirty feet behind.

Troyak pinched off his collar mike again, and spoke one word. "Koronet."

* * *

Back at Brigade Headquarters the reports were now as thick as the heavy sky. Another village in the north reported enemy horsemen, and the cavalry unit at Kostogor south on the road from Troyak's position indicated they were also under attack. Yet it was the silence that weighed most heavily on General Ozawa, the silence from Lenino Airfield, from Apacha and Malki. No one at those outposts could be raised on the radio, which led him to conclude something more substantial than a tribal raid was now underway. He took the liberty of sending a message to Lt. General Fuzai Tsutsumi at 91st Division HQ, informing him of the difficulties. He was told to do what he had already decided, wait for the weather to clear and send up planes to reconnoiter the entire road.

Then the radio hut reported the security mountain cavalry detachment at Kostogor had spotted strange aircraft, and what looked like large artillery observation balloons. An alarming picture was developing, but one the General was having real difficulty comprehending. Those were isolated and difficult mountain roads. How could there be so many attacks reported in that terrain, and all at once? The notion that airships and helicopters were leap frogging assault groups forward along the road to clear it for the main body never entered his mind.

Weather or no weather, he could see a threat on the map now, and took stronger action. "Colonel Azaki!" he shouted at a staff officer. The 14th battalion at Koryaki is to move immediately to Nachiki Airfield. The regimental group at Mitsunami will then move to Koryachi and await further orders."

Halfway down the long valley road to Nachiki, the 14th Battalion would run into Troyak and his Marines. They had halted the advance of Sergeant Kimmoura's 67th Machine Canon Company, blasting his lead vehicles to oblivion and then opening up with the Bullpup MGs and two 82mm Mortars. The sergeant thought he had run into a full battalion, and ordered the vehicles at the back of his column to turn about and head back to Dal'niy. Troyak was soon joined by the local Koryak cavalry militias, and so he took to the helicopters, leaping ahead over a high mountain ridge beyond Nachiki Airfield to take up a new blocking position on the road leading northwest.

When that report came in by radio, Brigadier Ozawa stopped for a moment. "Yet there are no attacks reported at Nachiki?"

"No sir, all is quiet there."

"Then the enemy must be using these observation balloons to float over the mountain passes and put troops on the ground behind our advancing units."

He had suddenly stumbled into the realization of what was actually happening. All his initial responses had been deftly bypassed in this manner, and now his troops were out on the long road to Nachiki like a string of pearls. But what to do? He had already moved one regiment northwest to Koryaki. Should he leave it there, or order it to press on to Nachiki? If there were attacks all along that road, as far as Lenino, then something more substantial was coming at him. Of course? How else could this port be attacked? The enemy certainly could not come here by sea, and so they were coming on the one road that would take them to Petropavlovsk, to *Kazantochi*, the land of volcanoes.

He briefly considered moving that regiment down the valley road to Nachiki. I am here to protect the ports and airfields, he thought. It appears that the enemy has already taken the landing strips at Lenino. Nachiki may be indefensible. They are already behind it with these balloons! So I will defend my primary assets here.

Now he looked to find Colonel Azaki again, but the man had already run off to convey his earlier orders. Cursing, he grabbed a Sergeant. "Go find the Colonel and tell him those last orders are hereby cancelled. The regimental group will wait at Koryaki as ordered, but the 14th Independent Battalion must return there at once."

So when Troyak and his Marines opened up on that battalion, realizing they were going to have a good fight on their hands, they were surprised when the enemy quietly fell back, then started withdrawing back up the road.

"I don't think they like us," said Zykov.

"What have you been eating?" said Komilov. "They can probably smell you way up here!"

Troyak said nothing, watching the Japanese infantry pull back with good discipline and then listening as the sound of their vehicles rumbled on the road below his position. He could see immediately what was happening.

"They're pulling out," he said in a low voice. "Notify home base. Enemy consolidating at Point Bravo. Proceeding to Sorka as planned."

Point Bravo was Koryaki up ahead, where the road winding around the mountainous bulk of Gora Ostraya finally reached the river that ran through that town and down to Petropavlovsk. That was where they were going to try and make a stand, and Mount Sorka to the northwest of that position was his next objective. They were going to flank the Japanese defense before they could even get it established.

At Troyak's signal, the noisome dark shape of the KA-40 soon appeared overhead, landing in a small clearing. His squads boarded and the helo climbed into the grey sky, heading northwest towards the looming stone shadow of Mount Sorka.

Part XI

Plan 7

"*The general who wins the battle makes many calculations in his temple before the battle is fought. The general who loses makes but few calculations beforehand, and rushes blindly into combat seeking a victory that may never be his.*"

— **Sun Tzu**: *The Art of War*

Chapter 31

Hajime Sujiyama was a stolid, bullish man, Chief of the Army General Staff. The samurai sword of his ancestors hung always at his side, and those ancient warriors were often on his mind, which wandered in the ancient castle of Kokura, where the old Daimyos of the Ogasawara and Hosokawa held sway. His mind was as sharp as the blades of Miyamoto Musashi, the famous *ronin* swordsman who always fought with two weapons at one time. He had been Minister of War when the fighting first broke out in Manchuko, and Campaigned with the North China Army. So now this alarming news coming from Kamchatka and Sakhalin was most disturbing. Today he would meet with Prime Minister Hideki Tojo to discuss the formal declaration of war with Siberia, and plan Japan's response.

"The announcement will be made formally this afternoon and broadcast from Tokyo," said Tojo.

"I was afraid our business in the north was not yet concluded," said Sujiyama.

"Yes," Tojo remarked with the slight edge of sarcasm in his tone. "Your prediction in 1937 that our invasion of China would be completed in three months was quite bold, and we are still there."

"Do not taunt me," said Sujiyama. "I can still feel the sting of the Emperor's rebuke. The question now is what we must do about this situation. That attack on the *Kido Butai* was insult enough, and it will be interesting to see how Yamamoto tries to explain the loss of an aircraft carrier to a third rate power without so much as five destroyers in its navy. As for me, it is time I returned to the Kwantung Army, and settled affairs in the north."

"Do not bother yourself with that personally," said Tojo. "I have someone else in mind. What is the latest report?"

"The Siberians have landed what appears to be two divisions on the west coast of southern Kamchatka. There is only one road to speak of from that region to the Pacific port at Kazantochi, and they have moved very rapidly along it, seizing all the landing strips. Now they are at Nachiki, the new airfield we were building there in the inland valley."

"How could they move so quickly? How could these sea landings have been carried out unnoticed?"

"Quite simple—no one was looking. The navy has settled at Karamushiro Island, just off the tip of Kamchatka, and now that the ice makes operations to the north troublesome, they discontinued regular destroyer patrols."

"The navy again," said Tojo with a dismissive shake of his head.

"The ice," said Sujiyama. "That was why the Siberians waited to make this attack. They are moving with ski troops, and by airship."

"Airship? What is the air force doing about it?"

"When the weather permits, they fly, which isn't often. But those old airships are more durable than we realized. We suffer now because we have simply underestimated the cunning and resolve of our enemy."

"Outrageous," said Tojo. "What will you do about it?"

"Whatever the Emperor commands. At present, the 4th Independent Mixed Brigade is holding the area around Kazantochi. Colonel Ozawa has asked for reinforcements, but says he will hold that ground to the last man, even if we send him nothing. But now that these new landings have also taken place on Karafuto, we simply must respond. Those airfields are valuable. They cannot be taken by the enemy, as he will certainly invite the Americans to use them in time. That is the real threat here—American troops and aircraft on Siberian soil. To prevent that possibility, and re-secure our northern holdings, we must now contemplate much stronger measures. The garrisons in place on Kamchatka and Karafuto will not suffice."

"Then what do you suggest?"

"I was planning to go there myself and assemble a corps to deal with the situation. Who is this other man you speak of?"

"Our little Tiger in Malaya, General Yamashita."

"Yamashita? He has not yet completed his work at Singapore."

"Exactly. He will if I leave him there, and then he will want to come home to take his laurels. Remember, he's a troublemaker. I want him isolated from any contact with the Emperor. I had planned on re-assigning him to the northern command in any case. So now let him take this position and deal with the Siberian Front. The orders have already been given."

"Without consulting me?"

"That is what this meeting is about. Do you object?"

Sujiyama stewed for a moment, then relented. "Very well, send Yamashita."

"And what troops can we give him?"

"They will have to come from the Kwantung Army. I will speak with General Umezu. There has been some Siberian movement along the Baikal front, but we believe it is nothing more than a feint. What they seem to be most interested in are the ports and airfields in Kamchatka and Karafuto. They must never get them, and if they do, then we must certainly take them back. In the short run, we can send elements of the 73rd Brigade in the northern Kuriles. Two or three battalions can go by sea to reinforce Kazantochi, and the navy is putting together a task force to accompany them. One good battleship in the bay should be able to provide heavy artillery support. The Siberians will soon see that landing there is one thing, fighting there another."

"Be careful, General," said Tojo. "This is territory where they have lived and fought for centuries. We can expect no help from the indigenous population, such as it is. It is amazing that they have the temerity to strike us like this, but this rebellion must be put down this week."

"A moment ago you criticized me for my own predictions concerning Northern China. Now you want all of Kamchatka secured in a week? It will take two weeks just to bring in reinforcements."

"Just see that it is done. But bear in mind that the Strike South camp will not permit any troops to be taken from those already assigned to offensive operations there. Any forces you give to Yamashita must come from the Kwantung Army."

"Three divisions should be able to do the job," said Sujiyama. "I will see the orders reach the appropriate commanders." He settled into his chair, thinking.

"And when we are done with the bravado here," said Tojo, "tell me what you really think."

Sujiyama looked at him, his hand on the haft of his sword. "I think that now we must fight like Miyamoto Musashi, with two blades, and win our victories on both fronts… Or lose them. Only time and the valor of our soldiers will tell the end of that tale."

"Which front gets the long sword?"

"The south, of course, even though all our victories will come from the south in the next few months. After that, the troops will sit on their islands and wait for the Americans. But we will be fighting in the north for a very long time."

"Then we must do so as Musashi advises," said Tojo. "Does he not say that to wield the sword well, you must do so calmly, purposefully?"

"We will do so," said Sujiyama, "respecting both Buddha and the gods as we fight."

"Of course," said Tojo. "But we must not count on their help. This war will take a good deal longer than any of us first thought or realized. Now we win, then we struggle not to lose what we have taken. Considering that an enemy as weak as Siberia would dare raise its hand against us, I can only imagine what the Americans will do when they draw their swords in anger. The attack on Pearl Harbor must have enraged them. Considering the losses we took in the carrier divisions, Yamamoto will be the one to apologize to the emperor, not me. It was he who insisted on that operation."

"That sword may be dented, but it is not yet broken. Just be certain Yamamoto uses it effectively. We will need the navy to cover and support the movement of reinforcements to Karafuto and Kamchatka."

"You may make that request directly to Yamamoto." Tojo rubbed his hairless head. "For now, find General Yamashita his divisions."

* * *

Karpov had carefully chosen his initial objectives. On Kamchatka, his troops had made amazing progress along the single mountain road, finally meeting Colonel Ozawa's defense as the road reached the open lowlands rolling down to the harbor. A bitter fight ensued, with three Japanese battalions in line, standing like a stone wall holding back the mounting pressure of the Siberian advance. One by one, more Siberian units arrived, as the men of the 92nd division finally came up.

The defense had been foiled in the long run because the Siberians had been able to meet it piecemeal. The battalions of the 4th Mixed Brigade had been strung out along the road and defeated trying to secure Nachiki air field. What remained of them fell back to Koryaki, to join the rest of the brigade, which was then set upon by the full weight of all Karpov's forces, nearly two divisions strong.

Eventually, the pressure on that wall was simply too great, and the Japanese were forced back to the southeast, taking heavy casualties. The Siberians overran Mitsunami Airfield, then used it to stage further air mobile operations with their Zeppelins. These troops were air lifted east of the port to open another front there, and stretch the available defense even thinner.

By this time, the navy had been alerted to the situation, and was finally assembling forces to intervene. Elements of the 73rd Brigade were planning to move from the island of Shumushu, ready to board transports for the journey up the long, ragged coast by sea to Kazantochi. One of Japan's old heavy battleships would be selected to lead the operation, the venerable *Mutsu*.

She was the second and final ship in the *Nagato* Class, laid down in June of 1918, and commissioned two years later in May of 1920. Displacing 46,690 metric tons at deep load, she was a big ship, 100 feet longer and 10 feet wider abeam than *King George V* after her most recent refit in 1936. Old and slow, the ship could push 25 knots on a good day, but she carried a good punch, eight 16-inch guns that had been on reserve for the *Tosa* Class Battleships that became the carriers *Tosa* and *Kaga* instead.

Mutsu once had the distinction of serving as the Emperor's flagship during the naval maneuvers of 1927, but aside from that, the most notable event in her early career was a bump on the nose with her sister ship *Nagato* in a minor collision. With fighting already underway in China, and plans brewing in Japan for more conflict, *Mutsu* got a major overhaul between 1934 and 1936, all new boilers, a better torpedo bulge, more armor, a taller pagoda style mast, more secondary guns.

In August of 1941, Captain Kogure Gunji came over from the heavy cruiser *Chikuma* to take command of the battleship, and he was about to become part of a most interesting entry into Time's new ledger of events for this history. Word of the Siberian invasion of Kamchatka had rattled the Japanese, eventually reaching Yamamoto himself in Tokyo, where he was conferring with Admiral Nagumo after the Pearl Harbor operation. The two men had been planning their next moves into the South Pacific, eyeing Rabaul as the beginning of a land bridge to their vital, yet isolated stronghold at Noumea on New Caledonia. The Siberian attack was completely unanticipated, but of course the Navy was immediately expected to intervene.

Initial accounts were scattered and incomplete, with the heavy weather impeding reconnaissance operations, but it was eventually learned that the Siberians had actually pulled off an amphibious landing on the southwestern coast of the peninsula, just beyond the limit of the ice pack. It had come out of the only port that still remained ice free in that region, Magadan, and soon reports were also coming in of air lifted troops landing all along the single road that led through the mountain valleys to Kazantochi, the port on the Pacific the Russians called Petropavlovsk.

With most of the fleet already tasked with operations to the south, only units in home waters were available, and among them were the battleships *Nagato* and *Mutsu*. It was determined that *Mutsu* would form the heart of a small task force and investigate the Siberian landing, putting a quick stop to it all with those big 16-inch guns. Her new Captain's old ship, the cruiser *Chikuma*, would also join the task force, along with the destroyers *Yugumo, Kazaguno,* and *Makinami*.

Mutsu's last assignment had been the inglorious duty of towing the old Italian built armored cruiser *Nisshin*, so that *Yamato* could enjoy some target practice with her massive 18-inch guns. That ship had already been sunk once in such trials, but like a man beaten to the floor in a bar fight, it was raised and floated again only to be pounded to oblivion by *Yamato*. After that, *Mutsu* was on standby alert status at Hashirajima in the Inland Sea, and was now called to join what was known as the "Kita Joyaku Naval Group."

Captain Kogure rubbed his hands at the opportunity, finally getting a respectable wartime operation under his belt. He led *Mutsu* out to sea on the night of February 11th, while all Japan celebrated the founding of the Empire, and General Yamashita gnashed his teeth on Singapore. It was a long 1200 nautical miles to the lower Kuriles where he met the remainder of the task force coming out of Sapporo on Hokkaido at mid-day on the 14th. They would then sail together to the Musashi Naval base on the southern tip of Paramushir, escorting transports necessary for the movement of troops north to Kazantochi.

While that operation was being prepared, the task force would depart and sail north to see what was happening on the western coast of Kamchatka. They set out on the foggy night of February 17th, expecting to reach the scene of the Siberian landings sometime after dawn on the 18th. It was there that they would meet the whispered legendary beast that had reportedly hunted Admiral Nagumo's carriers after Pearl Harbor—*Mizuchi*.

Chapter 32

Kirov had left Magadan to cover the landings, and was standing off the coast in the ice free zone when Rodenko picked up the contact. Fedorov was on the bridge that morning, starting his shift very early.

"Five ships, sir," said Rodenko, "bearing almost 180 true, and about 120 kilometers out. *Tunguska* is still up over the landing zone, and they just relayed the data from their *Oko* panel. They want to know whether they should investigate."

"Investigate? No, tell them to move well inland. We'll handle the matter, and inform the Captain."

Karpov arrived minutes later, somewhat bedraggled, the circles dark under his eyes. "Five ships? Any further data."

"Sir, *Tunguska* wanted to investigate, but I advised them to stand off and move inland. I've taken the liberty of sending the KA-226 out to have a look. It should be close enough to feed us imagery in about five minutes."

"Good," said Karpov. "Yes, there is never any need for *Tunguska* to confront enemy surface ships, which is what I assume this contact to be. What else? They certainly aren't transports, or fishing boats. What is the speed of this contact?"

"Sir," said Rodenko, "18-knots steady, and presently at 112 kilometers."

"Already inside our missile range for the Moskit IIs. The ship will come to battle stations. Mister Samsonov, ready on 100mm forward deck gun, and heat up the Moskit II system."

"Aye sir," as always, Samsonov was all business.

Nikolin soon advised that they now had a telemetry feed from the KA-226, and put it up on the overhead HD panel. "What are we looking at, Mister Fedorov?" Karpov folded his arms.

"That large ship is certainly a battleship… two twin gun turrets forward, two more aft… tall pagoda mainmast, single stack, clipper bow… That rules out *Ise* or *Fuso* class, as they had more turrets, and the aft turret configuration means it cannot be *Kongo* class—the guns are too closely spaced. Captain, I believe this is *Nagato* class, either that ship or its sister ship *Mutsu*. Those are 16-inch guns, and they'll have an effective firing range of about 30,000 meters."

"Very precise, Fedorov. See what a good team we will make? You identify the targets, and I'll kill them. But I'll be diplomatic about it. Mister Nikolin, send out a warning—in the clear please—and tell those ships they are violating Siberian controlled waters, and they are to withdraw immediately or be fired upon. Use that kana code you've been fiddling with. That should impress them."

"They won't respond to that," said Fedorov.

"I'm aware of that, but the history will record that they were duly warned off."

"You're concerned about how this gets recorded in the history?"

"Why not?" Karpov smiled. "Since I am now personally re-writing the history of the Pacific War, these appearances matter. The history will record that we did not attack them without warning—not that it matters all that much. They had no qualms with the Americans, and should not expect any different treatment, but I'll give them this one chance to turn away."

* * *

Captain Kogure would certainly not take that chance, or even perceive his present danger. He had no idea that his task force had even been detected, the low rolling fog and mist reducing visibility as they approached the coast. He was back on a battleship, one he had been assigned two twice before as a younger officer, but *Mutsu* felt and looked quite different to him now. In recent years he had moved from target ship *Settsu*, to cruiser *Chikuma*, to his present command, and now he was finally getting into the war.

"Warned off?" he smiled. "By the Siberians?" His deep laugh was shared by all the officers on deck. "Do not even answer that ridiculous message. We will answer it with our guns. The ship will increase to 24 knots. Signal Captain Komura on *Chikuma* to take station ahead. The destroyers will follow our wake. There will likely be no more than transport ships ahead, and they will make for good target practice. *Mutsu's* guns could use a little work. They have been silent for too long."

It was then that the first whine of an incoming shell was heard, Karpov's warning shot across the bow with two rounds from the 100mm bow gun on *Kirov*. He had allowed the range to close to 50,000 meters, the maximum range of that weapon with extended rocket assisted shells. For the sake of decorum, he put two such rounds out, and they fell well short of *Chikuma* as the cruiser took the vanguard of the task force.

The Japanese Captain was surprised, yet he still had a wide grin on his face. He had no idea how they had been spotted, but their gunnery was certainly nothing to be concerned about. He sent lamp signals to *Chikuma* ahead—return fire—and though Captain Komura had no sighting in the heavy overcast, he nonetheless complied, firing a single salvo from a forward 8-inch gun turret. A most unusual ship, *Chikuma* was the only sister of the *Tone* class, a seaplane tender aft, and a heavy cruiser forward where she had all four of her twin 8-inch gun turrets ready for action. A sleek looking ship, with twin funnels the kissed one another in a backwards swoon, the cruiser had a prominent swept bow, and could run easily at up to 35 knots. She had been a scout ship for the Pearl Harbor attack, and was therefore available with those seaplanes to investigate the situation at Kamchatka—a situation that was now about to spin wildly out of control.

Minutes passed with no sign ahead. The watchmen strained at their posts, eyes puckered against the low clouds, waiting. Then a bell rang from the high pagoda, and the watch shouted down—aircraft ahead!

"Aircraft?" the Captain did not expect anything of the kind. He rushed out onto the weather deck, seeing what looked like a plane on fire, climbing slowly up, and visible as a dull red-yellow glow in the sky. The movement was deceptive, for the missile coming at him was just in its boost phase, now about to tip over and come roaring down, so fast that it would outrun the sound of its own engines three times over, and seem a silent arrow of death, flung at them from some wrathful God of fire above. It was a sleek 10,000 pound lance of inertial radar guided chaos, and firing at this short range it was carrying a heavy load of highly flammable fuel.

Up it went, the silent fire in the sky. Down it came, cutting the stillness, piercing the low clouds and then spearing down onto the forward deck of *Chikuma* in a massive explosion. Karpov had reprogrammed the missile to make this top down attack, and were it not for the fact that it struck one of those four 8-inch gun turrets, it might have plunged right through the thin 36mm deck armor at that point. Instead it plunged through the roof of that gun turret, only 25mm thick, and the explosion obliterated everything within, detonating ready ammo, and sending its raging solid rocket fuel fire deep into the inner shell of the barbette.

The heat was terrible, and the ammunition already on the hoists to be raised up to the guns exploded, along with all the charge bags, and then the violence of that chaos ignited the magazine itself, blowing what was left of the turret completely off the ship.

The Captain stared in utter disbelief. There had not been a sound before that hammer struck, for the missile was too far ahead of its own engine noise, and when it exploded, it drowned all that out. Yet now the Captain thought he heard a low, residual growl, as if the dragon that had belched this awful fire at them was out there somewhere in the rolling mist. For the briefest moment he thought he saw the smoky shoulders of some great beast, but it was only the heavy black smoke from the fire that was now devouring the innards of that heavy cruiser.

A secondary explosion raged out again from the stricken ship, for the close positioning of all four turrets on that forward deck meant there were four gun magazines beneath that long bow. The same thing might have happened to *Kirov* had the Japanese flung one of their massive shells up into the sky to strike her forward deck. All those tightly packed missiles, their heavy warheads and nearly 200,000 pounds of missile fuel in the weapons would have literally ripped the battlecruiser to pieces.

Gunji Kogure raised his arm as if to fend off the destruction he was witnessing, then instinct prevailed and he spun about, wide eyed, and shouted an order to turn the ship hard to port. The officer of the watch relayed the order, and the helmsman was hard on the wheel. Slowly, the heavy bow of Mutsu turned, and then, to the despair of his soul, the Captain saw two more glowing coals in the darkened sky. They rose up, side by side, like a pair of smoldering eyes, the withering regard of *Mizuchi*, the terror of the seas, come to burn and break and kill.

Mutsu would now feel the demon's wrath, a pair of the heavy Moskit II missiles, again plunging down from above like angels of death. Fiery the angels fell, bringing deep thunder in the deafening roar of their own demise. One would strike the conning section and end all thought and fear in Kogure's terrified mind, the second fell very close to the tall pagoda mainmast, the explosion shearing away the supporting legs, the fires raging, smoke broiling up and up.

Then the massive metal structure began to fall, guy wires, cables and halyards snapping, the ship's ensigns immolated, the seething wreck collapsing down. Chaos without, the rage of fire within, this was the vengeance Karpov delivered that day, and now old *Mutsu*, bereft of command, her conning section blasted and burned, continued round in that wide 30 point turn, reeling like a headless knight that had been pierced by the fiery lance of its unseen foe. Much of the conning tower structure remained completely intact, protected by heavy 365mm armor, but it was all engulfed in that fire, killing every man there, devouring the oxygen in the air like some rabid jinn.

Neither ship would sink that day, though both were so badly damaged that they were definitely mission killed insofar as this operation was concerned. The fires would rage for an hour before exhausting themselves, leaving a charred and blacken hulk of most of *Mutsu's* main superstructure, and the ship had to be steered from the emergency engineering section. The forward deck on *Chikuma* was so badly damaged that she barely made it south to Musashi Naval base on Paramushiro Island, and they were forced to ground her there to prevent the ship from going down. Both were also effectively out of the war for a good long while.

The Captains of the three destroyers trailing in the wake of the bigger ships saw what happened, but could simply not believe it, and that day, the name *Mizuchi* was branded on their souls.

* * *

Aboard *Kirov*, Karpov was literally watching the effect of those missile strikes by using the telemetry camera feeds from his KA-226. It was hovering beneath the cloud deck, an unseen speck, running dark as it watched the scene from a distance.

"Well Fedorov, what do you think of your battleships now? That top down attack profile has certainly proven to be most effective. Look at those fires!"

"Yes sir, most effective." There was no enthusiasm in Fedorov's voice, and little excitement. It was clear to Karpov that the fire of battle was not burning in his *Starpom's* heart, and he thought he was most likely still grieving the loss of Volsky.

"I realize you may take no pleasure in all of this, particularly after what happened to the Admiral."

"There are men out there burning to death in those fires," said Fedorov.

"Correct," said Karpov. "And there are men facing death and freezing cold in Soviet Russia, millions of them. There is fighting in the streets of Moscow even as we speak, and the casualties will dwarf what is happening here. There are men dying in the Atlantic, their merchant ships torpedoed, sides ripped open and sunk a thousand miles from any friendly shore. The Germans have taken half the Canary Islands, while here, the Japanese run rampant in the Pacific. Who's going to stop them? The Americans are still trying to extinguish the oil fires at Pearl Harbor. Those fuel tanks have been smoldering for weeks now, and they are in no position to mount any offensive operation yet. But we are. We are ready, and with clear and important objectives here. This is war, Fedorov, and so you had better get used to this, and the sooner you harden your soul to the necessity of taking the lives of our enemies, the better. You, of all people, know what the Japanese will do in this war, and the merciless ferocity with which they will prosecute it. Their naval officers may still slip on white uniforms and gloves, but beneath them, their hands will be stained with the blood they have already shed. Understand?"

Fedorov gave him a grim nod, though he still felt burdened with the war, with the inevitable destruction and chaos it would unharness, with the loss of every life it would consume, just like those raging fires on *Mutsu*.

"I may be a reluctant warrior in your eyes, Captain, but that is only because my conscience has not yet died here. Yes, I see the necessity of what we now do, but I don't have to like it, or embrace it. This war will be terrible, and in many ways it is only just beginning now, but one day it will be over, and I want there to be a man left alive inside me when we finish. Understand?" He handed Karpov back the same word, and the Captain gave him a thin lipped grin.

"You may think I relish all this violence, or even take pleasure in it. I assure you, I do not. I see it only as a means to an end, and that end must be achieved. It will be victory, Fedorov, victory. Only then will we restore our lost homelands, and perhaps even see the re-unification of the Soviet Union. I plan on having a great deal of influence in that. You know, they tried to kill Sergei Kirov, which does not surprise me. Tyrenkov tells me he survived, and he's out there somewhere right now, planning the defense of what remains of Russia, and the counterattack against our enemies. That is all I do here, and its end will be victory. Keep that in mind, and those fires out there will be easier to stomach. That ship was coming here to do the very same thing to us if it could. You know that as well as I do."

"You realize this isn't over yet," said Fedorov. "You have shocked them here. They will not have expected this setback any more than they expected your attack in Kamchatka. You caught them off guard, and while most of their navy was operating in the south, but now they will have to respond. We must anticipate that their next move will be equally bold, and much stronger, both by land and sea."

"Then help me get ready to face it," said Karpov. "Help us win."

Fedorov gave him another nod of his weary head. "What else can I do, Captain? The prospect of defeat is too bitter a cup to contemplate now. Yet that does not mean the taste of victory here is sweet to me just yet. It may come someday, but for now, it is a sour cup alongside the one we force our enemy to drink here, and for me, the dregs of victory are still bitter."

"Well enough," said Karpov, "but when you are done with that, you might consider offering more pertinent advice."

Fedorov thought for a moment, then turned, folding his arms. "Time to move," he said quietly. "Our amphibious landing operations are over. We have very little open sea left in the Sea of Okhotsk. When they come north, we'll be bottled up here if we don't find more sea room. Get the ship to the Pacific—now—before they have time to organize."

Karpov nodded slowly. It was sound advice, but the tone in Fedorov's voice made it more than that. His Navigator was giving him a warning.

Chapter 33

Shaken by this heavy blow, the Japanese navy was at a loss as to how to proceed, like a boxer stunned in the opening round with a heavy punch. No one really knew what had happened, but by the time the reports filtered up to command level, they began to realize that this must have been yet another rocket attack, by the same ship, and with the same dreadful weapons that had struck at the *Kido Butai*. It was only now that the true measure of the threat the Siberians represented was beginning to register in Tokyo, at General Headquarters of the Combined fleet, now aboard the battleship *Yamato* as it was heading out to sea.

Yamamoto got the news, his brow furrowed, eyes dark, and with a strange light of presentiment in them. It was as if he were seeing something in that report that was not written there in the boldly typed script. For the briefest moment, the image of a wild thing at sea came to him, a shadow of a memory, or a nightmare. He had been in the heart of a massive castle of steel—like this very ship around him—and yet he kept hearing the thunder and roar of heavy blows against those walls and towers. Then fire… awful fire and choking black smoke… the dreadful glow of the flames on the sea… and then it was gone.

It was an old memory, and something new. It was a distant recollection of a battle he had fought in his youth, near Tushima Straits, against a sea demon that had vanished without the slightest trace. And at the same time it was something impending, something very close, another great battle, and though he knew the notion was ludicrous, he could not shake the feeling that it had been fought with this very ship. Could he be merely anticipating the inevitable result of these events, the inexorable sucking gravity of this war that would pull his ship into that nightmare like a maelstrom?

He cleared his thoughts, shaking the memory from his mind. Yet it was almost as if Yamamoto could feel the presence of a dark nemesis, sense it, perceive it on some inner level, though he could not clarify any of this in his mind. The report of the fate of *Mutsu* and *Chikuma* seemed a foreshock to events that had not yet happened, darkening his mind like a threatening shadow. There was a warning in this report, something that sent his pulse rising. He had heard the legends that Nagumo shared with him, heard the name *Mizuchi* whispered by the men in the lower ranks. He could believe nothing of that, but he could feel some grim reality in this report. It was a harbinger, an omen, a herald of unseen danger ahead, not for himself, but for the navy he commanded, and for his nation.

A battleship, and a heavy cruiser.... Such a loss, and so suddenly, so unexpectedly. That it had come at the hands of the Siberians was an outrage, and now he would be forced to answer it. Now the fleet would be forced to turn about and confront this new foe, and all while the Southern Offensive was still under way, still expanding outward into the South Pacific like the shock wave from a great explosion.

He considered what to do, noting what ships would now be available. Clearly the Siberians had a powerful warship at their disposal. Such a ship had been found by the Germans at Nikolayev when they captured that great naval port in southern Ukraine, the *Sovietskaya Ukrania,* nearly complete. Could they have built another similar warship, and then sent it into the Pacific by the northern route? It was from that direction that Nagumo's carriers were first attacked....

What to do? The immediate situation for the Army on Kamchatka is now regrettable. I cannot send a convoy of the 73rd Infantry north to Kazantochi as planned, not with this enemy warship at large. It must be found and destroyed, but by the time we do so it is likely the garrison on the main peninsula will be defeated. The Army will blame the Navy, of course, for failing to prevent the landing of the enemy troops that defeated them. But that doesn't matter. All that matters now is that this enemy exists as a proven threat. The Siberians can no longer be laughed off and ignored. They must be crushed.

His mind now turned to the ships, the long steel hulls of the battleships and cruisers, the sweeping flat decks of the carriers, the mad frothing rush of the destroyers—the fleet. A task force will not do now.

I must send a much stronger battlegroup. Yet here I am, sailing south to take up command at Truk. Who can I send?

His mind ran down the list of names. Who was available? Rear Admiral Kurita… Yes, Takeo Kurita has the 7th Cruiser Division now, and he was poised to operate in the Indian Ocean. I have canceled Nagumo's carrier raid there, which will mean that Kurita will be available, a most capable man. Yet a cruiser division will certainly not suffice. We will need a real show of force this time, with strong carrier based air support, and the Army will have to transfer aircraft in as well. We will have to darken the skies over the Sea of Okhotsk, fog or no fog. The ice free zone there is very restricted in winter. If this ship retreats to Magadan, then we will have the genie in a bottle. But I will have to send a wall of steel to drive it there, just as Admiral Togo deployed the full might of our navy at Tushima, and at Oki Island…

Nagumo has already gone on ahead with 5th Carrier Division for Operation R against Rabaul. *Kaga* and *Akagi* are both in the docks for their planned refit. That leaves only *Soryu* in home waters, and *Tosa* now joins her to reconstitute Carrier Division 2. Those ships will have to provide the carrier support.

There was still a good deal of strength left in the Inland Sea. *Nagato* is there, and would most likely be eager to avenge the insult to her sister ship. *Musashi* is there, sitting like a steel fortress at Hashirajima, more a symbol of our power than anything else now. I would have to obtain the permission of the Emperor to use it, as that ship has been formally designated the Emperor's Flagship now that I have taken *Yamato* to sea. Making such a request would be awkward, to say the least, and it would have to be done in person, so *Musashi* stays where it is for now.

There are plenty of cruisers and destroyers available. I could also recall *Satsuma* and *Hiraga*, our newest fast battleships, though I hesitate to do so. Those ships were built to run with our carriers. I'll want them in the Solomons…. *Ise* and *Fuso* could be recalled, as their work in supporting landing operations has been concluded. So that will be the order. I will build a new Northern Fleet, with the nucleus being those three battleships and Carrier Division 2. Kurita can plant his flag on *Nagato* or one of the carriers if he so chooses, and he can have the pick of the litter when it comes to the cruisers and destroyers.

So… What are the strategic consequences of this opening move by the Siberians? They will likely take Kazantochi, and by so doing gain a port on the Pacific. At the moment, Magadan is their principal naval operating base and it is deep within the Sea of Okhotsk. Any line of communications by sea to Kazantochi must run right through the Kuriles, where we could easily interdict and destroy it. So the only way the enemy will be able to supply Kazantochi is with that airship fleet they possess. I must admit, those old Zeppelins have proven much more useful than they ever were in the first war. However, they create a very limited supply line to that port. So I do not anticipate a major threat from there any time soon, unless…

What about the Americans? They might be very interested in that port as a base, particularly for its airfields. They could attempt to supply that place by sea, and would have the means to do so. Look what they are already doing to support the Soviets through Murmansk. Yet they do not control the lower Aleutians, and if we move quickly to establish a strong base there, the air power could serve us well. So this means the first counter move against the Siberians will be to launch an offensive into the Aleutians. I can support that with one of the light carrier divisions, and use the newly formed Marine Amphibious Brigades.

Next we have Karafuto, Sakhalin Island. The entire northern half is presently locked in the cold embrace of sea ice. So I do not expect anything more than a token intervention by the enemy there, as nothing can come by sea. Again, his airships prove useful, but they can only lift so much—enough to disrupt the oil exploration operations underway there in the north, and that could be a problem. So we will send troops available in Hokkaido to southern Karafuto. The new rail lines we have built there will be most effective in moving them north. What happens along the Amur River further inland will be up to the Army.

Very well, resolution of the Siberian issue will be up to Kurita. I will then continue with Operation R into the Bismarck Archipelago and Solomons, and we will continue to support the next phase of the planned offensive into the Dutch holdings on Sumatra and Java. Thankfully, the navy we have built is strong enough to respond to this new challenge. Pearl Harbor has bought us time, nothing more. Soon my main worry will not be the great bear to our north, but the eagle in the east, America. That is where our war will either be won or lost....

* * *

The Siberians continued to press their relentless attack at Kazantochi, struggling now to overcome the old fortifications they themselves had built to protect that place. At one point, an entire regiment was thrown at Fort Avacha at the north end of the city, and took nearly 30% casualties under Japanese artillery, supported by some timely naval gunfire from a few destroyers that had been in the bay. The old stone ramparts were also manned by unmovable Japanese troops. Trench lines were dug in the hard cold ground, and the action took on the flavor of the battle for Port Arthur, when the Japanese infantry took that at great price in blood from the Russians. The Siberians rushed these old fortified positions, but they would simply not yield, even after successive attacks by much superior numbers.

The airships tried to stand off and use their 105mm recoilless rifles against that small naval flotilla in the bay, but the dual purpose batteries on the destroyers simply outranged those rifles, and made any approach close enough to hit the enemy a very dangerous proposition. *Abakan* was damaged and forced to withdraw, and so the presence of these few steel warships in the bay had effectively neutralized the Russian airship division's presence over the harbor.

Two battalions of artillery in the Russian 92nd Division tried to reduce the fort, but without success, so the Siberians decided to simply bypass that strongpoint, taking to the high slopes of the imposing Mount Sorka volcano, and edging east to attack the city from that direction. Unable to be everywhere in sufficient strength, the Japanese could not stop the Siberians from eventually breaking through. The tough ski troops assembled, then made massive infantry attacks that swept down the slopes of Mt. Sorka like an avalanche, pushing into the town. There they were met by stubborn groups of Japanese infantry, fighting house to house.

Had the Japanese simply held in the buildings and cellars, they could have made a mini-Stalingrad out of the battle. Yet as the defense wore thinner and thinner, the increasingly desperate situation led the Japanese Sergeants to muster what little troops they had left and launch suicidal banzai charges. With the enemy already behind them in the city, the defenders of Fort Avacha fixed bayonets and came charging into the Siberian machineguns.

In all this action, Troyak and his Marines acted as a kind of storm group. They methodically advanced on the coastal fortifications at Dolinovka, east of the port, and the Black Death combined the suppressive firepower of their assault rifles and the precision targeting and penetrating power of the Koronet ATGM to reduce key enemy strongpoints. Then the stolid Siberian infantry would mount a battalion strength assault and carry the position.

Colonel Ozawa reported the situation to 91st Division commander, and though he was prepared to die there, he was ordered to embark as many troops as possible and return to Shumushu Island to the south. Six battalions had been under his command, but no more than two battalions made it safely south. All the rest died where they stood in those last hours, leaving much of the city a blazing wreck.

When Karpov learned of the casualties his divisions had taken to secure Petropavlovsk, he grimaced, then took a long breath. "What you have said about the fighting character of the Japanese is now made clear to me," he said to Fedorov.

"Yes sir, they will be tenacious and fierce opponents. Consider what just happened. We had the element of surprise, air mobility, overland speed with our ski troops, and yet in the end it was hand to hand in the streets of Petropavlovsk."

"And that is what the place will be called again," said Karpov. "I ordered every sign of Japanese occupation eradicated. Mitsunami Airfield is now Mokhovaya again, and Uji Airfield is now Zavoko. That is the way it will remain."

"What if they counterattack?" said Fedorov. "What if they persist and move troops there by sea? Those waters won't ice over, and *Kirov* cannot be everywhere. We can't sit there watching that sea route indefinitely."

"They will have to bring at least a full division by sea to retake that harbor from us now," said Karpov. "I will have the entrance to the bay mined in 24 hours, "Yes, they could try a landing, but I do not think the Japanese will send the force required to retake this place here any time soon. We paid a high price in blood for it, but Petropavlovsk is ours, and with it, we now have de facto control of Kamchatka, whether the Japanese know it or not. Now I will have a port on the Pacific in the spring, and with *Kirov*, the means to defend it."

Fedorov nodded, seeing the strategy Karpov was slowly working to bring about. He struck in the dead of winter, yes, the Siberians were always better then. He took the one place that had to be held to lay claim to that vast peninsula, and that was all that mattered. It was his now, and in spite of fears concerning what might lay ahead, Fedorov had an inner hunch that this first small victory was going to matter a very great deal.

Kamchatka had fallen, but now the battle for Sakhalin would begin, and there the Japanese would soon come to see that desolate northern land as more vital to their security than any of the distant islands they were now seizing with their Naval Marines. Yamashita would arrive, flying directly to Khabarovsk to assess the situation and gather intelligence on what the Siberians were doing. And then the Tiger of Malaya would soon become the white, striped death of a Siberian Tiger, for Karpov's war had only just begun.

Part XII

Too Many Cooks

"Too many cooks will spoil the broth."

— Proverb

Chapter 34

With Kamchatka's principle port and city secured, Karpov's Plan 7 now shifted to Sakhalin Island. Initial objectives would be in the North, where there were considerable settlements along the coast of the Tartar Strait. The only problem was that the pack ice in February would prevent any landings there by sea, and the operation would have to be entirely entrusted to the Air Corps. The entire might of the Siberian Air Corps was amassed for this operation. Three of the five airships in Kamchatka were recalled, leaving only the cruisers *Abakan* and *Angara* there to patrol the sea approaches to Petropavlovsk. The three bigger airships joined six others, three from Irkutsk and three more coming down with Karpov from Magadan.

These nine airships could combine to lift a five battalion brigade, Karpov's veteran Air Guard units, and this force was deemed sufficient to seize the initial objectives. They wanted Okha, which offered a modest port in warmer months. Further south on the east coast, particularly between the towns of Paromay and Val, the Japanese had been surveying for oil, which led Karpov to believe Ivan Volkov had given them information on where they could find it.

Karpov and Fedorov also knew exactly where the most productive wells would be found and developed, and so this region was a big part of the strategic plan for North Sakhalin, yet it, too, could not be reached by sea in February.

"I have given some thought to using ice breakers," said Karpov.

"Far too slow," said Fedorov. "The sea ice can extend out 200 miles from Sakhalin. If they are spotted trying to plow their way towards that northern coast, the Japanese could bring down enough air power to destroy the invasion flotilla."

"I can stop them with *Kirov's* SAM umbrella."

"Possibly, but that won't prevent them from trying, and they won't give up easily. They'll take their losses, endure the shock of facing our SAMs, then simply shift more planes from Japan and try again. Do not underestimate them. Your sea transport assets are few in number, and very valuable. You caught them napping with that surprise landing on Kamchatka, and you could only do this because the waters remain ice free year round in the landing zone you choose. But now they will be on alert. You moved almost two divisions to take Kamchatka, but you don't have that kind of muscle now for Sakhalin. As you have said, everything has to go by air. Attempt to get through that ice, and you are courting disaster. Should even a few planes get through, could you afford to lose a transport, or even two or three such ships?"

"Your point is well made," said Karpov. "Given the situation as it is, we will simply have to rely on our airlift capability. So this will be an operation lifting one brigade at a time, and *Kirov* will stand off in the ice free zone in the Sea of Okhotsk, and serve for A.E.W. picket duty, and air defense. Once we establish a lodgment in the north, we can move down the coastal roads and seize the oil development region, and then Lazarev at the narrowest segment of the Tartary Strait on the west coast. My plan will then be to build up forces and supplies in the Amur region, for a planned drive down that river to Komsomolsk, Amursk and eventually Khabarovsk."

"That's a long way to go in winter."

"375 miles," said Karpov. "The Japanese are not well established in Khabarovskiy Province. There is nothing there, and the river is the only way to move in the warmer months. So this buildup will not be opposed on the ground. Once established, we'll move as we did in Kamchatka, along the frozen rivers with ski troops and sleds, and by air. Once we do take Khabarovsk, we will have cut the Trans-Siberian rail there, effectively isolating all the Japanese garrisons in Amurskaya Province along that rail line."

"They'll still have the line running from Vladivostok, through Harbin to Chita."

"True, but we will have at least isolated the entire Amur River bend with that move."

"Yes," said Fedorov. "It is a bold move, but also very risky, a little like posting a knight in the center of the board in the opening game."

"Exactly," said Karpov. "And from Khabarovsk it is then only another 400 miles to Vladivostok. So what do you think of my plan?"

"I think its virtues could also spell its downfall," said Fedorov. "You will carry off the seizure of Northern Sakhalin easily enough, and possibly secure Lazarev as an access point to the mainland. But then we will have to wait until the ice breaks to use that as a logistical port receiving supplies by sea from Magadan, and it will certainly come under regular Japanese air attack. As for the drive along the Amur River, if it can be done swiftly, while the ground and river remains frozen, then you may get your division to Khabarovsk. When the thaw comes, anything you have in the open will get bogged down. I hope you have plenty of small boats. That's miserable terrain out there, just ask Troyak."

"We'll get down river before the thaw," said Karpov confidently.

"Yes? Then what will your troops find waiting for them at Khabarovsk? That's what concerns me. The Japanese will use the rail infrastructure from Vladivostok and Harbin to move forces there. In fact, I believe Harbin will be the key to their defensive operations. It will be the center of the wheel, and from there, road and rail connections branch out to all the major towns along the Amur River. This will be a much more difficult campaign than you may realize. You could be facing several divisions when you arrive, outnumbered two or three to one. Unless you have well established river transport, your forces will have to be supplied by air. And remember, Japanese airpower will go after any river traffic, and certainly challenge your Zeppelin fleet as well. Khabarovsk is well inland. *Kirov* would have to hover right off the coast in the Tartary Strait to project any SAM defense, and even then, only S-300 missiles have the range to matter, and we have only 61 aboard."

"I have considered all that, but remember, my men lived in this region for generations. They can live off the land if need be. I have no illusions about what we will be facing, but this is the only strategic move worth the name. We will make small moves first. This winter offensive attack only aims to secure one primary sector—north

Sakhalin. That's where we play out Knight to King Bishop three. Come spring, we will see how the board looks, and plan our moves accordingly. But we must eventually take Khabarovsk. Only then can we open that file and strike south to Vladivostok. I know it will take time. I do not expect this all to happen in just a few months. In the meantime, I have already seized a port and airfields in Kamchatka, and I plan on using these to make an offer to the Americans."

"I agree that those airfields could be useful," said Fedorov, "but to a limited extent. Weather conditions in Kamchatka will prohibit large scale air operations there. The waters off Petropavlovsk are the foggiest in the world. Furthermore, the real bastion of Japanese power remains on Shumushu and Paramushir Islands. They'll move fighters there, and right astride the routes any American bombers will have to take to reach Hokkaido. So, while you have Petropavlovsk, your campaign in Kamchatka must now transition to an attack on those islands. The northern Kuriles will become some of the most strategic islands in the war. And also consider Attu Island in the Western Aleutians. The Japanese took that in June of 1942, and I have no doubt they will try to do so again."

"A lot of gloom and doom, Fedorov."

"You wanted my best assessment of the situation, and I am giving it to you. Remember, in chess we are not the only one who gets to make a move. The Japanese will have counter operations to everything we do. And now, with this campaign in the north already under way, the Pacific war looks to be an entirely different game. But this is a war, Captain, as you have pressed upon me on more than one occasion, not a chess game. Everything we do must be carefully planned, because as you have seen on Kamchatka, we pay for it in blood."

"Yes," said Karpov, smiling. "It is war, to be certain. I gave them an ultimatum, and they ignored me. So now I will give them a war on two fronts. They will now have to expend resources, men, ships, planes, supplies, that they never had to use in the history we know. The Americans will not fail to notice that. Mark my words, they will soon come to appreciate what we do here a great deal."

* * *

The Japanese would also come to appreciate it, only not in the way Karpov hoped. It would soon be clear that they intended to contest his opening war moves with the same ferocity and tenacity that they applied elsewhere. In some ways, Karpov's war was premature. His opening was playing out to an optimistic beginning, but only because his enemy had been caught off guard. Fedorov's cautious warnings would soon become apparent to the Siberians, as the Japanese now met to plan their countermoves.

The grim faced Chief of the General Staff, Hajime Sujiyama, flew to Harbin to meet and brief the man Tojo had selected to lead operations in the north, General Tomoyuki Yamashita. Unhappy with his reassignment, Yamashita stewed in Harbin for some time, thinking he had been shamed and cast off to a do nothing outpost for his failure to take Singapore. The fact that the recalcitrant General Nishimura had been given command in his place galled him, as Tojo intended.

"Do not look so glum," said Sujiyama. "Forget Singapore, it was nothing. We do not even need it to continue operations as planned in the south. It will be isolated and become nothing more than a millstone around the necks of the British. The city is swarming with refugees. They will have a million hungry mouths to feed, and our air power will eventually win the day. Yet now, these new developments in the north are most troubling. Your campaign in Malaya was a masterful affair. Believe me, it was noticed, even by the emperor."

"Yet I will never live down the shame of failing to deliver the city."

"Nonsense. The Emperor has the same mind in this matter as I have just related. In fact, he has ordered Nishimura to consolidate his position, and the air force will pound the place while supplies are moved south. Nishimura was forbidden to attack it again directly, so now he is the one sitting in the humid jungle down there with nothing to do."

"No further attack on Singapore?"

"It will fall now by the indirect approach. Our next move there is Sumatra and Java, where the enemy is hoping to retain valuable airfields to defend Singapore. Once we have taken those, the place will fall like rotten fruit. So be glad you are here! This is where the real action is now. The Siberian attack has opened a second front, and one we did not expect to have to consider in our war plans. All our resources have been thrown into the Southern Offensive, but now we must fight with two swords. So you will take command of the newly reconstituted Northern Army."

"What army? There is only one division here in Harbin, and it does nothing more here than watch the rail lines."

"And for good reason," said Sujiyama. "Those rail lines are now the life lines of the Empire. Three more divisions will be assigned to your command. First, the 8th Cedar Division will be pulled from pacification duties in Manchukuo, then the 14th Shining Division will be recalled from Qiqihar in Mongolia. I cannot think of a more distant and useless place, and so those troops will come to you. Finally, the 28th Abundant Division, is presently stationed north of Harbin for internal Manchukuo security. It is yours, along with the 10th Iron Division, which has its headquarters right here in the city."

"Four divisions?"

"Precisely. So you will have an army to command after all, General, and one almost twice the size of the force you so ably led in Malaya. The enemy has just made his next move. Those obsolete Siberian airships are now landing troops in Kita Karafuto, the far northern tip of the place they called Sakhalin Island. Do not concern yourself with that. The Navy has troops on Hokkaido that will be moved to reinforce Karafuto. But we have learned that the Siberians also plan a move up the Amur River. They plan to take Bo Li!"

That was the old Chinese name for Khabarovsk, and Yamashita raised his eyebrows as he studied the map between them. "You will, of course, stop them from doing this, and then plan their complete destruction."

"But Bo Li is nearly 400 miles from these landings in Kita Karafuto."

"Yes, but that is what they are planning. We have this from the network of spies and informants established by our friends in Orenburg. They are going to move along the Amur River. See how it runs up from the south, parallel to the coast? In Kamchatka they moved great distances by using ski troops, and those infernal balloons of theirs. We believe they plan a similar move, while the river remains frozen. But it will take them a good deal of time to build up forces to do this. Their airlift capability is known to us, and it can move no more than a single brigade. So that gives you time to plan your own moves, and we have the roads and rail lines. When your divisions arrive, begin moving troops to Bo Li. Some could move overland by road, but it would be faster to use the main rail line through Urajio, and then go north from there. We expect they will attempt to sabotage that line, but it is well guarded, so you should not incur any major delays."

"And once I am there?"

"That is up to you, General. You may wish to push a division up the Amur river to see what they are up to. Follow that river and it will eventually lead you to Kita Karafuto. Our counterattack will come from the south on that island, and then your forces can join from the Amur River axis. Nothing can be done in the warmer months. The ground is simply one bog after another."

"Yes, very difficult terrain."

"No more difficult than the jungles of Malaya," said Sujiyama. "I am sending you the God of Operations. Masanobu Tsuji served you well in Malaya, so put his mind to good use here as well. There you moved in humid jungles, but here, like ghosts in the winter snow."

"How soon should I begin?"

"Move forces to their defensive positions as soon as possible, then consolidate and build up supplies this summer, and make your plans. I have every confidence in you, and I will relate the same to the Emperor when I meet with him in Tokyo next week."

"Tojo won't like that."

"Tojo doesn't like his own shadow. Forget about him as well. Focus your mind and energy here. You are Tomoyuki Yamashita, the Tiger of Malaya, and now you are the flashing sword of the north. I will see that the Army provides you with everything you need, transport, supplies, air support. There is only a little time before the spring thaw makes any movement impossible this winter. So it is likely your opening moves will be little more than defensive. Protect Bo Li—that is your first order of business. Build up your forces there, and along the coast at Vanino-Gavan, that we now call Hakucho. Nothing much will happen for some time, but when winter comes again, you must be ready to prowl—our Siberian Tiger. So bide your time, sharpen your teeth and claws. Let the summer pass as you make ready. Then, in the winter of 1942, you have only one thing you need to concern yourself with—the destruction of our enemies."

Chapter 35

It was one of the most difficult decisions Churchill would make in the entire war, and he stared at the letter he had just received from Wavell with an almost unbelieving expression on his face. The prospect being put to him now by his Theater Commander seemed preposterous, and yet, as he read on, the cold military logic in Wavell's arguments could not be denied. Now he sat with his newly appointed Chief of the Imperial General Staff, General Alan Brooke, relieved to have him at hand now instead of Field Marshal John Dill, a man Churchill never fully appreciated, and one he quietly maneuvered out of the chair he now gave Brooke.

Given the central role he would play in planning the war, Churchill had found it necessary to take Brooke aside and confide the one great 'truth' to him that had shaken the history to its very foundation. Brooke was absolutely amazed, as any man might be upon hearing such a story, but when Churchill handed him photographs of the strange Russian ship, the General had removed his eye glasses, and leaned in very close.

The shock of knowing he was looking at men and machines from another time, the far flung future, was almost too much to take. Churchill confided he felt the same way, until the reality of what he was looking at finally banished all the arguments his mind put forth as to his own insanity. With those men, those machines, the Allies could win the war.

At one point Churchill thought he would summon the Russians to London, and keep one at his side to navigate the stormy waters ahead, but the young Russian Captain Fedorov had convinced him of the danger inherent in the knowledge of future days.

"Knowing what once happened will not necessarily bend the course of this war to follow the same path," he had told Churchill. "In fact, simply knowing the outcome of any battle could become a fatal poison in the brew. It removes the uncertainty from your thinking, and could introduce a cavalier attitude to the decision making process that might be fatal. For it was only in the dark of the night, with enemies on every side, beset with fear and that awful uncertainty, that you could truly weigh the risks, and the consequences of the choices you had to make. I could hand you a book that would lay out every battle, every misstep and lost opportunity, every advantage before you, but that would take the passion of life out of you, and without that, you would never be the same man again. Understand?"

"I suppose I do," Churchill had said. "It would be like knowing the outcome of every flirtatious proposal you might make to a lady, and whether you might win through to capture her heart, among other things. Would a man risk his pride and honor to woo a woman he knew he could have at his whim? I think not. There would be nothing at stake, and he could therefore neither feel the elation of his conquest, nor the pain of his loss should he fail. Yes, Mister Fedorov, I do understand what you are saying."

So it was that Fedorov remained very careful and cautious with the information he had on the outcome of the war, and he had also privately urged Karpov to be equally reticent. "These men may know they can win this war, but not how, not by chapter and verse. They must write this history themselves now, with the sweat of their brow, and the blood of the men they send to do battle. Besides—from everything I have seen, this entire history seems to be a house of cards. Change one thing and the whole of it could come tumbling down. We have no way of knowing which events could cause such a catastrophe. We can speculate and guess, but never know to a certainty. Tell them everything, and the weight of all that knowledge could be too difficult for them to bear."

The weight had seemed that way to Churchill, and he eventually decided he had to bring someone 'inside' on the truth of the matter, someone with dignity, authority, and the broad respect of his peers— someone like Sir Alan Brooke. He needed a foil to his own mind on the war, and Brooke would become that for him, though he would once write of Churchill: "A complete amateur of strategy, he swamps himself in detail he should never look at, and as a result fails to ever see a strategic problem in its true perspective."

The two men would have a very tempestuous relationship in the years ahead, but it was one where something would arise from their interaction to define a new truth. Like yin and yang, they would both oppose and define one another at the same time, and something sublime would result.

"Well General," said Churchill, "We have a rather delicate situation here. Wavell wants Montgomery back for his big operation in North Africa, but the man has only barely warmed the chair in the Pacific."

A veteran of the First War, Brooke specialized in the hammering work of the heavy guns in that nightmare, developing a tactic that came to be known as "the creeping barrage." His thunder was heard at the Somme, and at Vimy Ridge, and after that war he moved on to the Imperial Defense College. There he met many of the men who were now running the war, including General Montgomery, who had 3rd Division in Brooke's II Corps in France. Both men saw eye to eye. In fact, it had been Brooke who quietly put forward Montgomery's name when the decision was made to relieve Percival.

"I recommended him wholeheartedly," said Brooke, "but it will seem a bit of a snub to Percival to have Monty say 'there, I've gone and fixed your little mess, and now I'm off to my desert again.' The problem is, Monty is just enough of an old goat to say something along those lines. He can be somewhat blunt at times."

"That is the least of it," said Churchill, handing Brooke Wavell's latest communication. "After all this shuffle and bother, Wavell wants to pull out of Singapore! He's of a mind that, in spite of every effort made to hold it, the place is now indefensible with the Japanese landing on Sumatra. Outrageous!"

Brooke studied the letter for some time, with Churchill pacing about the close confines of the War Cabinet Map Room beneath the Treasury building near Whitehall. Here was a perfect case of the danger in knowing too much. Churchill had learned the truth from

Fedorov as to the actual force disparity between the Japanese troops and those under Percival. He had then dispatched his close advisor Brendon Bracken to try and convince Percival to stand fast, but he remained a weak stone in the wall there. Montgomery had been the solution, but now, in spite of that intervention, events were already conspiring to undermine that whole effort. It seemed Singapore was a rock destined to sink, and the question now was what would it take down with it when it fell?

"I know on the face of things that your reaction would seem fully justified," Brooke said at last. "Quite frankly, I must tell you I personally never believed there was much hope of saving Singapore. Montgomery did a bang up job, stopped the Japanese right in their tracks, but now that island is no more than a solid rock in the stream."

"Exactly," said Churchill. "The Rock of the East. Do you realize the political and moral capital we've put in the treasury as a result of this one small victory? Here we finally find a General who can win in a good fight, and now Wavell loses his nerve and wants to simply give it all back to the enemy! And for what? Java? We couldn't hold Gibraltar, and losing it we virtually lost the Mediterranean, at least in the public's eye, even if Admiral Cunningham still holds sway in the east. To lose Singapore will mean we've lost the Pacific, and with the war there only months old."

"It may mean that to the man on the street," said Brooke, "but to those of us lurking in the War Cabinet, we must take a wider and longer view." Brooke quietly laid Wavell's letter on the table. "Yes, I certainly never expected to see things fall apart as they have," he said. "I was of a mind to send the British 18th Division to Rangoon instead of Singapore, but Monty made good use of it, and was bull headed enough to stop the Japanese. Yet now they have gone right around him with these landings in Sumatra. They've gone after the airfields he was counting on for air cover over the island. Without them, we'll be forced back to Batavia, and with the Japanese already on Borneo, Singapore will be sitting there like a pearl in a Japanese clam. It will be completely isolated. Mister Prime Minister, the fact of the matter is this…. For the moment we hold that island on the strength of our ground troops there, and the man who led that defense. Yet to hold it further, we will need control of the air and sea around it."

"You will recall my proposal to secure a lodgment in northern Sumatra?" Churchill wagged a finger.

"Yes, I do recall it, but there was simply no suitable port. Banda Aceh was the only prospect that could be supported from Colombo. Pedang on the west coast was just too small."

"Yet we might have made a good fight there on Sumatra."

"With what sir? The Australians have just recalled their entire first Corps from North Africa, and they certainly would not hear anything about sending them to Sumatra. Would you have us divert the 70th Division from Burma to Sumatra? That would be madness. It was all we could do to get the 18th Division to Singapore, but I think all we have done is throw good money after bad. Percival lost his battle before we gave Montgomery a chance to win it for him. He lost it on the Malayan Peninsula. The fate of Singapore always rested on the assumption that we could hold Malaya for at least six months. His Operation Matador decided everything when it squandered all his strength in piecemeal defensive battles followed by chaotic retreat. By the time those troops got to Singapore, they were beaten three times and ready for another good licking. It was a miracle that Monty pulled things together, but remember, he did that with fresh British troops, including the New Zealand Brigade Wavell sent him."

"But do you seriously propose we should now simply abandon the city? It would give the Japanese the greatest harbor in the Pacific!"

Brooke smiled. "They don't need it. All they wanted there was a moral victory."

"And we denied them that, while savoring the very same dish ourselves. Singapore was about the moral fiber of this Empire, of the fighting British soldier, and of the word we gave to our friends and allies that we would hold it safe and secure."

"All well and good," said Brooke, "but to the Japanese, taking Singapore was a defensive move to shore up their right flank as they push south. They won't be using it to carry out further offensives, as the only prize west of Singapore is Burma, and they already have troops there. That's also a defensive move, and one we should strongly oppose."

"Agreed," said Churchill. "If they push us out, they'll be knocking on the door to India."

"Possibly," said Brooke. "I rather think they will have other designs in the near run. They'll take Sumatra. The Dutch can't hold out for long there, and we simply can't get sufficient reinforcements there to stop them, but we might do better on Java. That's where they will turn next. If they take Java, and the islands leading east, then things point in a very dangerous direction—Australia. That's why the Aussies are pulling their troops out of the Middle East. They'll need them at home, and on New Guinea. We've also received disturbing intelligence that the Japanese are looking over the Bismarck Sea. That would be a prelude to a move into the Solomons, and once they have control of those islands, Australia would be completely cut off. They already have the New Hebrides. When the Yanks ever do muster up to get into the war, they'll have to operate from Fiji and Samoa. Now then... we might wail over the loss of Singapore if we take Wavell's advice, but consider the loss of Australia. It isn't Java we may be trading now for Singapore, it's Australia."

That remark so darkened the air in the room that Churchill remained silent, sitting with the grim prospects of their situation for some time. "I see it as plainly as you do," he said sullenly. "Wavell's arguments certainly sting. We can't control the Malacca Strait because the Japanese are sitting on all our airfields in Malaya. The front door is closed, and the only other way in is through the back door in the Sunda Strait between Sumatra and Java."

"And to use that," said Brooke, "we'll have to hold Batavia. You can be sure the Japanese know that, and Java will be next on their list. So even if we hold Singapore, those troops will just sit there, and with dwindling supplies, and no further air cover. After we lose that, the convoys won't get through in any case. We can't cover them from Batavia, which is 550 miles from Singapore."

"Then where do we stand? When do we dig in our heels and tell the other fellow no more. I had hoped we could do that with Singapore, and now you tell me it was all for nothing."

"Not entirely," said Brooke. "We've taught them a lesson on Singapore. We've shown them they aren't invincible—they can be stopped. Yet now we must learn the hard lesson they are teaching us—that control of the sea is the essential element in all of these maneuverings. That's what we've built this Empire with—the Royal Navy. The Army can't go anywhere without them, and that is the simple fact of the matter. It comes down to sea power, and control of the air space over those seas. The Japanese have gone and knocked the Yanks off their bar stool at Pearl Harbor, and it may be a good long while before they get up off the floor. In the meantime, the Japanese Navy is the undisputed master of the Pacific, and if we're going to stop them anywhere, we'll have to pose a credible threat to their sea power."

Churchill shook his head, regretfully. "I wanted to send a pair of heavy warships to Singapore, but this Russian Captain let slip they would go down in a Japanese air attack. A hard lesson indeed, General Brooke, but we're learning it. Our battleships have taken the hard knocks of late in this dirty business off the Canary Islands. So now it's down to cruisers and aircraft carriers. We'll be forced to fight the way we should have been fighting all along—by projecting air power at sea."

"Correct," said Brooke. "Admiral Tovey knows it. I had a discussion with him when he was in London a while back. He wants to send Somerville to the Pacific, with three aircraft carriers, and he wants a new dive bomber."

"That's the way the Japanese have pulled off their parlor tricks," said Churchill.

"Indeed," said Brooke. "I noted Wavell leaned on that rather heavily. He wants to try and salvage something from our stand on Singapore—the Army we sent there to do the job. At the moment, the

Dutch are sitting with about 25,000 troops on Java, mostly native units. The Aussies have a brigade there, and there's a battalion of Yanks in the mix as well. Wavell wants to pull out of Singapore while we still can, and get those troops to Java. To do so we'll have to be quick. In another week to ten days the Dutch will be pushed right off Sumatra. The Japanese have already taken Airfield P1 near Palembang. They haven't found P2 yet, but they will in good time. The 18th Division might just slip away from Singapore if we act quickly, but just barely. Otherwise, I'm afraid those troops are as good as lost. In another two weeks we'll never be able to get them out, nor will we be able to keep them supplied."

"And the civilians?" said Churchill with a look of anguish. "That is the other side of the moral issue here. There's a million people on that island. Do we just abandon them? Do we just leave them to the mercy of the Japanese? You know what they did at Hong Kong."

"Only too well," said Brooke. "Yet it comes down to losing Singapore now, or losing it later. It's only a question of time. Mister Prime Minister, we put up the good fight, but our enemy is smarter than all that. Mark my words—they'll take Java before spring, and then hop their way east towards Australia, whether we still hold Singapore or not."

Chapter 36

"My god man," said Churchill, "you make it seem as though we haven't a shred of hope in any of this."

"Forgive me if I sound jaded." Brooke stood there with complete poise, in spite of the gloomy mood that hung over the scene. "I'm a realist. I won't stir honey into your tea here, because the day I stop telling you what I truly believe, is the day I will be of no further use to you. As to Java, yes, I have my doubts about trying to reinforce it now. Assuming the 18th Division does get to Java safely, I would make arrangements to pull it off in due course. We could use it in Burma. If nothing else, such a maneuver might buy us time. We just might slow them down enough to let the Yanks get back on their feet. You know damn well that we can't beat the Japanese in the Pacific alone. We're just hanging on by our fingernails in the west. We need the Americans, and we need Australia. That's the long view of it all; the hard view. A million souls sit there in Singapore to pay the price for the tens of millions that will fall into the darkness if we lose this war."

The ticking of a clock on the wall seemed unbearably loud as Brooke waited. Then, slowly, Churchill drew back a chair and sat down. He reached into his pocket and pulled out a cigar, lighting it with quiet, methodical movements, his eyes fixed on the flame as it began to scorch and burn the tip.

"We can do both at once," he said. "Make quiet arrangements for the withdrawal of the 18th Division and the Australian and New Zealand Brigades to Java. Mister Curtin will likely want those troops back on Australian soil, and I agree that the 18th Division would be better posted in Burma. Montgomery won't like it, but we don't have to tell him anything until the orders have been sent. Get discrete word to the Governor that he should see to the arrangement of daily convoys to move as many civilians as possible off the island. The Indian divisions and the Malaya Brigade, along with all the Fortress troops, will stand the line. We will hold Singapore as long as we possibly can, but make it seem that contingencies compel us to reinforce the Dutch, particularly with the threat that an early enemy occupation of the Malay Barrier Islands would pose to Australia."

"You realize that by dividing our forces we risk both ends of this equation," said Brooke.

"True, but I once told the Australian Prime Minister that as long as we hold Singapore, the Japanese would not dare to attack his homeland, and that should they do so, we would respond by sending a battle fleet. It was only on the assurance that Singapore would be held that the Australian government agreed to join us in North Africa and the Middle East. Those troops were a godsend. Without them we could not have held the line there. We owe them. So now we must fight, as best we can, to retain some footing from which we can restore what we have lost when stronger forces become available. In the short run, I have finally scraped together that battlefleet I promised. Somerville's job will be to project as much air cover over the area as possible, enough to cover these withdrawals and deter a Japanese invasion of Java. If need be I'll send a full squadron of Spitfires over there. This is the least we can do, and all we can do for the moment. As for Java… How long can we hold there? Will we be having this same conversation in another two weeks?"

"Everything depends on Somerville. If he can cover Batavia, deter or prevent a Japanese landing on Java, then we might have the time to get our shirts tucked in and make a stand there as we did on Singapore. In this light, I'm of a mind we should leave Montgomery in the Pacific until the question of Java is settled. I told you the Japanese never needed Singapore, except to deny it to us. What they do need, however, is Java. If we do try and hold them off, expect a fight there, and for all the other islands leading east to Timor and Darwin. As for Somerville's prospects of forestalling an invasion, I very much doubt that. He would have to take his carriers through the Sunda Strait and into the Java Sea to oppose any landing on the north coast. That would be dangerous. He'd find himself boxed in, and if the Japanese move planes to Sumatra, he'd be under their land based air power."

"And if we lose Java?" Churchill's question betrayed his uncertainty. He took a long drag on his cigar, and now his wandering eye sought out his brandy flask.

"Then we will fight them from Darwin," Brooke said flatly.

It was what happened the following day that finally put the real fear into Churchill's soul. The Japanese bombed Port Darwin. Their attack was meant to prepare the way for planned invasions into the Celebes at Kendari and Makassar, and an attack aimed at Amboina and eventually Timor. It was thought that any naval forces worth the name that might be mustered in Port Darwin could be eliminated as easily as the American Navy had been humbled at Pearl Harbor.

When Churchill got the news, Brooke's words about trading Singapore for Australia were finally riveted home. Orders went out from the Chiefs of Staff immediately:

19 Feb, 1942
TO: ABDACOM
FROM: COMBINED CHIEFS OF STAFF

In light of Japanese operations now underway against Tarakan, Samarinda and Balikpapan on Borneo, and against Menado, Baubau, Makassar and Amboina in the Celebes region, it is anticipated that further enemy operations will be directed against the Malay Barrier Islands as early as 24 Feb, 1942. It is therefore ordered that:

1. JAVA should be defended with the utmost resolution by all forces present on the island. Every day gained is of importance.

2. You have discretion to augment defense of Java with available naval forces and with U.S. aircraft now at your disposal assembling in Australia.

3. Land reinforcements to be moved from Singapore should augment defense of points in your area vital to the continuance of the struggle against Japan, namely, Java, Bali, Sumbawa, Flores and Timor. Of these, Java, Bali and Timor are to be held with the utmost tenacity,

and every provision must be made to cover and defend the Port of Darwin on the Australian mainland.

4. HQ Fortress Singapore is hereby reinstated to overall command of General Percival, and will defend in place with the following forces now assigned as permanent garrison:
- 11th Indian Division: 28th Indian Brigade, 41st Indian Brigade
- Malaya Brigade, S.S.V.F. Brigade, and all Fortress Troops.

5. Insofar as available shipping permits, every effort will be made to see to the safe transit of civilians by sea to friendly harbors.

6. HQ staff and personnel assigned to General Montgomery will be withdrawn in such a manner, at such time and to such place within or without the ABDA area as the commanding officer may decide, but its timely withdrawal, concurrent with forces listed in paragraph 7, is essential, and will be given the highest priority.

7. Forces to be assigned to Java Command are as follows:
- All brigades of the British 18th Infantry Division
- 6th New Zealand Brigade
- 22nd Australian Brigade augmented by 2/26th Battalion
- Maori Battalion and all Gurkha Battalions on Singapore
- Dalforce units selected at Commander's discretion

8. JAVA CMD forces will coordinate with Commander in Chief, Eastern Fleet, Admiral James Somerville, especially in regards to all operations requiring naval air cover by the fleet.

9. In light of paragraph 7, control of Sunda, Bali and Lombok Straits is deemed essential to permit offensive or defensive operations as may be deemed necessary and prudent by the Commander, Eastern Fleet.

10. Every effort will be made by the Army to hold major ports on Java secure, notably Batavia, Semarang, and Surabaya, so that they may serve as embarkation points for relief and supply convoys routed to Fortress Singapore. To this end, the ports of Tjilatjap and Bantu on the southern Java coast should be held secure in the event operations in the Java Sea cannot be undertaken with reasonable expectation of success.

It was all bravado, except for the reality inscribed in that last line, and like all plans and devices in the whirlwind of war, these orders and dispositions would soon be put to a severe test. A powerful force was now rising in the southwest Pacific, and nothing Churchill or Brooke would devise was going to stop it.

* * *

It was immediately clear to Percival that he was now to be offered up as the sacrificial lamb on Singapore, as the command he had so badly managed prior to Montgomery's arrival was now to be stripped of its best fighting units. His situation would have been seen as hopeless, if not for the fact that the Japanese had also made substantial withdrawals to pursue objectives in Sumatra and prepare for operations against Java and the barrier islands.

To this end, the entire 5th Division was pulled off Singapore Island, leaving only the 18th Division holding the western segments taken during their ill-fated assault. The new commander, Nishimura, was not content to see his forces divided by the marshy Kranji river, and saw no point in leaving the 18th Division in place there. He therefore gave orders that it should withdraw on the night of February 20th and move to reinforce the positions being held by his own Imperial Guards Division. In his mind, the possession of the Causeway Bridge, which his troops and engineers had fought for so gallantly, was the one essential avenue to supply any Japanese presence on the island itself.

In the short run, with his divisions badly depleted, and no ammunition for the artillery remaining beyond a few rounds for each gun, a lull fell over the battle for Singapore, with both sides digging in and doing little more than probing at the enemy lines for purposes of reconnaissance. While Montgomery and the better units still remained on the island, he worked with Percival to outline the best defensive dispositions possible given the limited forces that would remain.

The 28th Indian Brigade still held positions on the northern coast of the island, blocking the way to the old naval base. 41st Indian relieved the Australians and took up positions astride the Mandai Road. The Malay Brigade took up positions on the defensive works formerly occupied by the British 18th Division near Tengah Airfield, and also stood up one of its battalions as a local reserve at Bukit Pandang on the Mandai Road. Elements of Dalforce, their ranks now swelled by over two thousand Chinese Volunteers, were forged into a makeshift screening force that now patrolled the northwest sector that had been the scene of so much fighting earlier. The S.S.V.F. Brigade took up similar duties along the exposed northeast and east coast of the island, and Fortress Troops remained in and around the city to act as a constabulary force and impose order on an increasingly frightened population.

No matter how discrete and quiet the withdrawal was, rumors were soon flying that the British were pulling out, and the frightened disorder in the harbor swelled to a near panic, until Montgomery gave strict orders to quell the disturbances until his troops could board available shipping for the transit to Java. It was a hard and desperate thing for the people to see the very same men who had come to their rescue weeks ago now leaving them, but the stalwart effort made by the men to stop the Japanese attack had at least bought the troops the goodwill of most everyone who came into contact with them.

"Tojo has a mind to get his hands on Java," a Captain in the 53rd Brigade told them. "Now we can't have that if we want to keep the supply convoys running in here with food and such. You just stand fast while we get over there and settle the matter."

It was a very narrow escape the night of the 23rd of February. Just a few days earlier on Feb 21st, a Japanese task force centered on the light carrier *Ryujo* had covered operations to land elements of the 229th Infantry Brigade of 38th Division, which had embarked from Hong Kong. Their target had been the port and airfields near Palembang on Sumatra, where fighting was already underway with Dutch garrisons sparring with Japanese paratroopers that had landed to seize Airfield P1. Once those troops were ashore, *Ryujo* had moved into the Malacca Strait to cover further operations against Medan in northern Sumatra. This left a brief window where the British forces could make their dangerous move by sea to Java.

To cover the operation, British squadrons remaining on Sumatra at Airfield P2 flew defensive missions, and the carriers *Illustrious* and *Indomitable*, already on the scene in the Indian Ocean, were ordered to slip in towards the Sunda Strait. Somerville was still delayed aboard HMS *Formidable* and would not get there for some days. Those land based planes, augmented by the F.A.A. squadrons off the carriers, were just enough to provide air cover.

It was also fortunate that Japanese surface units were out of position to intervene or interdict the sea transit. The *Ryujo* Group was still far to the northwest with Rear Admiral Jisaburō Ozawa's Western Covering Fleet, composed of five cruisers and an equal number of destroyers. Other Japanese surface units in the region were gathering at Balikpapan, where shipping was already assembling for the planned invasion of Java. Commander Ohashi in submarine *I-56* spotted the convoy, designated SJ.3 for "Singapore-Java 3." He was able to put a torpedo into the ammo ship *Derrymore*, but could do little more that night.

The following morning Montgomery's relief force, and now the heart of his new Java Command, would arrive safely in the harbor of Batavia and begin debarking. They had left much of their heavy equipment behind, leaving as many guns in place as possible to support the Singapore defenders. Yet they found that several of their own artillery regiments had finally reached Batavia to join them, diverted there in those halcyon days just before the main battle at Singapore.

Advised on the planned British troop arrivals, the Dutch forces in and around Batavia had begun moving east by rail towards Semarang, Cirebon, and Surabaya. Montgomery would then plan to send additional troops by rail east to bolster the Dutch defense as needed.

As it happened in the history Fedorov knew, Java fell in a matter of days once the rag-tag Allied surface fleet under the Dutch Admiral Doorman was defeated in the Battle of the Java Sea. This time, that battle might be very different. The Japanese might find a much stronger Allied naval presence ready to oppose the Java landings, including two fleet carriers.

On the night of February 24th, *Illustrious* and *Indomitable* moved back out to sea, intending to wait for Somerville and the remainder of the Eastern Fleet. Though the battleship *Royal Sovereign* had come round the Cape to Colombo, the Admiral elected to assign it to the vital convoys carrying the Australian 7th Division. The British had hoped to divert them to Rangoon in an attempt to save that city, and by extension, Burma, but Australian Prime Minister Curtin would not hear of it, demanding the unit return home.

Churchill relented, but made one last attempt to salvage this veteran unit for the impending operations now gathering like a bad storm in the Java Sea.

"Your government might see the defense of Java, a prize dearly coveted by the Japanese, and one for which we have put our most important base in the Pacific at risk, as being instrumental to the defense of the Australian mainland. For if Java and the remaining barrier islands should fall, it would be no great leap of either logic or imagination to see the Japanese putting troops ashore at Port Darwin within 30 days time.

"To forestall this dreadful possibility, I have ordered the stalwart defenders of Singapore to make a hazardous journey to strengthen the Dutch position on Java, and make another gallant stand on that wall, imposing themselves between the enemy and your homeland. Might the leading elements of the 7th Division now join their brothers on Java and fight side by side with Brigadier Bennett and his heroes of Singapore? Might they now join the New Zealand Brigade, which we have released at great sacrifice from our dwindling forces in the Middle East in this grave hour? If, however, your government still insists on repatriating these troops, then, at the very least, I strongly urge you to consider debarking them at Darwin, where their presence will act as a strong deterrent to invasion there, and also place them close to Port Moresby on New Guinea, where you will unquestionably need them should we fail to stop the Japanese here and now."

They were certainly going to be needed, because the Japanese offensive continued to sweep south like an unstoppable wave, and even Montgomery was going to soon wish he was back in the relative calm of the Libyan desert.

Part XIII

Feather Light

"Loyalty and honor are heavier than a mountain, and your life is lighter than a feather."

— **Samurai Code**

Chapter 37

It was an argument that John Curtin found difficult to dismiss. The movement of the British 18th Division from Singapore was certainly audacious and risky, and the fact that the 22nd Australian Brigade and 6th New Zealanders were also included in that withdrawal was difficult to overlook. Yet Curtin still had grave reservations. If Timor were to be taken by the enemy, Japanese air and naval units operating in those waters would sever sea lane communications between Darwin and Java, isolating the latter. Curtin therefore cabled Churchill:

"Deployment of our 1st Expeditionary Corps to Java is seen as a risky proposition, for it demands that all the barrier islands between Batavia and Timor be held as well. Enemy occupation of Timor, or any of the other islands, would effectively cut off our forces in Java, and make the prospect of their safe withdrawal to Australia a less than encouraging proposition. Notwithstanding the value of resources in Java itself to the enemy, it is the considered opinion of this government that any 'last stand' to be made in this theater would best be fought in Australia itself, for only here will there be found a base of sufficient strength to build up forces arriving from the United States, and plan the inevitable counterattack against Japan.

"To therefore risk our most capable and combat effective divisions on Java would seem to be unsound strategy. We would rather suggest that every available unit in theater should be moved to Australian soil as quickly as possible. To that end, we now find it necessary to insist the 7th Division return home, followed by the 6th Division, and request the immediate withdrawal of the 9th Australian Division presently operating in Libya as well. We will, however, strongly consider debarking this division at Port Darwin as you have suggested."

In trying to hold one cat by the tail by tussling for the 7th Division, Churchill was now about to see two others slip out the back door. It was all a clear case of supposed allies unable to come to a common view of the purpose before them. Upon receipt of his orders, Wavell had looked the situation over and come up with a grand plan employing not only those forces he was receiving from Singapore, but both the 6th and 7th Australian Divisions as well. One would be sent to hold southern Sumatra and keep open the left flank of the vital Sunda Strait that led to Batavia, and the other would go to central Java. While he was floating this grandiose idea past the Australians, Churchill had been wrangling to get the 7th Division to Burma, and Curtin was dead set on clearing the board of all his pieces and then setting up a new game on the home soil of Australia.

They were all like blind men about the elephant, each with a different view of how this massive, unwieldy animal should look. Yet it was not Churchill, nor Wavell, nor Curtin who would decide the matter. It was not even Brooke in his new post as Chief of the Imperial General Staff. Weeks ago, a Sergeant was managing the loadout of the 7th Australian Division in the Suez Canal. His name was Bill Thornton, and he was a stickler Stevedore with an eye for detail, and a short temper when anything that mattered to him was botched or overlooked.

Sergeant Thornton was supervising the embarkation of the Australian 7th Division, flipping through a clipboard of unit registries, cargo manifests and other information relating to the movement. It was his job to get the troops loaded on the troop ships, the guns and heavy equipment loaded on the cargo ships, and it was a fine art that was called "tactical loading." In a nutshell, it aimed to group ships with guns and equipment belonging to the proper brigades and battalions in the same convoy. If this was not done correctly, the troops would arrive without their equipment, and it could then take weeks for the division to sort itself out.

The interesting thing about Wild Bill Thornton, as he was called on the docks at Suez, was that he was not supposed to be there. He was to have been down with a bad case of dysentery, laid up for nearly a month, but in this retelling of events, the malady had not struck him, and he was fit and on the job when the 7th Division got orders to move.

Four separate convoys would end up moving the troops, some composed of just a few ships. The first of these was just a single ship, the *Orcades*, which had pulled into the harbor at Batavia in spite of an order from the homeland advising it not to disembark there.

Once *Orcades* arrived, Wavell wanted to unload the AA guns and troops all neatly mated up and sent off by Sergeant Thornton, so that they could "protect the aerodromes" on Java. The Australians advised him that once disbursed on Java, it would seem impossible to ever safely withdraw the unit. It was a bit like quibbling over the movement of a pawn in the early stages of the game. Once pushed forward, the Australians argued it could never take a backward step, and they feared it would soon be lost in the fray.

Behind *Orcades*, three other small convoys were strung out between Bombay and Colombo. These "flights," as they were called, were composed of larger troopships coming from the Suez that would first offload the men at Bombay, and then re-load them onto smaller ships for the final leg of their journey to Colombo and points further east. These were the heavy pieces in the division, carrying the 25th, 21st, and 18th brigades in that order.

Yet this was a chess game where there were two players on the same side vying for control of the Knights and Bishops. Churchill actually gave orders for the lead flight to divert north to Rangoon, only to find Curtin countermanding those orders and sticking to his guns that the troops should come home. One argument he would make was that the units had not been "tactically loaded," and if the division went to Burma or Java it would still not be able to organize for operations until all the other flights arrived and all the equipment could be sorted out. In Curtin's mind, the final destination of the first flight was going to determine where all the others would have to end up, and so his hand was heavy on the mane of that Knight's horse, and he tugged the reins firmly to lead it east to Australia.

This time, however, Curtain's argument could not be made, at least to Churchill. Sergeant Bill Thornton had seen to all of that in Suez, and the flights were all tactically loaded. In what would now become a perfect illustration of the maxim that amateurs talk strategy while the experts talk logistics, Thornton's intervention had swept away Curtain's arguments before they could matter. His methodical mind for logistics had seen the ships off in proper order, with all equipment correctly assigned to each brigade flight. Because of this, each flight was now capable of landing at any friendly port, and of functioning as a fully effective combat unit the day it arrived.

Yet Curtain did not know that, and assumed the hasty withdrawal from Suez would have seen the division embarked willy nilly, and scattered all over the seven seas. He had a subordinate issue a cable that *Orcades* should not debark at Batavia, and instead return home, and that all other flights should follow this same course.

At this point, another methodical man came on the scene at the quay in Batavia, demanding to know why the *Orcades* was sitting there idling about when it might be unloaded in a matter of hours. His name was General Bernard Law Montgomery, fresh off the boat himself and rubbing his hands together as he contemplated his new command and the defense of Java.

"Good show," he said when he learned this ship had the leading elements of the Australian 7th Division. 2/3rd MG Battalion under Lieutenant Colonel Blackburn and 2/2nd Pioneer Battalion under Lieutenant Colonel Williams would be a most welcome addition to the forces now building up on Java. He was lucky the ship was even there, for in the history Fedorov knew, it had been diverted to Oosthaven on the southern tip of Sumatra, where its units would act on orders to form a provisional brigade and advance north on Palembang and the vital airfields then under threat from the Japanese.

Montgomery knew the men of the 7th Division, for this was a unit he had in his corps in North Africa, and he also knew its fighting merit well. With it, and the troops he was already sorting out from Singapore, he had every confidence that he would hold Java secure.

"See here," he said, collaring the dock master at Batavia. "Get that ship unloaded at once. What is all this dawdling?"

"But sir," the man protested, "we're still waiting for authorization on that one. It's not yet on my clipboard."

"Damn your clipboard!" Monty fumed. "Get the men to work on it this very instant. I am your authorization, and I won't hear of any further mucking about. The Japanese will be on our backs in a hot minute, and those troops will do us no good on those ships. What if the Japanese bomb this port? They'll be sitting ducks. Now get it done!"

Faced with the wrath of a full General, and with Montgomery's unflinching will applied to the task, *Orcades* was summarily unloaded—the very day that the Japanese bombed Port Darwin. Curtin and the Australian War Cabinet were all caught up in the news, and the word sent back concerning the fate of *Orcades* never got through the chaos of that day.

Even Wavell had not been informed that the *Orcades* had debarked, and that the other flights carrying 7th Division had all altered course to Batavia. Australian officers on the scene came in to make a formal protest to Montgomery, but left that meeting knowing the meaning of yet another well-turned line in the annuals of history—*'ours is not to reason why, ours is but to do or die.'*

In effect, the efficiency of Sergeant William Thornton, and the meddling intransigence of Montgomery, had effectively taken hold of the Australian 7th Division by the nose. Even while Curtin and Churchill exchanged long cables laying out arguments and counter arguments as to why the 7th Division should or should not go to Burma, it was steadily moving to Batavia, and then one more unaccountable fact would determine its destination point once and for all—fuel.

It was going to come down to the level of fuel oil remaining in the ships after their long Journey from Suez. All the strategy and high level wrangling that had pulled in heads of state as far as Washington DC when Churchill appealed to Roosevelt to pressure the Australians, would come to nothing. Strategy was now the servant of a fuel hose. Once diverted in that odd meeting of Thornton's mindfulness and Montgomery's iron will, the flights of the 7th Division could not easily turn about to other ports. They needed more fuel to reach Australia, and Batavia was now the best place to find it. The only other place they could land would be Colombo.

By the time this was all realized by the higher ups in both governments, the 25th Brigade was nearing the Sunda Strait, and the Japanese were hastily preparing to launch a series of blows that were intended to deliver the real prize in this region, the resource rich island of Java.

* * *

In sharp contrast to the divided and sometimes chaotic dispositions of the Allies, the Japanese war machine continued to move with a single minded purpose, and ruthless efficiency. The forces they had arrayed to strike the barrier islands would form nearly three full divisions, a force the size of the army that had conquered Malaya. A full regiment of the 38th Division was already on Sumatra, forcing scattered British and Dutch units there to flee south to Oosthaven and get aboard any ship available in the harbor to make good their escape to Java. Among them was a small detachment of light tanks, the British 3rd Hussars, and it would soon employ the services of the *Orcades* to make the trip over to Batavia.

For the attack on Java, the entire 2nd Infantry Division would form the Western pincer aimed at Batavia, and it would be reinforced with a fourth regiment, the 230th 'Shoji Detachment' from 38th Division. This force was covered by the light carrier *Ryujo* returning from the Malacca Strait, light cruisers *Natori, Yura,* and *Sendai,* along with three destroyer divisions, (12 ships), and mine sweepers. Beyond this, the entire 7th Heavy Cruiser Squadron was present with *Kumano, Mikuma, Mogami,* and *Suzuya.*

The Eastern Task force would bring the entire 48th Division to attack central Java west of Surabaya, again augmented by a fourth regiment, the 229th Regiment of 38th Division. It would be covered by light cruisers *Naga, Kinu,* and *Jintsu,* another dozen destroyers, and the 5th Heavy Cruiser Division with *Haguro, Nachi, Ashigara,* and *Myoko.*

Yet that was not all. The Japanese were leaving nothing to chance here, and after its successful covering for Operation R at Rabaul, 5th Carrier Division sailed under Admiral Nagumo to support the attack on the barrier islands. This would bring the new fleet carriers *Zuikaku* and *Shokaku* into the Arafura Sea, escorted by battleships *Kirishima, Kongo* and *Haruna.* Another three heavy cruisers led the way, *Atago, Maya* and *Takao,* and the force was screened by light cruiser *Abukuma* with another ten destroyers.

All told, the Japanese were sending three carriers, three battleships, eleven heavy cruisers, seven light cruisers, 34 destroyers, four minesweepers and a number of auxiliaries. It was an overwhelming naval presence, and the reason why the Japanese advance had been unchecked up until that moment. It would also be backed up by no fewer than 420 aircraft based on land and sea. When it came to planning and execution, there was no quibbling, no equivocation, no misread orders at cross purposes, and nothing more than a skillful concentration of force and will that had produced one victory after another.

Against this irresistible force, the British would throw the best they had available, Admiral James Somerville with three of their new fleet aircraft carriers, cruisers *Exeter, Cornwall, Emerald* and *Enterprise,* with destroyers *Jupiter, Electra* and *Encounter.* The battleship *Royal Sovereign* had been joined by *Ramillies,* but those two ships would remain on duty as convoy escorts.

Soon the tide would break upon the distant shoreline of the barrier islands, and the last line of defense shielding Australia from possible attack. There, on the largest island rampart of Java, Bernard Montgomery, pleased to take the moniker of 'Rock of the East' upon himself, would hastily organize his defense. He had stopped Rommel at Tobruk, just barely, and then stopped Yamashita on Singapore. Now it was his to hold or lose this last bastion of Allied strength in the Pacific.

The Japanese plan was straightforward and strategically sound. Even as Prime Minister Curtin had argued his homeland was the only suitable base of supply that could host, sustain and build up a credible war fighting machine against Japan, the Japanese also saw Australia as the one place the Allies could use to mount a counteroffensive. Port Darwin was the closest location where sufficient port and airfield capacity permitted this, and the daring bombing raid that struck there was the prelude to operations now underway.

The decision had been made to sever the lines of communication between Port Darwin and Java, which would mean the Allies would then have to rely on the much more distant port of Perth for logistical support of the island. It was 1,750 miles from Perth to Java, but the route to Darwin was 400 miles shorter, and it was also much closer to resources in eastern Australia. The Japanese had two objectives in mind, both considered valuable for one reason only—their airfields.

The first was Bali, hugging Java's easternmost coast, and with a good airfield at Denpasar. The second was the large island of Timor, with good operational fields at both Dili and Kupang. Once taken, these islands would effectively cut off all forces in the archipelago between them, allowing the Japanese to occupy them at their leisure. These operations were principally intended to secure the left flank of the planned invasion of Java, and they would begin with a scrappy, if chaotic naval duel off Bali on the pitch black of a rainy tropical night.

Chapter 38

Badung Strait – 25 Feb, 1942

The airfield at Kendari on the southeast coast of the Celebes was the largest and most modern base in the region, placing Japanese aircraft in good positions to operate over Java. It had but one liability, that being frequent and persistent fog and rain. To assure uninterrupted air support for "Operation J," the Japanese therefore decided to invade and occupy Bali for its small but useful airfield at Denpasar. They would do so about a week later than these events transpired in the old history, but the outcome would be remarkably true to those events.

For this mission, a single battalion of the 48th division, the 3rd Battalion of 1st Formosa Regiment, was designated the Kanemura Detachment. It was hoped that this small force could slip in quietly undetected, but it was soon spotted and word was flashed to the local naval commander on the scene.

Rear Admiral Karel Doorman was determined to put his patchwork fleet to good use that day. Familiar with the Dutch East Indies from his youth when he served aboard survey vessels mapping the waters there, he eventually returned after the Great War and an abortive stint as a pilot. So it was off to the navy, where he was posted at Batavia, eventually working his way up to command the cruiser squadron composed of *Sumatra* and *Java*. Today he was aboard *De Ruyter*, a light cruiser of about 6,600 tons, with seven 5.9-inch guns and ten 40mm Bofors.

The first sign of a Japanese invasion fleet had been spotted in the Java Sea, but after his abortive attempt to impede the Japanese invasion of Sumatra a few days earlier, his little fleet was now divided into two widely dispersed groups. He had taken the light cruisers *Java* and his flagship *De Ruyter* down through the Sunda Strait to the relative safety of the port at Tjilatjap. That was where he was now, along with destroyers *Piet Hein*, and two American DDs, the *John D. Ford* and

Pope. The Admiral was hoping to have better luck when he got the news that an operation was now underway against Bali, and decided to launch a two pronged attack.

He would lead his small task force out from Tjilatjap, along the southern coast of Java, and strike through the enemy landing site like an arrow. At the same time, the remainder of his forces at Surabaya on the north coast, would sortie with RNN light cruiser *Tromp*, and USN destroyers *Stewart*, *Parrott*, *John D. Edwards* and *Pillsbury*. If he was able to drive the Japanese off with his own group, they would then run right into this second force coming into the Badung Strait east of Bali from the north.

Admiral James Somerville had not yet arrived on HMS *Formidable*, diverted by the hunt for a pair of German raiders near the Cape Verde Islands. This left the carriers *Illustrious* and *Indomitable* as the nucleus of the Eastern Fleet he was to command, now under the capable hands of another rising star in the fleet, Captain and Lord Louis Francis Albert Victor Nicholas Mountbatten. Men of his ilk tended to stack up names like that, and medals along with admission to select orders and societies to go with their titles.

The squadron had been well out in the Indian Ocean to conceal their presence from the Japanese, lingering in low rolling fog and clouds. As soon as they received word from Doorman that he had detected the Japanese fleet and was ready to sortie into the Java Sea, Mountbatten turned northeast running towards the Sunda Strait on the southern tip of Sumatra. Unfortunately, Doorman received word that the British fleet would not arrive in time to support him, and so he undertook to engage the enemy with this daring pincer attack.

He would be opposed that day by four Japanese destroyers of the 8th DD Division, *Asashio*, *Oshio*, *Arashio* and *Michishio*, escorting the Kanemura Detachment aboard two troop transports, *Sasago Maru* and *Sagami Maru*. Doorman would be late to the party, and the Japanese landing would already be underway when his southern pincer approached through the low clouds threatening rain, a little before midnight on February 25th. Cruiser *Java* led the way, followed by

Doorman in his flagship and the three destroyers. They caught the Japanese still lingering near the sandy coast of Sanur at 22:20.

Doorman was squinting through his field glasses, frustrated by the darkness and looming presence of the island of Bali. Then he heard the cruiser *Java* open fire ahead, and the entire scene was soon illuminated when the Japanese fired off star shells to see what they were up against. A confused action resulted, with both sides opening up in a high speed dual that came to nothing. Strangely, Doorman decided to barrel right through the strait heading north where he expected to find his second task force.

The Japanese, however, turned away to the south, where they found the three allied destroyers that had been about 5500 yards behind Doorman's cruisers. Captain Jan Chompff on the *Piet Hein* saw them coming, got rattled, and executed a sharp turn to come around to the south, firing his deck guns and launching torpedoes as he did so. It was then that an unaccountable thing happened. A crewman on the bridge of that destroyer lost his footing in that turn and fell onto a button that controlled the 'Make Smoke' command. Thick smoke poured from the funnels, and completely obscured the scene, frustrating the gunners on the American destroyers behind *Piet Hein*. Putting on speed to try and break through the smoke, the US destroyers emerged just as the Japanese returned torpedo fire against the Dutch DD.

They were firing the dread Long Lance, and its fabled accuracy, range, and power would not fail the Japanese that night. *Piet Hein* was struck a fatal blow, and peppered by accurate naval gunfire as she rolled to one side. The two remaining American DDs swapped gunfire with the *Asashio* in a brief five-minute duel before Captain Jacob Cooper on the *Ford* began to also make smoke. They had already fired off their port side torpedoes, hoping to hit the transports, but failing to do so. So now Cooper came about in an attempt to get his starboard tubes into play, and this brought him right across the bow of the Destroyer *Oshio*, and into heavy gunfire.

Destroyer *Pope* fired off five torpedoes, all missing wildly in that action, and Ford swung around behind her, still making smoke. In spite of that, the sea around them was erupting with shell splashes that were close enough to wet the decks on both destroyers, and they decided trying to turn back north to follow the Dutch cruisers as ordered would be most unwise. The Americans broke off, running south in the confused action that saw the Japanese opening fire on each other at one point, with the Captains of two of their four destroyers claiming kills that never happened. It was all too typical of night actions, and the high speed in those restricted waters led to the haphazard results.

With his train of supporting destroyers now out of the action, Doorman was alone with his two light cruisers, though help was not far off. This time the four American destroyers of the northern pincer led the way with orders to charge in and attack the Japanese anchorage. They made a brave torpedo run, confronted by a pair of bulldogs when *Asashio* and *Oshio* came around to challenge them. The Japanese gunfire was again very accurate, and the American torpedo strike a miserable failure. Of 21 torpedoes fired, fifteen would miss, four would fail to explode and two would be jammed in the launch tubes.

The US flotilla had the enemy outgunned with their combined sixteen 4-inch guns to only twelve 5-inchers on the two Japanese DDs, but simply could not get hits. In the meantime, the Japanese saw the thin illuminating beams of searchlights from one of the American ships, slowly fingering the darkness. This gave them a perfect target, and they quickly put two hits on the USS *Stewart*, damaging her engines and forcing Captain Harold Smith to break off and turn back to the northeast.

As the remaining US destroyers came about to follow, *Parrott* and *Pillsbury* nearly ran into one another, and that near miss also forced the *Edwards* to make a sharp turn to avoid a grand pileup. The whole mess lurched north, with the Japanese running parallel between those ships and the Dutch cruiser *Tromp*. Though they brought another six

5.9 inch guns into play, the Dutch could not get hits either, but the two Japanese destroyers had a field day.

Captain Jan Balthazar de Meester on the *Tromp* decided to make the same mistake the American destroyer *Stewart* had made, switching on her bright searchlight to try and find the enemy in the heavy darkness. As the flashing light searched about, it clearly revealed the position of the cruiser to the enemy, and both Japanese destroyers opened fire.

Asashio pummeled the bridge and conning tower of the Dutch cruiser, her guns firing rapidly, the shell casings careening off the forward deck. The experienced gunners would get no less than eleven hits in a brief, hot engagement that was going to put *Tromp* out of the action, and lay her up in Australia for months after for repairs. Thus far, these two intrepid Japanese destroyers had been attacked by three cruisers and seven Allied destroyers, and come off the better. Now the odds would shift even further in their favor when *Arashio* and *Michishio* came up to join the fray.

As she turned to fall off to the north, *Tromp* got in one good hit on the bridge of *Oshio*, inflicting a number of casualties and temporarily shaking that destroyer badly enough to cause the torpedoes it had just fired to miss badly. Misery loves company, and the American destroyers *Stewart* and *Edwards* were inshore of the action near in the vicinity of the damaged *Tromp*, now attended by the US destroyer *Pillsbury*. The four allied ships suddenly found themselves under attack by the two newly arriving Japanese destroyers, which ran right between the two groups in a brazen attempt to decide the battle then and there.

With the two sides passing in opposite directions, the Japanese destroyers were about to run a dangerous gauntlet of fire from two directions. It was a fast and furious gun duel, but this time the two undamaged US destroyers *Pillsbury* and *Edwards*, acquitted themselves by putting accurate and damaging fire on the lead Japanese destroyer, *Michishio*. Tromp joined the action and the Allies riddled the ship with hits that would kill 13 and leave another 83 of her 200 man crew wounded, and the ship itself foundering, and nearly dead in the water.

Once the ships were clear of each other, the darkness folded her cloak over the scene, and the gunfire ended. Neither side wanted any more of the other, and the *Arashio* maneuvered to position herself to take her damaged sister ship *Michishio* in tow. That ship was so badly damaged that it would have to be towed all the way back to Japan. *Oshio* would be laid up for at least six weeks with extensive repairs required on her bridge, but the other two Japanese destroyers suffered only minor damage. They could claim a tactical victory in having faced down a vastly superior Allied fleet, while successfully shielding the final stages of the embarkation of the Kanemura detachment at Sanur.

An hour or so after the guns had fallen silent and the smoke cleared, nature intervened with a hard driving rain. It was the kind of weather that would always halt any active operations by Allied forces, the darkness alone often serving to prompt them to settle quietly into defensive positions. For the Japanese, however, it was perfect fighting weather. They would use the cover of darkness and rain to steal up from the shoreline and through the groves of trees towards the airfield at Denpasar.

There they would find the place defended by a company of irregulars in an outfit known as Korps Prajoda. It was a native contingent, 600 strong, recruited from the local population. While mostly armed with spears instead of rifles, and officered by only a few Dutch regulars, the company at the airfield was backed up by a few old armored cars. Far to the north, the main body of this force would defend, stupidly, at the coastal town of Singaradja. The Japanese had long ago written that site off as a potential landing point due to the steep rocky shoreline in the area. Furthermore, it was the airfield they really wanted, and that is where they attacked with the full battalion now safely ashore.

Soon the natives of Korps Prajoda would be facing the veteran Japanese troops that had already fought and won in the grueling battle for the Philippines. It was no contest. The airfield fell that night, and little more than a week later, two companies of the Kanemura detachment would sweep the island and overcome the meager resistance of the remaining Korps Prajoda "troops" at Singaradja.

So it was that with no more than a single pinky on the hand of the Japanese 48th Division, just one battalion, the valuable airfield on Bali was delivered into their hands. They had done this while Montgomery was still busily sorting out the haphazard arrival of his troops from Singapore. With that airfield secured, the Japanese would prepare to move air units there to support the next stage of the attack on Java.

That same night that part of the plan would swing into motion. General Takeo Ito would take in the veteran 228th Regiment of the 38th Infantry Division, which had taken Hong Kong earlier, intending to seize the vital bases on Timor. Five ships would carry the regiment. *Miike Maru*, the largest ship at 12,000 tons, held the regimental HQ and support units. *Africa Maru* carried the 3rd Battalion, *Zenyo Maru* the 1st Battalion, *Yamamura Maru* the 2nd Battalion, with 1st Mt Artillery aboard *Ryoyo Maru*. With a force so small, the loss of any single ship could be disastrous, but the recent action at Badung Strait gave them confidence, and the little invasion fleet would be well covered.

This same force had just defeated a small combined Australian Dutch force on Ambon Island to the north, and now it would face a similar defense for the attack on Timor. To put the scale of the operation in perspective, Timor was an island roughly twice the size of Crete in the Mediterranean, some 340 miles long and 90 miles wide at its greatest point, compared to the 150 mile length of Crete. Its land mass would exceed the total of all seven of the Canary Islands, which had been fought over so bitterly in recent weeks. Yet to conquer an island of this size, with nearly a million native residents, the Japanese were sending a single regiment, three battalions, and the Allies were defending with even less.

If Prime Minister Curtin clearly perceived the importance of that island to operations then underway, the units and equipment Australia sent to defend it belied that assessment. In fact, the troops did not even have a reliable radio link from Dili to Darwin. Curtin's problem was that all of his core veteran fighting units had already been sent overseas, and the British always seemed to find one place or another where they were desperately needed. The rest of the Australian Army was ill equipped, barely forming and largely untrained. There were also many other places under threat, New Guinea and Rabaul being uppermost on the list. So the only forces that could be found were small ad hoc battalions given the code names Sparrow, Lark, and Gull. These three little birds flew out to face the might of the Japanese Army, but they could be no more than a brief delaying force.

Lt. General Sturde, Australia's Chief of Defense, warned against this policy, seeing it as a "penny packet" dispersion of otherwise valuable battalions. What he wanted was a concentration of force in Australia, and was much behind Curtin's insistence on recalling home the expeditionary divisions. His misgivings were soon proved correct when Lark Force went to Rabaul, where it arrived just in time to be overwhelmed and captured by the Japanese there in Operation R. Gull Force had already been met and defeated on Ambon by the same troops now coming to Timor. The last bird on the wire was a scrappy band of hearty defenders in Sparrow Force, which was also augmented with a company of Commandos that would prove particularly troublesome to the Japanese.

Elsewhere, Australia's real birds of prey, the tough, experienced divisions now enroute from the Middle East, were still mostly on the sea. The Eagles and Hawks were coming, but the question remained as to whether they could get there soon enough to matter.

Chapter 39

Timor – Feb 26, 1942

The landings at Timor were as audacious and brilliantly conceived as any of the other operations Japan had carried out. Utilizing a remarkable economy of force, the Japanese would send two battalions south of Kupang in a surprise landing, and then move north to attack the port. A third battalion would land near Dili in the northeast. These were the only two locations with airfield and port facilities worth having, and if controlled, the remainder of the island was largely irrelevant.

Major General Takeo Ito was arriving on the scene six days later than the actual invasion in Fedorov's history, but with the same exact force in hand. With Dutch Admiral Doorman licking his wounds from the action at Badung Strait, these landings would be unopposed. The southwestern group came ashore between 02:35 and 04:00 on the morning of the 26th, with 1st and 3rd Battalions of the 228th Regiment, 38th Division, under Asano and Nishiyama. They moved inland quickly, through thickening stands of Mangrove trees, with their first objective being the airfield at Penfoi.

They would not find it in working condition when they arrived. While Sparrow Force had found themselves all deployed to defend the harbor, when they realized what was happening they immediately began to move inland. At the airfield, the dogged Engineers of 2/11 Field Company, R.A.E., had set up nine dumps packed with fifty 500lb bombs each. When they set those off the resulting explosions heavily cratered the field, putting it out of action for the near run. It was ironic that this force had been seen by Wavell as essential to the preservation of that airfield for a way station for shorter ranged planes out between Darwin and Java. The Japanese operation there was precisely aimed at eliminating that asset, and claiming it as a forward airfield of their own. But the first act of the defenders was to blow the place to hell.

The main force was 2/40 Tasmanian Battalion, otherwise designated as "Sparrow Force," under Lt. Colonel William Leggatt. The Tassies had come a very long way to Timor, shipping into Darwin for a month leave before the war, where they soon ferreted out all the best pubs. Otherwise they trained hard, then lolled about, swimming in the Adelaide River where a Padre from a nearby Catholic Church would regularly hunt down crocodiles with a rifle. The men came to call him 'Crocodile Bill,' and some even took to barbecuing some of the Crocs he put down. When the Japanese hit Pearl Harbor, the fun was over and the troops shipped out on the *Zealandia* and *Westralia*, where they were finally told what had happened.

For some time, all they had seen of the enemy were occasional flights of fighters that swooped in to strafe the airfield at Penfoi. They had dug out weapons pits, laid barbed wire, and then waited for their turn on leave in Koepang to hit the pubs and quaff down some good French Brandy. All that was soon to be over, and now they would finally meet the enemy face to face.

Alerted to the landings, the main body of Sparrow Force moved out from Koepang, intending to clear the road to the airport, but ran into more unexpected guests. In the third Japanese parachute operation of the war, the elite 3rd Kure SNLF Battalion had dropped after sunrise, at about 10:45. The Japanese interpreted the Australian movement east as a retreat, but in actuality, it was meant to clear their lines of communications back to Koepang, where a group of engineers and auxiliary troops was still holding the port.

Lt. Colonel William Leggatt wanted to secure the special supply depot established along that road at Champlong in the event they might be forced to move further east. At this point, there was no real appreciation of how big the Japanese operation was, so prudence dictated the line of retreat should be secured first. The SNLF paratroopers had no idea there was a supply center at Champlong, but had landed to try and prevent just this sort of eastern movement, hoping to net the Allied defenders into the battle for Koepang.

Once he had moved east, Leggatt soon found that he could not keep the road open behind him back to Koepang. He therefore decided to press on to Champlong to try and secure those much needed supplies, but kept running into stronger detachments of enemy paratroopers, first at the village of Babao, and then on the Usau Ridge beyond.

"We've got to push on through," said Leggatt to his Company commanders. "Position the Vickers Machineguns to provide good cover fire. The Lewis Gun teams will move up with the rifle squads. Lieutenant—"

"Sir?"

"The Japs have worked up a roadblock ahead. Can your sappers deal with it?"

"Right away, sir." Lieutenant Stronach was a big man, and at his side was Sergeant Couch and Lance Corporal Kay. They rounded up four more sappers and crept into position to get closer to the obstacle, all under enemy fire. It was cleared away, and the Tassies tramped on through.

It was hard fighting, but they cleared Babao, and then pushed on up to that ridge. At one point, with the Japanese putting up stiff resistance, Leggatt came forward to see what was happening. It would be no good to let his men get pinned down on that barren ridge, and he could think of only one thing to do, his hard voice shouting out the order for all to hear—*"Battalion.... Fix Bayonets!"*

It was an order that had been heard on countless battlefields over the last centuries, for the bayonet was a weapon made more of dread than steel. Now, all along the line, the hard click-click of the bayonets being fastened to the barrels of those Lee Enfields broke the stillness. The sound brought back awful memories to Leggatt, a man of 47 years who first heard it as a much younger man during the terrible trench warfare in France. He would do now what he had seen so many times before when a unit was faced with a determined enemy in entrenched positions. He would attack, the old fashioned way....

The battalion mortars would open the attack with a good barrage, hoping to keep enemy MGs pinned down. Leggatt looked at his watch, waiting, and almost reflexively reached for a whistle to sound the attack, but he had none. So instead he raised his pistol and gave the order to charge—one last push. It was to be the last bayonet charge mounted by a battalion sized Allied unit in history, but he could not know that. Captains Roff and Johnston would lead the attack, and the Australians charged on up that hill, braving the enemy fire, and falling on their enemy like banshees out of hell.

The Japanese instinctively knew what was happening. This was *gyokusai*, the 'shattered jewel' attack made by units who could see no other way out of their dilemma, and meant to be one last attempt at victory, or an honorable death if it should fail. The men of the 5th and 18th Divisions had made just such an attack on Singapore, their ranks swarming across Tengah airfield into the riveting fire of Montgomery's stalwart defense. Such attacks often failed, but they were glorious, even in defeat, the very essence of warfare. It was men with rifles and flashing sharp steel, face to face with each other in the trenches in a moment of rage and terror that could leave only one or the other alive. Bayonets would clash with samurai swords wielded by the Marine officers, where the skill of those swordsmen was matched by the sheer brawn and guts of the Tassie soldiers.

For the men who made that charge, it was raw nerve and reflex, pushed on by the pounding pulse of adrenaline in each man's chest. Up that hill they went, arms extended, big hands gripping the haft of their rifles, leaping into the enemy trenches and giving them the hard stiff forward thrust with the bayonet. As if to underscore the terror of that deathly hour, at one point a platoon swept over the ridge and down into a hollow that had been used as a graveyard. There, crouching behind the makeshift headstones, stolid Japanese Marines lay in waiting, suddenly rising up like walking dead and joining the action. The charge swept into the cemetery, becoming a furious, ghoulish hand-to-hand combat among the tombstones.

Men will do things in the heat of such a moment that would be unthinkable to them at any other time. They fired their weapons until they were empty, then fought with the bayonet, man to man. When one Corporal's bayonet was bent and useless, out came his knife. It was hands on throats, head butts, ear biting work in that dead man's den, with the hard muscle and brawn of the Tassies simply overpowering the smaller Japanese soldiers, even though the enemy Marines were all trained in martial arts. But nothing was going to stop the Tasmanian Devils that day—nothing.

They swarmed over the defenders inflicting terrible losses on the enemy to clear off the last resistance. This was no small feat, for the men they had faced were elite Special Naval Landing Force Marines, all veterans of China and Malaya. 2/40th lost 80 men killed, and another 69 wounded in that hellish fighting, but they won through.

The mortar fire during the attack on Babao had set many of the village huts on fire, and pallid grey smoke hung over the scene when the action subsided. Sparrow Force had sustained 149 casualties, but they gave much worse to the enemy. As the sun set, it was finally over, the last of the Japanese falling back towards Champlong. Hundreds of Japanese paratroopers had been cut down, and they had less than a company remaining. In spite of that terrible defeat, they doggedly established yet another blocking position on the road further east.

Night fell, and now Leggatt had to make another difficult decision. His men had fought long and hard, and come all the way from Koepang. He still had no idea of the size of the enemy force he was facing, and as company commanders reported in, the tally of wounded men rose from 69 to 132, with many others down with malaria.

"Tough fight today," he said. "The men need rest, and any food and water we can get to them. We'll just have to get patrols out ahead, and try to move on to Champlong before sunrise."

He knew well enough that the enemy behind them were going to use these hours of darkness to good advantage. Word came that Koepang had fallen. There were only 111 men with the Fortress

Engineers and some of 2/11 Field Company, with another 320 men in the AA gun batteries and some signals and service troops. They were not able to hold up the main strength of two Japanese battalions, and the city fell near dusk on February 27th.

As soon as it was secured, the Japanese sent one reinforced battalion in hot pursuit of Sparrow Force on the road to Champlong. They would march all that night to the scene of the battle, moving like tireless spirits in the gloomy murk of the darkness. By dawn on the 28th, they had caught up with Sparrow Force on the road, but hearing of the heavy casualties taken by the SNLF troops, Colonel Nishiyama decided to try and pull a Yamashita with a bold bluff.

Two men approached the Tassie encampment under a white flag, and a meeting was arranged. There they told Leggatt that Koepang had fallen and 23,000 Japanese troops had just landed the previous day, including a full battalion of tanks. To add thunder to their story, they had moved up all the tanks of a single company that had landed with the troops, and while the Australians were deliberating, Japanese bombers swooped in to bomb the head of their column. This infuriated Leggatt, but he took some solace in learning that several of the planes had also unloaded sticks of bombs on the SNLF positions.

Yet there he was, between the proverbial rock in those stubborn Naval paratroopers, and a very hard place. All his wounded and sick were at the back of the column, and they would be the first to go if those Japanese tanks made a run at them. They were cut off from Koepang, and still blocked from reaching their supply depot at Champlong. If he decided to fight, the Company Commanders indicated they might have two hours before the ammunition ran out. With great regret, and realizing he could ask no more from his men, Leggatt decided to seek terms with the enemy. Had he known the caliber of the men he was facing, the cruelty and barbarity they were capable of, he might have thought twice about surrendering.

The Japanese first order of business was to force the Australians to gather up all the dead bodies of their fallen SNLF troops. They had them lay them in great piles, and then calmly poured gasoline on the corpses and set them on fire. It seemed a horrid and undignified way to treat their own fallen soldiers, something that shocked and reviled the Tassies. Those men had given all they had in a fight to the death, and now the Japanese officers seemed to regard them as carrion trash. One Japanese soldier even took out his knife at the edge of the burning pyre, and was carefully extracting gold crowns from the dead paratroopers' charred faces. It was as if their lives, and their service, meant nothing to them now. They were like empty, spent shell casings.

The stench of burning human flesh was never forgotten by the men of 2/40th that survived the war. They were then ordered to build the camp that would become their first prison, using the same barbed wire that they once strung out as a defense against this invasion. Their lot would be a hard one from that day on, making friends with hunger, thirst, cruelty, dysentery, gangrene and malaria. The troops were fed, but the Japanese swept weevil larvae and mice droppings into the rice bowls, laughing as the hungry men ate whatever they were given. The war was over for Sparrow Force, but their ordeal had only just begun.

Farther north, Colonel Alexander Spence was defending near Dili airfield with 2/2 Independent Company, a group of gritty Commandos who had special training in guerilla warfare. Each man had been handpicked for the unique skills required of a Commando unit. They were hardy young men, physically fit, bush-crafty, and able to live off the land. There were no slackers among them, and they wouldn't stop for tea, for darkness or weather in any circumstance where their lives counted on them fighting.

2/2 was a unit of strapping, bruising misfits, many who had been plucked right out of a brig or detention facility and interviewed for the job they would now be given. If someone wanted to pick a scrap with them, they had best beware. Now, after extensive training in Guerrilla tactics, each man wore a distinctive double red diamond insignia, and they would soon prove they were a real gemstone in the actions that followed. In the early hours, no one had been informed of the enemy attack at Koepang, as there was no radio link. When the transports carrying Colonel Sadashichi and the men of 2nd Battalion appeared off shore, they were first thought to be Portuguese ships bringing in long awaited reinforcements.

Colonel Spence suddenly heard the sound of gunfire from the Dutch Coastal gun positions. He got on a field phone and rang up the nearest post to see if he could find out what was happening.

"It's a Japanese submarine out in the harbor," said the local Dutch Commander, Colonel van Straaten, but it was soon apparent that something much more than that was going on. When the ships began disgorging Japanese troops, the company began to fall back from the harbor towards the airfield, screened by one group as a rearguard under Lieutenant Charles McKenzie, with 18 Commandos of No. 2 Section.

The Japanese were too bold in their attack, thinking to simply overwhelm the enemy defense and storm into the airfield, and the tough Australians, with good prepared positions, inflicted a fearsome toll. Those 18 men fought all night, answering enemy offers to surrender with their Bren guns. They held the position until just before dawn, when McKenzie gave orders to slip away after demo charges were set on the airfield. They finally broke off, only twelve able bodied men remaining, four walking wounded, and two more unable to travel and refusing treatment so as not to hold the others up. No. 2 Section then joined the withdrawal, but not before they had inflicted some 200 casualties on the enemy, the barrels of their machineguns so warm that they had to be wrapped with the men's shirts to be carried during the fight.

Another section of 15 men had been up in the highlands, completely out of touch, and were now heading towards Dili in a truck, not even knowing the invasion had occurred. They thought they would go into town to scrounge up some food for breakfast, but they were on a deadly road that day. Caught unawares, they blundered right into an ambush laid by Japanese troops, all captured before they ever had a chance to fight. Shortly thereafter, the fate they suffered would be a warning to the remaining men of the company. They had been taken by a small 50-man detachment of the 3rd Yokosuka SNLF, under

Lieutenant Hondo Mitsuyoshi. No one knew exactly why he would act as he did, or whether he had heard of the terrible losses suffered by the others in his unit that had parachuted to the west.

An incident occurred on the road when a Dutch militia group fired at the Japanese column. Enraged, Mitsuyoshi quickly sent a platoon to deal with it. Then he selected out four of the 15 Aussies, ordering an officer to force them to kneel in the road and shoot them one by one in the back of the head. It was a spiteful act of cruelty, all too common in this theater. Every army would have lapses and failings in the ranks, and atrocities would come hand in hand with war, but the Japanese army would prove to be specialists at the art of this depravity.

Five years earlier, they had set their troops loose on Chinese prisoners of war, and civilians, in the city of Nanking in one of the greatest atrocities of the century. Chinese were bayoneted, beheaded, raped, burned, starved, buried alive, and infants were even thrown into pots of boiling water. It was cruelty and barbarity on a scale to rival the atrocities committed by the Germans in their concentration camps. Over 200,000 were killed in Nanking, for the Japanese mindset seemed to regard a fallen enemy as subhuman, particularly one who would suffer the dishonor of surrender instead of fighting to the death. Just weeks ago, after the desperate defense of Laha Airfield at Ambon, scores of Australian and Dutch P.O.Ws were executed, many simply beheaded as they knelt, bound and blindfolded. The Naval Marines were again behind the incident, where over 300 prisoners were put to the sword.

There was a saying among these hard minded warriors, coming down through the ranks from the days of the Samurai: *"Loyalty and honor are heavier than a mountain, and your life is lighter than a feather."* A human life counted for nothing in those days. It could be taken at the whim of a Samurai lord, for the most trivial of reasons, and in many ways the modern Samurai of 1942 held the same mindset towards their enemies. Their lives were feather light. Whatever Lieutenant Mitsuyoshi's reasons were here, he took those four lives that day, and later, he had the remaining men herded into a shed and summarily beheaded, one by one.

The rest of 2/2 Independent Company soon saw that they were badly outnumbered, and learning of the demise of Sparrow Force, they knew they would get no help from the west. Yet Timor was a very big island, and they had a clear line of retreat, which they soon took, hiking up into the highlands. The decision was made to disperse the company into small groups, and to fight on guerilla style until relieved. Soon their only connection to Australia would be a single radio cobbled together from spare parts found and collected over months by signaler Joe Loveless. When it finally came to life and actually worked, they promptly dubbed the radio "Winnie the War Winner."

With 'Winnie' operating, the Commandos were able to make regular intelligence reports to the homeland, and also receive messages as to when they might expect secret shipments of air or sea dropped supplies. They soon became a band of shirtless bearded rogues, and the bane of the Japanese for long months. When asked if they wanted to be extracted, the men instead simply requested delivery of more ammunition for their Tommy guns. Their choice to fight on alone prompted Churchill to smile and give his own tribute, which would become the official motto of the unit: *"They Alone Did Not Surrender."* It would be a long year in the steamy jungles and tortured highlands of Timor before they would finally be pulled off in Fedorov's history. Yet here, in these altered states, that story would soon change….

Part XIV

A Roll of Thunder

"Thunder is good, thunder is impressive, but it is lightning that does the work."

— **Mark Twain**

Chapter 40

The Japanese plan for the invasion of Java would be dubbed "Operation J" in this telling of events. With Bali and Timor well in hand, the main thrust for the offensive was now about to begin. It would employ three full divisions, the first being the tough 48th Division under General Hitoshi Imamura coming from the Philippines. Among the best divisions in the army, the 48th had special training for amphibious landings, and had performed as expected on the Philippines, participating in the capture of Manila. It would be further strengthened by the "Sakaguchi Detachment," a regimental sized gift from the 56th Division in Burma.

This division would land well west of Surabaya at Kragan, push southeast and attack that city by indirect means, as the Japanese had done at Koepang on Timor. The Sakaguchi Detachment had a special assignment, ordered to drive south through the city of Surjakarta and along the south coast of the island to the port of Tjilatjap. If taken it was thought this would prevent any successful Allied attempt to evacuate.

The 2nd, "Courageous" Division, was a reserve unit taken from the Sendai region of Japan. As such, the 2nd was not one of the veteran fighting units of recent months. It had seen action on the Siberian front and China years earlier, but after being recalled home, it languished to a point that Prince Mikasa once said it had become the worst equipped division in the army. All that had to change, and quickly, and the man to change it was Yamashita's confederate planner and master strategist, Colonel Masanobu Tsuji, the man who had cherry picked the best fruit in the army to assemble Yamashita's 25th Army for the Malayan Campaign.

The 2nd had once been a "Square division" with two brigades of two regiments each. After its recall to Japan, it was made triangular, leaving one regiment behind to form a nucleus for forces being raised to replace it at home. For this operation it would be made square again by receiving the support of the 230th Regiment of the 38th Division, under Colonel Toshihari Shoji. The "Shoji Detachment" would land east of Batavia on the coast to block the enemy retreat and take a valuable airfield, and the remainder of the division would land west of the city near Merak on the Sunda Strait, and Banten Bay. This main force would send two of its three regiments at Batavia, and loop one further south to take Bandung in the center of the island, the location of the Allied Java Command HQ.

It was a well-conceived plan, and in Fedorov's history, with only the Dutch and a scattering of Allied units present, it became overwhelming force. This time, however, the entire British 18th Division was on the island, along with a reinforced brigade of Australians, two battalions off the *Orcades*, the 2nd New Zealand Brigade, and the Gurkhas. Allied strength on Java was now more than doubled.

It was for this reason that the entire 5th Division had been pulled off of Singapore Island after Yamashita's departure. Once perhaps the strongest division in the Army after Colonel Tsuji had buttressed it with the best units he could find, it had been badly worn down from the long campaign in Malaya, and the heavy casualties sustained at Tengah Airfield on Singapore. Now it could muster no more than a Brigade strength unit, with six battalions under Major General Takuro Matsui, formed into two regiments, the 11th and 21st. Most of the rest of the division was dead, and the living had been told the enemy they faced at Tengah Airfield had made a cowardly withdrawal to Java, and that now they would have the honor of hunting them down and finishing the battle that had been joined earlier. Now they would avenge their fallen dead.

Bandung, Java, HQ Java Command, 27 Feb, 1942

Montgomery had wasted no time taking command from General Sitwell and assembling his senior officers. He had commandeered a car in Batavia and drove immediately to Bandung, entering the city past the long rows of squat houses, their roofs looking like truncated pyramids, the streets lined with small rickshaws left idle in the disconsolate rain. One lone man was walking a main street, seeming a lost soul in the gloom. Everyone else was hidden away, huddled in shelters, fearful that the war was at last coming to their island. The rain seemed an outlier of worse things to come, and now here was this scrawny, determined man emerging from the weathered 1938 De Soto Sedan, a red beret cap and British Army jacket his only protection from the weather.

Behind him came Brigadiers Bennett, Clifton, and Blackburn, commanders of the ANZAC troops, the last to arrive. They would find Brigadiers Backhouse, Massy-Beresford and Duke of the 18th Division waiting for them in the bungalow that had been chosen on the southwest edge of the town near a once thriving banana plantation. Monty was all business from the very first.

"Well met, gentlemen, the last of the transports have unloaded and the disposition of the troops is well underway. Now it comes down to our plan for the defense. As I see things, we have two options. We know what the enemy will want here, and we can stand in such a way to deny it to him. That will mean we deploy to defend the key ports at Batavia and Surabaya, and the nearby airfields. Without them the enemy will have difficulty keeping themselves supplied. Unfortunately, these ports are all on the north coast of the island, and it does not seem likely that we will command the Java Sea."

"There's one good port on the south coast," said Blackhouse, "Tjilatjap. We'll have to hold that to the last. It's the only way we can get our own reinforcements and supplies in."

"Right," said Montgomery. "Your battalion is here in Bandung. Why don't you take it south by rail today and position yourself to control that port. Most of the Dutch garrison here has moved to the eastern portion of the island. They'll hold Surabaya."

"Not for long," said Bennett. "They've very little in the way of good equipment, and frankly, they're completely untested. If the Japanese hit us there, we can count on losing that port in short order."

"Then they'll need support."

"My 2/20 Battalion is at Malang," said Bennett. "The rest of the brigade is still at Semarang, another port we have to keep an eye on, and Clifton's New Zealand Brigade has reached Surjakarta. Do you want us to push on to Surabaya?"

"That's the dilemma," said Montgomery. "At Singapore we were able to concentrate our entire force and face down the Japanese along a very narrow front. Here we're sitting on an island that's 600 miles from one end to the other. If we try to hold everything, we could find ourselves outmaneuvered. The enemy will be able to choose their landing sites, and we can't simply sit in a central position and wait for them to come with any hope we can move reinforcements where they're needed in time. The rail lines here are useful, but they'll likely be hit very hard by the Japanese air power when this game tees off. So I propose that we select one sector of the island or another, and concentrate there, defeat the enemy landings in at least one instance. The question is where will that be?"

"Surabaya is closer to Darwin," said Bennett. That's where supplies will originate."

"We can also expect regular convoys from Colombo," said Montgomery. "I understand your point, but we'd have to move the 18th Division east rather smartly, and we don't have sufficient rolling stock, road transport, or perhaps even time. At present, things got rather muddled on the lift over from Singapore. The men are doing a bang up job getting sorted out, but I've had to rebuild the brigades as they arrived. Now we're strung out all along the roads and rail line from here to Batavia, and I propose we stay right where we are."

"Hold Batavia?"

"Precisely." Montgomery folded his arms. "The airfields here can cover the Sunda Strait, and Batavia is the nearest hop to Singapore. We mustn't forget Percival, and all those civilians in the city. If we can hold the Sunda Strait, the run in to Batavia under our air cover might allow us to receive supply convoys out of Colombo. If the Japanese take it, then Singapore is as good as lost. The Japanese have already taken Denpasar airfield on Bali, and they're on Timor as well. So we can't count on anything coming by air from Darwin, and frankly, I don't think we can expect much support from there in any case. No. Our line of communications will have to be the sea lanes to Colombo, or down to Perth. That will be Somerville's watch."

"Then you'll pretty much abandon all the barrier islands from Java to Timor." Bennett shook his head. "They won't like that back home."

"It can't be helped," said Montgomery. "We don't have the forces to even consider garrisoning those islands. I've a mind to see about using the Gurkhas to raid Bali. Word is the Japanese didn't put much more than a battalion there. If we can take that back, then we at least have a line through the Badung Strait to Surabaya, for what it will be worth."

There was silence for a while, then Brigadier Duke of the 53rd Brigade came out with the one obvious element in this plan that had gone unspoken. "You realize that if we concentrate here, then we're basically leaving the Dutch to wither on the vine out east. You know damn well that if we do hold Batavia, the Japanese will go all out for Surabaya. They'll have little other choice."

"General Duke, the Dutch expected to have to hold this entire island without us. They might be grateful if we at least keep half of it safe. We won't be abandoning them. If hard pressed, they can fall back on our positions here."

The others nodded, and there seemed to be no other dissenting voice. So Montgomery doled out his orders, and the die was cast. Japanese troop transports were already loaded and "on the water," but the determination of Dutch Admiral Doorman was about to force a brief delay in the invasion.

Java Sea, 11:40, 27 Feb, 1942

Regrouping back at Surabaya after the fracas at Badung Strait, Doorman had received intelligence that the Japanese were coming. Another man might have looked at his weary sailors, battered ships, all needing maintenance and repair, and given up the ghost, but not Doorman. Even if he had no business doing what he now set out to do, credit must be given for his sheer audacity. He was going to take out anything he had at hand, and give challenge.

So it was that Doorman steamed out into the Java Sea, his ships battered and bruised, many old four stack destroyers dating to the last war. His crews had little rest in the last 18 hours, but they stood to their posts, in spite of a general pall of misgiving that had fallen over the little fleet. They had just faced their enemy, outgunning them by a wide margin, with nine ships against four in the Badung Strait, and they suffered a convincing defeat. So nerves were raw as they set out, eyes swollen and tired, some men even falling asleep at their battle stations.

To make matters worse, it was a much weaker force in this last sortie than the one made by Doorman in Fedorov's history books. The entire British squadron, cruiser *Exeter*, and destroyers *Electra*, *Encounter* and *Jupiter*, had steamed off with the Australian cruiser *Perth* to rendezvous and support the arrival of Mountbatten and the two British carriers. If that weren't enough, the US cruiser *Houston* was no longer afloat. Captain Rooks had made his fateful decision to screen the *Antietam* and *Shiloh* in the battle of the New Hebrides, and his valuable piece was no longer on the board. So instead of fourteen ships, Doorman had only eight, mostly destroyers.

To bolster this force, he called on the four American destroyers that had returned to Tjilatjap. They would join the four that had returned to Surabaya, and he would also press the cruiser *Sumatra* into service, even though it had been laid up with engine problems for some time. So he would end up with a baker's dozen that day, the fleet limping out of Surabaya at no more than 26 knots.

The first American destroyer squadron led the way, with *Edwards*, *Jones*, *Alden* and *Ford*. Then came the Dutch squadron, the cruisers *Java*, *Sumatra*, *De Ruyter*, and two destroyers *Witte de With* and *Kortenaer*. Lastly he had the second US destroyer squadron, with *Parrott*, *Pillsbury*, *Stewart* and *Pope*. It was the last hurrah of what was once called the US Asiatic Fleet, and the final act in the drama the Dutch Navy would play in this campaign.

The Japanese knew the enemy was out there. Doorman's fleet had been spotted by search planes off the cruiser *Natori*, and the fleet was subjected to a probing air strike at 14:20 that afternoon. No hits were scored by the few Japanese planes that came in, and Doorman reformed and pressed on. He was going to meet a different mix of forces this time out, largely from the Western Screening Force led by Rear Admiral Jisaburō Ozawa. He had been well north in the Malacca Strait, but learning of the British evacuation underway from Singapore, he moved quickly south to interfere. Though he had arrived too late to stop Montgomery and his troops from reaching Java, he was now in a perfect position to cover the western segment of the Java landings.

Ozawa had a fairly powerful group, light carrier *Ryujo*, 7th Heavy Cruiser Squadron with *Kumano, Mikuma, Mogami,* and *Suzuya*; light cruisers *Natori, Yura,* and *Sendai,* along with 12 destroyers in three divisions of four each. One division, and all his mine sweepers, stayed with the invasion convoy carrying 2nd Infantry Division. The rest of his covering force was out to give battle.

Doorman could feel in his bones that he was going to be overmatched that day, but true to his roots in Naval Aviation, he put out a call for air support as soon as the lead formation of Japanese destroyers was sighted. The British still had 36 of the 48 Hurricanes that had been operating from Sumatra. Now they were based at fields near Batavia, and they ran to answer the call. They would join a group of 16 Blenheims, and a few Hudsons and a squadron of Buffalos in an effort to gain air superiority over the Java Sea. Against this force, Ryujo would put up 16 A5M fighters and 12 B5Ns, and there were several squadrons of land based fighters coming from Balikpapan, with 25 Zeroes, and another 11 A3M Claudes in the first wave of Japanese air strength. The drone of their engines tipping over in a dive was the opening overture of the Battle of the Java Sea.

Chapter 41

Destroyer Flotilla 3 under Rear Admiral Hashimoto was the first to sight the Allied fleet. He had been steaming as part of a wide screening line of destroyers, his flag on the cruiser *Sendai*, with destroyers *Fubuki, Hatsuyuki, Shirayuki* and *Shirakomo*. *Sendai* opened the action at 16,000 yards with her 5.5 inch guns targeting the lead US destroyers, *Edwards* and *Jones*. The Japanese DD Flotilla then put on speed and charged in at the tail of that column, their guns engaging *Alden* and *Ford*.

Further south, the 5th DD Flotilla under Rear Admiral Hara aboard light cruiser *Natori* swung up to the northwest to engage the Dutch. Destroyers *Asakaze, Harukaze* and *Matsukaze* were in a good position to make a torpedo attack, and they put down a spread of 12 Long Lance torpedoes, firing from 15,000 yards. Behind them came the heavy cruisers *Kumano, Mogami* and *Mikuma*, and their bigger 8 inch guns already had the range to begin firing.

These three cruisers, all in the same class, had been cleverly designed in 1934 with five triple 6.1-inch gun turrets to be classified as a light cruiser. Yet the ships were over 8,500 tons, and 646 feet long as opposed to a standard Nagara Class light cruiser of about 5,300 tons and 534 feet in length. The barbettes for those five turrets were also secretly enlarged so they could accommodate a bigger turret during refits if desired. It was a deceptive little shell game played by Japan early in the treaty years, when they felt snubbed to be allocated fewer ships than the so called "Major Powers" like the US and Britain.

So in 1937, these ships all had their facelift, receiving better 8-inch gun turrets to deftly move them into the heavy cruiser class. Later on, the lead ship, *Mogami*, would be converted to a hybrid seaplane carrier, with 11 planes aft on a long flight deck, and three turrets forward, much like the *Tone* class.

Those three ships combined for thirty 8-inch guns, and they were going to wreak havoc on the thin skinned old destroyers. The American Tin Cans charged into the teeth of that fire, making smoke as they came, but visibility was good, the seas steady, and the Japanese aim was dead accurate. In the swirling duel that followed, *Edwards*, *Pope*, *Alden* and *Ford* would all take damaging hits, with the first three sinking within the hour, and *Ford* dead in the water. The engineers managed to get the screws turning again, and *Ford* limped off, fated to run into light cruiser *Jintsu* and come under the guns of heavy cruiser *Haguro* as it passed very near the Japanese landing zone, en route to Surabaya.

The Japanese destroyers lunged in towards the center of Doorman's battle line, and the Long Lance torpedoes were again in the water, this time from the south. Yet the Japanese had little luck with this deadly weapon that day. One hit would take Dutch Destroyer *Kortenaer* aft, and the resulting explosion put so much damage on the screws and rudder that she would wallow helplessly for the next 40 minutes, eventually sinking at 18:20.

The line of three heavy cruisers then engaged Doorman's force, and the ensuing battle would close to 8,000 yards and see hits on every side. *Sumatra* was so badly damaged that one of her boilers exploded, and the resulting fires would gut that ship in an hour. The Flagship *De Ruyter* was pummeled by no less than five hits, and had only one main gun operational thirty minutes into the fight.

This Japanese gunnery was superb compared to the results another set of heavy cruisers had obtained in the old history. There they had fired over 1600 rounds, getting only five hits, with four of those failing to explode. Those ships had been of the older *Myoko* Class cruisers. In this action it was all *Mogami* class, and they had scored at least sixteen hits for roughly the same expenditure of ammunition, an average of one hit per hundred rounds fired.

This was combat at sea in WWII, and nothing like the almost certain calculus that *Kirov* enjoyed. It was all a haphazard affair, one part seamanship, one part sweat and skill, three parts sheer luck. Doorman himself was wounded, his bridge clotted with heavy smoke, and he realized that his brave charge had done all it could. He turned about, hoping to make Surabaya before his ship lost power, and the remaining four US destroyers wheeled about to lay a heavy smoke screen and cover the withdrawal.

The Japanese were more than happy to see them go, and not inclined to pursue. *Kumano* had one forward turret out of action, *Mogami* two turrets that had sustained heavy damage, and *Mikuma* had her aft turret jammed by a hit near the barbette that prevented it from rotating. It would send the entire squadron home after the invasion for the refits that would see *Mogami* move from a caterpillar to a butterfly. The loss of *Chikuma* in the north meant the fleet needed fast scout cruisers with search planes, and this class was always eyed with that in mind.

So the Japanese had done exactly what a covering force was supposed to do, and protected the invasion convoy, putting five enemy destroyers and the cruiser *Sumatra* under the Java Sea. They would not lose a single ship, and the invasion would now proceed as planned.

Doorman's surviving ships made Surabaya, and the haggard Admiral came ashore, his arm in a bloodied sling, realizing that he could do no more with his tattered squadron. He was, in fact, a Zombie now, for in the old history, his intransigence and persistence in leading his outgunned ships after the enemy would end with his death. This time he would have a very long night ahead to think about the men and ships he left behind. The four remaining American destroyers would slip off to try and reach Darwin, leaving him nothing much to fight with.

Doorman's fleet had bothered the Japanese invasion of Sumatra, failed to stop the landings on Bali, and was now convincingly crushed in the Java Sea. The strategic result of his actions was nothing more than a brave, futile defeat, and his many sorties resulted in the Japanese now having total control of the Java Sea. Yet the naval game was not entirely over. Mountbatten was too late to intervene here, but he would arrive the following day just as the landings were underway.

It would put him in a very good position to cause trouble, but at that moment he did not know that another Admiral was steaming west in the Arafura Sea, Chiuchi Nagumo, with the 5th Carrier Fleet.

Zuikaku and *Shokaku* had finished their work at Rabaul and now they came west, with three battleships, and trouble would not be half a word for what Nagumo had in mind.

* * *

That night, the 2nd Division convoy would make its approach to Merak, and the Eastern Covering Force moved into position to screen off any further sortie from Surabaya. The 48th Division followed it, with the Sakaguchi Detachment, and in the pre-dawn hours the ships deployed their paravanes and glided slowly towards their assigned anchorage sites. This detachment would be the first troops to set foot on Java at Kragan, a small fishing village on the north central coast. It had been chosen precisely because it offered a stretch of long shallow beaches, and was not near a port where the enemy might be expected to defend. As such, the landing achieved complete surprise, and was unopposed.

The troops moved quickly inland, reaching the rail line coming from Semarang through Lasem. Soon the remainder of the division would expand this beachhead east to Tuban on the road to Surabaya. One key objective were the oil fields at Tejapu, about 40 kilometers south of Kragan. This was assigned to Colonel Sakaguchi, as it was on the road to the large inland city of Surjakarta, which opened the route to the south coast.

The Dutch were the first to hear of the landings, and quickly dispatched their 2nd Cavalry Battalion positioned northeast of Surabaya to investigate. As it approached Tuban, it ran into 1/1 Formosa Battalion of the 48th Infantry, advancing quickly along the road in column.

Number 2 Armored Car Company was composed of 12 Alvis Straussler AC3D Armored Cars purchased from the United Kingdom in 1938. It was a speedy 13 ton four wheeled vehicle, with a hull mounted Vickers .303 MG and a turret mounted 12.7mm heavy machine gun. This small company stopped at Balud along the rail line near a bridge over the Solo River and began to set up a road block. The Japanese actually intended to cross this river at Bodjanegoro, about 30 kilometers west, but the position occupied by the Dutch was also on their list of objectives that day.

The only substantial fighting force for the Allies was well to the west, Brigadier Bennett's Australian Brigade, which was all that was left of the 8th Division forces that had been on Singapore. They were 100 kilometers from the Sakaguchi Detachment landings at Kragan, and Bennett now had to decide what to do.

There were two routes he could take east. One was through a broad valley that skirted south of a stubby peninsula formed by the mass of Mount Murjo. This road would take him to the small port of Rembang on the north coast, then east to the site of the enemy landings. The second route followed road and rail lines through another inland valley that would take him to those oil fields at Tejapu, and then on to Surabaya. There was high country between the two routes, with no good roads of any kind. Bennett's problem was that he would need to cover both routes. He got on the telephone to Brigadier Clifton, who was posted south at Surjakarta with the New Zealand Brigade.

"If we take the road to Rembang," said Bennett, the Japanese could swing through Tejapu and then come west. That would bottle my brigade up near Mount Murjo. I would have to split my brigade and send at least one battalion by the other route as a blocking force."

Bennett's problem was that he could not walk two roads and yet one traveler be. Splitting his brigade in the face of uncertain enemy strength was not wise.

"If you decide that," said Clifton, "then keep your main strength on the inland road to Tejapu. We know the Japs will want those oil fields. But I'll go you one better. I can take my brigade up to Ngawa, right south of those fields. Then we'd be in a good position to support you."

After contacting Montgomery, that was the order of the day, but it was specified that the airfields near Surjakarta and Semarang had to be garrisoned.

"We've heard the Japanese used paratroops on Timor," said Monty. "Furthermore, we haven't established that this is their main landing yet. Semarang is a nice cherry of a port. It will have to be held."

That order was going to split Bennett's Brigade three ways, and he wasn't happy about it. He sent his 2/19 Battalion up to Rembang on the coast, and then took his artillery and 2/26 Battalion by the inland route. 2/18th Battalion deployed along the coast near Semarang. He had one more battalion, but it had been sent well south on the road to Malang, the "support" Monty had decided to provide to the Dutch forces in Surabaya.

As for Clifton, he found rolling stock and put his 24th Battalion on the line east. The Brigade than pooled its transport and sent the 26th Battalion by road, leaving the 25th Battalion in Surjakarta. So these orders were going to set four battalions in motion, advancing on a front that measured some 80 kilometers north to south.

Even as these troops set out on their marches, the next alarm rang far to the west at Merak on the Sunda Strait. Japanese troops of the Fukushima Detachment of 2nd Division stormed ashore there, swarming the Dutch and British defenders that had been watching that vital crossing point to Sumatra. The Dutch had just escaped from Oosthaven, welcomed by the single British battalion there, 2/5 Beds & Herts.

Further north, on the other side of a knobby mountain peninsula rising some 1900 feet, more Japanese transports had appeared in Banten Bay. It was soon clear that this was to be the main attack against Batavia, and now Montgomery rocked on his heels. "They've split their forces in two," he grinned, "east and west. That gives us an excellent chance to defeat them in detail."

"Assuming this is all they have," said Sitwell, acting as his Chief of Staff due to his better knowledge of the scene there on Java.

"True," said Monty, but at the very least I think we can hem these landings in near Merak."

Then word came of the landing further east on the coast near a small hamlet named Patrol, and Monty's eyes lost some of their shine. "Any idea of the strength there? Any division identified?"

"It looks to be the leading edge of at least a regiment, but we have no further details. Collier's Royal Engineers are at the airfield at Kalidjati."

"That's what they want," said Montgomery, thinking. "They knew they needed Merak on the Sunda Strait to secure their communications over to Sumatra. But these landings at Banten Bay look substantial from all reports. I'm inclined to think this other landing to the east is merely a raid, aimed at securing that airfield. They wouldn't land that far east to make a go at Batavia. That's why they're in Banten Bay."

"Sir, we've got the Division Recon Battalion at Cerebon, and the 1st Sherwood Foresters on the road heading that way. Together with the Royal Engineers, we could put three battalions into that landing out east, and they'd be coming in from every side."

"Perfect," said Montgomery. "Make it so."

Those Royal Engineers were fairly well equipped. They had 27 squads in all, with 13 Vickers MGs, plenty of 3-inch mortars and even four Bren carriers. They set out towards the landing site immediately, and soon ran right into a much smaller detachment of engineers that were making right for that airfield. They would meet at Pagadan Baru on the rail line over the Punegara River, and a sharp engagement ensued.

The Royals reached the bridge first, with rifle fire from the advancing enemy snapping off the metal girders. They had no idea of the actual enemy strength, and there was soon help at hand to the east when the recon battalion came up in lorries and began to attack a small detachment of Japanese armored cars from march. They drove them back, but the Japanese were only falling back on the first of their three battalions of infantry in this landing, and their defense soon strengthened.

Out in the Sunda Strait, Mountbatten had sent a pair of destroyers to screen and patrol, wanting to know if the Japanese were making any movement into the Indian Ocean. DD *Jupiter* heard the radio traffic near Merak, and steamed up to investigate, but Lieutenant Commander Norman Thew was running into trouble. He had just lowered his field glasses, after seeing the vast sweep of enemy troops ships and thought he would have a crack at them. Soon they began to receive enemy fire from small caliber guns, and he gave an order to maneuver, when there was a sudden violent explosion.

"Torpedo!" a man yelled from below, and it was clear the ship had taken a hard blow to the starboard side. In fact, *Jupiter* had struck a mine, making her appointment with fate exactly on schedule, in spite of the many changes in the order of these events. The mine had been laid to help screen the approaches to Merak the previous day, by the Dutch minelayer *Gouden Leeuw*.

So while spared the grave risk of the fighting in the Java Sea, *Jupiter* would nonetheless meet its ordained end here in the Sunda Strait off the rocky coast of Java. The tabular record of movement would report her end almost verbatim as it had in Fedorov's history: *"During maneuvers to avoid enemy fire, ship detonated mine in position 6.45S - 112.6E and was totally disabled. Remained afloat for four hours before sinking. 84 of ship's company were killed or missing with 97 taken prisoner and 83 were either able to reach the shore or were rescued by the US Submarine USS-S38."*

Thus far, the enemy was ashore in at least three locations, but Allied resources had been close enough to reach them and move to contain the landings. But this was just the leading edge of the storm now blowing in from the Java Sea.

The real thunder was yet to roll.

Chapter 42

05:40, Sunda Strait, 28 Feb, 1942

In the early morning hours of Feb 28th, the distress signal received from destroyer *Jupiter*, along with the report that the Japanese were continuing their landings at Merak, prompted Mountbatten to act. Operating well south of the Sunda Strait, the flight crews on *Illustrious* and *Indomitable* were already beginning to spot planes for a planned airstrike at dawn. Mountbatten therefore decided to detach a stronger surface action group to move into the strait prior to that attack and scout the enemy position.

Destroyers *Scout* and *Tenedos* were already north of a small island group that sat in the middle of that strait, and they were probing closer to the Sumatran coast to ascertain whether the Japanese were making any use of the recently captured port of Oosthaven. Destroyers *Electra* and *Express* now led in a small task force to the south of those same islands, with light cruisers *Dauntless* and *Dragon*, followed by heavy cruisers *Exeter* and *Dorsetshire*. They soon encountered a screen of three Japanese destroyers south of Merak, and began to engage them with fire from the cruisers.

Captain Agustus Willington Shelton Agar, VC, DSO, was also a man to stack up names and titles, and he stood aboard *Dorsetshire*, watching the darkness ahead as the first salvoes fired. There followed soon after a slight quavering, which prompted him to look over his shoulder, thinking one of the other ships had fired behind him. All seemed quiet, so he looked forward again.

"That's *Exeter* up ahead, is it not?" he said to the Officer of the Watch.

"Aye sir, she hasn't fired yet."

Thinking it was no more than an echo, the Captain turned to watch as *Exeter* finally fired, her 8-inch guns lighting up her silhouette some 2000 yards ahead. The guns barked, followed by a long, low rumbling sound that the Captain thought was thunder.

"Mister Dawes, are we expecting rain?"

"No sir, clear ahead and with a good moon. She's nearly full sir. Should be good sighting once we close the range."

The hydrophone operator on *Dorsetshire* had heard the sound as well, but thought it was nothing more than the dull rumble of naval gunfire, or perhaps even one of the destroyers dropping a depth charge on a suspected enemy submarine. Captain Agar looked at his watch, marking the time 05:48, and gave the order to increase speed to two thirds. The small bright flash of enemy gunfire appeared ahead as the Japanese destroyers realized their peril and began to fire back. No heavy guns yet, thought Agar, all the better for us, but we don't know what's back of that destroyer screen.

It wasn't anything behind that destroyer screen that he should have been concerned about, for there was something in his wake that was far more dangerous. He had felt something like this an hour ago as they entered the Sunda Strait, a fluttering in the air, as if the pressure was changing, though the barometer remained steady. There came a trembling in the atmosphere, a quavering vibration that rattled the ship, setting lose equipment to shaking. The engines would rumble like that at times, protesting a sudden change of speed, but *Dorsetshire* had been fairly reliable of late. She was due for a refit soon, and the Captain hoped he would not have engine trouble now as he entered battle.

There was a loud boom, followed by a low growl, like the sound of a long distended roll of thunder, but the skies were clear, the wind calm, save for the vaguest sense of unease on the breeze, as if something was happening, a subtle shift, not in the weather, but in the earth itself. Captain Agar looked over his shoulder again, the hair on the back of his neck prickling up, as though he was being stalked by some unseen foe, but there was nothing to be seen, at least at first.

Dorsetshire fired again, and he moved out close to the edge of the weather deck to have a look with his field glasses, but he was not looking forward. Even in the urgency of the battle, the discomfiture he felt, an almost queasy sense of unease that was akin to dread, had prompted him to look aft, and there he finally saw something low on the horizon, a dull red glow much akin to what the sun might look like in the first red moment of dawn. Moving quickly to the chart table on the bridge, his finger tapped out the spot where he thought he was seeing the spectacle. There came a low rumble again, like that of a tea kettle just before it boiled, and the sound of a distant hiss in the sky.

"Must be a bloody volcano," he said aloud. "But this one has gone dormant, hasn't it?"

The Captain was an educated man, and new something of the world he was sailing in. The sea mount on his charts was in fact a cluster of small islands, Penjang, Sertung, and then a series of three peaks, Pertuban, Danan, and the highest being Rakata. They rumbled about from time to time, but seldom bothered anyone beyond that. Now it was the boom of *Dorsetshire's* third salvo that commanded his attention, and shaking his head, he turned to his battle without another backward thought.

Far to the southwest, the planes were lined up on the decks of the British carriers as the skies slowly began to lighten. *Illustrious* had suffered an odd collision with HMS *Formidable* in the old history, and repairs had kept her from this duty. But it never happened here. Somerville and Wells had taken *Formidable* on a private hunt, and so *Illustrious* was in fine fighting trim, her two newly installed radar sets alert to any sign of enemy planes. She had her flight deck enlarged by 50 feet, a new catapult installed, and ten more 20mm Oerlikon AA guns to beef up her defenses.

Just as *Illustrious* wasn't supposed to be where she was, an officer on her flight deck that morning was also off his appointed rounds. His name was Charles Bentell Lamb. He had come up through the Merchant Marine, then learned to fly with the RAF Coastal Command before being posted to *Illustrious*. He had a fondness for the old Swordfish torpedo bombers, spending many long hours in his Stringbag before it was finally replaced with the new Albacore. Before the war he had gained some notoriety as a boxer for the fleet, and now he was spoiling for another kind of fight, eager to get up and see what the Japanese were up to that morning.

Lamb was supposed to be in a jail cell in French North Africa, captured when he tried to fly in a special agent there, and his plane developed engine trouble and had to go to ground. He would have sat out most of 1942 there, waiting for his confederates to land in Operation Torch in November. But that had not happened either. It was just a small thing that had changed his fate, an errant tick mark on a flight officer roster that checked off someone else's name instead of his. So there he was, also in good fighting trim, and ready to board his Albacore, one hand reaching up to one of the wings as he completed his preflight inspection.

Then, strangely, he felt the wing vibrating under his hand, thinking the ship had finally turned to find the wind, but that was not the case. He looked aft, but the wake of the carrier was calm and smooth. Mountbatten had not yet turned, the elevators were still working, and the last of this flight was still being spotted on the flight deck.

But there it was, a trembling vibration that rippled now from his hand on that wing, down his arm and all the way to his boots. The metal deck was quavering, and he thought he felt an odd stirring in the air. He looked around, finding the near full moon clear and bright as it fell towards the horizon. He looked at his watch, seeing it was just a little after 06:00. They had been under its pale silver light for some time, and it would not set for another hour, at about 07:00. Then, in that last interval of darkness, the planes would take off to race north before sunrise at 09:30 that day.

Lamb was enough of an old salt that he knew something was wrong in that vibration. Was *Illustrious* teething from that last refit? Had the work crews missed something in her engines? He would not find a chart and realize that it was only the occasional rumbling of the volcano that lived in these waters, one of so many that rose in tall misty cones along the Malay Barrier.

* * *

The long archipelago that military strategists of the 1940s referred to as the "barrier islands" stretched over 2,500 miles from the northern tip of Sumatra to the eastern tip of Timor. It followed the subterranean line of a great subduction zone, where the Indo-Australian plate slowly folds beneath the Eurasian plate. The resulting pressures created over 130 active volcanoes in the island arc, and among them were some of the great terrors in the panoply of Volcanic Gods.

In northern Sumatra, the mighty supervolcano of Toba sits beneath a serene blue lake, the largest in southeast Asia, that now covers its massive caldera. At its center sits the misty island of Samusir, almost as big as Singapore Island, and white falls of water now cascade down to the lake where hot flows of lava once shaped the flanks of those sheer cliffs. When it last erupted, over 70,000 years ago, scientists say it may have been a V.E.I. 8 on a scale of 9, where no known eruptions of V.E.I. 9 have ever been found. Some believe it nearly wiped humanity from existence, reducing the population to perhaps fewer than 10,000 individuals.

The children of Toba dot the landscape of these verdant, steamy islands for thousands of miles. Rinjani, Child of the Sea, sits prominently astride Lombok east of Bali. Merapi the Mountain of Fire, dominates the rugged central mountains of Java. The legendary Tambora sits as the undisputed master of the Island of Sumbawa, and in 1815, just a few months before the battle of Waterloo, it produced the largest eruption known on earth in the last 25,000 years.

And then there was the demon of the sea, sitting right astride a dogleg bend in that subduction zone, where the thinner crust saw the fiery heart of the earth migrate upwards to produce another famous mountain of fire in the middle of the Sunda Strait, and one with a name that might now be a synonym for fear and dread—Krakatoa. These were the islands that had rumbled to bother Captain Agar that morning, and their stirring had quavered the wing of Charlie Lamb's plane, even though HMS *Illustrious* was 110 kilometers to the southwest.

In Fedorov's history, that volcano had last erupted in 1883, producing the loudest sound humans ever heard, resounding all the way across the Indian Ocean, and shaking seismographs the world over. Its explosive force was 30,000 times greater than the bomb dropped at Hiroshima, and its shock wave circled the earth seven times. The mountain itself was literally blown apart, but as terrible as its demise was, the volcano still refused to die. In 1927, it slowly began to rise again, a dull grey cinder cone emerging from the sea like some dreadful behemoth with a single glowing red eye. Called Anak Krakatoa, or the 'Son of Krakatoa,' it would grow at a rate of five inches per week, always restive, never really sleeping, like a man beset with fitful nightmares.

Of all the most explosive eruptions in human history, the top three were Tambora in 1815, Santorini off Greece in 1628, BC, and Krakatoa off Java in 1883—at least in the history Fedorov knew. In this timeline, more than human events had been found to change. Meteorological and geologic events had skipped a beat here or there as well. The 1920s earthquake in Japan that had damaged the hull that was being built for the battlecruiser *Tosa* had never happened, and now that ship was afloat as a converted aircraft carrier, standing in for the loss of *Hiryu* after Pearl Harbor.

No one had ever thought to look, not even Fedorov, for there was so little time in the heat of all these events, and so much data to reabsorb. He had focused on trying to analyze what had changed in the history they were now sailing through, and why, but a flip through a geologic reference to see what the earth itself had been doing had never occurred to him. Perhaps he simply assumed that these "acts of god," the storms, earthquakes, eruptions of the earth were all riveted in the chronology, destined to take place at their appointed times, but, as we have already seen, they were not.

The weather was so fickle that it could simply not be so harnessed. The wind would go where it wished, heedless of time's ledgers and the urgencies of human endeavor. The storm that delayed Halsey and hastened the arrival of *Neosho* had been early, speeding the gritty

Admiral into that confrontation with the *Kido Butai*, and sending *Neosho* to her fiery fate. That simple weather event had a considerable effect on the outcome of the Japanese attack on Pearl Harbor, though no one ever took the time to finger the wind as the real culprit that day.

The interval from the 1800s to modern days is but a wink in geologic time, so to have two major eruptions so close together like Tambora and Krakatoa was strong evidence that the barrier islands were rumbling to life, the earth there shaking, even as it has in modern times, producing some of the largest earthquakes ever recorded on the planet.

Eruptions on this scale could radically alter the flow of events in the history they affected. The dire and weighty matters of war and strategy produced volumes in the brief outbreak of violence that was WWII, but relatively little has been written on the life changing powers possessed by these fiery mountains, and the restless angry Gods that hunched beneath their glowing cinder cones.

Whatever force had moved the levers that day, it was moving again in the Sunda Strait, awakening from long troubled sleep, rumbling to life beneath the turbulent seas where uniformed men now steamed about in the rising swells on small metal ships, flinging even smaller hunks of metal at one another, and calling it history. The lines they would inscribe in that book would be nothing compared to the epic now about to be written by the Demon in the waters off Java that morning.

It was something that was never supposed to happen now. The violence inherent in that fractured spot in the crust of the earth was already supposed to have vented its wrath in 1883, but it had not done so. If Fedorov had taken the time to look, he might have discovered the grim possibility that was now rumbling to life. He might have learned that, for reasons he could never fathom, the eruption of Krakatoa in 1883 had never occurred in this time line, but better late than never, it was going to happen now, and it would change the entire course of these events.

Aboard *Illustrious*, Mountbatten was settling into the Captain's chair on the bridge with his early morning tea. Charles Lamb was sitting in his plane and ready to go find the sunrise, but he would never see it that morning. Something else was rising, from the depths of the earth, slowly throwing open the gates of hell itself.

Krakatoa was about to explode....

Part XV

The Gates of Hell

"Hell is empty, and all devils are here."

— **William Shakespeare**

Chapter 43

It began at 06:40, on the last day of February in 1942. The vague misgivings, thrumming vibrations in the air, and dull and distant rumblings soon produced a vast column of what looked like white steam, rising up and up, a massive veil over the Sunda Strait. In the little gun duel that was then under way, every man on either side with a view to the south and west took notice, some standing spellbound as they watch the rapid ascension of the steamy white cloud. High up, perhaps over 11,000 meters, it caught the wind, its top sheared away and smeared across the dull grey sky.

On the shore where the Japanese had landed on Java, the small, once bustling port of Anjer had long since ceased to be the little paradise of Palm and Banyan trees, with the sweet trade winds laced with spices. First came the headlong rush of soldiers and refugees coming over from Oosthaven on Sumatra, swelling over the quays and docks, hastening inland on the roads to Serang and Batavia to the east. Ships came and went, pulling up anchor and then putting out to sea, for the enemy was said to be very near.

At night, the dark silhouette of a Dutch gunboat lurked off shore, then fled north around the stony Cape Merak. Soon the silver grey night saw those glassy seas broken with the coming of over fifty transports, their holds laden with troops and equipment, the Japanese 2nd Infantry Division had finally arrived. Destroyers churned in the waters to the west of the landing site, soon to be challenged, first by the probing of the ill-fated *Jupiter*, and then by the larger task force led by Captain Agar on *Dorsetshire*. But he had been too late to prevent those landings, and now the old village Kampong huts were burning from the fires of war, and the dull tramp of Japanese infantry had swept over the sandy shore as they pushed inland, driving off a company of hapless Dutch defenders, and then the hasty defense mounted by the Beds & Herts.

When that vast column of steam vented up into the sky, the last gleaming light of the moon illuminated the silken white veil, and the moon itself fell like a massive blue pearl into the troubled waters of the Sunda Strait, as if fleeing from what was now to come. It set behind the island group that had sent this first warning up, and any man who gazed west was awed by the sight of the tall conical island, backlit by a violet haze that deepened to scarlet indigo at the level of the sea. The soldiers gawked for a time, then were urged on by the harsh throated orders of their officers. They had an invasion to see to, and no thought of what was now about to take place had entered any of their minds.

That morning, in the dark interval between moonset and the coming of the sun, the last of the landing parties cast off their lines, and anchors were pulled up on the transports. The first squadron was already heading north, hastening away from the rising sound of naval gunfire resounding from the west. Three of their guardian destroyers were already engaged, and out in the strait, a line of three more were hastening west like the winds they were named for, *Harukaze*, the Spring Wind, *Hatakaze*, the Flag Wind, *Asakaze*, the Morning Wind that was now about to become the breath of hell.

The pop of their gunfire was briefly heard, even as that vent of steamy sky reached upwards. Then the muffled report of the gunfire was suddenly smothered by the low growl of that isolated stony island in the sea, and this time something much more than steam erupted. The tip of the mountain's sharp cone belched with fire, and a huge billow of pinkish-grey smoke and ash piled up above those flames, surging into the sky with a loud roar. It cast a vast shadow over the glassy blue sea, which deepened as the column rose, a roiling mass of heat that carried the sulfuric taint of some long lost den of horror beneath the earth.

The ships at sea were caught up in a sudden wild disturbance of the water, not a wave emanating from the site of that eruption, but something affecting the entire area around the islets of Krakatoa, as if the earth beneath was heaving and bucking up, shaking the water above. The smaller destroyers lurched about in those wild seas, and on the bigger ship *Dorsetshire*, Captain Agar was forced to reach for a guide rail near the binnacle as his heavy cruiser rolled suddenly to one side. His gaze was now transfixed on the scene behind him, amazed by the spectacle of that darkening bloom of heavy ash rising above the volcano.

The day that had been slowly lightening, now darkened under that shadow, the impenetrable pall of Hades spewing forth until the gloom shrouded the entire scene. The smoky ash that blighted the sky gathered with unceasing volume, and tremendous speed, driven on by a series of thunderous reports, as if massive bombs were being set off. They were heard all over Western Java, and dazed villagers came stumbling out of their huts and houses, staring in awe at the fisting shadow of doom that now rose into the violet grey sky. That fading color soon deepened to shadow, and darkness blackened the sky in every direction.

Out on the weather deck of *Dorsetshire*, Captain Agar gawked as a fine haze descended all about the ship. He reached out his ungloved hand, surprised to find a sheen of ash whitening the handrail. In a matter of minutes, it had covered the cruiser from halyards to decks, a mantle of pallid grey-white ash that made it seem he was now Captain of some ghostly phantom ship.

The Japanese destroyers had careened about in that wild sea, and then turned rapidly northeast, as if they could sense the unnatural movement of the water beneath them was an omen far more dangerous than anything the British could be doing. The fume in their wakes seemed to underscore the chaos of the movement, but this was only the beginning, the first herald of the storm that was coming. It was only the first great eruption, which would persist until well after sunrise. Krakatoa was only just awakening from its long sleep, and for the next twenty hours, the gates of hell would be open, the host would issue forth, until it would end in a world shattering event that no man then alive could have possibly imagined.

At the bungalow HQ of Java Command near Bangdung, General Montgomery had been up early to follow the reports of the battle that was now underway. So far the movement of the Australians to contain the landings at Patrol east of Batavia had been smartly carried out, and he had come to believe that lodgment was not the main event. In the heart of Western Java, he was 250 kilometers southeast of Krakatoa, but when that first eruption burst forth, he soon heard the loud rumble, thinking it was the sound of a Japanese airstrike nearby. Then a messenger ran in with a cable from Batavia, and news of what was happening.

The boom of the eruptions could be heard clearly, growing louder with each report, as loud as heavy naval guns. Calls from Batavia, a hundred kilometers east of the eruption, claimed that a heavy ashfall was now blanketing the city, and frightened people were rushing about, throwing their meager belongings onto carts and rickshaws, and starting east on the road. The Japanese landings south of Merak were only 50 kilometers from Krakatoa, and there the rain of ash and pumice was far heavier, until the troops were themselves covered in ash, moving like pale ghouls through the thickening darkness. Even an hour after sunrise, the gloom was impenetrable, and all combat operations had to be immediately suspended.

Montgomery had one of his Brigadiers on the line in Batavia, learning that the city was not yet under attack. Then the line went dead, and a moment later there came a much louder explosion, the sound finally arriving from the distant mountain in the sea. It gave him a chilling, ominous feeling, and he wondered what must be happening there.

Windows were rattling in the city with each booming explosion, and battalion commanders further west, their men choking in the ashfall, were making frantic calls for permission to pull out to the east. Those orders were given, until the telephone system also went completely dead. The day that had promised nothing more than the thunder of war, had now descended into the wrath and chaos of nature, which was so all consuming of the sky that Krakatoa began to generate its own weather. Lightning streaked through the broiling mass of rolling black clouds, illuminating the bristling crown of the maddened Sea God.

As for flight Lt. Charles Lamb, safely out in the Indian Ocean, it was immediately apparent that he and his mates would not go out that day. All the planes on the two British carriers, still 150 kilometers from the eruption, were ordered removed from the flight deck and stowed below. Air operations were now completely impossible, and one seaplane that had tried to go up to see what was happening came plummeting down in no time, its engine completely clogged with ash.

Out in the Sunda Strait, Captain Agar had come about and was now withdrawing southwest. He would have to come within 25 kilometers of the volcano to leave the strait, and it would be a very perilous journey. Ships flashed lanterns at one another, until they could simply not be seen. Then the order was given to use the naval search lights, and long white fingers probed the ashen seas ahead and behind as the column proceeded at a cautious speed of 15 knots.

The ashfall was so heavy that it swept into any open hatch or stairwell, until the chalky white was tracked deep into the inner compartments of the ship. No one on deck could stay there for long, and the Captain was forced to rig out tarps on the open bridge to stave off the cinders that now began to fall in pea sized fragments, still warm to the touch. These would increase to chestnuts, and eventually fist sized clumps of pumice that fell continually.

At one point he had to give a steering order when the watchman called out an obstacle ahead. It was narrowly averted, and Captain Agar saw that it was a broad raft of pumice, which now covered the sea itself, giving the ocean a ghostly, milky-white appearance. To the men unfortunate enough to be on the high mast mounting their watches, it seemed that the task force was covered in hoarfrost, frozen ships on a frigid white sea.

That ash fall was going to spread for hundreds of kilometers on the wind. Soon much of Western Java was under the fallout, and later there would be reports of ash accumulating to a depth of half an inch on Cocos Island, 1,155 kilometers southwest of Krakatoa. Ships at sea in the Indian Ocean would report the blanket of fine dust and ash while steaming over 2800 kilometers away, and some reported ashfall as far off as the Horn of Africa, over 6,000 kilometers distant. The rafts of pumice that gathered in pinkish-yellow patches on the open sea would persist for over a year, drifting all the way to the African coast.

In the old history, the events already described had happened in May, and the mountain continued to steam and vent off and on, until late August when the final paroxysm came. Here, the pressure building beneath was nearly 60 years greater, which was not much in geologic time, but something unusual had happened beneath the earth. A subterranean eruption had forced a vast quantity of magma up, but it did not break the surface, forming a massive dike or plug in the deep wells that were driving the eruptive process. It literally 'kept a lid' on the mountain for those six decades, but all the while more and more magma flowed up, and the pressure building beneath Krakatoa was much greater than in the 1883 eruption that had happened in Fedorov's history. This time, the entire process was going to be collapsed into a much shorter, and more violent event.

The explosion was so massive that it created a sound that would circle the earth seven times with its incredible pressure wave. To every man in Captain Agar's squadron, it was simply ear shattering, so deafening that the crews were literally stunned, as if they had been struck by a hammer, the pain intense, their eardrums shattered. Many, were knocked unconscious, others cowered below decks with their hands over their bleeding ears in shameless fear. They had been through rough seas, wind and storm, but never anything like this.

It was a sound so loud that it would be heard 85 minutes later in Perth, over 1700 kilometers to the south, as a strong explosive bang. Nothing like it had ever been heard before. Tambora's blast of 1815 was terrible, but did not produce this same explosive sound. As if to proclaim itself as the new pretender to the throne in the long arc of volcanic islands, the Sea Demon beneath Krakatoa was bellowing with a roar that moved the air around the island with an awful wrenching pressure.

The column of the eruption poured out and up, towering into the sullen sky like a living thing, a monstrous demon of earth, smoke and fire. Its smoky shoulders rolled upwards with incredible force, and then massive hunks of earth were seen in the sky, soon plummeting down into the turbulent sea.

This tremendous outpouring of gas and ejecta would go on for many hours, the sky growing ever darker, until it was near pitch black by mid-day. By then, the 54th Brigade defending near Merak had retreated east to Batavia, and the 53rd Brigade stationed there was ordered to move east on the road to Kilidjati Airfield. There was nothing that could be done about the 31 Hurricane fighters still on the airfields near Batavia. They simply had to be abandoned, for they could not fly. Some of the crews made a vain attempt to move ten or twelve on flatbed rail cars, but the ash was falling so heavily now that even the rail lines were hazardous. In the end, most of the planes simply had to be destroyed.

On the other side of the equation, The Japanese had a much worst time of things. There was already ash to a depth of many inches all along the coastal regions where they had landed. Half of the transports had fled north, but the remainder hovered furtively off shore, where three brave destroyers still stood guard. When it was clear that the situation was going from bad to worse, General Maruyama ordered any further landing of supplies, equipment, or vehicles halted, and began pulling his troops back towards the coast. He was going to attempt to re-embark as much of his force as possible.

The troops moved like zombies, their faces and eyes swathed in cloth, shirtless, ashen souls stumbling through the utter darkness in long lines, each man with a hand on the shoulder of the one in front of him. Many fell from respiratory distress, collapsing in listless heaps on the roads and trails, and then the lightning flashed, thunder joining the constant rumble and roar of the volcano, and a heavy sulfuric rain began to fall. This created pools of ash mud and flows of tiny 'lahars,' a Javanese word that had been used to describe ash and debris flows from volcanoes ever thereafter.

Yet the cold lahars were not the flows to be truly feared. It was the sudden collapse of that massive volcanic plume that would pose the most danger, a pyroclastic flow that could originate from any of the big explosive eruptions now underway. It could form a fast moving current of hot rock, ash, and gas that would cascade down over the sea and spread out like a mantle of utter destruction, moving at the incredible speed of up to 700 KPH. To be caught anywhere near such an event meant almost certain death, and General Maruyama, having lived under the shadow of Mt. Fuji most of his younger life, knew enough about volcanoes to be mortally afraid.

A few battalions made it to the rafts and boats, desperately paddling back out to meet the waiting ships, which stood like frozen icebergs on a blanched white sea. At a little after 22:00, when the beginning of the end rattled the atmosphere so heavily that the movement of the air knocked the men from their feet, all the ships lurched about, their anchor chains barely holding them. Then came the noise that would be heard all the way on the other side of the Indian Ocean, a sound so powerful and intense that it shattered every window in Batavia, over 150 kilometers to the east.

Fifty kilometers from Krakatoa, at Anjer, it struck the men with a sudden piercing thunderclap, knocking them deaf, dazed and senseless, to the ground. As far away as 100 kilometers, the sound would be as high as 172 decibels, ear splitting, nerve wrenching pain, well beyond the threshold of endurance for any human being. It was as if each man had ice picks driven into their ears, and then all was deathly quiet—they would never hear another sound again.

There they wallowed in agony, blinded by the heavy ash, their eardrums burst and bleeding, their voices clotted and mute. The 2nd Division was deaf, dumb and blind, and yet that was the least of the afflictions that was now about to befall those men. The great upheaval from beneath the earth had finally begun. Up until that moment, the eruption had been emerging from cracks and fumaroles in the heavy cap of cooled magma that had sealed off the main chamber. Now it all gave way, and terror was not half a word for what would happen next.

Chapter 44

The painful irony in General Maruyama's retrograde movement to the coast was that each struggling step his troops took in the hope of saving themselves brought them closer to death. Thus far there had been a regular series of powerful explosions that produced surging pyroclastic flows out to 10 or 20 kilometers from the volcano, much of that activity becoming undersea flows. The paroxysm that was now underway at Krakatoa was so intense that it would collapse huge segments of the main island into the sea. The resulting tsunami would surge out in all directions, but was particularly amplified as the displaced seawater entered the Sunda Straits, a bottleneck formed by Java and Sumatra.

Aboard *Dorsetshire*, Captain Agar managed to gather himself, his head throbbing with pain. He was completely deaf, but his long years of experience at sea kept him moving, helping the helmsman up and gesturing to the heading he wanted. It was no good shouting orders, for no one would hear them. In fact, no man aboard those ships would ever hear again either, but the Captain managed with hand signals, slowly getting his men up and back to their posts to re-establish control of the ship.

Then the waves came, the first produced by the massive pyroclastic flows near the island. They were enough to raise the line of ships heavily as they fled, and as the dazed and deafened crews struggled to life again, the vessels were rocked heavily with its passing. They had been following one another closely due to the limited visibility and smothering darkness, with searchlights probing to see the nearest ship ahead. When the helmsman of destroyer *Electra* fell senseless to the deck, the ship veered off, her aft section now batted about by the first wave, while *Express* behind her was carried on like an arrow about to hit a wall. The encounter she soon had was devastating when the two destroyers collided, with *Electra* skewered amidships by the bow of the other ship.

Dorsetshire's greater displacement and wider beam rode out the first few waves easily enough, though the entire column was now scattered, with ships loosing contact with one another in the murky darkness and scattering in all directions. There was a gracious interval between those first two waves and the great wave that would follow them.

Captain Agar could see the direction the waves were propagating, and steered in such a way as to best ride them out, but they were merely outriders in the storm. A huge segment of the island was collapsing into the sea, and it would generate a tsunami that would be well over 40 meters high. When the great wave finally came, the might of the sea lifted *Dorsetshire* up like a bath toy, her bow tipping down and then riding wildly up as it finally passed. The ship careened down with a heavy roll, ash and sea creating a wild white haze all around her, but *Dorsetshire* righted itself and eventually ran true again. *Exeter* had also escaped and was well off to starboard, but the light cruisers *Dauntless* and *Dragon* fared a little worse, eventually managing to ride the wave out, but seeing many men washed overboard. As for *Electra* and *Express*, the wave smashed the two together in a much more violent collision, and both would be completely swamped. Their crews would descend in terrified silence into the sea, lost to a man.

Off the coast of Anjer, the first two waves rolled through the anchorage site of the 2nd Division, again sending all the transports into a dizzying dance on the sea. These waves were big enough to swamp small boats laden with troops, and overturn rafts carrying artillery and equipment. Men clung to rope nets on the sides of *Sakura Maru*, desperately trying to keep themselves from being flung into the sea. The great wave would soon follow, smashing everything in its path with that wall of unstoppable seawater.

General Hitoshi Imamura, the overall commander of the Japanese 16th Army, would suffer a very peculiar fate. He was aboard the transport *Ryujo Maru*, a little over 100 kilometers from the fiery mountain, and well on the other side of Cape Merak above Banten Bay. When it finally came, the tsunami was still powerful enough there to create a 30 meter wave, nearly 100 feet. The ship rocked so heavily that he was thrown from the deck of *Ryujo Maru* along with his Vice Chief of Staff, and no one saw the two men go overboard into the ash covered water. He had been maneuvering to help coordinate the withdrawal, but now the operation would be completely unhinged.

The entire landing site descended into utter chaos. Minesweeper No. 2 was literally lifted up and flung at the transport *Fushimi Maru*, landing right astride the forward deck, and then the two ships rolled into the sea and the transport's back was broken by the tremendous weight. Anchor chains snapped like tinsel, whipping through the water to sweep away smaller boats. Every deck of the 30 transports remaining there was heavily swamped, with 14 ships capsized and three others driven madly onto the nearest shore. The wave was so powerful that it would carry the *Dainichi Maru* twelve kilometers inland, where it would later be found on a jungle knoll, beached like Noah's ark.

The men of 2nd Division had struggled for hours to reach the coast, only to find a 40 meter wall of water surging in from the Sunda Straits, and carrying everything before it, boats, rafts, ships and men alike. Many of the troops had just recovered from the terrible sound, clustered in small groups on the shore, dazed and disoriented, only to find this new terror, a wave they could not even hear coming, sweeping them to their doom.

Seventeen transports would all be a total loss in the waters off Anjer and Merak, and with them thousands of troops from the 2nd Division would perish. Only 12 of the 30 ships would manage to stay afloat, but everyone aboard was so dazed and thunderstruck by the disaster that they were virtually lost as an effective combat force. In one fell blow, the mighty Krakatoa had done what Montgomery had spent hours with his maps trying to plan and devise. The entire Western Task Force of the Japanese invasion of Java was completely shattered.

The great wave surged inland at Lada Bay south of Anjer, and would roll 10 kilometers inland, sweeping all before it. People, homes, possessions, animals were all caught up in the massive movement of water, with a death toll that would be counted in the tens of thousands.

The water careened up the flow channels of streams and small rivers that found their way to the sea just south of Anjer, and into a broad, low valley, some six miles wide. It would inundate the entire area, creating a small lake there for weeks before the water eventually drained back to the sea. Farther north near Merak, the wave was powerful enough to sweep completely over the nine miles of lowland just south of the knobby wrinkled rise of the mountains that formed the Merak Peninsula. It would surge over the lower ground, all the way to Banten Bay on the other side of the peninsula, where more Japanese troops that had landed there would also be swamped and drowned.

Only the transports anchored well out in the bay had a chance to survive, for the peninsula shielded them from the direct assault of the tsunami. So a few battalions and auxiliary troops that still remained in those ships would live to tell the terrible story of what had happened to their division, but they would be called the *Mimi nai dansei* ever thereafter, the men without ears.

The great wave pushed completely through the Sunda Straits, around the small islands of Sebuku and Sebesi north of Krakatoa, and into the long bay running up to the port of Oosthaven on Sumatra. There it would crash ashore, sweeping away boats, launches, docks, warehouses, and the entire town itself, rendering the port completely useless. It was so powerful that it migrated all the way to Batavia, and was still 28 meters high when it reached that major port.

As for the British, they fared a little better, being much further inland east of Batavia when the thunder and water came. The one forward deployed battalion, 5th Beds & Herts, was completely wiped out near the village of Serang when it was caught by the wave as it slogged east through the grey ash and rain. But most of the remainder of the division had already been given the order to pull out of Batavia hours earlier, and they were on the long road east when the thunderous roar was heard. The men dropped their rifles, covered their ears in misery, but the sound was not so debilitating there, the head of the column already 180 kilometers east of Krakatoa, and approaching Cirebon.

There it eventually blundered into a company of Japanese infantry from the Shoji Detachment that had landed at Patrol on the north coast with the intention of seizing Kilidjati Airfield. This regimental sized force had already been engaged by the 1st Sherwood Forrester Battalion, and the 18th Divisional Recon Battalion, with fighting about 50 kilometers west of Cirebon. The commander, Toshihari Shoji, had received word of the disaster at Merak and Anjer, and now realized that his was the only Japanese force west of the main landings at Kragan, completely isolated.

He radioed for instructions, but was unable to get through. Seeing that his transports were still offloading supplies, he took matters into his own hands and decided to preserve his regiment, withdrawing back towards the coast. This detachment would end up being the only effective fighting force that was delivered by the Western Task Force, and he would later be commended for his initiative in saving those troops.

The British were starting to deploy to engage that blocking company when it slowly dissolved and withdrew, leaving the road to Cirebon open. So they pressed on, keeping a wary eye north, but found no further enemy presence. The ash fall was slowly thinning out as they reached that port, but the darkness persisted, and it would take all the next day just to sort units out and reassemble the battalions in some semblance of order.

Well south of that column, Montgomery had a real dilemma on his hands. All of Western Java was a zone of heavy ashfall, and anything that lived was fleeing east, creating massive jams of refugees on the roads and a humanitarian nightmare. The desperate natives pleaded for help and, where they could, the British rendered assistance. The war was over in that portion of the island, and while light ashfall was experienced over most of Java, the real debilitating pumice and ash ended near Montgomery's HQ at Bangdung.

Now he had to decide what to do with his Java Command Staff and a few battalions of the 54th Brigade he was holding in reserve. From all accounts, the chaos to the west was going to focus the remainder of his battle on the Japanese landing further east near Surabaya. Brigadiers Bennett and Clifton had already deployed there, and now he had most of his 18th division slogging east towards Cirebon. Word was that they found the rail lines operational there and could make good use of any rolling stock they could get their hands on. Krakatoa had pronounced its awful judgment on the strategies and plans of Generals on every side. Montgomery's plan to try and hold Batavia was now swept away with that thunderous eruption, and he set his mind on deciding how to proceed.

"There's nothing more we can do out west," he told Bennett on the telephone. "We'll have to come east and reinforce your defense of Surabaya. I'll move the division through Cirebon to Semarang as soon as possible, and take what's left of my reserve and headquarters to Surjakarta. It may be days before we can get sorted out, but we'll muddle through."

"What about Tjilatjap?" Bennett had asked. It was the only port open on the southern coast now.

"Blackforce is still there, with some local Dutch units and a few Aussie ships in the harbor. I can reinforce that position if need be, but I can't see any immediate threat to the place at the moment. The Japanese must be as shaken up as we are. The Devil only knows what happened to those troops they landed out west. What is your situation?"

"Not entirely satisfactory," said Bennett, with a characteristic understatement. "We're holding Semarang, but the Japs have taken Rembang further east, and I've just the one battalion blocking the coast road in the north. My lines stretch southeast from there. Clifton holds the oil fields at Tejapu, but his right flank is open, and there appears to be heavy enemy movement in that sector."

"They're trying to flank Surabaya," said Montgomery, "and I doubt if we'll be able to get anything over that way for days."

"My 2/20 Battalion is on the road northwest of Surabaya," said Bennett. "It's the only thing holding that axis at the moment, along with a company of those old Dutch armored cars."

Montgomery took a deep breath. "Frankly, unless the Dutch can hold on, it doesn't look like we can keep them out of Surabaya. Your 2/20th is likely to become caught up in all that."

"Right," said Bennett, "but I don't much fancy the thought of those lads in a Japanese prison camp."

"If need be, have them fall back through Surabaya to Malang. We're still holding all of east Java, but if the Japs do swing south of Surabaya, that could change. It may be that the best we can do is stand the line from Semarang to Surjakarta, and hold on to Tjilatjap as our principal supply port until I can organize a counterattack."

"Counterattack?" Bennett seemed surprised. All he had been doing since December was fighting one stubborn holding action after another. "That's going to be a problem. I'm all for putting up the good fight, but that port can be easily interdicted by the Japanese Navy. To keep it open, Mountbatten and Somerville will have to maintain a constant presence south of Java, and with Perth being their only good base of support well to the south. For my money, we should get the troops off this god forsaken island while we can, and hold the line in Australia."

"But if we move deliberately we can use that time to concentrate our entire force on Surabaya," said Montgomery. "7th Australian Division is at sea, and coming to support us. Run this last Japanese division off, and we've won this thing."

"But our boys won't be able to come in at Batavia now," Bennett warned.

"Yes, getting through the Sunda Strait is impossible. Tjilatjap will have to do. Then we can put them on the train to Surjakarta. By the time they get here, we should be ready for a decent push east to relieve the Dutch, assuming they can hold out that long."

Monty's dander was up, but his plan was overly optimistic. The Dutch would not hold, and that became the real problem. On the 1st of March, the Japanese landed at Karagajar east of Surabaya with three battalions of the Shoji Detachment supported by a recon battalion and two more engineer battalions and artillery from Makassar. Soon the city was flanked on every side, and Montgomery received the bad news the morning of March 3rd.

There was only one battalion of Australian troops supporting the Dutch garrison inside the vise around the port, and looking at his map Monty began to see a situation forming up that, as Bennett would have put it, was less than satisfactory. In spite of the catastrophic nature of the disaster, he had been pulling things together, and planning his next moves. The opportunity he saw in getting to Surabaya first had now slipped away. Fighting on the outer perimeter was tough going, and he could see that his troops would not get through.

If he had the Australian 7th Division in hand, that might do the job, but the disaster at Krakatoa meant Batavia was no longer there to receive them, and in the mind of Prime Minister Curtin, Tjilatjap would not do. He reluctantly gave the order to turn the convoy back to Colombo, the only other port it could possibly reach, and it would creep slowly back to the west, out of the battle, barely making port before the fuel ran out.

Now, with insufficient forces to really go on the offensive, Montgomery would be forced to heed Bennett's advice and fall back on his only port at Tjilatjap. Obsessed with the capture of Surabaya, the Japanese did not attempt to pursue his withdrawal. The Dutch, and the brave stand put up by 2/20 Australian Battalion, would hold on just long enough for the bulk of the 18th Division to get down to the south coast, where they began boarding any transport shipping available.

The Japanese navy could have made a decisive intervention here, but all the ships were north of Java, and many had been sent to the stricken region out west in the hope of rescuing stranded troops of the 2nd Division. The destroyers and cruisers were plying through the dull grey seas, braving the ashfall, and pulling out a few hapless survivors adrift in the flotsam. One man in particular, would soon be found, and by a very important ship.

On the 5th of March, a flotilla of cargo ships arrived from Perth, and were joined at sea by Mountbatten with *Illustrious* and *Indomitable* backtracking from their flight to Colombo to serve as a covering force. They looked like gaunt shapes carved from bone, with ashfall completely blanketing every exposed area of the ships. They began pulling the rest of the 18th Division off, and the battle for Java would be lost. In spite of the presence of those troops, and the Rock of the East in Montgomery, nature had pushed the history along with the sheer power of that mighty eruption. The Rock was pushed along with it, and soon Montgomery would find himself in Perth, contemplating nothing more than a long sea journey back to Alexandria where he hoped to get back in the swing of things for Operation Supercharge.

Java's fate had been decided, and Japan would occupy all the key barrier islands as they had in Fedorov's history, but something else had happened in the Sunda Strait when the mountain finally vented its wrath in that last massive detonation. It was going to change more than the weather across the globe in the months ahead, and its effect would ripple out like the shock waves and tsunami had from Java, reaching all the way to the North Pacific, where Vladimir Karpov was quietly plotting the demise of his enemies.

Chapter 45

Captain Takechi Harada stood on the bridge, still unable to believe the devastation he was seeing. All around him, the sea was frosty white, convulsing in the last throes of a great disturbance. The air itself was thick with ashfall, and the deep basso of some great thrombosis within the earth growled with an ominous persistence, a steady rumble that spoke of calamity. What in the name of all the Gods and Demons had happened here?

His ship, the destroyer *Takami*, was one of Japan's newest fighting ships, state of the art for her day, but now it seemed a deaf and blind thing in the heavy oppressive airs. All of the equipment was down, though engines were still hot and running smoothly in spite of the seas being clotted with ash. They had determined that there must have been a sudden, catastrophic eruption close by, for this island archipelago was infamous for its violent geology. A quick look at his charts named the likely suspect—Krakatoa.

At the moment, all he could think of was getting his ship to safety, and trying to find a way to navigate north away from the Sunda Straits to do so. They had been steaming about 110 kilometers northeast of the suspected eruption site, after passing through the straits and rounding the northwestern tip of Java at Cape Merak. They had been in a storm, skies darkening, winds up, with heavy lightning, and the ship was struck. The bridge blackened and systems failed just as they were cruising in the lee of a small island named Pulau Tunda according to their last charted position. Then the sound came, first a strange distended hum that descended into deeper tones, finally resolving to the awful roar and rumble they had been hearing for the last ten minutes.

The darkness intensified all around them, which they soon found was caused by a massive broiling eruption cloud to their southwest. It has to be a volcano, thought Harada, yet it was completely unexpected, as there had been no warnings or alerts issued. He wondered now at the fate of the other ships he had been maneuvering with before they broke off on separate courses.

Drawing a direct line from their presumed position to the volcano, the Captain saw that it passed right through that island, and then the northwestern tip of Java, reasoning that those land masses must have shielded his destroyer from the worst effects of the eruption, particularly the heavy wave sets that he could now see rippling over the sea. Like everything else that had been happening in recent days, it had come out of nowhere, changing the sea and sky in just minutes, and now persisted with its ear thrumming roar.

"Any word from engineering," he said to his first officer, Lt. Commander Kenji Fukada.

"They're still working, sir," said Fukada, tall and gaunt looking in his grey overcoat, and battle helmet. "We got hit pretty hard."

The ship was still rolling in the last residual swells, and with ash descending, darkness pervading, it had been impossible to see through the forward view panes. The wipers only smeared the ashen slurry to a dull opaque wash. He posted a watch on every weather deck, and seconds later the watch called out: "man overboard!"

They saw something bobbing on the white sea, only 50 yards off the starboard bow, which was the outer limit of visibility in the deep ash and gloom. It was the first sign of anything else afloat and alive, yet as he stared at it in his field glasses it seemed no more than flotsam.

When the watch finally made the sighting, the Captain came to all stop, grateful that the auxiliary engine and steering controls were still functioning. They had only been on the weather deck off the bridge for a few moments, but the sheen of ash was already coating their foul weather coats and rain ponchos, dusting their shoulders and then running in pale grey streaks with the rain.

The Captain craned his neck, to see the man pointing at the very same location where he had spotted the wreckage. He looked again, adjusting his field glasses, and now he saw not one man, but two, desperately clinging to the broken remnant of an old raft. One of the two was slumped on the raft, the other with an arm over him to keep the man in place.

"Looks like somebody else made it through this alive," said Fukada. "Shall I have KK get a boat over there?"

"At once."

The First Officer had referred to Katsu Kimura, the Sergeant in charge of the ship's small contingent of Naval Marines, always called KK by the officers. The word was sent down and some minutes later they watched as a small launch went over to the scene, the broad shoulders and stocky hulk of Sergeant Kimura prominent as he stood at the wheel, three helmeted Marines behind him in full gear. The word came back—two survivors, one unconscious, but both alive, and they were both in uniform.

That set the Captain to wonder what may have happened to the rest of his squadron. They had separated an hour earlier, each bound for different ports in the rising tension of those last hours. He remembered feeling that impending sense of doom. His operation had proceeded smoothly enough, but then, with a suddenness that stunned every man aboard, chaos reigned over the scene. Perhaps he could learn more from these men.

* * *

Out on the turbulent water, the one conscious survivor was elated when help arrived. They had seen the ship appear, moving slowly through the heavy ashfall and rain. It seemed a sallow grey specter, deathly still, and frosted over with the ash that clung to its mast and odd looking riggings. He did not recognize the ship, but realized it must be one of the screening force units—most likely a cruiser from its size. He thanked the Gods that they had been found, and the long ordeal, clinging to that broken raft in the choking sea, would finally be over.

Being well over 120 kilometers from the massive detonation of Krakatoa, they had been spared the wrenching pain and deafness, though their ears were still ringing from the loudness of the event, even at that distance.

"Thank god you have found us," he gasped when the small boat reached them, still bobbing in the high swells. He could see friendly troops there, four men, one using a grapple to secure the tattered raft, two others throwing life preservers. "This is General Hitochi Imamura!" he said with the last of his strength. "Take him first…"

* * *

General Imamura… Captain Harada was quite surprised when his chief medical officer came to the bridge, a bemused look on his face, and related that information.

"A General? An Army General? Out here? Did he say what ship he was on?"

"*Ryujo Maru*—a cargo ship from the sound of it. God only knows what it was doing out here in this mess." The doctor folded his arms, Lieutenant Isamu Hisakawa, coming over from the *Atago* when this new ship was commissioned. The Captain found him a competent, no nonsense man.

"He's resting quietly now, but he was quite talkative for a while. He wants to know if we have any information from 16th Army General Staff—says they were operating out of Balikpapan."

"16th Army?" The Captain scratched his head. "Japanese Army?"

"That's what he says. They both have on military service jackets and uniforms, and the one man is well decorated. If he isn't a General he's something else, and fairly high and mighty. What do you make of it, sir?"

"All I know, from the last orders I received, was that we were to get back to port. Then all hell broke loose. What was this man doing out here? I wasn't aware the army had anybody that high up in this region."

"He says they were way down above Banten Bay when their ship was taken by a tsunami from that eruption. They both went into the drink and managed to grab onto that broken raft."

"But we're 70 kilometers north of Banten Bay."

"Looks like they had a pretty rough ride sir. They must have been pushed all the way up here by that tsunami."

Captain Harada sighed. He was a careful man, and the fewer unanswered questions in front of him, the better. "Very well… I'll go down and have a look at them. I need to see Chief Engineer Oshiro. We've got to get the ship back on her feet. We barely have engine and steerage control. Everything else is down, and we can't raise anyone else either. Gods are angry today, Doctor. Whatever happened out there, it's created a real nightmare. Give me ten minutes and I'll see you in the sick bay."

* * *

"You are Captain of this ship?" The man squinted at Captain Harada, his eyes still red and swollen from the ash and seawater, face haggard, though he was a portly man, with a substantial belly. The Captain bowed politely.

"You are safely aboard the *Takami*," he said. "I am Captain Takechi Harada. What has happened to your ship?"

"That I cannot tell you," said the man. "I was swept overboard… wait—what did you say your name was?"

"Harada, *Itto Kaisa*, Captain of the First Rank."

"*Itto Kaisa?* Don't you mean *Kaigun-daisa?* And how very strange, another Harada. My Deputy Chief of Staff is from that family. Perhaps you are a distant relative? In any case, I am *Rikugun- Chūjō*, Lieutenant General Imamura, Commander of the 16th Army now conducting these operations. You have done us a very great service, along with that sailor in the other room who helped keep me from drowning on that raft. I owe the navy a great debt. Thanks to you and your ship, I was fortunate to survive, but it is imperative that we reach a friendly port as soon as possible. I must ascertain what is happening on Java."

Doctor Hisakawa said he was talkative, thought the Captain. Yet the more he looked at this man the stranger he felt. There was something about him, stirring some old memories to life. He stared at the man's uniform, seeing the prominent gold stripe, well soiled now, and the two silver stars on his shoulders. But he knew something of the Army ranks as well—a Lieutenant General should have three stars, and they were supposed to be gold on green.

"Where are you from?" the man asked.

"Sendai," said the Captain.

"How strange, Miyagi Prefecture, I grew up there as well. I still miss the trees on Jozenji Dori. I always loved to walk there. In the winter they would shimmer with a thousand lights for the Pageant of Starlight." The man forced a wan smile. "Yet I have traveled far and wide since then. This war will likely take me even farther before it is over, but I should not complain. I could have been a meal for the sharks out there, assuming any will survive in that hell. It was terrible... the sound... the sea...that terrible darkness."

The Captain nodded. "From what we can determine, Krakatoa must have erupted, and very suddenly, right there in the middle of the Sunda Straits. There was nothing in any report or communication to indicate a hazard there, or any state of elevated alert for that volcano."

"Nature will do what it wishes, we must simply try and stay out of its way." The man frowned. "That's what my Deputy Chief of Staff would always tell me. I'm afraid the 2nd Division on Java was on the wrong side of that advice. The casualties must have been very heavy from that tsunami. Well, I put it there, and so I suppose I must bear the responsibility."

"2nd Division? From Camp Asahikawa? They had units out here? We were not informed."

That confusion aside, the Captain was deeply struck by what the other man had just said, not for any sense of its eloquence or wisdom, but it was something he had been told long ago—by his grandfather.

'To live a long and happy life, a man must be wise, lucky, but also careful enough to stay out of nature's way.' He tilted his head to one side, looking at the man very closely. A powerful sense of recognition swept over him, and now he realized it was the uniform the man was wearing. It reminded him of his grandfather's old army uniform—yes—even the rank insignia was much like that on this man's shoulders.

"Be thankful you are in the navy, and with nothing more to worry about than the doings on this single ship. In the Army, things have been very much different since this business in China started. I was Deputy Chief of Staff in the Kwantung army once—sorting out all the messes that other Generals would create. Things were not so bad in the Kwantung. No volcanoes there. Now I have a mess of my own making to sort out, so you must get me to a friendly port right away. I must make my report on what has happened directly to the Imperial General Headquarters. It looked like we had things running very smoothly, but who could have expected this?"

Captain Harada, blinked, quite surprised.

"Imperial Headquarters?"

"Yes, a stuffy place full of sour old men, if you want my opinion, but they will need to know what has happened, and Combined Fleet as well, if they don't already know it. We must have lost many ships in that tsunami, and I'm afraid we won't have much left of 2nd Division now. We will have to pull reserves from Nishimura's troops at Singapore. A brigade of the 5th Division is already forming up—excellent troops. I had that division a year or so ago, and they fight like tigers."

"Well… General… We were headed for Singapore when that volcano blew. I don't think we caught the worst of it. I suppose we were lucky after all, and managed to stay out of nature's way. Yet my ship still took damage—nothing all that serious from what the engineers tell me. It is simply a matter of time before we can get everything up and running again. In the meantime, I'll be making way with some caution here. It isn't only nature we have to worry about. The Americans and

Russians have just had a good fight in the North Pacific, and something tells me things will be going from bad to worse here soon. Odd thing… this is the second mountain to blow its top this week. Something in the Kuriles erupted three days ago, and all of Hokkaido is under this same goddamn ashfall."

At this the General seemed quite surprised. "I had not heard that," he said.

"Yes… Well sir, we'll get the decks swabbed and be on our way soon enough. In the meantime, try to get some rest."

"Just a moment Captain… Did you say the Americans were fighting with the Russians?"

"That is what we heard, and both sides lost ships, if the rumors are correct."

I see…. And where did you say you were heading?"

"Singapore."

"Impossible! Shouldn't you rejoin the Western Screening Force? We will need to get to Balikpapan, or perhaps Makassar. Singapore is out of the question. That is Nishimura's command now. Yamashita was brilliant, but sadly, he failed to finish the job."

The Captain had started to edge towards the hatch, but he stopped again, turning his head. "I suppose I could get you up to Balikpapan, but why in the world is the army sending units there with all this trouble on Taiwan?"

That was going to end up being a very long story, and one we have heard before in this saga. It was going to be two men talking at cross purposes at first, each one failing to understand what the other was really saying. Yet if Captain Harada was listening closely to what this man was telling him now, he might have heard things that would have alarmed him a good deal more than those nostalgic memories of his grandfather. It seemed more was shaken than the earth, sea, and sky when Krakatoa vented its wrath. If Anton Fedorov had been in that room, he would have certainly picked up on the things the older man was saying about Yamashita at Singapore, and the 2nd Division on Java.

As for the General, he might be forgiven for knowing nothing about an eruption in the Kuriles earlier that week, for that had happened in a time he knew nothing about.

At that moment, however, the urgent business of the ship would pull Captain Harada away, though the encounter left him with a very strange feeling. For his part, the Major General might be forgiven for not knowing there *was* no Japanese destroyer by the name of *Takami*. That was the name of a mountain, and most destroyer class ships in the IJN were given poetic sounding names associated with wind, sky, sea, clouds, waves, frost or mist. Mountain names were typically reserved for bigger capital ships like heavy cruisers, and sometimes carriers. *Kaga* and *Akagi* bore such names, as they were special ships converted from older battlecruisers.

Yet there was *Takami*, real as the grey rain still falling on her decks, and she was a very special ship indeed, though not one a man like Hitochi Imamura would ever be familiar with—not one even Admiral Yamamoto could name. Her full designation was JS *Takami*, and there was a third letter after her hull type, DDG-180....

The War in the Pacific Continues....

Volume II in the alternate history of the Pacific War as rendered in the *Kirov Series* will follow soon. It will present the story of JS *Takami* and the fateful decisions they must make. When the shock of what has happened to them is finally realized, they must answer the question of who's side they will support in the war. Meanwhile, the action in the Pacific continues with the Battle of the Coral Sea, Halsey's raid on the Marshalls where he battles a pair of Japanese ships that never were, then Yamamoto launches Operation FS and the landings on Fiji begin, leading to the US landings at Suva Bay and the climactic Battle of the Koro Sea. Karpov's summer offensive on Sakhalin Island is also covered, and finally the battle between *Kirov* and an unexpected challenger in the Sea of Okhotsk, (another 45 chapters in all to be released Oct 1, 2016 for kindle and trade paperback.)

KIROV SERIES - SEASON 1: *Kirov*
1) *Kirov*
2) *Cauldron of Fire*
3) *Pacific Storm*
4) *Men of War*
5) *Nine Days Falling*
6) *Fallen Angels*
7) *Devil's Garden*
8) *Armageddon* – Season 1 Finale

KIROV SERIES - SEASON 2: *Altered States* (1940 – 1941)
9) *Altered States*
10) *Darkest Hour*
11) *Hinge of Fate*
12) *Three Kings*
13) *Grand Alliance*
14) *Hammer of God*
15) *Crescendo of Doom*
16) *Paradox Hour* – Season 2 Finale

KIROV SERIES – SEASON 3: *Doppelganger* (1941 – 1942)
17) *Doppelganger*
18) *Nemesis*
19) *Winter Storm*
20) *Tide of Fortune*
21) *Knight's Move*
22) *Turning Point*
23) *Steel Reign*
24) *Second Front* – Season 3 Finale

KIROV SERIES – SEASON 4: *Tigers East* (1941 – 1942)
25) *Tigers East*
26) *Thor's Anvil (Sept 1, 2016)*

Other Kirov Series Battle Books:

Foxbane
The War in the Desert, 1941-1942

Vendetta
*All the great steampunk action as
Karpov and Volkov duel for control of Ilanskiy*

Discover other titles by John Schettler:

Award Winning Science Fiction:
Meridian - Meridian Series - Volume I
Nexus Point - Meridian Series - Volume II
Touchstone - Meridian Series - Volume III
Anvil of Fate - Meridian Series - Volume IV
Golem 7 - Meridian Series - Volume V
*The Meridian series merges with the Kirov Series,
beginning with Book 16, Paradox Hour*

Classic Science Fiction:
Wild Zone - Dharman Series - Volume I
Mother Heart - Dharman Series - Volume II

Historical Fiction:
Taklamakan - Silk Road Series - Volume I
Khan Tengri - Silk Road Series - Volume II

Dream Reaper – Mythic Horror Mystery

More information on each book is available at:
www.writingshop.ws

Made in United States
Orlando, FL
10 November 2025